THE BIG HOUSE

First published 2024

Copyright © NJ Miller 2024

The right of NJ Miller to be identified as the author of this work has been asserted in accordance with the Copyright, Designs & Patents Act 1988.

All rights reserved. No part of this book may be reproduced, stored in a retrieval system, or transmitted in any form or by any means, digital, electronic, electrostatic, magnetic tape, mechanical, photocopying, recording or otherwise, without the written permission of the copyright holder.

Published by NJ Miller Books

ISBN: 978-1-3999-8805-6

Cover design by Nick Hunsley
Internal design by Andrew Easton

THE BIG HOUSE

BY NJ MILLER
A SEQUEL TO '23'
C/O - Comedy,
Crime & mistake
making dept.

OMG WTF

For Lulu and Soph…

The best damn wingmen a girl could ask for.

'Baby, she turns out to be a natural freak,
Popping pills and smoking weed.
And when she's sweet sixteen she packs her things and leaves
With a man she met on the street.
Carmen starts to bawl, bangs her head to the wall.
Too much love is worse than none at all.
There but for the grace of god.'

Machine

HEADING NORTH

It didn't sound appealing when she suggested it, in fact it sounded excruciating. But it was my parents' fiftieth wedding anniversary, and my mother wanted a big family holiday to mark this momentous occasion. So, I gave up my summer and I danced to her tune – I owed her one, in fact I owed her several. "Time to give something back, Raquel," she told me, before winking with both eyes.

Being stuck in a house in the middle of Scotland with my family was a horrifying prospect. After last year, I just wanted a drama-free summer, but my barriers were down when I agreed to this. I had been very weak at the time – that time was two days before my period, the 'witching hour', and just three minutes after my weekly weigh-in. Let's just say that Zumba is a lying bitch, and the bathroom scales are Zumba's smug friend.

So, when Mum had rented a beautiful house that housed sixteen for four weeks over the summer, I had signed my life away and agreed to be a part of this torturous 'staycay'. I couldn't be arsed to argue – I was still traumatised after the weigh-in, just trying to process the fact that I had convinced myself that my husband had been on the scales just before me and somehow the digital window had become stuck on his colossal weight. When he pissed his pants laughing and told me he hadn't been on a set of scales since 2011, my chips, pardon the pun, were down!

And, yes, Mum was now using words like 'staycay', she wore Nike Flyknits, and we were doing Zumba together on a Tuesday. She was also still riding my dad like a horse and telling me in great detail all about it, which is just what every daughter wants to hear. Mum had got her 'oomph' back while mine, well, mine was in the bin.

THE BIG HOUSE

The relocation of all the 'crazies' from Cheshire and Ireland up to Scotland, albeit a temporary arrangement, was an idea that had everybody excited, everybody but me. I'd tried my best to look at the positives; it was easier to focus on what could go wrong but actually there were some things I possibly could look forward to. I'd told myself I could cook up a big Scottish storm in the spacious kitchen, which had an Aga and a large collection of copper pans. A walk-in cold room would be where I could hang freshly caught pheasants and swig wine from the bottle, when Mum was acting up, which inevitably would be daily. I could even forage in the estate grounds whilst wearing a straw hat, I would have mud on my face in a sort of sexy, Celtic way. The brochure had described wild mushrooms, berries and interesting edible flowers, and there were apparently chickens providing fresh eggs every single day. I'd decided I would befriend them and teach them to lay on the doorstep so I wouldn't get wet if it was raining. A kitchen garden was better than any farmers' market providing an abundance of fresh produce, so work assignments would be a doddle. This place was a foodie's paradise.

I could also exercise and shift some of this lard. Apparently, the walks in the local area were breath-taking, and perhaps I would see a muscly local bending over in a kilt whilst I was jogging, which would certainly brighten up my day. Then I considered the children; this would be educational, they would return to Cheshire brimming with information about the Wars of Scottish Independence, plus they could call each other 'Cunty Bollocks' and nobody would bat an eyelid.

Dave and I, well, we could make love in a big old Caledonian bed and afterwards he would read me a poem by Robbie Burns by a crackling fire. Yes, I'd decided to embrace this experience and make memories with my family, opening myself up to a new life. I would stop being negative because there was so much to be grateful for and I was just being a crank.

THE BIG HOUSE

Plus, I did have plenty of making-up to do after my misdemeanour the previous summer. It wasn't an affair, it was more of a crush, but I did have a 'thing' with my neighbour who turned out to be a criminal, which was extra hurtful for Dave as a police officer. Dave seemed to have moved on from it, telling me he had accepted my relentless apologies, mostly embedded inside pies, casseroles and lovely big toasties, but I still wasn't fully convinced everything was firmly back on track.

Old Tom and Babs, my dad's musky old cousin and his new refugee wife would also be joining us this summer. They now had a little flat in a small village about ten minutes from my parents' cottage and were enjoying married life, with Tom spending his afternoons watching the racing channel and booze-snoozing. Babs was still highly addicted to cleaning so she'd got a couple of jobs around the village that kept her busy enough during the day and then in the evening she would make some sort of cabbage-based meal that she and Tom would enjoy together; they were really quite content. However, not content enough to say no to a free Scottish jaunt, so they were joining us, and as usual Old Tom had made sure I knew he was watching my every move.

"Let's just hope you can keep your hands to yourself on this holiday, young lady." He'd sniggered as he constantly reminded me of the mistakes I was trying to move on from.

"And try not to hump the local drug dealer if you can manage it." He winked at Babs who nodded and chuckled at his crap jokes as if he were Peter Kay himself. It was comments like this that made me want to swap his back tablets for Es, the absolute git.

It really didn't help that a number of people were privy to what I did; they knew that I had dipped my toe into other waters and that I had broken the law. But, in the end I did the right thing, so they would need to remember that – nobody is perfect, and mistakes happen.

THE BIG HOUSE

Roger and Mel were also joining us. Mel had taken a sabbatical from work and was apparently focusing on herself for a year, so she had a lot of free time. I almost coughed up my spleen when she first said it; she had focussed on nothing else her entire life. She had also become quite spiritual, meditating in the mornings and looking directly at the sun without her sunglasses on to become in tune with the elements. According to Mum, she had taken to permanently walking around with no shoes on to reconnect with the earth via the soles of her feet. She would need surgery on her retina and specialist flip-flops for plantar fasciitis if she carried on with this malarkey. When Mum had emailed her a link to the Scottish mansion, Mel's PA replied within the hour confirming that she would love to be a part of such a special trip. My suspicions were that the PA needed a break from Swampy the lawyer and she packed her stuff weeks in advance desperate to become free of this gobbledygook. Naturally, we were flabbergasted – Mel usually couldn't even make a quick lunch date without huffing and sighing about her diary that was always full to the brim with important lunches and swanky dinners. But now she was on a quest to find herself, Mel felt that this was the universe calling her up to Scotland – God's country, apparently.

CeeCee and Gary, Dave's parents, had agreed to come over for ten days too, although they'd not been impressed at the thought of a British summer.

"It's facking freezing up there, we ain't built for temperatures like that, Raquel," they'd said when we invited them. CeeCee's knees were only just about holding her up and that was only due to her exposing the knobbly old things to the Portuguese sunshine every day.

"Any longer than a few days, my darlin', will only send me backwards." Her sweet cockney accent made her moaning almost bearable. Gary on the other hand was becoming quite cantankerous and a bit of an old woman himself.

THE BIG HOUSE

"And make sure that they have the heating on, Raquel, we'll seize up like statues otherwise." I think he had hoped we would all go to Portugal, causing him minimal disruption to his routine and zero cost. Gary was thrifty, never going anywhere without a calculator.

"And ask if she can get rosé, I only drink rosé these days." Let's be real here, CeeCee would drink whatever colour the wine was even if it were luminous green, but I'd added her rosé to my shopping list to keep her quiet and happy.

"Is there a downstairs toilet? I don't want to be legging it up two flights of stairs every time I need to go – when you need to go, you need to go." Gary had also checked, really piling it on and being quite difficult.

"It sleeps sixteen, Gary. It was built in the time they all had rickets; I doubt the toilets are all on the third floor." I'd sighed as I'd tried but failed to appease him.

"He shit himself on the beach last week, Raquel – when you need to go, you need to go."

"Quiet, women, for fack's sake." Gary had shushed CeeCee, clearly a bit pissed that this information was being bandied about. I'd shuddered at the vision of Gary soiling the beach because he'd misjudged the distance between his wind-break and the toilet block.

The phone call to the 'Portuguese pillocks' had been tedious, and I was a little annoyed that it had been left to me; they were Dave's parents after all, and I had my own very tricky mother to deal with. Each time I'd spoken to them recently they seemed a little more difficult, but I suppose that's what happens as we age. Maybe I noticed it more because we didn't speak to them a lot, but then when we did it's like they'd got another five years older.

THE BIG HOUSE

Arif, my parents' housekeeper/surrogate son, had never been to Scotland, and although I liked the kid and I did have a connection with him, it seemed a bit much that he would also be joining us once his studies were complete. He had a place at a local college learning English and maths, but he still worked and lived at Duck Cottage. I would have thought that he'd want a break from Mum and Dad, perhaps some time to relax and enjoy himself. But no, his big brown eyes lit up when Mum had told him about the Scotland trip. He'd asked if he would be able to stroke the Loch Ness Monster and that's when I knew for sure there was zero chance of him getting into university.

Morag, Mum's best friend from school, and her husband Robbie owned the house we were staying in and had kindly offered it to us for a reasonable fee to help with the upkeep and repairs, so it seemed like a good deal all round. They had rented a beautiful apartment in Edinburgh for the summer so they would be quids in while we would get to pretend we were aristocrats. It had been the perfect solution as Mum was really desperate to get the whole family together and Morag was really desperate to get the damp-coursing done

* * * * *

On the first Tuesday of the school summer holidays, an annoying petty argument broke out between my girls just as we were about to leave. Michaela had re-looked at the sleeping plan and made the late suggestion that she should have the entire top floor to herself. There were two rooms and a bathroom on the top floor and naturally we had made the decision that two of the kids would sleep up there leaving the other two floors to the adults and two other kids. I say kids, but even though two of them were eighteen and over they would still make a racket with their big trainers and inability to whisper. Apart from the

THE BIG HOUSE

obvious extra agility these young 'uns had, any late-night music or phone calls could be done without disturbing the adults/pensioners who valued their sleep and general peace and quiet like gold dust.

"The whole fucking floor? No chance! It's probably haunted up there anyway, you'll wet the bed, love." Suzy immediately spat out her dummy and stomped into my bedroom, where I was folding and packing four weeks' worth of big knickers.

"Mum, she's changing the sleeping arrangements. It's not fair! We agreed I would be on the top floor."

Michaela followed her in and flopped down on a pile of shirts I'd ironed last night. "I need my own space for my studying, there are plenty of other options. She's thick as two short planks so she wouldn't understand."

Suzy yelled back. "I don't need to be educated within an inch of my life, you rancid little bookworm – I have a life, I have a plan."

Michaela threw her head back in laughter. "I really hope you're not thinking of relying on your looks to get through life, you're not all that."

I shut my eyes and sighed. I really could not be bothered with yet another argument over a load of pointless shit; I was completely exhausted before we'd even left the house.

"Listen, you two, I don't give a toss where you sleep, I don't care if you sleep, all I want is for you both to grow the hell up. Do you think I want to go on this holiday, do you? Do you think this is my idea of fun? I am doing this for the family, for Granny, because she will love this, all of us together, especially when it's an important anniversary for her and Granddad. None of this is for me, I just want to stay at home and watch *Married at First Sight*. So, unless you both calm the hell down and stop fucking whining, I am turning off your phone contracts for the whole summer. Got it?"

THE BIG HOUSE

They were taken aback. I didn't normally swear at the kids. But they were both old enough to know better – Suzy was eighteen now, and Michaela, well, she'd always had the mental age of a sixty-year-old. I'd had enough and I wasn't joking – this time I meant it, and they knew it.

They both left the room quietly. Michaela beckoned Suzy into her bedroom, and they spoke in hushed tones. Whatever was said, they behaved cordially after that and there was no mention of the sleeping arrangements again that day. Michaela had recently joined a young writers' association and had committed herself to an online course over the summer. She figured that if she could start getting something published at the tender age of sixteen, it would help her secure a place at the university of her choice when the time came, and I didn't know where she got this drive from. She was never without a book and now she was never without her laptop. I think she fancied herself as a war correspondent, and who was I to stand in her way? Suzy on the other hand did the bare minimum – she'd just finished a BTEC in business studies and had repeated her maths GCSE having failed it miserably more than once. Business had been an interesting choice for Suzy; initially, Dave and I were quite impressed, but then we found out that a hockey player with a diamond earring she had taken a shine to was doing that course and it immediately became clear. She had all the business acumen of a mouse wearing a top hat and, although I could guide her, I couldn't force her into anything. The only books Suzy read were the instructions for her Apple products and even they baffled the girl.

We decided to take both cars to Scotland. Dave might have to pop back and forth for work reasons, plus we had so much stuff, really taking everything but the kitchen sink, that we would need them. I chose to do the first part of the journey with Sam, leaving Dave to

THE BIG HOUSE

deal with the girls until we got to the services in Kendal and then we would do a swap. My Sam was beside himself about the trip, excited that he would get to fish in his own garden in the huge lake. He'd get to spend time with his dad who was apparently the best thing since sliced bread, and he would have Arif to play football with whenever he wanted. There was talk of all sorts of trips, one being the Rob Roy MacGregor memorial, just the boys, no girls allowed, but I clocked Sam yawning rather deeply during the discussion so I suspected he would feel unwell that day. A trip to Ibrox Stadium would be another matter – he would certainly be up for that.

Now Sam was thirteen he was on the cusp of becoming a proper fully fledged teenage dickhead. The other two were already there and almost overnight they just stopped being nice. I dreaded that day when the god of hormones came down and took the nice Sam away. But I told myself you couldn't avoid it, it happened to them all. Suddenly one day, your kid looks at you like something they'd stepped in when all you'd said was a simple 'Hello.' It happened earliest with Suzy, who'd only just been twelve. I'd sat in my car as I always did, waiting for her to come out of school. I had a snack for her, as usual, and nothing had changed at my end. I saw her in the distance with a group of other girls and she seemed to be looking for me so, as normal, I waved out of the window but she sort of looked straight past me. I then got out of the car and waved a bit harder, still she didn't see me, so I then got back into the car and flashed my lights. She was almost looking straight at me, but she just could not see where I was. I presumed it must be the light or maybe she needed glasses, either way, I decided to walk over to her and make my presence known. I was only a few metres away when she used her hand to shoo me away. Shooed away like a stray dog actually, with a flick of the hand and a tutting noise. I was confused – perhaps she

THE BIG HOUSE

had been in a drama class and was still in character. But sadly, this was an intentional move.

When she got in the car I was told in no uncertain terms, "Your waving is so embarrassing, the way you do it is so cringe. Who taught you to wave like that? And why are you flashing your lights? What are you thinking? Nobody flashes their lights unless they're mental – are you mental?"

I shook my head, mortified at being berated by my own daughter.

"And I could see you, I am not blind, I was busy. God, you're so impatient – is there something wrong with you?" she'd shrieked.

I planned to stop for wine on the way home.

"And then if things couldn't get any worse, you get out of the car. You're not allowed to get out of the car, you have to stay in the car. And please do not wear that jumper again, it's so bright. Everyone was laughing. Oh my God!" she'd screamed.

I'd looked down at my funky neon number from Zara, now an offensive weapon that I would be wearing on every school run until it dissolved with old age, and when that happened, I would buy another one.

And from then on, it seemed like everything I did was wrong. Everything I said was wrong and my daughter, who used to hold my hand and tell me I was the most beautiful mummy in the world, now endured my presence with a face like a slapped arse.

When it came to Michaela changing, it was a little more subtle because she was already quiet. With her, she just became an eye-roller and a sneerer, she swapped words for facial expressions, mostly miserable ones. I only had Sam left so couldn't have him changing on me too soon. He still laughed at my jokes and looked happy to see me when I picked him up. But the hormones were starting to make changes to Sam, and although he was still my boy, alarmingly, he had started to grunt.

THE BIG HOUSE

Dave took all of this in his stride because he was Big Dave who was easy-going and matter-of-fact. "Kids will be kids, they'll grow out of it," he'd said. He would say this whenever I angrily told him about the negativity I endured from the kids every day. "Embrace the madness," was another pearl of wisdom he'd deliver when I had been scowled at so hard that my skull almost cracked.

If I am to be completely honest, I almost lost my marriage last year. I nearly threw away the type of man some women never even get to meet, never mind marry. I had to live with that, and it was harder than I thought. I had to remind myself every day after what had happened that I'd been lucky to be given another chance. I'd hoped that if I kept my nose out of trouble, we would eventually forget what I did – yes, we, not just him. Every day, my thoughts would take me back to the day when I made my husband's eyes leak. I didn't like to say cry, that was too sad, so I had a new term that kept the shuddering to a minimum.

We had made some changes to our relationship after my unfortunate and inappropriate friendship with our neighbour. They were positive ones, particularly for Dave, who had taken us rebirthing our marriage very seriously. We'd been seeing a therapist, pouring our relationship woes to a 'know-all' called Julian, who I'd found online and whose reviews were very encouraging. Julian had instructed Dave and me to have a date night on a Wednesday, he'd also set us homework to have sex once a week no matter what. He'd said, "Even if you have to do it in the car, it must be done, it's imperative to the process." Dave found this exhilarating and almost aimed to make sure we did do it in the car every week; me, not so much. I did not enjoy my head bashing against a steamy car window and the fear we would be spotted by someone we knew made me feel sick. But I did what had to be done because I had let Dave down very badly and because Julian told me to.

When Julian had asked us to report our progress after the first

THE BIG HOUSE

month, I was sure he enjoyed listening a little more than he should have, and unless he had a glue stick in his pocket, I think we may have had a problem on our hands. Still, I persevered for my marriage and for Dave. Julian was full of it – he had all the answers, he'd been there and seen it all, but it was entirely possible that he went home to a blow-up doll called Roxy and she was his rock, his inflatable rock.

My opinions on Julian really didn't matter in the grand scheme, I had to be seen to be trying and making an effort. It could have been King Charles lecturing me on staying faithful and being honest, and I would have just listened and agreed obediently.

The second month, we were asked to write a list of three things we would like to change or improve on within the relationship. Dave misread the intention and it'd caused much embarrassment.

He'd proudly presented his well-thought-out list and looked to me for advance approval on the effort he had put into to his homework. Julian had read it out loud sounding more and more startled as he went:

1) Would like to watch porn together
2) Do role play (possible nurse's outfit)
3) Give anal a try

Julian had become very sweaty at this point and used a hanky to dab his forehead.

"Okay, Raquel, what have you got on your list?" With a thunderous face and a very tight bum hole, I'd handed over my carefully thought-out reflections.

Julian read it as Dave became redder as he realised what he'd done.

1) Spend more time together as a family
2) Travel and visit some bucket-list destinations
3) Get fit and healthy together

THE BIG HOUSE

Dave quickly snatched his paper back and re-read the initial instructions. His face had dropped and his mouth was agape. "Oh, shit, I thought you meant in the bedroom, Julian. You don't specifically say what this is in relation to, though, mate. I mean, did you mean in the bedroom or what?"

Julian, ever the therapist, had said: "It means whatever you wanted it to mean, Dave." The realisation had dawned on Dave that he had not only bared his perverted self to the room but also that he may have to go on a diet.

"Raquel, is there anything on Dave's list that you don't think you can do?" I'd cocked my head at Julian, the silly little man. I took the list from Dave's hand and screwed it up slowly into a tight ball, throwing it towards the small waste-paper basket in the corner of the therapy room. It would have been so fucking cool if it had gone in, but no, it hit the wall and bounced back, hitting me in the face, and then landed right onto my lap. Julian was flustered but nodded slowly, perhaps he felt this was a sign to compromise – I did not.

"Okay, let's move onto Raquel's list, Dave. Will you be able to achieve the things on there, do you think?" He'd tried to steer the conversation back to actionable resolutions.

Dave had nodded, putting his arm around me. "Yes, mate, all of them. Totally."

"Let's leave it there." Julian literally hadn't been able to wait to get us out of the door. This had been a very uncomfortable session for all three of us.

As we'd got into the car, Dave, clearly feeling guilty for being a deviant and not doing his homework correctly, said, "Hey, love, shall I take you to that new wine bar on Saturday night and then for tapas at that Spanish place you like?"

I looked at him dead in the eyes and made it clear.

THE BIG HOUSE

"It is NEVER going up there."

* * * * *

Apart from that awkward incident, therapy had helped. We had been to three European cities together, twice with the kids and then Paris just the two of us. We'd also been down to Rick Stein's restaurant in Padstow, which was on my bucket list – sad I know, but I needed to know what all the hype was about. On the health front, I had started Zumba and Dave had gone keto. We'd been making an effort, and it was working. Whilst Dave had lost masses of weight, I'd tried to lose masses of weight and we did more together, in fact we kept ourselves so busy that I did not have the time to think about what I did.

Although things were fine on the surface, I did still feel as though I was walking the tightrope at times. I felt that if anything reminded Dave of my behaviour, it might push him away. He had never indicated this was the case, in fact quite the opposite. It was me who felt anxiety because I was the one who had created the problem.

Dave being the kind of guy he was, never mentioned my indiscretion with the neighbour or once threw it in my face. We just erased the memory, and we pushed on together as a couple. Perhaps that was why I was apprehensive about Scotland. I didn't want the likes of Tom reminding him of what happened or that Roger might get into his head – I still would never fully trust him, especially after he'd grassed me up last year. I just wanted to enjoy myself and have a relaxing summer holiday, but as this was me, Raquel Fitzpatrick, I worried that somehow trouble seemed to follow me wherever I went.

THE EAGLE LODGE

Kendal Services were at the next exit along the M6, an hour or so before the Scottish border, and where we'd agreed to meet for lunch to break up our long trip to God's country. I wasn't going to allow anybody to eat food from the services so had brought cool boxes full of sandwiches for everyone, and to make it bearable before the full onslaught of everyone decamping at the rental.

We pulled up next to the burgundy Jag, with Mum, Dad, Tom and Babs all looking straight ahead, unable to meet my eye whilst tucking into a KFC family bucket with their stupid greasy faces. I banged hard on their window with my clenched fist. "What are you doing? I made lunch for us all!" Mum lifted her sunglasses and put the window down.

"Good afternoon, Raquel," she said calmly.

"Never mind 'good afternoon', why are you all eating that? We agreed to have a picnic before we entered Scotland – I brought all the sandwiches!"

Dad put down his crispy thigh and wiped the grease from his chin with his handkerchief.

"Sorry, darling, we couldn't resist. It really is finger lickin' good, you know. Colonel Sanders had a point," he said sheepishly.

They all nodded and continued to gnaw away at their bones, there was no getting through to them. I turned to Dave who appeared to be in conference with the kids. He looked back at me and then quickly away again. It was at that point I knew that they were planning on jumping onto the KFC bandwagon.

"Oh, just take them," I huffed, giving Dave the green light and consigning my picnic to staying in the boot. "Get me a frigging Zinger then while you're at it." Dave gave me the thumbs up. Well, if you

THE BIG HOUSE

can't beat them join them, I thought. And I had really pushed myself at Zumba last week – not only did I 'Shake what mamma gave me', which is what the absolute wanker of an instructor ordered us all to do whilst wearing a headset and false eyelashes, but also afterwards, I had a vodka slimline tonic and not the large glass of white I had been accustomed to in previous weeks. So, I would have a Zinger because I bloody well deserved it.

Mel's car pulled up just as I was handing out baby wipes to the chicken eaters. I was quite surprised at my sister and her new look.

Before she'd been a well-covered girl with wild blonde hair and a good sturdy pair of legs, but now she could only be described as slim, possibly on the skinny side. Her unruly hair had been cut into an actual style, one that I suspected didn't even involve a comb in the morning. Her official look, the one she had been born with (I am sure she wore court shoes from Russell & Bromley with her nappy), was now a much more casual thrown-together ensemble, with a soft lounge pant, high-top trainers and a blazer. She looked sun-kissed and fresh, actually appearing to be younger than me (how annoying). A scowl appeared across my face and I didn't know how to feel. It was like I was sixteen, and an overwhelming feeling came over me to trip her up. It had been revealed during my brief obsession with Matt, that fifteen years ago Mel had kissed Dave and he hadn't told me. He hadn't felt the need to tell me because she had been drunk and he'd been tired. While I was upstairs breastfeeding a child at the time, my dear sister had taken her opportunity to pounce on my husband.

It was no biggie, really – Mel had only told me to make me feel better, citing that we all make terrible mistakes which were possible to move on from. I'd readily accepted that at the time, but now she was here, and we'd not spoken much lately, I thought about it a little more.

I quickly glanced at Dave, who was nibbling a chicken wing, leaving

THE BIG HOUSE

the bun and the chips on one side. His face broke into a smile, a really wide smile as he looked at Mel. I gazed down at my burger, well, the remnants of it, and then back at her. She had definitely not been on the Zingers.

I snapped out of my sulk. "Mel, you look great. Really great."

"Hello, you." We hugged, and then before I could have any sort of conversation the children all swamped her with love and affection. She was the fun aunty that said yes to everything, the one with the money, the house, the job, and now she was the thin one.

I looked into her car but there was no sign of Roger the codger. But Sir Walter, my sister's right-hand 'mandog' sat regally on the front seat observing the interactions.

"Where's Roger?" I asked her, as she hadn't let us know it was just going to be her. She sighed. "He's not feeling one hundred percent, his sciatica flared up last week and then he got a boil on his…" She stopped herself. "He said he'll join us when he is feeling better."

I should have felt relieved, I mean, he was a piece of work and I would get to hang out with my sister but for some reason I wanted him there as a buffer. I didn't feel completely comfortable with her and her close relations with my Dave! Then the thought came into my head – had she lost weight for Dave? Was she still holding a torch for him? Was this the real reason he was off the carbs, for Mel? Shit, what if they were planning on having me sectioned under the Mental Health Act? I mean she was a lawyer and he was in the police so it would be pretty bloody easy for them to think of a way to get me out of the picture. And where was Roger? Perhaps they had already eliminated him. A boil and sciatica were probably a ruse when really, he was handcuffed to a radiator in a cellar somewhere being nibbled to death by rats.

As my warped mind took me to places I should not go, I noticed the kids had all piled into the back of Mel's car. A car with actual Wi-

THE BIG HOUSE

Fi – I couldn't match that. So, there was no arguing, no discussion, she would drive them into Scotland, and I would travel alone with the smell of un-eaten egg sandwiches to keep me company.

As we crossed the border, I did feel a sense of freedom. I know it sounds silly but there was something about entering Scotland that felt different, as if we were going somewhere things would be simpler. The air was clearer, the grass was actually greener, and I do believe that everyone was more down to earth. People said it how it was and if you didn't like it, you could 'stick it up ya wee arse.'

Mum called me from their car to check on my progress and she started the winding-up mission very early that day.

"What's for dinner tonight?" she asked abruptly.

"I beg your pardon," I said through gritted teeth, rising to the bait.

"Dinner tonight, we're all wondering what we're having."

I gripped the steering wheel and glared at Mum as I sped past the Jag. Again, she peered over her sunglasses – it was a new thing she was trying.

"Oh dear, what an angry face you have. If the wind changes, you'll stay like that. Somebody may be hitting the menopause, methinks." I heard Dad mutter the word "Yikes!" clearly remembering this as a particularly tough time for all involved.

I had a recollection of Mum in her late forties, drenched in sweat at a family christening and the priest asking her if she had been caught in the rain. "You should have used an umbrella, Suzannah, you're absolutely soaking," he'd told her, not knowing that this would be the day his career and his life would be crushed.

I remember Dad shaking his head to try and save the arse of this brave-but-stupid man but alas, it was too late.

Mum, whilst almost self-combusting not only in a blind rage but with her hormonal changes too, gave this man the dressing down of

THE BIG HOUSE

the century. She marched him outside and told him to look up. When he did, and there was not a cloud in the sky, proving there was no rain, she then went on to ask him what qualifications he possessed to be in charge of christening children and demanded to see the paperwork.

He was rifling through a filing cabinet looking for his CV whilst two families waited rather impatiently, ready to hand their babies over to the Lord. There was a free bar and a hot buffet next door so the bit where the kids got dunked was of the least importance.

She ended the scene by explaining to the congregation from the pulpit that Father Charlatan (as she'd re-named him) would be re-thinking his vocation. "We've established he would do much better as a bus driver, haven't we, Father?" Charlatan nodded, his top lip trembling as he realised he had just taken on something much darker than 'Old Nick'.

"What an insensitive and foolish man, to comment on my body temperature knowing full well I am going through the change. He has no place in a church. You need sensitivity, intuition and the ability to communicate to be a priest – he's got a long way to go."

How on earth a twenty-something-year-old Catholic priest knew anything about the shutting down of Mum's reproductive system was beyond me, but he'd know better for next time.

"Mum, I will have been driving all day and I have everything to unpack when we get there. You're seriously asking me to cook tonight? Come on, woman. And I'm not going through the change, I don't think." Actually, come to think of it, I had developed a big front bum and my hair was becoming very dry. So much so, a man referred to me as a clumsy Worzel Gummidge when I rolled my trolley over his toe at the supermarket recently.

"Whoa whoa, you were the one who said you would be in charge of all the cooking, in fact you insisted on it," Mum reminded me, jeering through the window as they pulled alongside me in the next lane.

THE BIG HOUSE

She was right, I didn't want her involved in the kitchen. I was territorial and I would be damned if I allowed Mum to slip her boring salmon in tin foil and new potato bollocks onto the table. But I needed time to settle in, find my bearings, and it had been a long drive.

"Not on the first bleeding night, Mother – we have the picnic in my boot. Surely, we can eat that?" I suggested.

Dad tried to help me out. "Yes, fantastic idea, we'll have a carpet picnic, it's been years since we did that, and it feels like a holiday thing." The rest of the passengers were noticeably silent, clearly not relishing the thought of eating their dinner on the floor cross-legged.

"Nobody else got anything to say? Would anybody like me to perhaps wipe their arse or peel them a grape? "I gestured through the window to Tom and Babs.

"They're both asleep, Raquel. The excitement of the holiday has got the better of them, bless their hearts."

"Sure they haven't passed on, Mother? You'd never know the difference." The line went dead and then I saw Dad pull into the slow lane as Mum poked Tom aggressively with an umbrella. Dave called me soon after from his car, which was in front of me.

"I forgot to tell you, love, Julian has sent through some homework to complete in Scotland."

"Has he?" I queried. That was strange; we had finished our sessions with him a while back and I'd paid the final bill. We'd gone as far as we could with therapy so now it was time for Jules to stand down, leaving us to fend for ourselves.

"Err, yeah, he says that we have to christen every room whilst we're there and apparently you're not allowed to moan at all."

I chuckled. "Very funny, Dave! I could probably manage the first one but you know moaning is part of my vocabulary so I would end up being totally silent."

THE BIG HOUSE

"Now there's a thought, only thirty minutes until we're there, love, let's try and make the most of it."

Dave was getting into the spirit of the holiday, which was nice and exactly how it should have been. Lately I felt like I'd been treating him like a china doll, not the thick-skinned rhino that I had married. I couldn't have anything rocking the boat, not even the tiniest of things that would put Dave off me once and for all. I wondered when I wouldn't feel so insecure and when I could go back to being the old me. I had even started to wear a bra in bed, not an underwired one of course, but a soft sporty thing that at least stopped the old girls from clapping together during the night.

* * * * *

The Eagle Lodge was off an A road about twenty-five miles north of Edinburgh. Once leaving the main road, it was a good five minutes on a windy lane until eventually, just along to the right, was the big beauty that would be our home for a while.

I crunched down the gravel driveway, which was a beautiful sound. Once a 4x4 skids to a halt outside a huge house, you know you've made it and you can pretend you're Kim Tate arriving home after a long day of riding, mainly men, to death.

Morag and Robbie, the welcome committee, stood in the doorway to their palatial home. They were both in their seventies and looked a little worn. Morag was beaming widely but Robbie didn't look as jolly as I remembered, appearing a bit downtrodden and tired.

Putting Robbie's misery to one side, I took in my surroundings; it was breath-taking and regal. It was a house, but it could easily have been a hotel because it was bloody massive. It had grey stone turrets, and below, thick ivy cascaded down the vast walls and slightly covered

THE BIG HOUSE

the edges of the old windows. The gardens were set significantly lower than the house to avoid flooding from the lake further in the distance. Although it was summer, the breeze provided a pretty decent current to this huge body of water to what was the backdrop of The Eagle Lodge.

"Fuck me sideways, this is something else," Old Tom muttered; he was originally from money but was as in awe of this place as the rest of us. He staggered out of the car leaning on his stick and breathed in the fresh air whilst Babs snored with her mouth open in the back of the car.

"Yes, this will do nicely." He patted Mum on the backside as he said it and she didn't even flinch, now clearly immune to his inappropriate behaviour. If he tried that with me, I would sweep the legs.

"So, family, have I done us proud? Isn't this the most beautiful holiday home we have ever stayed in?" Mum was beaming from ear to ear realising she had really done it this time, but in a good way for a change.

Morag came down the steps of her lodge with her arms outstretched to greet Mum. They'd been friends for a very long time and had attended the same boarding school together, and they had pretended to be cousins but there was no blood between them. Once they had gone off to separate universities, they had maintained their friendship by writing to one another. Being pen pals must have been a very annoying way to communicate. Imagine sending a letter to your bestie in, say, June and then weeks later in July you finally got a reply. In this day and age, shit happened daily, sometimes hourly, so by the time the letter had reached the sorting office, the likes of current teenagers would have shagged three people, been arrested and had two different hairstyles already. Thank the fucking Lord for WhatsApp so we know what's happening in real time.

THE BIG HOUSE

"Suzannah, how long it's been, we have so much to catch up on. I have missed you, so so much," Morag sighed.

Mum threw herself into Morag's arms.

"I'm here now and I sure have plenty to tell you," she said, raising her eyebrows in my direction and Morag gave me a knowing smile. Mum and her big gob, I bet she couldn't wait to get the gin out and reveal my darkest secrets. Luckily, Morag had always liked me, and she was certainly trustworthy; I knew she was definitely that.

I had once, and only once, had a sexual encounter with Morag's knob of a son, Miles. He was their only child, and when we holidayed together in the South of France in the middle of fucking nowhere there wasn't much else to do. We were all stuck in a crumbly old gîte in the back end of the Loire Valley; I had requested we go to an all-inclusive in Tenerife like everybody else, but I was told 'No! We're doing something classy and something cultural and you'll need to get used to it.' The trip had started with two days stuck in the car with my parents and lungs full of pipe smoke before arriving at the most silent and mundane holiday home that smelt strongly of French farts.

Mel was at university so had avoided this one, but I had been coerced into joining a two-week wine-tasting trip, which was to be broken up by the odd visit to flea markets and cathedrals. I only really went because the boredom was a small price to pay for a good all-over tan to show off to my mates back in Blighty. The plan went badly wrong. It was raining, so no lovely tan for me, and my parents conveniently 'forgot' to tell me that Morag, Robbie and Miles would be joining us. We were all crammed together playing board games and eating blue cheese whilst the French rain battered the windows of my summer prison.

Eventually after eight days of this hell, the sun did make a brief cameo. The parents immediately went off to a vineyard in a yellow

THE BIG HOUSE

Citroën Dyane that they had hired to make them look French. The combination of them talking to each other in English but with French accents and Mum being all continental infuriated me. So, once they had gone, to shake off the cabin fever, Miles and I, well, we polished off an entire bottle of cognac by the pool. After that, we broke one of the French antique beds during an afternoon of 'honky honky', and since then I have never been able to look him in the eye. We've all gone there with a family friend, and we've all felt the hideous cringe afterwards. He was my family cringe.

* * * * *

I really did not want anybody to find out about this, not my sister, hell to the no, and especially not Mum. She'd felt that Miles was a real catch, and she would have been very keen for me to marry into this Scottish dynasty, but I knew different. Miles was not a catch; he was actually one you would throw back and he was trouble. I saw Miles for what he was during that trip, which made it all the fouler. On top of his horrible personality, he was also ratty-looking with slicked-back hair, and he had tiny little hands. Half a bottle of brandy somehow blurred my vision and I overlooked all of this on a balmy afternoon in Southern France.

"Merci, Madame, très bon!" he'd said after the disgusting deed was done and he lit a cigarette in the bed. And then, before our parents returned, he'd rinsed the safe and stuffed his pockets with a fistful of his father's francs without batting an eyelid. "They'll not notice, the stupid old fools." Meanwhile I'd hunted around the room for my knickers and my dignity; the former were never recovered; the latter had always been a little iffy. And that wasn't the end of it – during that two weeks, not only did Miles shoplift at a vineyard, taking a vintage

THE BIG HOUSE

bottle of something very special and rare, leaving the staff thinking we were a group of travelling thieves, but he also certainly had something to do with the disappearance of some traveller's cheques his mother had saved for a boot full of Bacardi and Lucky Strikes to take home. They'd turned the gîte upside down, even checking under the carpets of the car while Miles just lay by the pool wearing stolen sunglasses giving literally no shits at all. He was quite frankly revolting, and I had let him do unmentionable things to me all because of cognac. Anyway, shit happens when you're a teenager, so I had put it out of my mind and hoped not to see this 'wee rat' for a long time. I'd also set a new rule after that: I would never sleep with a man who was smaller than me again, it's just all kinds of wrong.

After returning home, I'd had an attack of conscience and written a sneaky letter to Morag in complete confidence telling her that her sticky-fingered son was responsible for all things that went missing in France and maybe even Central Europe during 1995; I felt she needed to know. She replied with a very short note on stationery decorated with thistles telling me that she would forever be grateful for my courage in coming forward and that she would deal with it in her own way. She also asked that I never mention this to another soul and to destroy all evidence. I'd tried to burn the note with a joss stick but after two hours and just one small scorch mark, I flushed the note down the loo, proving I was the soul of discretion.

So, Morag and I had a special little bond based on that. I had been in their company a number of times after the holiday, but Ratboy was never there and France '95 became a distant memory. So, if Mum decided to tell her about my indiscretions, I felt they would be safe enough with Morag, which was something at least.

* * * * *

THE BIG HOUSE

Mel was annoyingly underwhelmed by the house, but I suppose she was used to all this pomp so didn't get giddy like the rest of us. She lifted a very small suitcase from her car and allowed Sir Walter to do a massive poo on the lawn whilst she gazed across the lake. She was more interested in the gardens than the actual house, taking some photographs of the grounds for her Insta apparently. Again, my hands made their way to my hips, unimpressed, as I watched my stupid sister plan to tell her followers how grateful she was to the universe. Then, she nipped back to the car and put her yoga mat under one arm, ready for her spiritual awakening. Cock.

"You need to pick that shite up, Mel. Don't forget the big steaming shite," I called after her loudly in an attempt to shame her to anyone within earshot. "Get that for me, will you?" she said, ignoring me, and appealing to Dave to help.

And then she threw a roll of dog poo bags to him and he went over to the poo and actually picked it up. I wasn't impressed. I didn't want her giving Dave disgusting things to do – that was my job.

Robbie took my lightest bag and carried it into the hallway. He seemed a bit off, a little quiet, and not the loud and gregarious character that I remembered from my childhood. He had a handlebar moustache and a big belly – if that doesn't say fun, then what does?

"Welcome, welcome to The Eagle Lodge." He ushered us into a magnificent hall. The room was vast, with triple height ceiling; even the skirting boards were almost a metre high, and an oak mezzanine that wrapped around a double staircase was a sight to behold. It was a little bare, there were gaps on the walls where paintings should hang; perhaps a few more antiques filling the space would have made it look less sparse. But bare was good, bare meant tidy and easier for me to keep clean.

Mum took in her surroundings, she had been here many times

THE BIG HOUSE

before, usually for Hogmanay when Robbie and Morag would have a fancy shindig for all the oldies.

"I have missed this place, it's been, what, five years?" she said, trying to work out how long it had been.

"Not for the last three years because of the coronavirus-19, and not the two before because we both had our hips done," Robbie explained, using the full description of COVID as so many people of that age did.

"And how are your hips, you two, are you both back at it, in full swing?" Mum glared at Dad who had already started with his innuendoes.

"Don't be so disgusting, Phillip, and get the rest of the bags."

Dad scurried off back down the steps to help Dave and Sam make the many trips up and down the driveway with all of our luggage.

Morag offered to show us around so we could get settled in our new home for the summer, whilst the kids had already started exploring by shouting down the corridors to see how far the echo would take them. We left them to it because I wanted to get to the important stuff.

The kitchen was the one place that I was looking forward to the most but turned out to be a let-down. The cold room had been disconnected, apparently it cost a fortune to run so it was now a big cupboard. I was to use a couple of quite substandard fridges that had seen better days in a room down the corridor. The Aga had been playing up so that had been sent away to be repaired and was replaced by a horrible-looking thing that had no place in this glorious house. There was a gap where the coffee machine had once lived, this had apparently 'blown up' a couple of months before nearly burning the house down. But not to worry, Morag had bought some Nescafé sachets that created a cappuccino if you added hot water and stirred really fast. The copper pans I'd been told about were nowhere to be seen and a new set of Ikea pans sat in a box on the counter. My expectations of a palace kitchen were disappearing with every cupboard I opened.

THE BIG HOUSE

Morag could see my disappointment; my face did not know how to lie, so she took me to a place that she knew would impress me. The kitchen garden just outside the back door gave me feelings I only normally got from that first glass of wine on a Friday night or a glimpse of Idris Elba running in slow motion. I kid you not, this was a place that I would happily end my days in.

There was a Victorian greenhouse that housed aubergines, tomatoes and a variety of chillies. There were fruit plants, herbs and big deep pots of potatoes ready to be dug, as well as neat symmetrical rows of lettuces, leeks and onions. This was heaven! And then, she introduced me to 'The Girls' – four plump chickens in a good-sized run, strutting up and down waiting to produce the freshest of eggs.

"We just call them Sister Sledge – we could nae be arsed to name them all." Morag threw in some potato peelings as she introduced me to the hens. They all rushed over and devoured them, which I never knew was a thing.

"They'll eat fucking anything, this lot, absolutely anything. Be careful it's not too spicy though because you'll taste it in the yolks."

Morag was an expert on hen-keeping and she talked me through how her kitchen garden had kept her sane. Perhaps I wouldn't buy eggs from the Spar after this, perhaps I would buy myself an allotment and spend the afternoons there smoking roll-ups and tinkering with compost.

"I do all of my thinking out here, Raquel, it's therapy. There's nothing better on a summer's evening than an hour in this garden with a Bacardi and Coke." She smiled at me knowing she had hit the spot with this one, we were kindred spirits, Morag and me. An early evening drink in complete and utter silence sounded like bliss!

"What's the Wi-Fi, Aunty Morag?" Michaela had come out to find out the absolute most important thing in the world to her. Morag

THE BIG HOUSE

laughed nervously, fiddling with her earrings.

"Oh, my wee darlin', you'll need to go into Robbie's office and log on to his big computer if you want to get onto the worldwide web. We don't bother with wireless up here, it's only dial-up."

"Sorry, what?" Michaela's face dropped, she almost dry-heaved. Could this have been a bad dream? Perhaps a silly joke? Surely Morag had not omitted to tell us that The Eagle Lodge was not connected to the outside world!

What happened after that was akin to hearing on the news that the country was under attack. People were running to windows and holding up phones. Sam flew past me with a bag of wires with a look of terror on his face. Suzy completely lost it and slapped a suit of armour around the face on the landing. Mum was herself a bit put out and shouted to Morag: "Christ, can I still use my emojis?" I wasn't happy either, hoping to watch *Married at First Sight* in bed on my iPad and I needed to be able to submit my work easily. This also put a huge amount of pressure on me as a parent if my children were bored – they would turn up the moan meter to 100.

I mean, you couldn't write it. I wanted to bloody write it, I was a writer, but if I wanted to send any sort of document without physically connecting, I'd need to download the document to my phone, walk up the lane and turn left, walk for three minutes and then stand on top of a dog-shit bin and hold said phone in the air. All of this was too much trouble, it was a backwards way to live. I would just drive into the town and sit in the bar of a hotel where the Wi-Fi was not only free, but it was fast, too. However, this plan would not help the girls or Sam, they were literally cut off whilst they were in residence.

Mum made a small inspirational speech to try and gee up the troops.

"Now listen up, you lot, they didn't have the internet when Morag and I were girls and we had the time of our lives spending summers

THE BIG HOUSE

together. We weren't shackled to the worldwide web and we turned out just fine. So, this break can be a digital detox, it will do us all good, I heard about it on *Loose Women*. Let's get the Monopoly out, let's go on walks, let's re-connect as a family." And then she clapped herself, the only one who did.

The only responses were glares and grunts. Mum beckoned us towards the kitchen to introduce us to the first instalment of 'digital detox'.

As the realisation set in that things were going to be little different up here in the Scottish abyss, I was forced into yet another skin-crawling situation, and this one was way worse than no Wi-Fi.

"Oh, Miles, you can come in now," Morag called.

I thought perhaps I had imagined it, surely she couldn't have said what I thought she did. But she did, and before I could prepare myself by gouging out my eyes with a spoon, Miles slithered in holding rounders set under one arm and a French boule set under the other. He still looked like a river-dwelling creature.

"Alright, guys, I'm Miles. I brought you some stuff to help you get over the lack of Wi-Fi. I kind of suspected you would find it difficult."

He smiled sympathetically at the girls, but they just sneered back at him.

Suzy grimaced at the outdoor games and flounced off up the stairs screeching an "Oh. My. God!" in frustration.

"You remember Miles don't you, Raquel? Lovely little Miles, we holidayed together in France." Mum smiled and I gulped. Miles was not lovely and by Christ I certainly did remember him.

"Errr, yeah, I think so, rings a bell, erm… how are you? Are you staying close by? I was told you'd moved away, so what are you doing here?" My voice was almost panicky. He was very smooth in his response.

THE BIG HOUSE

"Well, I'm here now, Raquel, and I'll be just on the back orchard if anybody needs anything at all – just say the word. I stay in the cottage there, just a minute's walk."

I was speechless. There was a small gate that said 'Orchard' on it and he would be on the other side of it. Yuck and fuck, I did not want to see him at all, not once, not ever. If Dave ever found out I had slept with this creep he would feel sick and it could derail everything. Yes, it was years ago but still, this would be very awkward having him around the place. Nobody could find out this information, so I had to hope that Miles had forgotten about it. Why on earth wasn't he abroad? What a great bloody start to the holiday this was turning out to be.

Dave took the kids into the local town for an ice-cream and Wi-Fi whilst the rest of us got settled in. Mel had found her spot by the lake where she could lay down the yoga mat and perform eye-watering poses in a flesh-coloured all-in-one. Mum and Dad sat at the huge dining table with glasses on the end of their noses writing a plan of potential outings for the holiday.

Tom and Babs were spending the rest of the day in bed recovering from the journey, which was mind-boggling as I wondered who went to bed to recover from sitting down for seven hours?

I decided to get my meal-planning done and the unpacking of my very important kitchen gadgets. Just as I was putting my Magimix in place, I felt a hand on my shoulder.

"Really good to see you again, Raquel, it's been a while." Miles had reappeared.

"Okay, good to see you. Sorry we won't see much more of you as we are a very private family." I lied – we weren't private at all.

"I think we will see each other quite often over the next month, actually." He said this quite creepily.

"No, I don't think so, Miles," I replied forcefully.

THE BIG HOUSE

His face broke into a smile and he sighed. "It's good to be home, I was away for quite a long time you know, Raquel, I missed this old place," he said as he looked around, marking his territory.

"I thought you were supposed to live abroad. I thought you had some job in another country. What's brought you back here?" I asked impatiently.

"I never lived abroad. My parents told people I was in Hong Kong because they were ashamed by me." He laughed and shook his head.

"Ashamed about what?" I enquired, wanting to know what specifically it was from the long list of embarrassments he'd probably caused them.

"Where I've really been for all this time."

"And where have you been?" I wondered. Perhaps it was Wigan and they didn't want anyone to know. He smoothed back his con-man hairstyle with his minute hand.

"The big house, Raquel, eight years. Got out at Christmas, been living here ever since."

"The big house?" I frowned.

"Aye, prison, jail, the clink. We call it the big house up here." He pulled up his left trouser leg and showed me a grey plastic ankle tag. "Got this for my trouble too, I have to be in the house by nine."

I grimaced.

"Does it electrocute you if you try to run off?" I wondered hopefully.

"No, I believe you're thinking of a dog collar, Raquel."

That was a shame, I would have loved to see him sizzling at 9.01 pm – that would have been a damn good watch.

So that's where he'd been and that's why Robbie looked knackered and pissed off. Who wouldn't be with a son like Terry Duckworth? Although none of this was my business and I didn't care one bit about Miles and his unsavoury lifestyle.

THE BIG HOUSE

"Oh dear, sorry about all that. But now I have to get on with my private family holiday. So, take care now," I said, setting some boundaries with him.

I turned my back to him, going back to my unpacking, secretly thrilled that he had paid the price for being a thieving scumbag – he deserved to be locked up just for his breath. He stood for a while before he took a cigarette from behind his ear and put it between his non-existent lips. He then gave me a message that was worse than a dose of the clap.

"Matt says hi by the way."

I felt a cold shiver go right through me.

"Who's Matt?" I asked, praying he meant Matt Hancock.

He lit the cigarette and laughed out loud.

"Your ex, that's who." And with that he left the kitchen in a puff of smoke.

CAMEL TOE

On Wednesday morning, I had set my alarm for 7 am. I wanted to enjoy the garden and the hens with a coffee and to be left with my own thoughts before everyone was awake. Dave was tucked up in bed peacefully sleeping, oblivious to his wife's antics again. Seriously, though, could I really be held responsible for this situation? I had done nothing wrong. Did I really need to inform Dave of a sexual encounter I had in another country many moons ago? And this Matt business was no doubt my mum's fault. She had probably told Morag about my indiscretion and Miles had overheard it. He was possibly trying to wind me up and play games with me. I decided it was best to completely blank him and buy a padlock for our gate just as a safe measure. It did feel strange, though, to be confronted by yet another mistake from my past. It looked like I had a type, and that type was 'dodgy'. This would be yet another con artist I had fallen for, and I wasn't comfortable with how it would look, particularly to Dave, which is why I needed Miles to stay well away.

I went outside, sitting in an old deck chair admiring the vegetable beds and listening to the light clucking of Sister Sledge. The sun was rising but there was still a slight chill in the air, which smelt faintly of heather. For the first time in years, I had not been greeted by the pings from my phone telling me when my period was due, no notifications to inform me that my current account was running low or some stupid app I downloaded whilst drunk asking me to record my weekly intake of alcohol. This was certainly a digital detox, and it was heaven.

When the silence was interrupted by what I can only describe as a crowd of idiots joining me in my sanctuary, I felt utterly robbed.

Mum was first out, in her tartan pyjamas, clearing getting into the

THE BIG HOUSE

theme of the holiday, then Dad followed in a silk robe – a robe with the TK Maxx label still attached, he was doing his bit for the Playboy Mansion.

"What the… what are you two doing up?" I asked them, unable to hide my frustration. Dad pulled up a couple of chairs next to me.

"We don't want to miss these beautiful mornings and we ended up falling asleep early after the long journey." He groaned as he lowered himself onto the seat of a deckchair.

"This is my time; I want to be alone actually," I huffed.

"Good morning, 'Moody'!" Mum plonked herself down with no intentions of leaving MY GARDEN.

The back door swung open again and Dave, rubbing his eyes, walked out wearing only his boxer shorts. He breathed in the Scottish air and stretched.

"I really don't know how you do that, darling." Mum shook her head at my husband and put her sunglasses firmly over her eyes.

"Morning, everyone. Nice day for it!" Cheerful Dave walked around the garden, practically naked and completely unbothered by it, smelling the plants with interest.

The door opened again and this time my three children appeared, squabbling about who'd pissed on the toilet seat whilst shoving and pushing each other quite nastily. Then, as if it couldn't get any worse with this gaggle surrounding me, a sash window on the first floor opened and Old Tom appeared and shouted down.

"Have you lot never heard of a lie-in? We're trying to sleep up here. Oh, sod it, we're coming down then. Raquel, Raquel – are we having a cooked breakfast? I'm starving and you didn't do a proper dinner last night."

Dave looked over at me sympathetically, realising I already needed some time to myself.

THE BIG HOUSE

"Raquel isn't doing breakfast this morning, we are going into town for a walk and a coffee, aren't we, love? Just the two of us?" he said, coming to my rescue.

I nodded. We hadn't discussed this at all, but it sounded like a great plan to me.

"So, you lot help yourself, the fridge is full!" Dave told everyone. And after that, Dave went inside to get dressed and the others were left in shock that they would have to cook their own meal and wash up afterwards.

When Dave and I headed over to the car, Mel was upside down on her yoga mat showing the Scottish hills her camel toe. I caught Dave glance in her direction as we left the driveway, and I didn't like it.

"Why don't you get a yoga mat and join her?" I asked, jealousy getting the better of me.

Dave shrugged. "Nah, it looks painful." He was completely unaware of how uncomfortable I felt at him ogling my sister.

"I don't know why she wears flesh-coloured leggings; her legs look like sausages. It's unsightly for a woman of her age, don't you think?"

I tried to get Dave to say something horrible to make me feel better, but he didn't engage.

"I think she looks great at the moment, and good on her for getting healthy. Maybe you should join her, Raquel, you could get some yoga stuff in town."

I was miffed, how dare he? I bet he'd like to see that, both of our camel toes glistening in the morning sun. I would check his search history and if I found the word 'sisters' on a murky-looking site, then he'd be for it.

We drove into what I expected to be a picturesque town. I was hoping to be offered a wee dram on the high street and hear the bagpipes from the hills, that would have got me in the holiday mood,

THE BIG HOUSE

but it turned out to be fairly basic. Of course, there were a few twee souvenir shops with ceramic Nessies in the window and coffee shops lined the high street, but it was early and the town hadn't woken up so our only option was to head to The Hotel and join the residents for a spot of breakfast. The name of this establishment was actually 'The Hotel', I found this interesting. Could have been a genius move I suppose when it came to Google search, but quite boring in every other way. Dave and I weren't really properly dressed for a hotel breakfast and my hair looked like I'd been in a fight. Dave had his slippers on with a pair of shorts, so eyebrows were understandably raised in the foyer as we waited to be seated.

"Room number please, sir?" A pretty little waitress wearing an apron looked down at Dave's footwear as she tried to establish where we had come from, not looking like their usual patrons.

"No, love, we're not guests, we're just her for a coffee and a bacon sarnie if you've got one."

She smiled kindly. "Perhaps you would like to sit in the lounge in that case, we serve non-residents in there." Dave readily agreed, particularly when he saw how formal the dining room looked. People were properly dressed, they had shoes on and hair that had been combed. We didn't fit in.

We sat in the window facing the street and ordered coffee and sandwiches. This was like a breakfast date and we deserved to have it in a nice hotel, even if we had been shoved in the corner of the bar.

"Oh, look, there's Morag and Robbie." I looked out of the window and saw the owners of The Eagle Lodge marching up the street with towels under their arms.

"Morning swim by the look of it. Such a nice couple although he's a bit glum, don't you think?" Dave noted, and I agreed.

"Maybe they're members of a local country club, something like

THE BIG HOUSE

that, they seem like country club types," I mused, but Dave frowned.

"All the way here, over an hour's drive for a swim. Seems a bit ridiculous does that, Raquel." He shrugged and turned away from the window and changed the subject.

"Let's try and really enjoy this break. We needed to get away from Cheshire for a bit, I think. It's going to be lots of fun."

"In what way will it be fun, Dave?" I wondered, clearly not as convinced.

"In every way: kids, family, fresh air. Mum and Dad are coming up too, and it's been ages since I saw them. Apart from the lack of Wi-Fi, what's not to love?"

I snorted.

"The cooker is a fucking joke, the fridges are tiny and the kids are bloody furious about the Wi-Fi, obviously. And Mel, well, she's being strange and I've totally gone off her."

Dave laughed at my rant. "You can't go off your own sister and who cares about the kitchen, we'll make it work, we always do."

"Will we now?" I didn't agree, I was feeling all annoyed again, I needed to cheer the hell up. Dave put his hand on my leg affectionately.

"Yes, we will. Honestly, we need to thank our lucky stars that we're even on holiday after last year, we both dodged a bullet," he said seriously.

I reddened, it was the very first time Dave had brought that up and I felt rotten. He was right, had it not been for him, things could be very different. He saw my shame and quickly moved on from this to try and lift my spirits, although unknowingly he'd hit on something even more shameful.

"Eh, what about that cousin of yours, Miles? Do you know him well? You've never mentioned him before, seems a bit shifty to me."

At this point I could have revealed to Dave that I had done the deed

THE BIG HOUSE

with this awful man and I'm sure normally he would have been fine and we'd have laughed it off because everyone has a past after all. But I just couldn't bring myself to add this to my list of disastrous decisions when things still felt a bit rocky between us, even if it was when I was young, drunk and stupid. Also, it was entirely possible that Miles had forgotten about what we did and so Dave would never have to find out.

After all, when you meet a man you know you will eventually marry and they ask how many men you've slept with, how many of us give the actual true figure? Sure, if you've been what I would call a good girl and have allowed just a handful of locals to deflower your 'lady flower' then your number would probably not exceed double figures. However, I digress; if like me you were a teenager who grew up in the nineties your 'number' would be kept in the deepest and darkest part of your brain and it would read more like a landline number. I couldn't fit Miles into my number and I didn't want to. The thought of Dave realising his wife was akin to a crumpled five-pound note that had been in many a trouser pocket certainly was not an option. Dave was only aware of the people I was not ashamed to have slept with and that list housed seven men and one rather unattractive woman. The rest would never make the cut for obvious reasons.

So, with all of that, it was best that I kept this particular smelly skeleton locked firmly in the closet. So, I answered the question with a grey lie, not a white one because with hand on heart, I could not genuinely say this was not for my benefit.

"Oh him, he's absolutely not my cousin, Dave. My mum and Morag are not related, they pretended to be when they were younger and now it seems to have stuck. Anyway, I barely know him, he wasn't really around when we were kids, I can't recall ever really being around him." Dave screwed up his face.

THE BIG HOUSE

"But hang on, you went on holiday with him didn't you, to France?"

I pretended to be confused, that the recent foggy memory I'd been experiencing had muddled my holiday memories. "Possibly, or it could have been Mel, I forget, he's very forgettable." Dave shrugged and left it at that.

Breakfast arrived in the nick of time and Dave's attention was immediately taken by two soft white rolls arriving stuffed with crispy smoked bacon and runny fried eggs accompanied by a steaming pot of fresh coffee. The holiday certainly started here – a lovely breakfast served in a hotel with my husband!

But then Dave did something that really annoyed me, ruining things. He carefully removed the bacon and egg from his roll and placed the roll on his saucer. This was the new ketogenic Dave, slimming down for some reason or perhaps someone!

"Oh, just eat the bread, Dave, you're on holiday. No diets on holiday, right?" I tried to sabotage his determination, which was a petty move. But he shook his head, "No chance, not undoing all of my good work."

He then pushed the bread towards me, the chubby one, and said: "You have it if you're hungry, love." And then he sipped his black coffee and nibbled on the bacon fat. I had been carb shamed; that bread roll might as well have been a breakfast-time Scotch the way I felt eating it. I recalled every hip rotation and squat I had done at Zumba, that had surely earned me a bacon roll on the first morning of my holiday. But I didn't enjoy my breakfast now that it had been tinged with guilt.

As we sat and watched the world go by, Morag and Robbie eventually emerged from an alleyway across the street. Morag with a turban on her head and Robbie wearing a towelling robe, both carrying wash-bags under their arms. They then got into a very old and battered Vauxhall Vectra and drove past slowly enough for me to realise they were arguing. Morag seemed to be reading Robbie the

THE BIG HOUSE

riot act whilst he had his head in his hands. Eventually she stopped shouting and then floored the Vectra, leaving a trail of exhaust fumes outside the hotel window.

"Trouble in paradise!" Dave clocked it. "Wonder if we'll still argue at that age, but what have they got to argue about? Makes you wonder, doesn't it?" He mentally drifted off, probably dreading the next thirty years with his 'carb monster' wife.

After breakfast, the little town began to show signs of life. We wandered up and down the streets hand-in-hand looking into the shop windows and listening to the lovely Scottish accents of passers-by.

The butchers, Ferguson & Sons, opened their doors just as we walked past, and I decided to go in and get something deliciously Scottish for dinner. I would pull out all the stops and I would open the good wine. Dave was right, we were here now so let's get this damn party started. Dave and I took a haunch of venison from Ferguson's son, and I got ready for an afternoon of cooking.

Back at the house, the mood seemed pleasant. Sam and Dad had set up by the lake with the fishing gear. Sam had a little half tent that he could sit underneath if it started raining and a proper fishing chair that professionals used. It was a nice little camp, very cosy, and I knew that Sam would be happy down there with or without Wi-Fi.

The girls had decided to walk into town and meet Arif at the train station. I suspected that they were using the collection of Arif as an excuse to sit in a café for three hours prior to his arrival to inform the world of their non-communicative status. They both barged past me on the driveway and were still quite frosty, possibly believing I had known all about the Wi-Fi problem before we came.

Little did they know I was probably more upset than any of them. I couldn't watch my shows, I couldn't see what James Martin was posting on his Instagram (my guilty pleasure) and I wasn't able to

THE BIG HOUSE

watch chiropractors cracking people's bones on TikTok, another of my secret delights. It was a new way to live although probably much needed.

Mum and Mel were having a heart-to-heart in the library, a small room off the main hall with some very shabby chairs and just a handful of books taking up only one of the many oak shelves. The huge bay window overlooking the lake had a padded window seat framed by some heavy curtains – it was a beautiful room but could have done with some care and attention. They sat in the window whispering, and I saw Mum stroke Mel's face. I dropped my meat and bits onto the hall table and tiptoed over to the door, which was slightly ajar. What was my mother doing stroking faces? Had she been at the gin already? She wasn't a stroker, she was more of a prodder, so something was certainly up.

"Sorry darling, you can't always have what you want. I'm afraid that you'll have to let this one go, it's just too complicated." Mum's tone was unusually soft and caring, especially as I normally got the Anne Robinson approach which was anything but.

Mel then sniffed and tears fell, which Mum wiped away with her own sleeve. I'd have had a used dish cloth if it were me.

"Mum, it's all I have ever wanted and it's not fair."

Mum cupped her chin and there was only one of them now.

"You need to put it to the back of your mind, you cannot waste any more of your time on this, it's not going to happen and it's just simply not meant to be."

Mel sobbed again.

"I just thought, well, I believed that I would finally get what I wanted for a change, how come Raquel gets to have it all?"

I shook my head – what the hell was she on about? She had a mansion, her dream job and a wardrobe that was worth more than

THE BIG HOUSE

my house. And now she even had a waistline and a jawline, she was always so spoilt.

Then she stood up and came towards the door, I quickly positioned myself behind a coat stand as if that was going to disguise me.

"I will find a way, Mum, just watch me. It might not be a conventional arrangement but I am not bothered what people think anymore."

And then she stomped upstairs leaving Mum looking at her sleeve with dismay. Whatever it was that Mel wanted, she seemed very determined to get it. I just hoped for her sake that it didn't belong to me because I wasn't very good at sharing. She should have learned that after I caught her trimming the hair of my Girls World that time. Mel's fringe left her forehead that night and ended up in a neat little pile on her bedroom floor. "A fringe for a fringe" I told her the next morning when she screamed into the mirror at her lovely new hairdo!

I took my shopping into the kitchen before I was spotted snooping. Mel had been very distant over the last year, and because I was concentrating on my family, I hadn't really had too much contact with her apart from the obvious 'Hi, how are you?' And 'Mum needs locking up' text messages. Surely to God admitting her kiss with Dave hadn't resurfaced any lingering feelings, had it? Had he reciprocated and were they struggling with their feelings? Last year, they had joined forces and planned my freedom behind my back, of course I was grateful. They had also stood side by side when I unfortunately became a drugs runner for a couple of days. I know this sounded ridiculous, but I was starting to wonder if my mess had somehow brought them closer together.

I decided to do something I never thought I'd do. I walked up the lane for full signal and decided to message Roger. I didn't like my sister floating around the place with no responsibilities, and her husband would be able to shed some light on just what the heck was going on with her.

THE BIG HOUSE

Hi, where are you? Are you joining us?
Not sure I'm welcome. Regards, Roger
Of course you are, why would you say that?
She doesn't seem to want me anymore, Raquel. Regards, Roger
Stop writing Regards Roger, and of course she wants you, please join us, she's miserable without you.
She said that? Regards, Roger
Yes, so get your Irish arse over here. Chop chop, Paddy. (Axe emoji)
I'll need the address and some directions.
Sending a pin now.

If Roger felt that Mel didn't want him anymore, who did she want? Just who was she being all thin and beautiful for? Had Dave finally realised that I was the wrong sister, the manky one? My infidelity had turned me into a suspicious and bitter person, making me doubt my own family as a result of my own actions. Back in the kitchen, I chopped the shallots aggressively with my mind racing. I ground herbs and spices with such force that smoke almost arose from the pestle and mortar. I spent the entire afternoon in the kitchen, and had I not been in a state of paranoia it might have been fun. Eventually I gave in, and after cracking open a fruity bottle of red as the clock struck 3 pm, to make the gravy, I helped myself to a couple of glasses which calmed me down – temporarily.

As I was setting the huge dining table ready for our first proper dinner together, I heard somebody whistle across the hall. Miles the cretin was lurking.

"Are you whistling at me?" He nodded. "Don't whistle at me, that's very rude." He laughed.

"Still a feisty one, then." I rolled my eyes.

"What do you want? We're having a private family dinner." My tone was unfriendly but I didn't want him around us.

THE BIG HOUSE

"Sorry, sweetheart, I just thought I'd pop by and see if you have everything you need."

"I told you yesterday, we don't need anything and this is a family holiday. We don't need any more visits, we're absolutely fine," I told him, eager for him to get lost.

"Don't you like me?" he asked, already knowing the answer.

I got impatient, not having time for this on top of everything else.

"Look, I have no feelings about you, I hardly know you, Miles. I just don't think this is appropriate, really."

"You mean because of what went down in France? Honky honky, eh!" He winked.

I gasped, Jesus God above, he remembered.

"Miles, this is just a bit inappropriate. I was under the impression this would be our house for the summer, and you keep turning up. And please, never ever mention the France thing or say honky honky."

He sighed.

"Okay, message received and understood, darlin'. It'll be our little secret. Anyway, I have something important for you. I've left it in the greenhouse."

Maybe he was returning my knickers from France 95 that I never did find, but Lord knows I wouldn't fit into them now. Presumably it would be some chicken feed, perhaps some slug pellets for the leafy beds? Whatever it was he didn't need to come into the house to talk to me about it – he was becoming an absolute nuisance.

"Right, I'll get it later, whatever it is, now I really have to get on and get this table done for this evening." I picked up my glass and turned to go back into the kitchen.

Miles moved towards me. I stepped back, having a horrible feeling he was going to kiss me, but instead, he took my half-full wine glass from my hand and, very cheekily, he downed the lot.

THE BIG HOUSE

"Shiraz, South African, right?" I watched in horror as Miles put his mouth around my glass, and then guessed the grape and country of origin correctly. I hid my admiration for his palate because as much as I hated to admit it, it was impressive.

"Never you mind what wine that is, off you go, go on, out."

I ushered him towards the back door, the only entrance he was good for, and I shut it firmly. Perhaps I should have had more respect for the fact that this was his parents' house, but we'd paid bloody good money to stay here and surely we had a say on who walked in without knocking. Little wanker.

I lit the candles, polished the glasses that although were not the expected crystal, still twinkled. I set the log burner going because even though it was summer these rooms were so big that you never actually felt warm. I felt very satisfied that this grand room would now be the setting for our first family dinner.

I knew Arif had arrived and was upstairs unpacking. He had landed himself the unfortunate position of being next door to Suzy on the top floor where he would also have to share the shower room with her and all of her shizz. When I say shizz, I'm talking fake tan, body moisturiser, face moisturiser, body scrub, face scrub, face mask, hair masks, hair spray… you get the gist. This girl did not travel light. There was probably a small space on a window ledge for his lone bottle of Lynx Africa and that would be all he got. On arrival, Michaela had discovered there was a single room without a view but had a small desk and chair for her to type at, so the miserable little bat bagsied that for herself.

I whizzed upstairs to greet our new guest and to ask him to keep an eye on the venison whilst I had a much-needed shower that would wash away the disgustingness from my interaction with Miles.

Arif came onto the landing beaming his entire mouthful of metal.

THE BIG HOUSE

This was a recent thing and it was all down to Mum. She had told me in her very caring way: "I simply can't look at him smile anymore; he's got more teeth than Istabraq. Something needs to change."

She had marched into Cheshire's most elite orthodontist and persuaded them to put fixed braces on Arif's top and bottom set – for free.

"He did his bit for the refugee crisis, and I managed to get him a seat on the parish council." Mr Fang as I imagined he was called, had done as Mum asked and he also got his picture in the paper with the headline, "The kindest dentist in town."

I couldn't bloody believe it – I was four grand down due to a slight wonkiness in Suzy's teeth whilst Mum had managed to get Arif a total freebie. "He'll have a better smile than Rylan Clark once those braces are off," she said proudly as yet another job to get Arif the life he deserved was ticked off the list. Other ideas included him getting a degree, passing his driving test and the one that I really had doubts about: writing a book about his life. "It would be a bloody bestseller, the things this lad has gone through." She was 'on one' that day, determined to get justice for the boy who ironed her pastel pants.

"I'll get onto it; in fact, we'll publish the damn thing ourselves if we have to. This story needs telling." Mum thought she was on hold to Salman Rushdie's agent at the time, but it turned out to be a takeaway in Cheetham Hill.

Apart from his metal mouth, Arif was still the lovely dorky Syrian he always was, with a positivity and gratitude for his life that the rest of us lacked.

"Hello, Mrs. I just love Scotland United Kingdom." He smiled as I hugged him.

"Arif, good to see you, now just come with me a minute, will you?"

I beckoned him down three flights of stairs and into the kitchen

THE BIG HOUSE

to keep a good eye on the dinner. I would do the small talk later. He was the only one I could trust with the venison, nobody else had a bleeding clue. I left him next to the bad oven with a can of Coca-Cola and a basting brush.

Once showered and dressed, I nipped to the greenhouse to collect some chives for my cauliflower and to check what Miles had been droning on about earlier. Just propped up by a red chilli plant leaning against a pot was an envelope with the word 'Rackel' on the front of it. Which illiterate moron had written such a thing? I wondered.

Hiya babe, hope you good. It's been a long time since we seen each other. It's not so bad in here, made some mates and got me-self a job in the kitchen, that's thanks to you that is. Big Mike who runs the kitchen has taken me under his wing, he's a proper ledge and he really knows his stuff. The ingredients we use is not as good quality as what we had, the veg is all frozen which you wouldn't like and it made me a bit sad too.

I've got that picture from the magazine of me and you holding that fish in the supermarket. I put it on the wall of me cell to remind me of what a laugh we had. Someone laminated it for me so it can get wiped clean if anyone spills something on it. Ha ha.

So strange right that I met your cousin Miles in here, he recognised you straight away from the picture and it turns out we have something in common, ya dirty mare. Ha ha.

Anyways, I don't think I will be getting out anytime soon because there has been some trouble with me and some of the screws and I know my sentence is getting extended soon. Meh

Hope you can write back cause I don't get many letters. Me Nan used to send me one every week but I've been told she's got a memory problem so it looks like she's forgot about me now.

Oh, by the way, could you write down the recipe for that beef Wellington thing we made? The guvnor said if we all behave, I could try

THE BIG HOUSE

and make it for Christmas dinner. But instead of the beef fillet, we'll have to use tinned tuna cause this is prison, so it has to be cheap.

Any recipes would be good because in this prison the guvnor likes his grub and he is nicer to us when Big Mike gets creative. He spends his weekends watching re-runs of MasterChef and he once appeared on Come Dine With Me.

Miss our street. Sorry for everything.

M xx

My mouth was wide open and I felt like I'd stopped breathing. What a bloody cheek, how dare Miles allow Matt to contact me like this. And what did he think we were going to become, pen pals? I couldn't exchange letters and recipes with an inmate, this was ridiculous. I grabbed a fistful of chives and I shrieked so loudly it almost shattered the glass of the greenhouse.

"And he's not my fucking cousin!"

What were the chances of this? Somebody up there was having a right laugh at my expense. I once saw a medium who told me my guardian angel was a narcoleptic and I was actually starting to believe it.

I wanted rid of the letter immediately, so I dropped it down the drain just outside the back door and sent it on its merry way to the sewers where it bloody well belonged.

I was left wondering what to tackle first now. It was only the second day of the holiday and already the problems were stacking up. The fact my sister was being super weird and talking about somebody she could not have, somebody who I worried sounded very much like my Dave.

The fact that two creeps I'd had dalliances with had been sharing a cell in some Liverpool nick which had a laminated picture of me on the wall - wearing a wedge.

THE BIG HOUSE

The small matter that my husband was looking thinner and younger by the minute leaving me feeling insecure and uncomfortable.

Or, and this one really hurt, I had already missed two nights of *Married at First Sight* and one of them was the first commitment ceremony. Since we'd got north of the border, everything had literally gone south.

I decided I would serve up the dinner, have more red and work out what to do when I was a little bit drunk. That was the clearly the best plan!

* * * * *

"I say Raquel, this is a bloody feast alright." Old Tom raised his glass at the head of the table appreciatively, God knows why he was seated there, he was anything but a lord. But, he was right, I had done very well and was feeling pleased with myself.

"Pass that cauliflower cheese back to me, please, it's so creamy, so cheesy." Grubby old Tom used his own fork to help himself to more sides instead of the serving spoons I'd laid out.

"Mm mm, these potatoes are so crispy. What did you cook them in? Goose fat?"

I nodded as I watched Dad crunch into one of my King Edwards with his knife before covering it in my port reduction.

Even the kids were impressed, their moaning temporarily paused as they happily tucked in. The venison was rare, the sauce was rich and this was the sort of meal that deserved to grace the table in a Scottish castle, so at least I was good at something. It was a satisfying feeling watching a group of people enjoy something I had created – I was a feeder, that's what I was. The only person who pushed it around the plate and didn't even make at least a noise of appreciation was Mel.

THE BIG HOUSE

She sat at the end of table playing with her food with a sullen look. She didn't even gasp at the height of my Yorkshires, which were towering; in fact, she stabbed it with her fork and then looked away as if she were disgusted.

Now perhaps it was because I had smashed a lot of the red during the cooking process, along with feeling inferior. It could also be that I felt pretty freaked out after reading the letter from jail. But to be honest, I was in the mood for a row, and she was my target, especially when I knew something wasn't right.

"What's up with your face?"

She looked up.

"Yes, you. Eat up, yoga girl, you'll need your strength for this new bloke you're chasing after," I said bitterly.

Mel said nothing. She glanced at Mum, her pensioner in shining Marks & Spencer armour.

"Raquel. This is not the right time for this – leave her and eat your dinner." Mum was protecting her so I wondered if she knew about Dave?

"Not the right time for what? A bit of sisterly bantz? You eat *your* dinner!" Mum raised her eyebrows, not liking my tone.

The table watched this trouble brewing with anticipation. Tom actually moved his chair to get a better view.

"Leave her alone, Raquel, she's going through rather a lot." Dad stepped in, which was, a bold move from him. I could take him down in ten seconds with the things I had on him.

"Shush you, eat *your* bloody dinner, Dad," I slurred.

Tom nudged Babs and whispered: "Told you, no respect, in my day..." I shoved the cauliflower his way and he immediately stopped mid-sentence and dug right in.

"Going through what? What exactly is the problem with her this time?"

THE BIG HOUSE

Mum responded sharply.

"That's rich coming from you, Raquel, perhaps we should do this in private?"

I was shouting now because she was all the way down at the other end of the table.

"Do what in private? What's the big secret? As if I don't know!"

I looked over at Dave, but he was busy draining the gravy boat and not really paying any attention to us so maybe he was oblivious to her feelings.

Mel stood up and left the room. I shouted after her.

"That's right, run away, go on, go show your camel toe to the neighbours."

"What is camel toe?" Arif asked confused.

Michaela leaned over and said: "Vagina, Arif, do you know what a vagina is?" And then she pointed to Suzy's crotch who quickly slapped her hand away.

Everyone was uncomfortable after chef's outburst and finished their dinners quietly. The kids all made different types of disappointed faces at me before excusing themselves and moving to the garden to play Giant Jenga, taking Arif with them and out of the firing line. Dave quickly followed, picking up the boule set and grabbing his wine, running for cover from yet another one of my episodes.

"She gets like this, best to keep away from her," Suzy whispered to Arif as they let the room. Arif turned back and winked at me, something he had definitely learned from my dad. Arif knew I was a nice person; he knew I wasn't the witch I was made out to be.

Dad came over and sat next to me, whilst Mum was giving Barbara a lecture on British cheeses and Tom had fallen asleep at the table. Sir Walter lay by the fire – he didn't follow Mel upstairs, which I took to mean he was on my side too.

THE BIG HOUSE

"Now listen, sweetheart, I try and keep out of female issues but you need to be there for your sister, like she was for you." He topped up my glass, knowing it would make it easier to take this.

"Something's going on, Dad, I can feel it. Why is no one telling me anything?"

"Because it's sensitive and we figured you had enough on your plate, you know, after the neighbours and you and Dave."

"But what's so sensitive that I can't know about it? Don't I deserve to be aware of what's happening in my own family?"

"You'll need to speak to Mel about that, but hey… go easy on her, she's got some difficult decisions to make."

"I'll bet she has, realising that me and Dave are stronger than ever!"

Dad frowned. "Just go and speak to her."

I climbed the stairs, wondering what I was walking into. Dad wouldn't send me into the lion's den with no warning, I would try to go in with an open mind.

Up on the first floor, Mel had taken a small room overlooking a courtyard I hadn't ventured out to as yet. It was in a corner of the house that was not only isolated but felt haunted too – she clearly wanted to be alone. I knocked, there was no answer. I pushed the door open to find her on her side lying on an antique bed with two freaky Victorian dolls sitting on the ledge next to her. I broke the ice:

"Your mates are a bit quiet." She turned over. I gestured towards the dolls. She smiled.

"Yeah, well they're good listeners, they don't shout at me over dinner."

She sat up and pulled her hood up over her head. She looked about fifteen again, not the forty-eight-year-old lawyer who wore pencil skirts and had a Mulberry City briefcase.

"Mel, why isn't Roger here and why are you being so odd?" She

THE BIG HOUSE

shook her head and then put it into her hands.

"Being healthy is a strange concept to you, isn't it? Unless I'm absolutely lamped every night and chewing on a pasty, you think something's off."

"That's rude, I'm not lamped every night and I've significantly reduced my pastry intake, thank you very much," I said defensively, pulling my T-shirt down and my jeans up to stop my belly making an unwanted appearance.

"Look, Raquel, I'm having some relationship problems right now. I would appreciate you giving me some space."

"Why do you need space?"

"Because this is my business and right now I need to keep it that way. I have some decisions to make and I need headspace."

"So you've come on a family holiday to spend time on your own? Seems a bit selfish to me. It's our parents' wedding anniversary and you're making it all about you."

"You have no idea, Raquel. And selfish is a bit rich coming from you considering all the help I gave you last year. I am here for Mum and Dad's anniversary and was actually planning a celebration for them that will be unforgettable. Now if that's all…" She gestured to the door.

'If that's all' is something a toffee-nosed lord would say to a lowly peasant as a polite way of saying 'fuck off'. But my sister had that about her, an air of authority and a way of making me feel like a sweaty wench.

"Well, where's Roger, your husband? Has he really got sciatica and a boil?"

She shrugged.

"Probably, but that's not the reason he's not here. He's not here because he's not enough for me anymore." She lay down again and that

THE BIG HOUSE

was my cue to leave. I wasn't going to force her into telling me what was going down, but clearly she had serious marital problems. I knew what that was like so I didn't press her. The thing I couldn't shake was that we normally shared things, so this made me even more suspicious as to what lay at the heart of her issue.

I left the room, none the wiser. I didn't like the new Mel and I didn't feel comfortable with her being thin and single.

In light of Mel's strange new personality and my husband being preoccupied with his new healthy lifestyle, I decided that the letter I received from Matt had to be ignored for now. Revealing this would be like picking the scab from a particularly nasty wound and watching it bleed all over again. The best thing to do was to sit on this, hoping it was a one-off and that it would just go away.

THE BASEMENT

Morag popped over on Thursday morning to show me how to use the dial-up connection and the printer for the massive old PC down in the cellar. Her hair was wet again meaning she'd been for another swim at the country club, but I didn't know why she hadn't just found one closer to the apartment she was staying in because Edinburgh must have loads of upmarket spas. She had long hair, which I found a bit odd for an older woman, but she wore it in a ponytail with a checked scrunchy so perhaps it was the trend up in Scotland. Although her hair was a rich chestnut brown, the greys at the root were very prominent – I'm talking at least a couple of inches of actual whiteness. She could have done with a trip to a salon in the city to sort that out but perhaps she was going natural, growing it out as grey hair was now a cool thing, but not the two-tone badger look she had going on, it needed to be all white to hit the mark. Once a stylish woman, mastering Scottish chic in every way, Morag was now looking more shabby minus the chic.

After following her down some very steep stone steps and my face being stroked by many cobwebs, I did not relish sitting at the battered old desk on an armchair that was far too low to type in comfort. There was a sofa in the corner mostly covered in a cotton throw, no doubt hiding all manner of stains, and I would sit there with my laptop until my article had reached its final destination, using a flattened carrier bag or Mel's best coat as a barrier between my arse and the smelly seat. I needed to get started on an assignment for a summer tart that *Woman's Own* wanted to include in their 'Picnics for Dummies' feature. I re-read the brief from my agent, Jane, to make sure I was on the right track.

THE BIG HOUSE

It has to be easy; it has to be so doable that even a person with no head or hands could make it, Raquel. They want a showstopper that looks the part but can be perfected with minimum effort.

Apparently the 'working mums' of Britain are pissed off at the 'stay at home' mums who are always outdoing them at every outdoor event.

And they're running another feature alongside about how to get ready for a night out in the back of your car, so it's all about busy parents keeping up with the lazy ones.

Hope Scotland is treating you well and say hi to your mum from me. We love her!

Jane Aldgate

If you're wondering how my London agency knew anything about my mother, then I'll tell you how. Without my knowledge or permission she organised a Zoom meeting with my agent, asking her to use one of Arif's home-cooked Syrian dishes as a feature. It would have apparently meant the absolute world to him if his 'boiled sheep's head surprise' appeared in one of the broadsheets.

Jane had told Mum she would mention it to her clients, and then after that they had a good old chuckle about the fact that I didn't have my maths GCSE and that I had lied on my CV pretending I had got a C. According to Jane, it was a sackable offence, but she said she would ignore what she knew because 'Mum' was just so funny. Thank you, Mother, for almost having me fired. Honestly, I could have killed her.

So my feature was to help us normal mums 'keep up with the Tabithas'. You know the types I'm talking about – those mums who manage to do everything without breaking sweat or a nail. They prance about the place in Lycra but somehow manage to look like they've just stepped out of L'Oréal's headquarters. They seemed to sew all their own labels on, bake their own gluten-free bread and their children have

THE BIG HOUSE

a master's degree before they leave the breast. Making a picnic look 'Insta ready' was a doddle to the Tabithas, and even though there was no doubt a gnarled mother-in-law chained to a beam in the attic who did all of Tabby's tasks, everything looked like 'Tabitha darling' did it herself. So I would help those knackered working mums struggling to get through the day without a pint of wine of an evening and I would make sure they didn't feel inferior at the Girl Guides' picnic.

The cellar was dingy, I could imagine that back in the day, during the time of *Outlander*, there had been a few Englishmen that took a good beating with a mallet down there, it had that sort of vibe. Morag told me that it used to be a wine cellar, but they had decided not to collect wine anymore and to use it as a study.

"Why not, you crazy woman?" I asked her, failing to hide my dismay. "If I had a wine cellar like this, I would romp around the globe picking up rare little quaffable gems and then I would section the wine shelves to suit my mood. Day drinking, drinking with friends, drinking with people I wanted to impress, special occasions, the run-up to my period and a very bad day section – that would take up one whole wall."

"Raquel, you'd normally do it by the region and the year, dear, but each to their own." She laughed, looking fondly at the empty shelves once filled with award-winning wines from around the world.

"My wee Miles became somewhat of an expert, you know, he would source the stock for us, travelling the world, actually. It all started after we all went on holiday to Southern France, do you recall?" I pretended not to hear her, and I stroked the big PC as if it were an animal, not wanting to be reminded of Miles slobbering in my ear.

She continued, "We returned to France a few times after our visit and Miles started learning about the different grapes, he took a real interest in the vintage, and because he was so good at it, we started our

THE BIG HOUSE

business doing wine tastings here at The Eagle Lodge."

"Miles was the sommelier?" I couldn't believe stinky Rat Fink was good at something so important.

"What a great skill to have," I quickly added, not wanting to seem too surprised.

"Yes, he was quite the man about town in the wine business for a while." She said this with a fond look in her eyes, a distant memory no doubt before he was sent down.

"Ah, and then he went away to work abroad?" I hoped Morag would tell me something about his absence at the pleasure of His Majesty and I think she almost did but then she thought better of it.

"Er, yes, he went over to Hong Kong and he worked his wee socks off, so he did."

I smiled sympathetically. "How exotic – lucky Miles."

She nodded and looked away, her cheeks pink with embarrassment. She left me after that, telling me she needed to check on Sister Sledge and then get back to Robbie who'd be needing his brunch right about now.

Left on my own, I noted that there was a lone small rectangular window, which offered no light at all. Apart from the desk, armchair, sofa and a lamp that looked a basic buy from Argos, the room felt bare and not a place my creative juices would flow. I decided I'd only come down here if I absolutely had to. After I had sent my recipe over to Jane, I quickly sent a text message to Roger, praying it would go through. Having had time to think on last night's conversation, Roger appearing could only make things worse if Mel needed some space. If anything, it could then drive Mel into Dave's arms if she needed comforting, which I wanted to avoid.

Mate, so sorry to do this at short notice but in hindsight I am not sure you should come. Wait for further instruction but for now, stay put.

THE BIG HOUSE

P.S. Please send an original copy of 1984, as Michaela is studying it so it will get me brownie points in your intellectual world of book nerds.
Regards, Raquel

I then legged it back up to the kitchen, eager to escape the cold and creepy basement. Although speaking of creepy, I wasn't impressed with who I found Mum chatting to over a cup of tea.

"Er, how did you get in?" I asked Miles.

"Don't be so rude, Raquel, I let him in," Mum frowned.

"What does he want?"

"Charming, I am here you know," he said, looking quite hurt.

"Can we help you?" I asked impatiently. His presence was making me edgy.

"Miles and I are just catching up. You get on with your day," Mum said, sensing my distain.

What did he want this time? Hadn't he got the message when I told him to do one? I hoped to God he wasn't telling Mum about our sordid afternoon in France because she would do something embarrassing with that information and make me the absolute laughing stock of Scotland.

I was still scarred by the time I got my period on the way to school so I had to call her from a phone box and ask her to meet me in the car park at lunchtime with two regular-sized Tampax. That was enough back then to control the flow, now I would need a traffic cone but that's another story. Anyway, she came early and dropped off a carrier bag full of sanitary products, including a whole roll of kitchen towel, at the school reception and she stapled a piece of paper with my name onto the front of it.

Anne, the senile receptionist just gave it to a brown-nosed prefect who then delivered it to my maths class, mid-lesson. Now back in the day, we didn't have a lot to keep us amused so if any lesson was

THE BIG HOUSE

interrupted, it was big news. So, all eyes were on me and the big bag of period paraphernalia.

I went to a Catholic high school in the nineties so having the piss taken out of you was an important part of the curriculum. Plus, I was in the bottom set for maths, which was like attending a drop-in centre for the criminally insane most weeks.

It was when Scott Lee stuck one of my Always Ultras, the ones with wings, to his forehead and headbutted the desk to see how thick it was that I knew this was going to be a difficult day. Somebody else then left the room to get a glass of water, and on their return the boys dropped a Tampax into it and cheered when it expanded as if it were a magic trick. Following that, the spare pair of big knickers, that mother had so kindly added to the 'bag of embarrassment', ended up in John Watson's mouth, stuffed there by a couple of the girls who had seen and heard enough of the nonsense and were possibly rejoicing it wasn't them enduring the sheer humiliation that day. The class descended into chaos and eventually the teacher called for help on the classroom phone using the words.

"Send help, Anne, 8E have gone bloody berserk."

Yes, Mr Ryan, 8E had gone bloody berserk because your dickhead prefect was tripped over on his way to my desk and the contents of the bag ended up on the floor next to a table of horny teenaged underachievers who struggled to even use an abacus.

Of course, this was more interesting than fractions – this was the closest thing to a fanny these lot had ever been.

My mother had caused carnage that day. I'd asked for a discreet meet-up between mother and daughter to drop off some items that would neatly fit in my inside blazer pocket with no drama. Instead, what she brought could have soaked up the entire River Thames, followed by the estuary.

THE BIG HOUSE

By lunchtime, the whole school knew I had my period and I was relentlessly ridiculed about it until the sixth form. So no, Mum could not ever find out about Miles and me because she would somehow leak it out with her loose lips.

Mum stepped out into the garden with Miles, and Dad watched them from the window whilst massaging his temples.

"You don't like him either, do you, Dad?" I could tell, the temple massaging usually came when Dad was feeling uneasy.

"Not particularly, no – and he needs a good bath if you ask me," he added, much to my delight. "I'm taking your mother for lunch today at the hotel in town. Keep an eye on Tom and Babs, will you?"

"In what way?" I wondered what I was supposed to do with them.

"Keep them fed and watered, make sure they get some fresh air, they have a tendency to stay in bed all day if you let them."

I agreed already planning to pass this job over to the kids because I had a tart to make and artistically photograph by two o'clock.

Dave and Sam were out on a jaunt that day, having got up early to explore one of the lochs nearby and they wouldn't be back until early evening. Michaela had barricaded her bedroom door so she could get her teeth into an essay about George Orwell, and she asked not to be disturbed. It was nice that people were doing their own thing and we were settling into the holiday. She had complained a couple of times that having no Wi-Fi was slowing her down, but she had some of his books which was all she really needed.

I went to ask Suzy to help although I wasn't going to hold my breath. "Right, lady, you and Arif are responsible for getting Tom and Babs outside for some fresh air. Perhaps you could take them into town for a cream tea."

"So, can we have some money then? I'm not paying for their lunch."

My eldest was co-operating, perhaps the fresh air had got to her

THE BIG HOUSE

brain or possibly the thought of being able to sit online for an hour or two whilst pretending to babysit the oldies was the real reason. Either way I handed her fifty quid and booked them a taxi for the short journey into town. There was no way Tom and Babs could have walked it without one of them face-planting, and then it would be me having to sew their noses and lips back on and I really could not be arsed with that.

Eventually, the day trippers headed off and Mel had taken herself down to the lake for meditation and mindfulness. That left me in peace at last in the big castle, which was much needed as I wanted to concentrate on caramelising onions and rolling out pastry. When cooled, I placed my finished tart on an old wooden board that I found in the back of a cupboard – it was rustic, it was a thing of beauty. The onions were sticky and a deep red, the mozzarella was gooey and oozed over the sides of a perfectly golden puff pastry – I had made that myself but the 'working mums' would use a shop-bought sheet. I sprinkled some freshly chopped basil over the top and drizzled some of my mega-expensive olive oil over the dish. It looked like a posh pizza and with a chilled glass of dry Riesling sitting nicely on the corner of the board. I went to fetch my camera to take a half-decent photo and tick this assignment off.

I set up in the kitchen garden using the edges of a raised veg bed as a platform for the tart. I took loads of shots but eventually I managed to get one with Sister Sledge in the background and the bright green tips of some camera-ready carrots to complete the shot. I'd attended a photography course during the autumn so now I was getting pretty good at this.

Project over, I sank into a chair, ate some of the tart and enjoyed a glass of the Riesling because I was on holiday after all.

Just beyond the wall, I heard the crunch of some footsteps walking

THE BIG HOUSE

past the gate that led to Miles's cottage. For crying out loud, surely he wasn't going to ruin yet another one of my peaceful moments. I braced myself waiting for the old bronze latch to lift but the footsteps went past the gate and towards the cottage. Okay, so he had a visitor, perhaps he had a girlfriend, a female rat who he had invited to his nest. That would be good, he would have a distraction and it would stop him appearing. I got up and crawled on my knees to peer through the gap and into the cottage, nosiness getting the better of me.

The cottage was actually a lovely little building and it sat very neatly in the corner of a small, cobbled courtyard; this was certainly previously the residence of a housekeeper or groundsman, and whoever had designed this estate did a very good job with the configuration of The Eagle Lodge. Sitting opposite the bungalow was an old barn, which was now quite run-down, but I imagined the horses that lived there happily in times gone by. The front door of the cottage was open, and whoever had walked past the garden gate was already in. Miles was at his kitchen sink with a teapot and he was talking to somebody sitting behind him. My thighs hurt like hell squatting like this but I stayed there long enough to see who the tea was for.

Sitting directly across from Miles and sipping hot tea from a china cup was my sister, Mel.

I couldn't hear what was being said, the cottage was close but still too far away for that. She stayed for about ten minutes before making her way around the side of the big house and back to her meditation point.

I just couldn't work out why Mel would drop by for a chat. I crept back to my spot undetected and decided to try to find out more.

I sliced up the rest of the tart and covered it in foil. This would make a good snack for in-between meals.

I left it for a good half-hour before wandering down to the shores

THE BIG HOUSE

of the lake to find Mel and see how she was.

"You joining me for some soul cleansing, Raquel?"

I laughed, and sat on the edge of her mat looking out onto the rather choppy lake, there was some weather coming in.

"Nah, just needed some fresh air, I've been working all afternoon."

"Ah, work, a distant memory. You know, I've not even checked my emails since we arrived." Mel seemed quite proud of this.

"Wow, that's insane."

She nodded; she didn't care about work anymore.

"Have you been out here all afternoon?" I asked, and she nodded.

"Yes, it's my happy place, I love it."

"Have you seen anyone at all? I've been stuck in the basement for the last couple of hours writing."

She shook her head. "Not a single person since breakfast, absolute bliss."

It was strange enough she'd popped in on Miles but even stranger to be lying about it.

"There's some onion tart thing inside if you're hungry?"

"No, I'm okay for now, thanks."

I stood to go back up to the house before making one final attempt. "That Miles is annoying, right? Always popping in uninvited. I caught him pestering Mum this morning."

She feigned confusion. "To be fair, Raquel, I haven't seen him at all since we arrived. He's not really on my radar."

"Lucky you, he's an arsehole."

She shrugged. "Don't let negativity ruin your day, Raquel." And then she turned back to the sun, legs crossed, eyes wide open, breathed in deeply.

I knew at this point, she needed more of this 'headspace' she'd apparently become so fond of.

THE BIG HOUSE

I had managed to send my photographs and recipe over to Jane after many attempts using the Elizabethan Wi-Fi, when I heard movement in the grand hall.

Tom and Babs were sprawled on the sofas, bags full of shopping, and they had big smiles on their faces.

"What's got them so happy?" I asked Suzy and Arif who were also looking rather amused.

"We couldn't get a taxi and Tom had a good few drinks with his lunch, so he was unsteady on his feet. We have had to give them piggybacks all the way up here."

"Yes, piggyback is lot of fun." Arif seemed thrilled to have learned a new phrase.

"Piggyback… piggyback." He kept repeating it and then laughing hysterically.

"What's so bloody funny?" I mouthed to Suzy.

"Oh, nothing really, Mum, we just had fun, that's all."

"So they had a nice time?"

"Yes, they have a few local purchases to take home with them and they had fish and chips out of the paper on a bench – we didn't bother with the cream tea, it was stupid money. And then we went to a little pub and we put songs on the jukebox. It was actually a laugh."

Suzy not scowling and not glued to her phone was a revelation.

Tom and Babs looked quite dishevelled; they'd had an afternoon out alright. Tom had a can of Irn-Bru in one hand and a small bottle of Scotch in the other. Babs was clutching a bag with a reel of tartan inside and she had something called Tablet wrapped in paper which she was licking like a lolly.

"They're still alive so well done to the pair of you. You're good at this. You can do the same with your nan and grandpa when they get here on Saturday."

THE BIG HOUSE

CeeCee and Gary were arriving at the weekend, but the house already felt quite full. Living with this many people was hard work, and although people were filling the dishwasher I seemed to be the only one who emptied it. There was a huge pile of laundry building and even though Mum said she would help, 'fingering other people's smalls' was not really her thing apparently.

We had jacket potatoes that night with a salad from the garden, it was the perfect easy tea. Dave had a block of cheese with his salad, as potatoes were the Devil in his new world. His arms were thinner, and I missed those big and bulky protective arms that used to make me feel safe.

Mel seemed more upbeat this evening, which was confusing. It was almost as though Miles had somehow cheered her up. I wondered, had Miles told her about his friendship with Matt and did she see this as a way to take me down once and for all? Maybe this was my cue to tell Dave about the letter but I just couldn't bring myself to do it. I had also walked in on a conversation Mel and Dave were having about 'good fats', which made me feel even more left out. These two seemed to have more in common with each other than their spouses, and when Dave asked to borrow Mel's tape measure to see how many inches he'd lost, I almost shouted out, 'measure your dick with it, give us all a laugh.' But I didn't, of course. He had never given a shit about his body before, in fact he had been quite proud of his rotund figure and likened himself to a 'rock hard Humpty Dumpty.'

Mum and Dad were telling me about their lunch out with Morag and Robbie and their afternoon of chatting about 'the good old days'.

"It was absolutely wonderful. Me and my bestie catching up over a steak Diane."

"Bestie? Oh, Granny, what have you become?"

Michaela sarcastically reminded my mum that she was not 'Gen Z' and she should not use their language.

THE BIG HOUSE

"Okay, gal pal – that's what we said back then." I don't know which was worse.

"Yes, it was a fantastic and enjoyable afternoon catching up with good friends," Dad added, putting his arm around Mum. Their relationship was so much more natural and relaxed, the sniping had stopped from Mum's end and the philandering at Dad's. It was an excellent turnaround; they were a fine example for us all to keep working at it.

After dinner, Mel sat and played Scrabble with Arif. She would have had more success playing I spy with David Blunkett. Arif's English was limited in the speaking sense, but when it came to writing it was nothing short of a disaster.

"What is this word Arif – sameer?"

He shrugged before explaining: "I sameer my chips with sauce."

Mel sighed. "Ah, you mean smeared." She removed the letters, not allowing him any leeway on account of English being his second language.

"And this, this makes no sense. Fajeena?" She pointed to the board. Arif again explained this in context.

"The girl, had a, how you say…? er, a sore fajeena."

He pointed to Suzy's crotch and said, "Fajeena, yeah?" Sam immediately stood and went to his friend's aid sparing him further embarrassment.

"You can't say that, mate, please don't say that." Sam quickly removed the letters that were supposed to spell vagina. Arif looked forlorn. It was worth a good few points and I am sure he felt this was just a biological term that was acceptable. Womb is fine. Ovaries are okay, we can even say testicles without recoiling, but vagina is taboo, we don't bandy people's vadges about at the dinner table, not the British.

THE BIG HOUSE

"I am sorry if I offend, it is new word I learn other day," he reasoned.

The table roared with laughter as Suzy covered her 'fajeena' with her napkin. Dave took it upon himself to try and teach Arif the correct pronunciation of vagina, which was wholly inappropriate as he split it into syllables and keep repeating it over and over again. Sam then kindly wrote the word on a piece of paper which Arif put it in his pocket, no doubt for googling purposes on the big PC in the dead of night. If he could reach a happy ending with Wi-Fi that slow, then good luck to the lad.

Just as I was bringing out a tray of hot chocolates topped with whipped cream and a Cadbury's Flake stirrer, there was a knock at the door.

"Who the fuck's that at this time?" Dave asked grumpily, inheriting my distain for guests without warning. Everyone moved to get a better view of the door that Dad had got up to open.

In the porch way, a figure shook a very wet umbrella in front of their face before revealing a red runny nose and bloodshot eyes.

"Hello, everybody, I think I'm coming down with cold, I do hope it's not coronavirus-19."

Interception failure. Roger had not received my message to abort mission.

STORMZY

The weather was just the tip of the iceberg for the drama that ensued over the next two days. Once Roger, his luggage and his ailments were inside the house, Mel had the mother of all meltdowns, screaming and shouting at everybody. As she hadn't actually given Roger the address to the house, she was confused at how he'd managed to rock up here. Realising somebody had to have helped him out, she initially focussed most of her angst at Mum, convinced she'd poked her 'bleeding big nose in yet again'.

I sat back, nibbling a cold potato skin, wondering whether Mum would just take one for team. She did not, in fact she immediately pointed the finger at my dad, shouting, "All the lads together, eh, Phillip? Is that what this is?"

Dad was confused as to why he was suddenly suspect number one. "Don't you start on me, Suzannah, I wouldn't dream of betraying my daughter." They looked at each other and then at Roger, waiting for him to grass up his secret ally.

It would be round about now that he would normally throw me under the bus and enjoy every minute of it, but to my surprise he didn't. He waited for the shouting to stop whilst dripping rain and snot onto his collar in equal measure. His beige raincoat, possibly once belonging to a flasher from the eighties, was belted up tightly and defiantly. He had no fashion sense, none at all.

"What the hell are you doing here? You know I wanted my space," Mel fumed at him.

He sighed deeply, his beard was quite short, his hair had been cut, he had lost his look of Jesus, he was going more for the 'charity worker' look – like the ones that stop you on Deansgate and ask if you care

THE BIG HOUSE

about anybody but yourself.

"I came to make amends; I want to talk to you but you wouldn't answer your phone so you left me little choice."

"How did you know where I was?"

"I found the address on your PC." And with that white lie I breathed a sigh of relief.

"Follow me! You can stay one night and that's because it's raining, that's it!" Mel barked sharply, angrily gathering her things from the table.

He shuffled behind her towards the bottom of the main stairs and looked back at me giving me a discreet nod. Dammit, I owed him one now and he would certainly call it in one day. I thought back to sending the abort mission message whilst in the cellar, a foolish mistake, one that I may eventually pay for.

"Okay, people, come on, off to bed, tomorrow is a new day, show's over." Mum ordered us off as if she were the house mistress in a school.

The wind still screamed around the house and rain beat relentlessly onto the windows, so I was glad to be getting tucked up. There were trickles of water on most of the sills, which were rotten and needed replacing.

Just as I was locking up and switching off the lights, the doorbell went again, so I went to answer it, who the fuck was it this time. Standing in nightclothes, drenched to the bone, were Morag and Robbie. The old Vectra they drove was parked on the grass verge slightly out of view of the house.

"Gosh, what's happened? Is everything alright?"

"There's been a flood at the apartment. The whole building is in dire straits, everybody has been evacuated; we have no idea how long it will be before we can get back in."

My initial thoughts were 'what do you want me to do about it?' but

THE BIG HOUSE

I had been trained to have better manners and she was Mum's best friend after all.

"What's this, what's going on?" Mum appeared in her dressing gown having heard the commotion as I ushered them in.

"They've been evacuated from their place in Edinburgh, Mum, flooding apparently," I explained, and Mum immediately ran to Morag's aid.

"You're soaked, you must be freezing, Morag, let's get you out of these wet things." And then she turned to me and said: "Right, you, soup and sandwiches I think are in order." And she flicked her hand towards me like I was a servant, clearly becoming a bit too comfortable in this big house.

"You what? I'm knackered. I've already cooked and cleaned the kitchen tonight." She gave me the look that meant I knew I would have to oblige.

Robbie and Morag took off their coats and sat in front of the fire that Mum had stoked up, adding another log. I leaned against the hob in the kitchen stirring a shop-bought tomato soup that I had brought for an emergency only. It was an interesting role-reversal that after handing over thousands to the owners of this house to use it as our own, we were now looking after them. The flood sounded serious enough, but surely it would have been easier to just find a hotel in Edinburgh instead of coming back here. If they wanted home comforts, they could have gone to Miles's cottage because they did own it, after all.

I grilled some bread with cheese on top and plonked it into two bowls of the soup before carrying it to the table on a tray. Robbie had poured himself a glass of Scotch and had put his enormous feet on a pouffe in front of the fire. I grimaced at the sight of bare wet hairy feet sizzling by the fire like a Gruffalo. Horrible!

THE BIG HOUSE

"They are staying here until the apartment is back up and running, Raquel, just a couple of nights. Add them onto your meal plan, will you?" Mum told me before squealing, "me and my gal pal, roomies again."

I headed to bed, unable to take any more drama.

"What an utter fucking piss take," I whispered to Dave as I got into bed. "We've only been here two days and already it's gone tits up. Add them onto my meal plan? Can you believe she said that? I mean they're loaded and now I have to cook for them and probably wash their clothes. Some holiday this was turning out to be. I'm just a skivvy, that's what I am, a glorified skivvy."

Dave stayed annoyingly quiet but still I needed to vent even if the ventee was unresponsive.

"And another fucking thing, your stupid bloody parents are arriving tomorrow afternoon with all of their 'requirements and demands', plus your dad keeps shitting himself so that should be tons of fun. Whining, then shitting, then moaning."

Dave faced me. "Go to sleep, Raquel, you're actually winding yourself up."

I turned off my night light and sighed, I was tired of tomorrow before it had even arrived.

Arif had affectionately named the aggressive wind and rain that battered The Eagle Lodge, 'Stormzy'. And because of Stormzy, it was decided that we would all stay in and do something as a group. Mum had bought herself a lounge set from The White Company and teamed it up with M&S's version of the UGG boot, her look for a grey day. You knew when Marks & Spencer have been involved, they always added extra grip and a good sturdy zip. A sensible version of what were really very expensive and slippery slippers. But as a friendly word of advice, never wear UGG boots in the snow, I made that mistake and went arse

THE BIG HOUSE

over tit in the middle of the street. I then got a lecture from an off-duty nurse who said she was sick of strapping up sprained ankles after 'UGG accidents', it was becoming a drain on the NHS.

* * * * *

"Here comes Katie Price's Nan," Dave muttered as she entered the room.

"Right, troops, I have a surprise for you all. Is everybody listening?" she trilled loudly to get our attention.

I held my breath. If this involved Miles, I would make my excuses and get drunk in bed. Mum stepped aside to reveal a couple of pretty young Thai girls wearing black tunics in the hallway.

"Meet the ladies from the Thai Angels Massage and Spa everybody. They are here to do some fabulous things to our bodies; all that pent-up tension will be released with their magical hands."

Dave's mouth dropped open, Tom looked up from the *Racing Post* raising an eyebrow, and Dad spat coffee into his lap. The two ladies looked at each other, wondering whether they should run.

Mum realised she needed to explain in a little more detail because we had no idea what was going on.

"We are all having massages, bone-crunching deep tissue massages that leave us feeling wonderful. Treatments will be in the library, two at a time."

Actually, I quite liked the sound of this, somebody walking on my back and cracking my neck. Perhaps Mum had come up with a great idea for once. This could be a very enjoyable treat. "Not for me, Mum, that may mess with my body tuning." Mum scoffed as Mel the misery, tried to turn hers down.

"Oh, I'll tell them to be gentle with you, Melanie, you'll be fine,

THE BIG HOUSE

they are couple's massages, it should be intimate and romantic."

Roger looked uncomfortable, as romance and intimacy was possibly something he was having trouble with. His wife was also treating him like a peasant, and to my surprise I was starting to feel sorry for him. That morning, she had walked into the lounge and shouted the word 'peppermint' at him. It was a good few minutes before I realised that she wanted a drink and this was not his new nickname. He jumped out of his chair and stood straining mint leaves into a teapot before delivering it to Mel who did not even say thank you.

"Just have the couples massage, Mel, the ladies are here now so it would be rude not to." I winked at her, she didn't like it and she stared icily in my direction.

Morag and Robbie were sitting at the breakfast table, observing the rowdy family interactions. Surely this was too noisy for them, and I didn't understand why they weren't busy calling the building for an update on the apartment or looking for a hotel. Sam was kicking a football to Arif across the hall, and I felt guilty that their house was being used as a sports hall. But really, I should not have to answer to them and we should have the place to ourselves.

"Wait 'til it stops raining, boys, you might break something."

Dave stepped in, realising somebody had to.

"Where's that huge piece of art that hung over the fireplace, Morag? Churchill, wasn't it – an oil painting?" Mum asked, noticing something was missing.

Morag looked up at the empty space. "Oh, that old thing. We put it in storage, we were thoroughly bored of it."

"What time are you picking up your parents from the airport?" I checked with Dave.

"Not 'til five-ish, why? Can't you wait to see... what did you call them again... my stupid bloody parents?"

THE BIG HOUSE

"Yeah, sorry about that." I blushed, realising it had just slipped out.

So, by this evening the numbers would be at sixteen. I'd have to make some sort of casserole, an easy one-pot job to feed everyone. I asked Suzy and Michaela to go to Ferguson and Sons and pick up some sausages.

"Dad will drop you and you run in, as it's torrential out there."

Michaela shook her head. "Mum, I am literally getting to the nitty gritty about Lewis Carroll and his liking for LSD."

Mum's ears pricked up immediately.

"That is a scandalous accusation, Michaela, can't somebody just have a good imagination without being accused of being a 'crackpot'?" Mum said, quite put out that her childhood was being tainted.

"I think you mean crackhead, Suzannah," Dave corrected her – if anyone knew the lingo, he did.

"What about crack whore? That's a good one," Tom added, seeing this as a game of words involving crack.

"LSD is very different to crack guys, it was used as a creative tool," Michaela said, as if she were a guru on the subject.

Dave curled his lip; he was not happy at all that his baby girl knew so much about narcotics and their uses.

Arif saved the day: "I will go, I like butchers, I like meat shop." So he, Dave and Suzy drove down into town to pick up three-dozen sausages for my Sicilian stew, leaving Michaela to destroy the innocence of Alice and her 'trip' to Wonderland.

Dave and I decided to take the second massages after he was back with the shopping. The two beds of bliss were set up in the library and the ladies waited, joining their hands together in a praying motion as we entered the room. There was light music playing from a CD player on the floor and incense burned, filling the air with scents from somewhere like Koh Samui. We both lay on our fronts with our faces

THE BIG HOUSE

squished through holes in the bed and the masseuses began to work on our backs. Something about the noise of the rainfall made it feel more relaxing and slowly I drifted off into a cosy state of deep sleep. Forty minutes later I was awoken gently by a whisper in my ear. "Turn over, please." As I groaned with stiffness and hauled myself over for the last few minutes, I looked over at Dave's bed, I hoped he'd enjoyed it as much as I had. Sitting on the bed grinning at me, skinny legs hanging over the side of the bed was Old Tom. He was having his neck rubbed.

"Oh my God!" I pulled the towel over my bare bits. "How have you got in here?" I demanded.

"Dave was interrupted, got a call so he had to leave. I took his massage; blimey, you are a snorer, I've heard quieter hogs."

I turned to my masseuse for back-up but she shrugged and giggled.

"Do you think they do extras, Raquel?" Tom winked, completely unbothered that it was a disgusting suggestion.

"Not for you, mate, definitely not for you."

I left the massage room feeling completely violated, my relaxing full body massage now tainted with a voyeur on the next bed.

"Mother, why did you let him in there, I was practically naked?"

"Oh, don't be a baby, we didn't want to waste the slot." She shrugged.

"Why didn't you send Mel in, surely that would have been a better option?"

"She's having hers with her husband, it's a couples massage. Keep up!"

I went off upstairs to grab a shower and met Dave on the landing looking a bit agitated.

"Dave, they replaced you with Tom, what the hell was he doing whilst I was..."

He stopped me.

THE BIG HOUSE

"Don't go mad but I have to go back down south today, I'll be as quick as I can. It's work, I'm sorry, love, I really am."

"But it's nearly the weekend," I said, as if that would make a difference. Dave frowned.

"People still break the law at weekends, love, there is no holiday for crime. Look, I'll be as quick as I can, okay," he promised.

I processed this for a moment: there was me, chief cook and pot washer, my bone-idle daughters who would once in a blue moon do something helpful, Mum and Dad who were generally just silly and couldn't be relied on as solid support, and now Morag and Robbie who didn't appear to be making a move to go back to Edinburgh. My sister Swampy and the wet wipe Roger who were arguing until the early hours were now both sulking so I couldn't see them doing much, and to be fair, Tom and Babs were happy in their bed eating gherkins and watching YouTube so wouldn't help but didn't create much mess. But with CeeCee and Gary added into the mix with their useless knees, lazy bowels and unable to regulate their own body temperatures, I wasn't sure there was enough rosé wine in the castle to keep their moaning under control, I would need to squeeze some blood from my finger into a glass of white if we ran out.

As I went through the guest list and everyone's requirements, quite frankly I was ready to wear lead boots to the lake. How would I cope? Especially without Dave to calm me down. Everybody was useless and more of a liability than anything else. But then I remembered, I was living with the sweetheart that was Arif. Okay, technically he wasn't working and this was his holiday too but if he wanted to be part of this family then he would need to roll his sleeves up. We could do this between us, and Dave wasn't much use anyway at the practical stuff, just the emotional support.

"Fine, Dave, but get your arse back here as soon as possible." He

THE BIG HOUSE

was relieved, I could have clawed him to shreds him like an eagle, but I didn't.

"You'll be okay, I know this isn't what we planned but something's come up. I'll be back before you know it."

He packed his overnight bag as I lay on the bed wondering just how loud my snoring had been and whether Tom had recorded it on a Dictaphone to taunt me with.

"Try not to shag anyone whilst I'm away," Dave joked, but it stung a little bit.

"I promise that if I get desperate, I'll interfere with that suit of armour."

He laughed. "You know that's from a fancy dress shop, don't you? It's not even original. There's a sticker on the back that says, 'Bargain Costumes of Glasgow'." I shook my head in disbelief.

"Disappointing and makes it all seem a bit naff. Plus, the pans are from Ikea and the wine glasses are pub grade. I thought we were hiring Balmoral's little sister," I sighed.

Dave nodded in agreement; everything did seem sort of 'cut back'. Things were missing all over the house and now they were back staying here and sort of hovering.

I offered Dave a quickie against the radiator before he left. I made a deal with myself that when he was away, I would always ensure we had some sort of sexual interaction beforehand. It was insurance, really, but he politely declined saying that he was not in the mood after such a big breakfast. I'd only seen him eat one sausage but I let it go, trying not to feel rejected. The real punishment for my behaviour was never ever feeling safe in my relationship. Who knew!

Currently my suspicions fell on my own sister, and before Mel it had been a woman called Cath from work who Dave had mentioned only twice but it sent me into a spiral causing me to stalk her on

THE BIG HOUSE

Instagram for three weeks. Eventually I accepted it was unlikely they were together as Cath was in her mid-sixties, a foster parent plus her sister was a nun. Before that it was a Tesco delivery driver. She was very attractive, had a look of Suranne Jones, sort of surly but sultry, and when Dave told her a joke outside of her van, she touched his arm and giggled. I was so livid, I left her a one-star review for rudeness. I know she'll probably wallop me if I ever see her again and rightly so. Over the past few months, I'd become a jealous mess, was insecure and what my Aunty Pauline would have described as 'living on me nerves'. Cheating on my husband had an unexpected result; it affected me more than it did him.

I watched through the bedroom window as Dave put his sports bag in the boot of his car. I watched him, looking for clues. He'd turned down a quickie, what was that about? There weren't many men who would say no to that – a quickie requires no emotion and zero aftercare, something was definitely up. And then, just as he opened the car door, somebody caught his attention beyond my view. I pushed my head out of the bedroom window to see who he talking to. Miles sucked heavily on a cigarette whilst chatting to Dave about God knows what. It was a brief conversation, but it was enough to make me worry. Just looking at them together was a horrible thing. As Dave pulled away, Miles looked up to the window that I had my head wedged out of and he waved with a smile. And then after that, he repeatedly pointed to his watch and mouthed the words 'tick tock'.

The massages were still underway when I returned downstairs. Mum and Dad were sprawled out on the sofas murmuring about being taken to another place both physically and mentally. Tom kept cocking his head from one side to the other exclaiming, "It's a miracle, I could only look forward before this."

Mel and Roger were in the room undergoing their treatment and

THE BIG HOUSE

the children had opted out of the activity claiming it would be utterly gross to lie in the same beds as the rest of us.

I found Arif and ushered him into the kitchen. "Can you help me? With cooking, laundry, that sort of thing?"

He nodded, "Of course. It would be pleasure."

"The thing is, Arif, I didn't anticipate how much work would be involved in a house like this. I am feeling a little overwhelmed, especially with so many of us."

He felt my pain, understanding the issue. "Give me half-hour, yes, I solve problem."

I shrugged, "Okay, every little helps." And then I was transported back to a world of rage thanks to Tesco bitch and her tight buns.

Not much later, Arif rounded everyone up. "Okay, people, I have new arrangement, and everybody need listen." Arif stood on a chair with a clipboard in his hand and a pen behind his ear.

"This is big house, does everybody agree?"

They all nodded and muttered in agreement.

"So to make sure all work does not fall on Raquel, we need to help. Yes?"

More muttering.

"I can't hear you, people."

They finally relented and shouted, "Yes."

Not enthusiastically I might add.

"So here is job list, it will be put on wall in kitchen. Everybody must perform one job per day and then make a tick when completed. That way, life will be, how you say... tickety-boo."

Everybody frowned, why was Arif talking like a cockney barrow boy?

Suzy chimed in. "We've been watching some DVDs of *Only Fools and Horses*, we found them upstairs. He seems to like the way they talk for some reason."

THE BIG HOUSE

"Say it people, come on… tickety-boo!" Arif shouted at us all.

We all shouted 'tickety-boo' and I found it very funny. Not just that I suddenly had a lot less to do but the fact these two had learned how to use an archaic DVD player.

Arif continued: "So, list goes a bit like this: bin-emptying, meal-prep, washing up and drying pots, clearing table, hoovering and polish, toilet cleaning, laundry, shopping, entertainment, feed Sledge Sister and collect eggs."

"Who in merry hell is Sledge Sister?" Roger whispered to me.

"Three black women that live in the basement practising Motown," I replied in a hushed voice, and he looked at the cellar door bemused.

Arif continued: "Walking Walter, bed changes and lastly watering vegetable garden at night, if Stormzy go away."

"And who is this Stormzy he talks of?" Roger leaned in again.

"He's Sledge Sister's manager."

He looked at Mel, who smiled at me. She wouldn't normally support me taking the piss out of Roger but things were a little different now.

"Oh, and another thing: you can't do same job twice in three days," Arif proudly exclaimed.

Another crushing blow for those who thought they could get away with only doing things they liked.

He then Blu Tacked the list to the fridge and headed straight upstairs with a bottle of toilet cleaner wearing rubber gloves having bagsied the bogs first at the start of the holiday when they would be in a better state. He really was a genius.

"I'm tired just reading that list, what a bossy little devil, I thought we were supposed to be on holiday." Old Tom squinted at the list on the fridge.

"To be fair, Tom, it's a pretty good idea. Between all of us we can have this place running like clockwork," Dad jumped in, clearly

THE BIG HOUSE

impressed by the delegation idea. Up until now, it had been very unorganised, leaving me with the lion's share unless people were told otherwise to help.

"There's nothing on there you can't do, Tom, it's a little light exercise," I said, making it clear to Tom he'd better co-operate.

Barbara walked up to the fridge and put a tick next to something, she then headed out to the utility and re-appeared with a Henry hoover which had seen better days.

"Watch her with that, she's got history." Mum laughed as she always did at other people's misfortunes.

Sam followed and put a mark on the list before putting on his waterproof coat and heading out to the kitchen garden with an egg basket to sort out the hens.

Michaela and Suzy both ran towards the kitchen barging into each other and trying to trip one another up. They eventually agreed to be in charge of entertainment for that evening and to walk the dog when the rain stopped.

Quite honestly, Arif had really come up with something pretty fantastic and it brought us all together. I would try and continue this at home; wishful thinking perhaps but worth a shot if I threatened to cancel their phone contracts…

Later that afternoon, I headed over to Edinburgh Airport to collect Dave's parents. They were landing at teatime but I set off earlier to get some time alone in the car with Wi-Fi to catch up on my emails. Sitting in peace with my feet on the dash was bliss. I had a good half an hour to relax without anybody bothering me. An email that had been sent the previous day but had been trapped in 'no Wi-Fi' purgatory until I hit a town pinged into my inbox.

THE BIG HOUSE

Raquel,

Good work on the tart, looked bloody delicious. Photos were fantastic too, well done.

Now, you are probably going to find this a tad annoying and I know it's August but with you being in a Scottish castle, it could be an opportunity for you to do something Christmassy and get ahead of the game. Nobody can afford to hire places for shoots at the moment so yes, I am being cheeky but at least your meal will be paid for, just send in the receipts!

Would be great if we had some Christmas dinner shots on file in such a grand location, your Mum did a video of the place you're staying at for me and I was blown away. In fact it was her that suggested you did a 'Christmas luncheon', perhaps we should put her on the payroll LOL. Anyway, it will be less work for you and I in the autumn when other jobs are rolling in. Plus, as usual, I'm going on a month-long cruise and I am turning my emails off until the end of September. My agenda will be mojitos for breakfast and the captain's Cumberland for lunch, ha ha.

In other news, the recession is hitting pockets hard so Good Housekeeping are going back to basics and want a menu inspired by wartime staples. Maybe some offal, something cheap and nasty that won't break the bank. You'll need to do a bit of research on what was available back then, they want authenticity.

Happy hols.

Jane

My agent Jane was married to the captain of a cruise ship, so every year she sailed off somewhere exotic for free and was treated like an A-lister. I envied her; when her husband was home he was completely off work with no interruptions, no calls, he was off-shift and somebody else steered the ship – literally. She was right, though, nobody in this

THE BIG HOUSE

industry had the budget to hire expensive places for shoots so at every opportunity writers like me were being asked to use our initiative when it came to locations. A Christmas feature in this house would be a triumph but where would I get a turkey in August and how would I decorate the damn place with festive trimmings? I'd find a way to deal with it, I always did.

I reclined my seat slightly, the Portuguese pillocks still hadn't landed, as they'd promised to send me a message. I pulled down my visor to dim the light a little and was surprised to see a yellow Post-it note staring me right in the face.

Matt is waiting for his reply, drop the letter in the greenhouse by tonight. It wouldn't be good for him to be re-interviewed. Clock's ticking.
M

I sat bolt upright, grabbed the note and screwed it up. Miles had been in my car, he was pressuring me, threatening me even. Why was this happening to me... again?

I tried to stay calm but it was difficult, my breathing becoming more rapid as my mind raced through my options. So, Matt was lonely with his wife gone, his cellmate released and now the only thing he had for company was a laminated picture of me and him in happier times when he was a free man who could eat food that hadn't been farted on. He was possibly annoyed that we were on holiday and he wouldn't see an ice cream, a beach or a real woman in the flesh that he could touch without being coshed on the back of the head. It made sense that he wanted contact so if I just wrote him a little note once, just to quieten him down then it might keep him going for a month or two. If I ignored him, he may spill his guts saying that Dave let the others go to save his wife and then we'd all be for it. This was all Gina's fault, surely she could have somehow got a letter to him up the arse of

THE BIG HOUSE

one of her associates. She should have, at the very least, let him have a laminated picture of her wearing Burberry nipple tassels. Everybody knows you can get anything in and out of a British jail – it has a better system than DPD.

I had read in *Take a Break* only last month that in one well-known serial killer's cell during a random search they found a photo copier, a massive old-fashioned one that was almost as big as a Corsa. Prison staff were apparently 'bemused' as to how it got in there.

So if the Yorkshire Ripper's protégé could take images of his bare arse in a re-created branch of Staples, then I'm damn sure Gina could have contacted Matt if she had wanted to. I decided I would write him a note, deliver it to Miles to pass on and then I would be able to relax for the rest of the summer. One short letter wouldn't hurt. No point in bothering Dave with this, he had enough to do, and I didn't want anything to push him into the arms or up the fajeena of another woman.

After virtually carrying CeeCee and Gary from the terminal to the car because they had seized up after a couple of hours of sitting down on the flight, I drove them up to The Eagle Lodge biting my tongue the whole way.

We had to do two toilet stops, one because somebody actually needed it and the other was just a feeling that materialised to nothing, but all of that was no problem compared to having to return to the car park of the airport because Gary thought he'd dropped his money whilst getting into the car. It turned out that he had dropped some money and I am so glad I went eight miles out of my way because of a flipping two-pound coin. I thought we were talking about perhaps two hundred quid in a money clip, but no. It cost me more in fuel to go back.

I then had to listen to a twenty-five-minute phone call between the

THE BIG HOUSE

both of them and their Portuguese neighbour who was actually from Hull about a spider plant that had to be checked on every day because she didn't like being on her own. 'She', they actually called a plant 'she'! The neighbour was equally as mental because she agreed to leave the blinds open during the lunar eclipse. "It would be a shame for her to miss it," said Maude the clown who lived opposite them on the complex. I went through an entire bag of Midget Gems during that journey, one after the other, just to take the edge off.

Back at the house, almost every job on the list had been done, so now people were doing their own thing. The dinner was prepped, the table was set and the girls showed CeeCee and Gary their room on the first floor overlooking the lake.

Arif was waiting for me in the kitchen with a pinny on. "What next, Mrs? I am ready." I asked him to brown off the sausages whilst I nipped down to the basement for 'work reasons' and that I would be back in no time. I sat at the desk and typed a letter on my laptop, connected it to the printer and waited impatiently for the stupid old thing to produce. There were some envelopes in the top drawer of the desk; I double-checked what I'd written just to ensure it was positive and something to keep Matt going.

Hello Matt, good to hear you are keeping well. Ever so sorry to hear your sentence has been extended – if you improve your behaviour, they might reconsider. Perhaps you could teach the inmates to read and write. That's what happened in a film I like, The Shawshank Redemption. Andy Dufresne, the main character, made lots of friends after some initial problems in the shower. Anyway, he ended up living on his own boat next to the Pacific Ocean after his release. So think on, it's not all doom and gloom.

Sorry to hear that Gina has not been in contact, I'll be sure to let

THE BIG HOUSE

you know if I see her and I will pass on your regards. I am sure she is safe and enjoying life, so you mustn't worry about her, she seems very resourceful. You really should concentrate on yourself, Matt, focus on what's happening on the inside and take it one day at a time. Big Mike sounds like fun, perhaps stick with him, learn some more about cooking, it will be good for you to be able to make your own meals once you're out and in a half-way house or whatever they call them. If there is a prison gym, maybe you could beef up for when you get out and then you could move to Tenerife and work in a holiday complex as a fitness instructor.

Ask the prison to get you a copy of The Shawshank Redemption, that will cheer you up and give you hope. But don't use that photo of us to cover up your escape route. (If you watch the film, you'll see what I mean. Ha ha.)

I enclose a recipe for a red onion tart, it's pretty easy to make and it goes a long way. If parmesan is too expensive, you can swap it for cheddar cheese, any cheese, really. Not sure you'd be allowed a fruity white wine to complement this, perhaps a fizzy water with a wine gum in it would work just as nicely.

Good luck for the future.

R

I'd made sure I didn't use question marks as they would insinuate I wanted a reply, but overall it was cheery and simple so should do the job. I had considered saying he wasn't missing anything on the outside and that he was better off where he was. I almost said the country was a joke and it was being run by incompetent fools but thought better of it. If somebody intercepted the letter it could be deemed as me inciting hatred, I could cause a prison riot. The 'guvnor' would probably get shanked and it would be all because of me. So I kept it light and I thought that would be enough to get him off my case. I popped the

THE BIG HOUSE

letter in an envelope and left it in the greenhouse next to the chillies and carried on with my evening as planned.

After dinner, Mel and Roger were on washing and drying duty, and Mum and Dad were laughing like school children whilst throwing socks at each other doing laundry duties. Morag and Robbie had clearly decided they were not involved in the chores list and had taken a walk to Miles's cottage to catch up with him. I'd wondered if they were going to see about staying there or were just saying goodbye before they went back to the hopefully now fixed apartment. The rain had calmed a little and the weather for the following morning was apparently good.

"Are you off home tomorrow?" I asked Roger, who was washing a pan vigorously with a scourer. He looked up apprehensively to Mel.

"He can stay until the weather has fully calmed down," she said without looking at him. I was about to say that tomorrow's forecast was fine, but I realised, if she really wanted him gone, he wouldn't have been in the kitchen at all.

He went back to his scouring, grateful for another twenty-four hours of grovelling.

Back at the table, which was being cleared by a grumpy Tom huffing and puffing and mumbling something about the war under his breath, CeeCee and Gary were sat looking tired and underwhelmed.

"How are you both?" I checked.

"The only fing is, darlin'…, it's the bedroom, really."

"The bedroom?" I frowned.

"Yes, the bedroom." Gary sighed whilst shaking his head.

"What about it?" I enquired. There could be nothing wrong as it was on the first floor, less stairs to climb than the other floors, it had a great view and it was next to the toilet. What the hell could the problem actually be?

"It's not so much the bedroom, darlin', it's the bed actually."

THE BIG HOUSE

CeeCee rubbed her kneecaps for added effect.

"The size of the bed, Raquel, that is our issue, it's too small you see. We like to spread out, I need to be able to lie legs akimbo for my joints to work the next day. I mean, it's only a double, we measured it," Gary explained.

"What with?" I asked.

"A tape measure, never go anywhere without a tape measure, do we, Cee?" he replied, and CeeCee nodded.

"Never."

I sighed, "Oh dear, unfortunately there's a full house and the only Super King bed is in the master you see."

Gary cocked his head to one side. "The master, is that the one with the en suite?"

I nodded.

"And who is in there? Is it an able-bodied young person without arthritis?"

I looked at the floor because only the floor would understand my hidden fury.

"That's where Dave and I sleep actually, Gary." They both looked at each other and shrugged and then CeeCee said in her softest and cutest voice:

"Ah, well, that's it, then, we'll just have to get on with it, Gary."

That big room and large bed had been my little nugget of luxury during my stay. Originally, it had been allocated to my parents but, due to the size of Dave and me, Mum had given it up in a rare act of kindness.

"You two take the big room, you'll never sleep otherwise," she'd said whilst sizing us both up. And then I heard her call Dave 'Chubs Maloney' as she walked off making Dad piss his pants.

During the following two hours, Arif and I moved four weeks' worth of clothes, all of mine and Dave's toiletries, books, cosmetics

THE BIG HOUSE

and personal items over to the small double. We then changed the sheets in the master, cleaned the en suite, carried up a plug-in radiator, kettle, cups, teabags, a jug of milk and retrieved an electric blanket from the attic. After all of this was done, Cee and Gary settled into their new room and announced: "This will do."

By eight o'clock I was ready to immerse myself in a swimming pool of Pinot Noir. Even though Dave had lost a considerable amount of weight he was still the widest person in this house, therefore when he returned, I would spend my time hanging off the edge of the bed losing insane amounts of much-needed sleep.

I called him from the bath in the shared bathroom that Tom did his mucky business in.

"Come back soon, for God's sake," I wailed.

"Why, what's up?"

"Don't know where to start but just know that I hate you."

He laughed. "How lovely! I take it people are being hard work?"

"There are no words, Dave, I miss you."

"A couple of days and I'll be back."

"A couple of days?" I shrieked. "No, please, no." I noted that he didn't say 'miss you too'. Small things like this got to me.

"It's work, my hands are tied. I have to go, speak tomorrow."

I sighed and reached for my glass; I would need a lot more of this stuff to help me get through until his return.

"Okay, Dave. See you soon. Love you," I said but the line had already gone dead.

I started to wonder if Dave was really at work and whether he still loved me. Or, was Dave in the back of a Tesco van doing a delivery of a different type?

I had no idea; I had no right to ask and no solid reason not to trust him.

HARD TIMES

Although I was a food writer, I now had to photograph my recipes too due to declining budgets across the board within mags. But every now and then, if I felt there was an interesting angle, I would write and produce something I felt was worthy of a read. Not just a recipe or a description of a dish; something with a little more substance. I would send over my creative extras to Jane at my agency to keep on file just because sometimes there would be a blank space in a publication that needed filling quickly. Normally because a journalist had missed her deadline and was face down in a pile of Charlie in some guy's flat south of the River Thames. These young journos were about as reliable as a regular Tampax on a heavy day and they were flaky as filo too.

I was a safe bet when it came to reliability – if I said I would do something, I always did. This is one thing you develop in your forties: a good strong work ethic and the ability to say no to Class A drugs on a Tuesday afternoon. We parents had school runs, we had piles of washing to turn around; we didn't have the flexibility to go down with 'fashion flu' every week, that just wouldn't do. But what we normally didn't do, was to go the extra mile or take risks. We did what was on the brief and then when we were done, we put our phones in airplane mode and would then drink the same amount of wine as Gazza did on a match day.

So now I'd had this idea to accompany the wartime recipes, I was going to make sure it was worth reading. It was Sunday afternoon when I finally managed to sit down with Tom for the interview I had planned. He didn't take much persuading, he liked to talk and he liked to drink.

"What year were you born, Tom?" I asked him.

THE BIG HOUSE

Tom sank back into an armchair next to the fire and began to tell me what he remembered about his childhood and what he ate during the war.

"I was born in 1937, two years before the war started. It ended when I was eight."

"Can you remember anything about the war?" I was interested to know.

"Of course I bloody can: it was frightening, people were terrified, you don't forget that in a hurry. I remember seeing the planes flying over our house, it was a very edgy time. Men went away to defend the country and the women and children stayed at home. But my father couldn't fight as he went blind in his left eye just before the war started."

I wrote some of this information down on my pad. He leaned over and peered at the page before glaring at me.

"You may think that we had it easy but we didn't, Raquel. You know people were jealous because Father stayed at home, they thought he was a coward. That's what the bastards called him, you know, and didn't help at all that his name was Howard. I was ribbed terribly."

I didn't react, I tried not to laugh but he could tell I wasn't buying it and he defended his father. This was clearly a sore point and he was transported back to classroom where the chanting must have been excruciating. I decided to pry a little more:

"But he was definitely blind in his left eye, Tom, you're absolutely sure of that?"

Tom staggered to his feet and poked his walking stick my way.

"Don't you start with me, lady, you sound like them. Yes of course he was, he definitely was!"

I passed him his drink which calmed him immediately and he sat back down and continued.

"He had no sight at all in that eye, he couldn't have fired a gun,

THE BIG HOUSE

steered a tank, he'd have killed his own men with such limited vision. And anyway, Mother was a bit suspicious initially so well, we did a few tests of our own, Mother and I."

"What tests, eye tests?" I was instantly interested.

"Before you start, we created our own tests, something a bit more practical, and he *was* blind."

"Go on, Tom, what sort of practical test did you do?" He went red, possibly realising what he was about to say was very unconventional and possibly illegal.

"It seems a bit mean now but Mother wanted to be sure. So, just to prove it, every now and then we would throw a cricket ball at him from somewhere on his left. Sometimes from the landing, often from a window whilst he was out in the garden or, just to make it completely unexpected, from behind a tree when he was out hunting. He never flinched you know, and he had a permanent black eye."

I grinned. "Okay, well that sounds quite extreme. But this article is actually about the food you ate during war times."

Tom grumbled to himself, he was furious that he had given me his Achilles heel, 'Howard the coward' was definitely some solid gold piss-taking material for my back pocket.

"So, you were a wealthy family, big house, lots of old money. Did the war affect your diet the same as it did the people with less?" I tried to focus back on the article.

Again, he got quite uppity.

"Now listen, just because we had money didn't mean we got any more than anyone else. I didn't see a banana until the fifties, you know. We were all rationed, we could only have what was allocated."

"Okay, so what was your typical weekly diet whilst you were rationed?"

He smiled as he took me back down memory lane, even though the

THE BIG HOUSE

country was a mess, his father was clearly a shirker with a very strong left cheek and his mother, well she sounded like an absolute hoot if I'm honest.

"Mondays we had tripe in milk. Tuesdays would be liver and onions. Wednesday would be a sandwich of corned beef, something tinned because Mother had her WI meeting on that evening and she didn't have time to cook. Thursday would be brisket, possibly with cabbage or another vegetable grown in the garden and Fridays we had fish, always a cod supper. The chip shops stayed open during the war and everything was cooked in lard."

He licked his lips at the thought.

"On Saturdays we went to my granny's – she lived alone but she somehow managed to feed us well. Granny would make scones, she made her own jam and there was always plenty of other preserves in her cupboard. So I think you would call that an afternoon tea, really."

That sounded quite lovely, a memory that he clearly cherished. He continued:

"On Sundays we had a roast but as I remember the meat was very tough, it wasn't like it is now all pink and fancy, it went in the oven for hours on end. On Monday at lunchtime, I would run home from school because I knew there would be bread and dripping from the beef fat on the Sunday."

I scribbled this down very quickly; he was giving me a lot of good stuff to go on for my menu-planning.

"Were you happy, back then, Tom? I know there was a war on, but you seem to recall it fondly." He nodded in agreement.

"Life was simple. You had what you had and got on with it; yes, we had a big house but it was always cold and it was quite lonely. Sometimes I would be jealous of the families of eight stuffed into terraced houses and sharing beds, sharing slices of bread sometimes.

THE BIG HOUSE

But you see, they were warm, they had each other. And when the country was under attack and their fathers went away, sometimes for good, they had each other."

I looked back across the grand hall at all the different people scattered around that I had been complaining about. He was right, family was important, there was safety in numbers.

"In answer to your question, dear…"

"Which one?" I'd asked so many, I couldn't remember.

"About me being happy, keep up, you sloppy girl."

"Sorry."

"I was generally happy in my childhood and then I was alone for many years which made me unhappy but now…" Tom added, looking around the room.

"I am happy again, because of all this."

I touched his arm, it was an arm-touching moment that this rather grubby man had somehow managed to verbalise the meaning of life. He had managed to melt me, the ice-maiden of Cheshire. An absolute breakthrough. But quickly, he pushed my arm away and handed me his empty glass.

"And don't think it's because of you or my cousin and this lot. It's because I love this massive house, it reminds me of when I was rich. Now toddle off and fill up this glass up like you promised."

I had enough to go on for the *Good Housekeeping* menu, I would google the bits I didn't have but whether or not this drunken mess of a man had dangled an emotional moment in front of my face before brutally ripping it away, it made me take stock. These people were my family, we were making memories and when I looked back on it in, say, thirty years, did I want to remember this as the time I ruined it with my misery? I would thank Tom one day for this. Listening to the old guy talking about his life when the Germans were bombing the

THE BIG HOUSE

shit out of us, when we were rationed to three sausages a week and when he was envious of the poor because they were rich with family.

I was also excited to get cracking with the recipes because this was a time when we used butter, lard and full-fat milk. There was no choice, people needed their own version of fast food. Eggs straight from the chicken's bum, free range and organic, veg that was grown on allotments or in their own yard, and berries from bushes within walking distance of the house. They ate bread dipped in fat for their school lunches, it kept them warm, it fed their brain. Perhaps an article that went against calorie-counting was for once the way forwards. We take what we can from the land and we survive, that was what they did when life was simple. I would definitely be best mates with Bear Grylls after all of this foraging talk, and if Dave was playing away then Bear and I would marry on the steps of the Imperial War Museum and I would be awarded the George Cross for cookery.

On Monday morning, I awoke with some positivity. I jumped out of my now small bed and was downstairs cooking breakfast by eight. The storm had finally passed on and the sun was shining. It wasn't exactly balmy but when the sun came out, it turned out that Scotland did have a summer. Dave would be back soon enough and his parents had stopped moaning after discovering the case of rosé I had bought especially for them. I also hadn't seen creepy Miles in a few days so things were firmly looking up.

In light of my new carefree attitude, I had arranged to take my three and Arif to a beach about an hour's drive away as we could do with feeling some sand between our toes and some fresh air in our lungs. The others had their own plans and we decided to meet at the hotel that evening for dinner. Morag and Robbie were finally leaving today to go back to the apartment, which was now dry, but I'd been asked by Mum to feed them beforehand.

THE BIG HOUSE

"There will be no lunch for them as I am out for the day," I firmly told her.

"Perhaps you could do something in the slow cooker for them so they have something warm before they leave," she tried again, clearly feeling sorry for them.

"Perhaps they could make their own lunch in their own apartment in Edinburgh. How about that?" I snapped.

"Raquel, you know there's been a flood. Don't be unkind."

"Unkind? I don't work here, Mum, I'm on holiday and their son lives over there, literally next door, it's absurd they've even come back here in the first place when we're subletting it."

"Foul mouth and a sour puss, it's not attractive, you know. I'll make them a salmon fillet with some new potatoes. They'll really enjoy that." She smirked as she said it, knowing full well I felt that combination was very Rosemary Conley.

"How did the interview about the war go, Tom?" Dad broke up the row by changing the subject. Tom had felt all important that he had been chosen to be the subject of an article and had showed off to the others as if he were some sort of celeb. I mean it wasn't really him I was interested in, it was his mother's suet puddings that I wanted to get my hands on but she wasn't here so he would have to do. Cockily, Tom told Dad about his 'Parky' moment in the chair.

"I educated your daughter on living through the war as a young boy. She had absolutely no clue what we went through, completely oblivious until I filled her in. You know, Phillip, they don't know they're born these days."

I rolled my eyes, I knew plenty about the Second World War actually because I had been to my GCSE history lessons and I had ridden a stinking two-day coach to Normandy with the school. I still had the remnants of a rather vicious love bite that I acquired on the

THE BIG HOUSE

back seat from one of the reprobates in my maths class. In my defence, I did get a B+ in the end so the hanky-panky that went down was clearly worth it.

"We had very little back then and we were afraid all the time," Tom continued.

Suzy casually looked up from her crumpet: "Sounds just like lockdown!"

The gasps of disbelief from the older diners travelled around the breakfast table at what Suzy had said. Tom nearly fell off his chair, Gary almost choked on his chucky egg, Dad looked at my mother, mouth willing her to say something, anything. I waited for the crescendo that would follow.

It was Gary that started.

"Sounds like facking lockdown, are you hearing this?" he yelled in my direction. I was, after all, her parent. "Is this the same lockdown that involved sitting in the house consuming truckloads of banana bread and making videos of yourself making it? Is this the same lockdown where the government had cheese platters and orgies in between meetings?"

Suzy looked sneakily at me and smiled, knowing what she'd been doing by dropping this bomb of her own that was blowing up the breakfast table.

CeeCee started her own tirade of 'woe me'.

"You have no idea, young lady, what went on during the war, do you? What are they teaching you at these schools? The war was a very difficult time for my parents and their parents, they didn't have an endless supply of Pinot Grigio to drink whilst wearing pyjamas all day, they were dodging bombs and hiding from Nazis."

Suzy shrugged. "Basically, Tom said they were in fear of their lives and there was a limit on food. Exactly the same as lockdown."

THE BIG HOUSE

Bizarrely, Roger semi-agreed. "Actually, everybody, she does a point. I went into Selfridges food hall during the pandemic, I had to queue might I add, I went to get two loaves of sourdough, one with black olives as we thought it would pair nicely with a speciality cheese that we'd managed to get from the raw dairy and the other plain to have toasted with pâté and suchlike. I risked my life really because my immune system isn't what it used to be but I went down there all the same. After two bloody hours, I was told by customer services that we were rationed to only one loaf per person and that was it. Do you remember that, Melanie?" He painfully recalled his worst day of 2020.

Mel nodded. "Yes, it was awful, actually. We did try to bake our own but it wasn't the same." And then she put her hand on his shoulder comforting him. I nearly pissed my pants. They might be on the brink of divorce but they had a shared PTSD over a posh loaf of bread which just about summed them up.

"Rich people problems, right there," Gary seethed, still purple with anger and yelling at Roger who jumped out of his skin and grabbed Mel's hand.

"Quite honestly, Grandad, I think what we suffered during Covid was probably much worse than anything anyone went through in World War… what number is it again?" Michaela played dumb, clearly stoking his anger.

Gary slammed his spoon down onto the table.

"What number? Jesus Christ, child. World War bloody Two, the second time the bastards tried to ruin us! And when your dad gets back we need to have a sit down about all this, this is just not on."

The kids couldn't hold it in any longer and they started to laugh, Sam was in hysterics and Suzy and Michaela high-fived each other on a very successful wind-up mission.

"They're messing with you, Gary, they don't mean it." I assured my

THE BIG HOUSE

father-in-law that apart from Roger, who welled up over the rationing of his artisan bread, the others were just taking the piss.

Gary smiled through gritted teeth but he was certainly relieved that his grandkids weren't as thick as mince. I quickly gathered up the kids to make our exit and head to the safety of the beach.

* * * * *

Helensburgh Beach was breezy. It wasn't particularly pretty and the promenade was sparse in the way of gift shops, ice cream parlours and the sort of thing you would normally find on a quintessential British seafront. It was more like a normal town that just happened to be by the sea. I did, however, witness a young boy being berated quite severely by his father for answering back; that is certainly something that reminded me we were on a British beach. If you've been to Blackpool as a child in the summertime, which being a Northern child was a rite of passage, you will have seen kids being blasted by parents wearing 'Kiss Me Quick' hats whilst puffing on a Lambert & Butler. It was the sweets that did it; kids from my era didn't get to stuff our faces with dangerous amounts of sugar very often and when we did, we went completely 'doolally'. There were kids being pinned up against fruit machines, lamp posts, moving trams, even being told, 'You've ruined the whole holiday, now get your face straight before I do it for ya.'

This particular family were locals, and bollockings sounded much better in Scottish – the boy was told off royally and his father gave it to him outside Betfred. I nodded at the man and smiled just as a sort of parent-to-parent thing. He frowned at me and then asked, "You alright, hen? What the fuck do you want?" Not as friendly as I'd hoped and I hurriedly moved us down the beach before he straightened my face for me.

THE BIG HOUSE

There were other tourists scattered around but it wasn't too busy with it being a Monday, and we found a lovely spot to eat the chips out of trays with wooden forks whilst sitting on a tartan blanket and looking out to sea. Eventually, after being persuaded by Arif who'd never been to the seaside, they all braved the waves. It wasn't exactly Bondi but they seemed to have plenty of fun. I wasn't sure if Arif's country was land-locked but he was absolutely fascinated by the water all the same. The four of them waded through the waves, splashing each other with their jeans rolled up. I hadn't noticed Suzy check her phone once since we'd left the house that day and during the journey my passengers actually looked out of the car window and took in their surroundings. This involuntary digital detox was allowing conversation to flow, and it was refreshing to get more than grunts out of the kids.

I lay back onto the blanket and looked up at the clouds, missing Dave. I felt anxious when he was away, just a bit vulnerable in a pathetic sort of way. So I made a decision to call Julian and book a session for a number of reasons: I wanted to be better, to understand my own head and I needed to talk to somebody who wasn't bored of listening. Yes, couples therapy was a two-man job but sometimes we need some one-on-one advice. It couldn't hurt to get a top-up, and truthfully it was just me who seemed to be struggling right now.

"Mrs Fitzpatrick, hello there. What can I do you for?"

'Do you for?' Was I calling Kevin Webster's garage or my therapist? That was very unprofessional, I felt.

"Hello, Julian, I was wondering if I could book your next session. It would have to be on Zoom and it would be just me."

There was a pause. "Okay, trouble at mill?"

"Not trouble as such, I just feel I may need some guidance. I'm feeling well, a bit off, really." There was a rustle down the line.

"Let me grab your notes and remind myself of your situation."

THE BIG HOUSE

I heard the flicker of some pages and a few murmurs. Definitely for effect as we were probably his only clients and he'd been waiting for this phone call for months.

"Okay, yes, I see. Here you are: infidelity, lying, mid-life crisis, self-sabotage." I glared at the phone as the pig read out my latest CV.

"Yes, sounds like me," I said meekly.

"So, why just you, Raquel?"

"'I'm the one with the problem," I admitted.

"You've not gone and done it again, have you?"

"No, I have not! It's not that and to be honest that is quite offensive. Surely you knew after meeting me all those times that it was a just a one-off."

There was an uncomfortable pause.

"Unfortunately, in my game, one-offs are very rare, Mrs Fitzpatrick."

"In this case Julian, that's what it was, I learned from my mistake actually."

"So why the session, then?" he probed.

"I am suspicious of Dave; I feel as if he is going to stray. It's affecting me quite a lot. Is this normal?"

"Well, you took a brick out of the wall and now the wall is weaker. So, yes, I would say that is normal."

I hated his analogy – what a massive cock. But a massive cock who had a point.

"How does tomorrow at ten sound? We can do some work on rebuilding the wall."

"That is fine, send me the link."

I have no idea why I was putting my fragile mind in the hands of this man; he was not my kind of person. In fact, he had not really mended us at all if I was still feeling broken. Perhaps a female therapist would have been better. I mean, if I showed a woman a picture of Matt

THE BIG HOUSE

cutting the lawn, it would all make sense. She would also understand that Dave had been very complacent and what I did had a lot to do with that. But what if she had a slutty secretary look? That would send me under, plus the thought of going over my issues with another stranger was too much, so I decided to stick with Julian as he already knew it all.

I was tackling my issues head on and although we had made progress, Dave and I were not there yet. I drove home from Helensburgh with a good feeling, I was taking steps to sort myself out.

CRASH

I ended up dropping the kids back at the house to change for dinner and then I nipped into town to the butchers to discuss whether they could get me a frozen turkey in August. Suzy had told me their accents were very strong so I decided a face-to-face discussion would be better than on the phone.

I had no idea who Ferguson was and who were the sons, but they all had buck teeth and rosy faces and were equally as friendly as one another. There was a bit of a queue, as they were having a surge on burgers with the sunshine making an appearance. Eventually when I hit the front the smallest of Ferguson's sons, God this was a mouthful, laughed in my face when I asked him for a turkey.

"No chance. I can do you a big chicken?" he offered.

"Well, I need it for a Christmas dinner."

"Now?"

"I'm a food writer and I need to get this done now because, well, we're in a house that lends itself to Christmas and…"

"Why can't you do beef?" he suggested.

"I could but a turkey would look better for the photos."

"It's very dry is turkey." A lady behind me with a roller in her fringe decided to give her two pennies' worth. "We like to have a nice piece of sirloin for our Christmas."

Ferguson nodded approvingly. "Aye, turkey can be pure shite if you overcook it."

A large man behind the lady came to the counter and also spoke to me. "Have you ever tried a goose, darlin', now there's a moist bird and I like a moist bird." They all laughed.

"A goose could work, I suppose, can you get me one of those?"

THE BIG HOUSE

Ferguson nodded. "Aye, in September."
"But I need it by Wednesday," I explained.
"No, then!" He was very direct.
"Have you thought about doing pheasant? We can get those whenever you like and even get everything delivered to you tomorrow," another Ferguson appeared and offered, trying to be helpful.
Roller lady grimaced. "Too gamey for me, plus I found a bullet in one, almost lost me fucking crown. You'd better off doing a nice big ham, dear. Do you know how to cook gammon?"
I nodded, "That's a good idea, I'll order a ham and some pheasants, that's Christmassy enough, thanks for your help everyone."
Ferguson went off through the plastic curtains to get his order book, and as he did so I could see the big silver tables where they did all of their chopping and skinning with big silver hooks on the wall where they hung the carcasses. It was the stuff of nightmares for the vegan lot, no wonder they had curtains. A man was mopping up a rather large pool of blood with his back to me just next to the doors of a cold room and he wasn't a Ferguson. I recognised the stature, the slight stoop and the rotund belly busting out of his white coat.
Why was Robbie working in the butchers? He had been a property tycoon and had sat on the board of a number of companies as far as I knew. This was a big step down, mopping up guts for The Fergusons.
"There's an English woman out there who wants to make a Christmas dinner in summer, she's pretending she's a fancy food writer but I think she's just a bit loop the loop," I heard him tell Robbie whilst chuckling. "Reckons she has to take photos for a magazine. We really do get them in here."
Robbie mumbled something about emptying his bucket, he must have known it was me and then kept well out of sight, edging backwards with every word.

THE BIG HOUSE

"I'll deliver to order if you give me your address. Thanks for your custom."

I filled out the form and left quickly – I didn't want to speak to Robbie if I could help it. I had enough going on without taking on their problems, but I would mention it to Mum and she'd get to the bottom of it. It was becoming clear that Robbie and Morag had money problems and I was pretty sure that Miles was responsible.

That evening, we had dinner booked at The Hotel, a taxi brought down Tom, Babs, CeeCee and Gary and the rest of us walked. It was a nice evening and it felt good to be out and about. There was a sign just outside the reception diverting 'wedding guests' to an upstairs function suite to celebrate the unity of a Mr and Mrs McManus. A big girl in a turquoise jumpsuit was already crying on her way up because her Spanx had given her indigestion and she hadn't even got started on the buffet.

"Who gets married on a Monday?" Mum scowled at the sign.

"Someone who's done it before, I'd imagine," Mel said judgementally.

"Maybe it's just cheaper," Tom added.

"Stop it all of you and come on, we'll end up getting our heads kicked in at this rate." I ushered the group away from staring at the wedding party any further. We had a large table booked in the dining room of The Hotel that spanned the back wall, one side was a fixed bench and the other a long row of rickety chairs. Mum was in her element and she ordered a two bottles of house champagne on arrival.

"It's actually our wedding anniversary," she told everybody in the dining room whilst swishing her chiffon scarf about like a Hollywood actress. Was she trying to steal the bride's thunder? It was likely.

"It's not your actual anniversary until later this month, Mum, stop stringing it out, woman."

Mum held court on end of the table with her stories of how Dad had

THE BIG HOUSE

chased her and basically begged her to date him until she eventually gave in. "There was a long line of suitors you know, I was in demand."

Tom chipped in, chuckling: "It was the same queue for the chip shop, it just so happened you lived next door."

"I did not live next door to a chip shop, Tom. Don't be ridiculous, you bad man, we had a driveway and topiary." Tom laughed – he loved a wind-up.

"Phillip virtually stalked me for months. He had a car you know, not many young men had their own car back then."

"So it was a Jag that swung it then, Granny?" Michaela questioned my mother's materialistic approach to dating.

"Well, I had nice clothes, a bus didn't cut it when you wore fine linen."

Michaela shook her head, this attitude was very dated to her, she was more of a 'it's what's inside that counts' type. "So if he hadn't had a Jag, you would have swerved him?" she asked.

Mum laughed loud. "He didn't have a Jaguar back then – if he'd had a Jag, I'd have been pregnant after one date. It was an Allegro, I think, a gold one and for that reason, I kept him waiting."

Michaela nearly vomited, Granny was a gold-digging trollop and she wasn't afraid to admit it.

"We had some fabulous times, didn't we, Phillip? Driving around the countryside, just the two of us, never a cross word."

Dad nodded but I knew for a fact that it wasn't all plain sailing back in the day.

"And our wedding was on a cruise ship, we didn't go with convention, oh no. We were married at sea by the captain of a cruise liner."

I already knew this because Mum had a large picture of her and dad on the day next to a captain in his white suit and hat. It was a sort

THE BIG HOUSE

of *Love Boat* vibe, their wedding – Mum looked like Farrah Fawcett and Dad like Peter Sutcliffe because big beards were a thing back then.

"Did you have boyfriend before Grandad?" Suzy was curious as to whether Mum had any allure or just jumped on the first fat-walleted man.

"Of course I had boyfriends, I was taken out by many a man."

"And did you… you know, ever do it or did you save yourselves in the olden days?"

Mum swigged down her champagne and got a little uncomfortable. "Suzy, what do you take me for, I was a good girl. People are like animals nowadays, but we held back."

CeeCee gazed at Gary with hearts for pupils. "We got married in the East End, a proper knees-up at the local pub, didn't we darlin'?"

"It's all we could afford. I wasn't on the taxis then, I was a mechanic and we didn't have much – we cut our cloth accordingly, not like now with everything shoved on the plastic." Gary rubbed his forehead.

CeeCee put her curly blonde head into Gary's chest and shut her eyes. "But it was the happiest day of my life: a few sausage rolls, my brother on the joanna and the man of my dreams."

Everybody oohed and aahed. Not me. Roger chipped in with his romantic memory, one that didn't involve a plaster or some phlegm.

"Melanie and I had a private, quiet wedding, didn't we, my sweet?"

Mel was still angry, I could tell. But Roger didn't appear to be going anywhere and they sat next to each other so she was softening and she nodded in agreement.

"We flew off to the Seychelles and we grabbed a couple of locals as our witnesses. Just wonderful apart from the sunburn – I almost lost my nose," Roger reminisced.

"What, no family at all? Why, that seems a bit sad, Aunty Mel?" Sam was shocked.

THE BIG HOUSE

"She wouldn't have wanted me there, I might have stopped her," I said before I could stop myself.

"Sometimes I wish you had," she replied.

Roger's shoulders dropped at that comment, and he shifted uncomfortably in the chair as the entire table waited for him to respond. I almost wanted to hug him as Mel sipped her water showing absolutely no remorse. Roger struggled to find the words, he went to say something a couple of times but nothing came out.

"Well I for one am glad they got married, actually, I think they make a great couple!" I said coming to Roger's aid, feeling bad that Mel was being such a bitch to him and in front of all of us. Then to seal the deal I lifted my glass to clink it with Roger's. Looking taken aback, he slowly lifted his and clinked me back.

I remember when Mel had told me she had agreed to marry Roger over the phone one evening. When I'd asked her why, she'd said, "Because I love him." And when again I asked why, she'd told me to "FUCK OFF" before slamming the phone down. But even after that response from her sister, she still did it anyway. She hadn't told us she had done it until they got back from what we thought was a holiday and they'd announced it over a lunch at Duck Cottage.

"Oh well, looks like I will never get to be the mother of the bride and wear the outfit I had always planned on." To my confusion, Mum had been very upset.

"What about my wedding two years ago, Mother? Didn't you wear it to that?" Had Mum forgotten her other daughter getting married when I stood in front of her and married Dave?

"Oh that, I didn't wear it to that, no no, that was just something from Debenhams that I picked up in the sale. No, I have a bespoke silk suit that I was saving for a special occasion, a really really classy event," she'd explained with no shame.

THE BIG HOUSE

"So not my wedding, then?" I'd fumed.

"Your reception was in a garden centre really, wasn't it? So, no, I guess not."

To appease Mum, Mel later had a fancy event in a marquee in the grounds of a 16th-century hotel just outside of Chester so Mum finally got to wear the special silk suit after all. Sadly, though, one of my girls had left an open jam sandwich on Mum's chair just before she sat down and, combined with the warm butter, it left an indelible stain which made it look like her bottom had leaked. What a shame.

All of this love talk and romance was making me feel better and I realised this is what it would be like if Dave had left me. Me listening to everybody droning on about how happy their relationships were after I had chucked mine away carelessly. Me, alone at a family dinner, probably after meeting two sex offenders in one day on Tinder to see if I could 'get back on the horse'.

My cousin Jolene, nearly fifty and single, had been on Tinder since it started; her parents were into country and western so this could have had a large impact on her dating journey. Jolene and I spoke once a month on the phone, as she lived in London, with me keeping in touch out of guilt really because I had done some terrible things to her when we were kids. Standard stuff like putting earthworms under her pillow, Nutella in her knickers, etc. Our childhood was a bit boring so I'd spiced things up, it just so happened that Jolene was an easy target, and being an only child was a bit of an oddball. Anyway, once we'd passed adolescence and I'd apologised for my behaviour, we still kept in touch and she used me as a sounding board for her dating woes. Last month's call was her explaining to me that she had dyed her hair platinum and actually purposely put on weight because she was going on a date with someone she had dated three years before and she thought a different look may result in a better outcome. This

THE BIG HOUSE

is how slim pickings were out there in the midlife dating scene. If it didn't work the first time, you went at the same guy again in some sort of disguise. That particular relationship ended fairly quickly because Jolene showed him her Billy Ray Cyrus memorabilia and he immediately realised who she was before exiting through a toilet window. I didn't want to become a Jolene, annually visiting Graceland alone whilst wearing cowboy boots from River Island.

Once the desserts had arrived, I was over this meal. Plus, I really didn't fancy what was the equivalent of Instant Whip so I gave mine to Sam and went for a wander around the building. This wasn't a bad little place, it was clean, it had original features which hadn't been messed with and so it felt authentic. The odd antique took my fancy, a sword on the wall in a glass box with a lock led me to believe that this was a genuine throat cutter passed down through the family that owned the establishment, and a fox wearing a top hat and smoking a pipe sat on a high shelf in the corner of the morning room. I liked this sort of stuff, this was character you didn't get in the Marriott in, say, Milton Keynes, unless of course you counted a pile of sick authentically delivered to the door by a guy attending a conference who was likely called Chris Smith. I stepped out onto a stone patio and looked back up at the building – I liked this place, it had something.

"Show us yer tits," a man grunted, and I recognised that voice. Luckily it was the only person who probably wanted to see my tits – even I didn't want to see the damn things. I leaned over the stone balustrade and pushed up my cleavage. Dave laughed.

"I wasn't talking to you, there's a hottie behind you."

I stupidly checked just in case, relived to see he was joking. "You're back, and thank God!"

"You missed me, then?"

I nodded. "Meet me in the dining room, they're all in there." He

THE BIG HOUSE

made his way into the foyer and I walked around to meet him.

"We would have waited for you if you'd said you were coming back, we've eaten already."

"I wanted to surprise you and I made good time. Stu has taken over running things so I managed to get away." Dave was dressed smartly, he smelled good and he seemed happy to see me, to see everyone, actually, but especially his parents. He ordered a double vodka tonic and set about joining in the festivities and being the fun guy he always was.

After a cheeseboard and more boring family stories, Dave came back from the toilet to announce we had been invited to an event in the function room. He had met a man at the urinal who had very kindly invited the whole family to his wedding reception, the night-do which was well underway upstairs.

"We can't go to the wedding of some randoms, Dave, that's just ridiculous." But my words were wasted as my entire family had already left the table and were heading upstairs.

"I just need to powder my nose and do my lips." Mum headed off to the toilets to get herself ready to crash a wedding with her best face on. I was adamant that I would not be involving myself in such a stupid idea but after ten minutes sitting alone with the rind of some Stilton for company I thought, 'Oh, fuck it, if you can't beat 'em' and up I went to see how the Scots tied the knot.

"Loving it, loving it loving it, I'm loving it like that," blared out on the speakers. What a set of lyrics. What a load of shit, and I would not allow myself to slide across the dance floor like a demented frog to keep up with the rest of them. God knows I loved the nineties, I embraced that shell-suited era with a high pony and a pint of sea breeze, but I would not lower myself in terms of its popular music. Yes, I knew rhythm was a dancer but it was definitely not as serious

THE BIG HOUSE

as cancer. Wedding DJs somehow reduced man, woman and child to shamefully display the most embarrassing dance moves they could muster up.

'Tim's Choons' was the name of the man they'd hired to put a 'dickhead spell' on the wedding guests and Tim did a grand job. Dave winked as he glided past me at some speed whilst moonwalking backwards holding a tray of green shots that were somehow on fire. Over at the bar, my dad twirled around on the toe of his tasselled moccasin with a crowd of complete strangers cheering him on.

"Sausage roll? Chicken wing?" The beaming bride approached me wearing a beautiful lace bodice with a straight satin skirt and a pair of Adidas trainers. She was well into her forties, so this was not her first rodeo, she understood the middle-aged foot thing we were all dogged with, heels just aren't worth the aftermath. She offered me a snack from her plate even though we'd never met. I was completely ashamed as I looked at the rest of my wedding crashing family in sheer horror.

"Er, no thanks, and I am so sorry, I don't even know your name. Your husband invited us, he met mine in the toilets and, well, there's a few of us. I feel really bad."

The bride was not fazed, she had Branston Pickle on her chin and she slapped me on the back.

"On yer go, hen, have a blast. I don't give a fuck." And then she handed me her plate before skidding across the dance floor on her knees because Kylie basically told her to.

I endured this wedding of strangers for as long as possible but there's only so much a person can take, so when the slurred speeches started, I decided to leave. I had a Zoom at ten so would sit this night out. Dave had even managed to get himself a mention from the best man. He quite cleverly incorporated 'the guy we met in the bogs' into his speech, something about him being the bride's secret boyfriend

THE BIG HOUSE

and it got a big laugh, so Dave took a bow. The kids had all immersed themselves into the camaraderie of the whole thing so there was really no point on me ruining their fun. I made the decision to walk back up to the house and to go to bed with my book, not bothering with a goodbye to avoid being forced into doing the locomotion.

"Where are you going?" Mel asked me frostily as I passed her on the stairs.

"I'm going home, can't be arsed with all this."

"Neither can I, the music is a disgrace."

I shrugged, "Well it's not your wedding so it's not your choice."

Roger appeared behind her rubbing his ears, he too was struggling with the bass.

"Are you okay, Roger?" I checked, feeling unusually sympathetic towards him.

He nodded though he was still shaky from being the target of Mel's hate campaign.

"Perhaps you should talk in private, the small hotel bar is nice. Why don't you go in there, both of you?" I led them down the remaining stairs and almost shoved them into the bar. I needed them to reconnect because I wanted her off my radar when it came to Dave, and if truth be known I didn't like to see Roger being kicked around like a kitten.

The walk back to the house wasn't too bad, the moon was unusually bright that evening. When I saw the front door to the lodge, I was home and dry. I did jog the last bit, I think we all do that just in case there is a lunatic on the prowl and then we drop the keys in the dark seconds before an axe makes contact with our skull. Cranium intact, I managed to get in and take off my coat.

The silence wasn't at all comforting, and the fact nobody was there felt strange. The appeal of big houses certainly diminishes once you are in them alone. Perhaps this wasn't the life for me, perhaps I did suit

THE BIG HOUSE

my new-build and the sound of traffic trundling along the main road on a daily basis. I decided to take a cuppa up to bed, that normally relaxed me, so I flicked on the kettle and waited for it to boil, my eyes were darting around the room feeling as though I were being watched.

Just as I was heading upstairs with my brew, I heard a creak, not just an old house creak, but what sounded like footsteps across the landing.

"Who's there? Hello, hello?" I shouted up, willing myself to be brave but struggling to swallow. However, I thought, if they were upstairs, I could get outside before them. So with car keys in hand I planned my escape route, and unless they were a relation of Usain Bolt, they would never get to me in time.

I heard another creak at the top of the lower stairs, they were getting closer. I edged backwards towards the front door and began to open it but for some reason still clutching my mug.

"I'm... I'm calling the police," I stuttered.

I could see a shadow looming on the landing. "Last chance lunatic, show yourself."

Morag appeared cautiously at the top of the stairs in a pair of cobwebby dusty blue overalls looking down at me like I was the actual intruder. Her hair was in a bun, and she had a scarf wrapped around the back of it with a neat little knot at the front.

"Jesus, hen, you scared me half to death creeping about the place. I thought you were out for the evening with your family."

I was quite put out. Why was I having to explain my comings and goings to Morag? We weren't sharing the house with them, we had rented it from them – there is a big difference. What kind of arrangement had Mum actually made with her 'bestie' as this was not any conventional agreement.

Morag made her way down the stairs to join me, saying nothing

THE BIG HOUSE

and walked straight past me towards the kitchen. I looked on open-mouthed, what did he think she was doing? She turned back and said: "Well come on then, you better join me in the office."

Down in the cellar Morag cranked up the big computer and after a series of high-pitched beeps the link stabilised. She double-clicked on a file that said 'Dordogne' and slowly an image appeared on the screen of a rustic French farmhouse.

"There she is, Le Moulin," she said with a smile and a satisfied sigh.

I shrugged, still none the wiser. "Very nice, are you going on holiday? What's this got to do with you sneaking about?"

She frowned, perhaps the word sneaky was a bit out of order in her own home but so was acting like Michael Myers.

"This is our future, mine and Robbie's. This is where we will be headed this autumn, for good – we're moving to France."

She swivelled round on the office chair and I sat down, interested to hear more.

"Robbie and I have really been through it, Raquel. I am not one to speak bad of my own but we need a fresh start and Miles needs to stand on his own two feet. He's nearly fifty now, we cannae spoon-feed the boy any longer." She shook her head.

"I know he's been inside, Morag, he told me with some pride," I said, deciding it was a good time to admit what I knew.

She rolled her eyes. "Aye, he did a stint in the big house, not that it's taught him anything, wee shite that he is."

He was a wee shite and he did deserve to be abandoned.

"So he doesn't know about the French house? You're just going to leave without telling him?"

"No, Raquel, I'm not that cruel," she explained. "We will tell him when the time is right, just before we go when everything is almost done so there's no room for persuasion. But in the meantime we have

THE BIG HOUSE

to save all of our pennies, tighten our belts, we still haven't sold this place yet although we have a decent offer to consider. Miles, well he has a way of extracting things, especially when it comes to Robbie. He needs cash for this investment and that business deal but they never work out and he always blames somebody else. We're too old for stress like this so we're off. We'll give him some cash from the house sale but apart from that he's on his own."

She switched off the computer at the socket and unplugged it at the wall, perhaps she thought hackers wouldn't infiltrate her emails this way.

"You see, Raquel, there was no apartment. We've been staying in a caravan up the road, but after the big storm we were completely washed out. The damn thing almost slipped into the lake." She laughed, God knows why.

Morag was a positive woman, she had that 'see the bright side attitude' which I did not care for. I liked her for it but it didn't suit me.

"We've been showering at the leisure centre you know, Raquel. There's no water pressure up at the site, just a shitty little trickle to wash all of our bits."

I nodded to show sympathy, but actually, some horrible images of Robbie's unwashed unmentionables showed up in my head.

"Anyway, we don't want to waste money on renting anything fancy, we'll need it for fine wine and cheese in our retirement, you get it, right?"

I nodded in agreement, of course I would rather spend my retirement surrounded by the finer things in life, although it wasn't really fair on us being dragged into this mess.

"Is that why Robbie is working at the butchers in town? I saw him there this morning."

"Aye and he's not happy about it, but he agreed to take a little job

THE BIG HOUSE

over the summer to keep the bank balance topped up. He delivers meat for them to the local restaurants and cafés, sometimes he helps when it gets busy in the shop."

"He looked quite annoyed when I saw him, like he didn't want to be there," I told her, but Morag just shrugged.

"He lent Miles twenty-five thousand a few months ago without me knowing, we'll never see that again. The rows we've had about this, Christ we nearly got a divorce – if he wants to give our money away, he'll have to bring some in, simple as that."

Perhaps he'd think twice in future now he was driving carcasses about and mopping up guts. Morag was a good, fair woman, she was calm but she was also stern, so I wouldn't want to cross her.

"We can also transfer our things in the butcher's van over to a storage unit in the evenings after Miles's curfew kicks in, it works quite well."

She caught me staring at her roots, they really were fascinating. She became self-conscious and ran her fingers through the dull hair.

"I've let myself go, I know. But it's been a hell of a time, it's hard to look good when you feel bad. When we're all packed up and ready to go, I'll be straight down the salon for a full colour and layers and back to my old self."

She was right. Even though I'd done a few Zumba sessions and swapped some of my wine for gin and slimline, I still felt like a broken-down old bus and there were many days that I looked like one too. A neon scarf and two tons of mascara cannot hide a shit day.

"Raquel, if we stay in Scotland, he'll wipe us out. It's very hard to say no to your only son. And that's why we're shipping things over to Le Moulin gradually, so he won't clock what we're doing. I couldn't handle him begging and pleading for months on end – this is not easy for me but it's the only way."

THE BIG HOUSE

I recalled the missing art and the fake antique, the empty shelves in the library. Things were slowly being shipped across the channel to their new home.

"And your mum's been helping, she's been real rock, she has, she was the one who made me realise that I had to do what's right for us. She said kids suck all of the energy away and leave you completely deflated."

I raised one eyebrow. So my mum knew all about this and this was a mercy trip to help out her mate. Well, well, well! And if anyone sucked the life out of stuff it was my mother, she was a complete mother-sucker. Ah, a lovely new word which I would keep and use regularly.

"Anyway, me darlin', this has to stay between us. I can't risk Miles trying to stop it or, much worse, coming with us. Now I need to finish boxing a couple of piles in the loft, so you never saw me! Robbie will be by in the van to collect me in half an hour."

"Could I ask you a favour, Morag? Could you leave a couple of boxes of Christmas decorations by the door from your loft if you have any? Just a few bits so I can decorate the table for a work project I need to do."

"No problem, hen."

She made her way back up the stairs leaving me to digest what I'd heard. Mum had been made aware of this a long time ago, so they must have plotted this together. All those lies she'd told me about the grand kitchen when she must have known the copper pans would be missing; I planned to buy her a significantly cheap gin in the next shop. Morag continued her secret packing in the loft, and I eventually got into bed and drifted off. Visions of Miles stamping his tiny feet as his parents left Scotland in a Citroën wearing berets filled my dreams.

The family didn't arrive back until 1.30 am, I know this because they woke me up with their drunken yelling on their way to bed. Suzy

THE BIG HOUSE

was howling about the fact she'd been looked up and down by a girl who was thinner than her and Dave was heaving his mother and father up the first flight because they'd been sitting down for too long. I heard Tom and Babs planning some sort of Syrian sex sesh: "You run the bath and I'll get the pickles," is what I heard from his mouth outside my door. There was nothing from Mum and Dad, perhaps they were still at the wedding. Eventually all was quiet and a very tipsy Dave did a fifteen-second fart before getting into bed next to me whilst still wearing his blazer.

That was it, I was awake. Nobody could endure all of that racket and stay in a state of relaxation. I put on my night light and decided to read a chapter of my book. It was very good, actually – the story of a footballer's wife who somehow became the manager of her husband's team. Dave's phone suddenly pinged and lit up on his nightstand. It was nearly three in the morning, I decided to check who it was in case it was an emergency. I leaned over him and grabbed it, he didn't stir at all.

On the screen was a picture of a blow-up kangaroo, Stu his colleague was holding it whilst laughing with his thumbs up.

Meet my new bird, boss, she's a bit jumpy! Off to Tasmania tomorrow. Hope Scotland is treating you well.

Stu

I frowned, was this same Stu he said he was with this morning? The same Stu who had called him into work? How the hell could Stu have got to an Australian sex shop that quickly? And, judging by his tan, he'd been there a while. So, if Stu was on the other side of the globe having sex with inflatable animals, then who had Dave been with for the past three days?

WHAT A PLUCKING PHEASANT DAY...

The house was silent when I crept down in to the basement to get on my Zoom call with Julian. It turned out that Mum and Dad had decided to take a room at The Hotel so they could have breakfast together and a bit of 'them time'. The bride and groom had a massive barney so the bridal suite was going cheap and they snapped it up. Mum had messaged me at 8.30 am to say they were going shopping and would be back later that afternoon.

It was chilly that day so I took a blanket and a cup of tea to keep me cosy whilst I tried to rebuild the crumbling wall that Julian had likened to my marriage.

With everything plugged in and in place, I clicked the link expecting to see a tank-top-wearing Julian sitting at his grey desk in Cheadle, the place that Dave and I used to visit each week. I was put off to see a Hawaiian shirt and a can of Lilt staring back at me.

"Hi there, Julian, are you on holiday?"

Julian moved a palm from his shoulder and positioned the screen away from the glare.

"Yes, I am currently working from Barbados."

"Oh, okay." I struggled to hide my distain. It did not feel right being therapised by a man wearing such bright colours and on a beach. This was a serious business, but he reminded me of Mr Tumble.

"My methods remain the same no matter where I am in the world, Raquel. Don't be put off; in fact, be cheered up."

He leaned forwards and looked at my environment. "I thought you said you were also on holiday?"

I looked behind me. A sofa and stone walls, a bare bulb hanging from the ceiling, it looked like I was being held hostage. "Well I am,

THE BIG HOUSE

Julian, but this is the only place I can get a steady connection, the basement of our holiday home."

He leaned back with his hands behind his head, I could just tell the air was warm and smelt of pineapples. "So, why don't you start at the beginning?" he instructed me.

I wrapped the blanket around me, tucking my knees up for warmth, and I told Julian exactly how I had been feeling since our last session. He slurped his Lilt a few times and wrote things down in his pad waiting patiently for me to finish.

"So, really, Julian, I live in fear that I will lose him. If I did, well it will serve me right, I think."

Julian nodded.

"What are you nodding for? You think I deserve to lose him?" I gasped, my anxiety rocketing.

He spluttered, "No, no sorry. It's just an understanding nod. I understand you, that's all."

"What do you think? What shall I do?"

Julian put down his pen and leaned forwards. "Perhaps you should be telling him all of this and not me."

"Sorry, what? I thought we were rebuilding walls, Julian," I said, confused.

"Yes, rebuild it by being honest. Tell him you think he's going to run off, tell him that his weight loss is causing you paranoia. Tell him that you feel old and fat."

"Err, I don't remember saying that," I told him, looking unimpressed.

"Did you not, oh well, that is just my interpretation," he mumbled nervously.

"Oh, is it really?"

"I don't think you should bottle things up. You need to be vulnerable and transparent."

THE BIG HOUSE

"Ugh, they say that on *Married at First Sight*," I sighed.

"What's that?" he asked, looking at me blankly.

"It's a dating show where people get married without meeting each other. The experts use science to match people together and…"

"That sounds very silly. In my professional opinion."

"Well, it isn't, it's very good," I insisted, not sure why I was using my therapy session to pitch some reality show to him.

"It sounds like the arranged marriage concept, which is dated and oppressive."

"Oh, come on, it's on Channel 4; it's entertaining. Anyway, what if me opening up puts him off me and it drags up all the bad stuff I did?"

"Then perhaps you killed it. But you won't know unless you talk to him, will you? We're stabbing in the dark here, Raquel. Let's leave it there for today."

I felt nothing – not lighter, not better, nothing. I was still in the same place I was before the session. This cost me £120 to watch a man slurping a drink I suspected had been banned from a balcony in the Caribbean.

"I have a slot next Friday at the same time if that suits. We can see how you've progressed."

"Yes, see you then, Julian. Goodbye."

I headed upstairs, frustrated to feel no further forwards and wondering why I hadn't seen a can of Lilt in decades. But I had to focus on 'Christmas dinner' so most of the day would be taken up with food prep from my end and people nursing their sore heads at the other. A little later, Ferguson's son turned up in his little van with my delivery and he'd added some extra bits for my Christmas-in-August dinner.

"There's some pork meat in there for a stuffing and we found a bag of chestnuts in the bottom of me ma's fridge – could be handy."

I smiled, that was very thoughtful. I did wonder how often his ma

THE BIG HOUSE

cleaned out her fridge, though. He helped me carry the pheasants into the kitchen and gave me a little tip. "Be careful not to tear the flesh when you're plucking, be gentle with them, keep the skin intact for a lovely moist bird." I smirked, I mean, how could you not?

"Which one are you? I mean which of Ferguson's sons are you so I can use your name in future?" He reached into his white coat pocket and handed me a business card.

Angus Ferguson
Master Butcher
07700 900929

I put it into my apron pocket. Before he left, he said, "Just call me if you need anything, anything at all." And then he put his hand on my shoulder momentarily. I looked at the hand and then back at him.

Now, a young old butcher with buck teeth was not really my bag, neither was a man who had blood under his nails and spat when he talked, but quite honestly, I felt flattered. Perhaps he saw me like a sort of Nigella, a striking English chef with a shapely figure, a woman who knew exactly what to do with a bag of chestnuts.

I chopped and stuffed, marinated and peeled that afternoon, although I was still feeling quite freaked out that Dave had lied about Stu. But I decided to let it go – I had to think like an adult, not spiral, not overreact, only deal with problems as they occurred instead of overthinking them.

The family had decided to sit by the lake that afternoon, and there were cans of Coke and many packets of Walkers crisps being carried down to placate the hangovers and for once I felt smug that did not apply to me. The weather was actually lovely, it was still jumper weather but the air was warm and the sky was clear. Arif, who could only

THE BIG HOUSE

manage a pint of Budweiser at most, made a selection of sandwiches and used his clear head to create a picnic to keep everyone going for the afternoon and saving me having to make lunch while I focused on my prep. My parents were in Edinburgh when Mum called me from Marks & Spencer to give me an update.

"This is a wonderful idea, having a family Christmas. It'll just be stocking stuffers, though, Raquel, we're not doing big gifts."

"Mum, this was your idea so don't play games. And we don't need presents, this isn't actually Christmas," I reminded her.

"Get into the spirit, will you, I'll be expecting the works. I wonder if we can get a snow machine from Argos. I think we'll have a look."

"Do *not* get a snow machine, you're going too far." But she couldn't hear me, or she didn't want to, getting it into her head that this was actually Christmas.

Dave walked into the kitchen just as I was chopping the head from the third pheasant.

"This looks gruesome, I wish I could unsee that." He pulled a face and looked away as he heard a snap.

"Do you think you'll have to go back down for work again?" I casually asked, trying to sound calm.

He shrugged, "Maybe, I'll just have to see if they can cope without me, depends what comes in."

"Who's in charge when you're not there?" I asked again, just wanting to check I hadn't got mixed up.

He started juggling with three satsumas dropping two of them within seconds. "Erm, Stu, mainly."

I rinsed a bird under the tap. "Oh yeah, Stu with the ponytail?"

Dave laughed, "You don't like his hair, do you, love?" I shook my head.

"Yeah, it's Stu who manages things when I'm not there. He's a good lad."

THE BIG HOUSE

I continued with my prep. I had to think what I did now, my next move had to be decided with my head on straight. Besides, this wasn't proof of infidelity, I tried to tell myself. Yes, there was a discrepancy in Dave's story that was extremely concerning but he was a police officer and his operations were supposed to be secret. Perhaps there was another reason that Dave was lying – I had to consider all other possibilities before I tackled him on this. Maybe this was a delayed message from weeks ago and Stu was back from Australia. Was Stu involved in something covert, something so top secret that he had to pretend he was away? I mean none of this was likely and the evidence was pointing to something that would make me very angry but people who lie are suspicious of others, people who cheat think they are being cheated on. Dave left the kitchen; he couldn't stand to see any more birds being dismembered so he went for a lie down and left his phone on the kitchen top. I decided to check this message again, seeing if I could decipher it more clearly during the daytime. But unfortunately, and mysteriously, it had been deleted. In fact, his entire chat with Stu from day dot was gone. A stress rash appeared on my chest; this was not a good sign.

I needed fresh herbs and fresh air after that so I made my way out to the kitchen garden and began snipping away trying to bury my dark thoughts. Sister Sledge ran straight over to me as I got close to their pen so I threw them some carrot peelings which they pecked at viciously. This was a peaceful place, a quiet spot for contemplation and reflection. I was calm here and able to think until I could smell an unwanted guest lurking close by. I am still of a generation where I think that smoking looks cool. I'm not talking about the type of smoking that leaves you with yellow fingers, brown teeth or a hacking cough. I am referring to the glamorous smokers, the ones who can pick it up or leave it, the ones who only smoke cigarettes that are all

THE BIG HOUSE

white, not the ones with the orange tips – they're saved for the people in my maths GCSE class. The classy smokers have a few puffs socially, they smell of fresh cigarette smoke, not the stale two-day-old stuff, and then once they have finished their weekly smoke, they stub it out underneath the pointed front of their Jimmy Choo shoe.

Miles was a scummy smoker. His smell hit you ten minutes before he arrived in the room and his breath made you want to lean back and do the Limbo whenever he spoke. My basket was full of sage for my stuffing, rosemary for my potatoes, and some thyme that would complement my Christmas carrots. Even over the top of my fragrant basket, I could smell the ashtray that was Miles. I tried my best to hurry over to the back door to avoid having to chat to him, but he must have been wearing wheelies because he glided across that kitchen garden so quickly and stopped me before I could trap his little fingers in the door.

"Afternoon, darling, not seen you in a while. You've had a delivery, do you want it now?" he asked, leaning one of his arms on the door frame revealing a wet patch under the arm of his Iron Maiden T-shirt.

I turned to him, grimacing, the last thing I needed on what was essentially Christmas Eve was any sort of gift from him.

"Is this absolutely necessary? Do we really need to keep meeting like this? I've explained to you that I just want to be left alone. I do not need any gifts, deliveries or conversations with you, *comprende?*" I said, firmly.

Miles reached into his inside pocket, he pulled out an envelope, and he placed it on top of my herbs. "As I've told you before, don't shoot the messenger. Have a nice day, sweetheart." He smiled, flashing his stained teeth before gliding away.

Oh, what now? The shit was coming at me thick and fast, surely I deserved some respite. I put the letter in my back pocket, dropped the herbs off in the kitchen and headed upstairs to one of the bathrooms

THE BIG HOUSE

with a lock to see what the delights Miles had in store for me this time.

Hiya babe, me again. Thanks for the letter. I appreciate you taking the time to write to me. I am not enjoying it in here, sometimes it's a laugh, but mostly it isn't. Last night my new cellmate decided to start a dirty protest. I wouldn't mind, like, but the screws have no intention of moving me so I am in a sticky situation. Ha ha.

Plus it's curry night tomorrow so just imagine the amount of protesting he'll be able to do after a plate of Big Mike's Jalfrezi.

I've been having a think, and you have access to stuff I can't get to. I need you to get Gina's sister to visit me. For obvious reasons I haven't been able to speak to Gina with her being on the run but I know her sister is in the UK although she hasn't replied to any of my VO's, she might have moved and I don't have her number. I miss my wife so much and it seems a bit unfair that you lot got to go free and I'm stuck in here, I just need to find a way to communicate with Gina through her sister. Her name is Gemma Wild and she lives in Liverpool, she'll listen to a woman. If you need help Miles said he can do whatever we need.

Not putting pressure on you but it's getting to the point where I am thinking about telling the real story to a solicitor. It was my birthday last week, I am 42 years old. I will be 50 before I get out of here and that's not cool. At least Big Mike made me a birthday muffin with a candle in it, well a match actually. He used the juice from the tin of some chickpeas to bind the mixture together. I told him I'd tell you about it cos I knew you'd be impressed.

Speak soon, Matt.
X

P.S I asked the governor if we could get a copy of the Shawshank

THE BIG HOUSE

Redemption and he slapped me across the back of the head, I don't think they like that film in here.

I screwed up the letter and dropped it into the toilet, I waited until it was fully submerged in the water and then I did a piss on it before flushing. I really did not understand what this guy was hoping to achieve by getting in touch with his wife or her sister. This is what happens when you have a flirt with a thicko, this was my punishment for having a dalliance with a moron. Where was his logic? He surely must've known that when committing crime and getting caught the punishment would be tough, that's why they called it 'hard time' not 'good time'.

Unfortunately, unless I complied in some way, there was a strong chance it could be me who would be me staring at turd-covered walls. His sign-off of 'speak soon' also made it clear he'd keep writing unless I helped him. I have to say, however, amongst my fury, that Big Mike sounded like a good guy, plus he clearly had some skills in the kitchen. I love a man who can cook even if he is behind bars.

Once I'd had a few days to decompress, at some point, I would have a nosey on Facebook to see if Gemma Wild looked approachable. I supposed I'd have to then ask Miles nicely, to message her and politely request she get her arse to the nick. I needed her to agree to this so daft Matt had something to look forward to, even if it was just a visit from his wife's sister. It was better than nothing and this would surely keep the silly sod from penning anymore daft notes and sending them my way. Not your typical thing to tick off the to-do list by any means, but doable if I just kept my focus.

The potatoes were parboiled, the gravy was simmering nicely and the ham was studded. The pheasants were quite fiddly, something I didn't normally cook, and being such small birds with little meat it took lots of effort to make them look festive. My prep was done and it

THE BIG HOUSE

was time to take off the apron and move onto my next task, which was to keep the family at bay to buy me some time.

"Would anyone like anything at all?" I hollered across the big hall.

"I'll take a cocktail actually, Raquel, seeing as though you're asking, something festive." Old Tom lowered his *Racing Post*, always on the scrounge for more booze. Christmas cocktails brought back some tricky memories for me as it was only six months ago that I had made a complete show of myself at the 'Eat' Christmas party. I didn't normally show up to this sort of shit but my agent felt it was right that I showed my face to at least one event per year for networking purposes. After an early dinner at a trendy brasserie, we headed over to a small jazz club in Soho and the evening started off as quite a nice introduction to the Christmas period late in November. A festive cocktail on arrival called 'Santa's little helper' got me in the mood. It slipped down so easily with its mix of clementines, cranberries and something else which I later discovered was the equivalent of absinthe. 'I'll just stick to the cocktails, I'm not doing wine' was the last thing I remember saying before waking up in the back of an Uber with a sax player called Griff, who had agreed to shepherd me back to my hotel as he was going the same way. It was only 10 pm! According to my fellow writers on the group chat, I was the life and soul for an hour and a half but after that I got a bit messy. Bringing up the turkey roulade into a drain behind the club was apparently when the decision was made to send the old girl home. Yes, I was the oldest there and the first to fall, which was mortifying. A Christmas cocktail would be made of two components from now on, fruit juice and vodka, that would be it! I handed Tom a jug of Smirnoff and orange juice over ice and called it a 'Tinseltini', instructing him to hand out glasses to anybody interested apart from Sam, of course. I then made my way over to Miles's cottage where I was going to have to strike a deal with the Devil himself.

IT'S THE MOST WONDERFUL TIME

Miles's cottage was really pretty, with climbers covering the walls made up of the lovely green ivy that grew on The Eagle Lodge plus some crisp white flowers. It was sad that a lovely old lady wasn't living out her days here, instead of the travesty that a thieving little troll had bagged it.

"Raquel, to what do I have this pleasure?" Miles smirked, wearing a blue towelling dressing gown. I don't like men in dressing gowns unless you've just had sex with them, it's very difficult not to imagine what's underneath it with the lack of buttons or a zip, just a flimsy belt was holding in all the gubbins.

Miles smiled and lit a cigarette. I looked down at the table and there was an ashtray that overflowed with his little orange friends, sitting on top of a pile of magazines mainly about finance. "I wondered how long it would take you to see sense," he said, before inhaling deeply. And then in attempt to look sexy and clever, he blew a smoke ring.

"I have no idea what that means but I have a job for you."

"Tell me more."

"If I find the account of a certain individual on Facebook, could you contact them please?"

"Okay, why can't you?"

"Because I just need to stay out of it."

"What do you want me to say?"

"Ask her to go and visit your friend Matt in prison, they are related and she's not responding to him," I explained.

"He is your friend too, though, Raquel."

"No, he's not a friend. But that doesn't matter," I muttered.

"So what's in it for me, if I do this?" My heart sank, how stupid I

THE BIG HOUSE

was to imagine this guy would do anything for nothing.

"What do you want?"

"Where do I start?" he looked me up and down.

"Oh my God, no!" I stepped back. He laughed, a little too loudly actually.

"I'm joking darlin'."

Relief washed over me. "So what, then?"

"There is something you can do for me, actually. My mum and dad are up to something and they've closed ranks on me. This house is my inheritance and I need to protect my asset."

I looked blankly at him, determined not to betray Morag.

"Find out what they're up to. Your mum will tell you, she knows everything about everyone, right?"

"Okay, I will see what I can do," I said.

He put his little hand out, expecting me to shake it, but I didn't want to touch his grubby hand.

"Nice doing business with you, Raquel, I think we make a great team."

"There's no business deal here, Miles, I'm just doing your mate a favour, just a very small favour and after that there will be no more letters no more contact and we all get on with our own lives after this is done," I told him firmly, setting my boundaries.

Miles smirked, "If you say so, sweetheart."

I left the cottage, feeling sick. Him being the middleman wasn't ideal. Dishonesty oozed out of his pores. Dave would be furious if he knew, but Dave didn't need to know this, he'd been through enough. Although it seemed like I wasn't the only one keeping secrets in our marriage. It was about then that I had started to miss home, I was stifled and unrelaxed, this wasn't a holiday, it was an ordeal. And this time, I couldn't go to Mel with this or my parents, I really was on my own.

THE BIG HOUSE

As I pushed open the kitchen garden gate to get back into the house, Dave was standing on the step outside the back door, his arms folded in a policeman/bouncer stance which was intimidating. He wasn't smiling, in fact, he looked quite stern. "Where have you just been?" he asked very directly.

I babbled; I did that when I felt pressure.

"Who, me? Oh, I've just been to ask Miles, my cousin, well he's not my cousin, if he knows where the rest of the firewood is, we're running out of logs, you see."

Dave nodded slowly, a sort of tight smile appeared on his face. I could tell he didn't believe me because he knew I would rather burn my parents as fuel than speak to Miles.

"Just thought you should know that your mum and dad are back from Edinburgh. The kids are going into town for a bit and I'm gonna take Roger and my dad for a few games of pool at one of the locals. So you've pretty much got the place to yourself," he said, looking at me with disappointment.

It made me feel sick to the stomach. We had promised to be honest and to not hide things from one another, and I was doing it again. But really, how many times could Dave compromise his integrity because of my mistake? My only option was to keep this from him and hope I could make it go away. And that when the time was right, he'd be honest about whatever he'd been hiding too.

"Okay, darling, enjoy yourself. See you in a bit." Why did I use the word 'darling' with an emphasis on the g? That wasn't our vocabulary, I wasn't from Chelsea or a man with a jumper draped over his shoulders. That made it even weirder. He left the kitchen and even from behind I could tell he was suspicious.

Julian had told me to tell Dave everything, to be open and honest, to keep the lines of communication clear, but Julian wasn't married to

THE BIG HOUSE

Dave and Julian wasn't in danger of losing everything, so Julian could stick it up his arse. I decided it wouldn't do to upset the apple cart and to ruin a family holiday. Of course, it wasn't the perfect scenario but I just had to push through.

I set the table and dressed it for the following day. I used some cuttings from the garden to create my Christmas scene, even managing to find some red candles and a sparkly tablecloth in a box Morag had left out. I'd shut the curtains and nobody would be any wiser we were six months away from the big day.

I'd let the family know that Christmas lunch would be served at 2 pm tomorrow. What happened up until that point was completely up to them, should they fancy playing cards, or just having a lie in, I wasn't actually expecting them to perform the normal Christmas duties. Mum was over-excited, I told her to calm down.

"Well, this is the only Christmas that we'll actually get with our family after you lot buggered off to Portugal and left us, so I'm taking this one seriously, Raquel."

I groaned, she had complained incessantly for the latter part of last year about it and clearly was still smarting. On numerous occasions I had assured Mum that with the decline in the calcium levels of both of Dave's parents' bones, it wasn't fair to ask them to join us in minus-degree temperatures for any length of time, Christmas or not, and that we had to make the journey to them once in a while. I also tried to play it down to appease her:

"I mean, what do the Portuguese know about Christmas, Mother? They can't decide if they're Spanish or African so you can't trust them with a Brussels sprout. I am not looking forward to it, I would much rather spend it here with you." I'd lied to her before we'd jetted off.

Adding insult to injury, Mel and Roger had decided to spend Christmas in a Swiss detox clinic where they would celebrate the

THE BIG HOUSE

birth of Jesus Christ our Lord with a fizzy water and some colonic irrigation. So my parents' only option was to spend it with Uncle Tom and his new wife Babs at a carvery.

"Thanks to you, Raquel, your father and I ended up in an all-you-can-eat buffet at a Harvester on the outskirts of Wigan town centre. Tom insisted he had it all in hand and that was the result!" She'd moaned when I'd called her on Boxing Day. I couldn't stop my eyes from crying with laughter but quickly composed myself knowing it wasn't a laughing matter.

"Mother, if you think the easyJet and Mateus Rosé are two things that appeared on my Christmas list, then you are mistaken. You do know but my Christmas dinner involved frozen roast potatoes and Robinson's raspberry jam masquerading as cranberry sauce?"

Mum had to sit down when I told her this, I knew how to get her to feel sorry for me and when she was assured that I was miserable, she got back to her Boxing Day and left me alone.

I mean it was all true – spending last Christmas in an English pub on the beach in Portugal wasn't how I wanted to spend the day.

"I love what they've done with the sprouts, they're almost like mash. I must get the recipe. And these potatoes are so crispy and delicious. Ooh, who's Aunt Bessie? How do you think they achieve this gravy, I could eat this as a soup, blah blah." I'd tried to be enthusiastic.

Gary and CeeCee needed to hear this so that they felt they provided a lovely Christmas for their son and his family. I had been so complimentary about their hospitality during our stay that I think it may have gone to their heads. Upon leaving the Algarve, I was handed a book of photocopied recipes from the different Portuguese establishments that we had visited during our six-day stay, all run by Brits who could not speak one word of anything other than English. Recipes involving Bisto gravy granules, Colman's packet sauces and a

THE BIG HOUSE

very snazzy trifle recipe who's top-secret ingredient was '7 Up' (shush don't tell anyone), was handed to me in a folder that was deemed more valuable than the Bible itself.

Putting my food snobbery to one side, we had some fantastic card games, we were party to some hilarious conversations with punchlines straight out of *Phoenix Nights* and I got to meet other crocodile-skinned oldies who had fled the UK for a better quality of life. Everyone was always smiling out there, I put it down to the sunshine. We all think 'yeah whatever, same shit different country' when people move abroad but the sunshine has a magical effect on so much in life. Imagine this; walk down the beach, it's 85 degrees, somebody says hello, you genuinely feel the inclination to say hello back, there's a bottle of chilled rosé waiting by your lounger and your husband has a tan. Let's change the temperature to 12 degrees with drizzle and set the scene on the Lancashire coast, we'll swap that rosé for a flask of milky tea and your husband is the same colour as Tipp-Ex. Needless to say, everyone in their complex was happy.

If only that was the case on this holiday. After Dave came back from the pub, he and CeeCee went for a walk around the gardens because apparently, she wanted some air and some time with her boy. It was just to be the two of them, so Gary had taken himself off to bed early so he could be 'up and at it' for his mid-summer Christmas. They were ages, I checked out of the window a couple of times to see where they'd got to. But they positioned themselves inside the half-fishing tent because it was spitting. The chairs were very low, and after the chat Dave had hauled her up with both hands, almost falling backwards into the lake. They'd walked back to the house hand-in-hand because she looked all shaky and pale.

On Christmas morning, as people were calling it, clearly taking this more seriously than I had anticipated, Dad was very busy making

THE BIG HOUSE

a tray of Buck's Fizz. My mother had stacked a pile of presents underneath a cheese plant in the library. Arif, who was more than happy to be involved in a traditional British celebration, was helping Suzy, bless her, who normally didn't see daylight until perhaps eleven or twelve o'clock to make bacon and egg sandwiches decorated with what they thought was holly, but was actually a sprig of ivy.

"Do you think one of those presents is Wi-Fi?" Sam asked, praying that Mum had somehow boxed up a permanent and strong connection in a shoe box as a gift.

"No, love, I do not!" And he duly sighed.

The whole family got into the spirit of the day apart from CeeCee, who claimed she wasn't feeling well and had decided to watch telly in bed. She had apparently doubled-dropped her codeine prescription and couldn't see straight.

"She mistook the suit of armour for an intruder and kicked it in the nuts! She gets like that when she overdoes the pills," Gary told us whilst trying to bash out the dent in the metal groin. "Best she stays in bed today."

It was a shame she missed it, but we had a fun day regardless, filled with lots of laughter, so much so, I almost forgot that this was a work project. The pheasants and their wild mushroom sauce photographed beautifully, the shot of the sticky ham smothered in a marmalade glaze next to a roaring fire was in my opinion the most Instagram-able shot of all time. I didn't put any of this on social media, I was not that sort of person – although I was incredibly impressed with my work, nobody likes a show-off.

Mel positioned herself at the opposite end of the dining table to Roger as they had been rowing again that morning. I saw Roger screw up a document that Mel was showing to him and he stuffed it into his own mouth and started to chew. I watched this transpire through the

THE BIG HOUSE

kitchen window with Mum standing behind me, and I have to admit we both had to stifle laughter. It was very unusual for Roger to do anything quite so rock and roll, and when he almost choked to death Mel had to thump him on the back to release it from his throat.

I turned to Mum and asked her, "What the hell is going on there?"

She tapped her nose a few times annoyingly saying, "Snitches get stitches." And that was all I got.

Once we sat down for dinner, Roger had already had two pints of Guinness and a whisky and he was being quite the court jester. He had three attempts at being witty, all of them failed but he gave it his very best. I know he was probably suffering but this new Roger was amusing. Mel rolled her eyes or made a nasty groan each time he made any noise and eventually, to my surprise, Dad gave her a public bollocking.

"Now that's quite enough, young lady, pipe down," he hissed sternly.

Mel went bright red and I revelled in it; it was about time she was put in her place. Even though I was delighting in not being the problematic daughter for once, Dad was right and this situation was becoming quite uncomfortable. She stood up to leave.

"And don't you dare storm off and ruin this fabulous Christmas. You might have your issues, Melanie, but there's lots worse off than you." He shot her a stern look and she promptly sat back down, while I couldn't suppress my smug 'hee hee' face to her to show her that I was still a petty teenager at heart.

After the feast, we played games. Some idiot had brought the game Pie Face so we spent at least an hour having shaving foam splattered into our faces, much to amusement of Arif. He was not familiar with silly board games, and he thought it was all highly amusing.

Morag had left out a box of crackers, so we had a good laugh and some naff jokes and I was now the proud owner of a black plastic

THE BIG HOUSE

moustache and a miniature bell. Who comes up with this shit, I'll never know. But anyway, it was Christmas so I was in decent spirits and I was forgetting my troubles for one afternoon.

Dave and Mel ended up on washing-up duty which put me slightly on edge because there's something about doing the washing and drying in partnership with somebody that connects you. I stood out of sight watching them passing crockery to each other wondering if this was the future; I would be wallowing in a bedsit crying into a stained yellow pillow wondering what they'd had for dinner at a classy bistro Mel would have taken him to.

I decided that tomorrow would be a positive day, tomorrow would be a mentally stable day and no matter what my hormones were doing, I would get my act together. I had to stop these stupid thoughts that were becoming more frequent.

Later that night, we watched a DVD, it was a Christmas special of *Only Fools and Horses* at Arif's eager request. He had become utterly obsessed with Del and Rodney and even though I was pretty sure he couldn't understand most of what they were saying, he thought it was the funniest thing on earth. He and Suzy sat next to one another, having become good friends. I could never have predicted that she even had the patience for Arif and his broken English and endless questions, but she was actually being very nice to him. Suzy wasn't normally a very kind girl, not at all, and I put it down to the Wi-Fi thing. These phones, tablets and games consoles had so much to answer for and I wondered how many parents had never ever got to see their children's true personalities because technology had swallowed them up.

As everybody went up to their beds, I handed Gary a small jug of milk in case he wanted a 3 am cup of tea.

"What a super day. Thanks, Raquel, lots of fun."

I hugged him, grateful he had been a little more positive that day,

THE BIG HOUSE

which was needed. I know they both had their aches and pains plus they were a long way from home but they weren't that old, there was still a few years of fun left, surely, even if they did seem a bit more unsteady recently. Gary then stumbled on the bottom step and spilt some of the milk on his slippers.

"Oh, bollocks, who put that there?" he said to a two-hundred-year-old step.

"Give the milk to me, Dad. I'll take that, you take yourself," Dave sighed, and then walked behind him to block any potential fall. I watched as two generations of boiled eggs climbed the stairs together to bed.

FACECOCK

The Christmas meal had gone well, everybody had enjoyed it and Mum was satisfied she'd eventually got her family Christmas. But it left us all a little jaded, so for the rest of that week we all agreed to do our own thing. Mel and Roger had been to some art galleries in Glasgow, Mum had spent time with Morag, mainly in the attic at night, and seeing her go up and down the loft hatch with trays of gin and tonics made me smile. Dad and Gary had both spent a whole day trying their hand at fishing with Dave and Sam's guidance and when Gary got a bite the entire family legged it down to the shores to see what it was. Turned out that the hook had just got caught on a rock or something so there were no celebrations when nothing surfaced. But the following day they tried and tried again and eventually Gary caught a trainer.

Both Mel and Dave had continued to be off with me, I wasn't sure if they were in on it together or whether they had separate beef. I still felt an iciness when either of them entered the room and at some point I would need to address it, but I just wanted to relax for a few days after the effort of the Christmas meal.

I have officially renamed Facebook, and it will now be known as Facecock which is another word for dickhead. Break it down and it basically means the same thing. Mark Zuckerberg must have been chuckling into his lobster thermidor when he thought this one up.

'I know, let's create a club for the bored, the jealous, the show-offs and the busy bodies (affectionately known as Karens) and then we'll let them all loose to express their feelings on literally any subject.' It's the most intriguing social experiment that I have ever witnessed.

I had skipped the Facebook era and had headed straight to Instagram, so when I delved into this world properly for the first time,

THE BIG HOUSE

it was an absolute gift. Yes, I want to know your intimate business but I don't ever want to actually talk to you in person. Cryptic messages which were actually just a transparent form of attention seeking were in full flow even from my own village – my neighbours were letting it all hang out on Facecock. Linda from the bottom of our road wrote, 'Some people need to remember where they came from.' And she added an emoji with one raised eyebrow to make it all the more mysterious. When she received a flurry of responses from intrigued do-gooders, such as 'What's up, babe?' 'Are you okay, hun?' Linda just responded, 'Don't ask.'

I sat in the bar of The Hotel and I spent a good hour delving into the lives of people I knew or used to know, finding out about their personal business and they had no idea I was there. I found out that the woman who works in my local Spar is never speaking to her best friend ever again, stating 'You never know someone until you live with them.' That was supported with a punch emoji. And again, when other Facecockers asked if 'hun' was okay, they were told not to ask. Hysterical, really.

I have also been made aware that the secretary from Sam's school is currently in Bodrum. She has been sick eight times after a dubious shish kebab she ordered from room service. As of 6 pm yesterday it was coming out of both ends. There was a picture of her big clammy face to support this and a toilet roll strategically placed behind her. Poor lamb.

And thank goodness that Caroline Watkins from Wilmslow had the nouse to let the town know that Tesco Express were running low on semi-skimmed. We should all whizz down quickly to avoid disappointment. Edge-of-the-seat stuff, this was.

'Two dodgy black men seen running through the woods. Take care out there, ladies.' That came from a dog walker who thought she was

THE BIG HOUSE

doing the local females a big favour. Blatant racism from one of the housing estates just a couple of miles from me, I was embarrassed to live near this person, ashamed, in fact. But this sort of thing was alive and kicking outside the big cities and unless Nelson Mandela himself explained why this statement was utterly unacceptable, it would go straight over their white-hooded heads. The two super-fit guys who were most likely training to represent Britain in the Olympics were now seen as predators waiting to steal handbags full of vape sticks and panty liners. These are but a few reasons I renamed this platform Facecock, it was apt.

Amongst my amusement, I did manage to find a large number of Gemma Wilds in the Liverpool area. I also found a few in America and one holding a machine gun on a high security complex in Bahrain. But I knew which was the correct Gemma Wild because there was a picture of her baby shower, and Gina, the dastardly sister, was smack bang in the middle in black hot pants with 'legs that went on for days'. That was the actual caption underneath.

So there she was, she was Matt's link to his wife. This was his best shot at being able to communicate with Gina. He was right, they must have been in touch somehow in a low-key way, Gemma and Gina sounded like the female version of the Krays, the Burberry bond would stay strong and nothing would break it. I screenshotted the profile and forwarded it to Miles, I had added him to my contacts under the name Angus Ferguson so if absolutely necessary we could communicate. I was good at this deception thing, or so I hoped.

On the following Tuesday morning, I asked Dave to join me in Helensburgh, having had such a lovely day there with the children when we went before. I wanted to spend some time with him away from the house, in the hope it might help us reconnect. I had almost bagged a date day, just the two of us, when Mel piped up.

THE BIG HOUSE

"We'll come, if there's room," she said as my face dropped.

"It's a seaside town, it's not posh, Mel," I said, trying to dissuade her.

"Define not posh?" Roger asked, concerned.

"Erm, there's no Harvey Nichols," I told him, hoping that would be enough to make him stay home. Roger looked at Mel, willing her to withdraw the offer.

"Raquel, we're coming. It's about time the four of us went and did something together." She insisted, which was an interesting move from Mel, but if she did have designs on Dave then perhaps this was a way to be close to him, in plain sight. If they had feelings for one another then perhaps they planned on telling Roger and I in a public place where we would think twice about attacking them.

Roger moved towards the window and gauged the weather with his flu radar. "We'll need to get wrapped up so we don't catch cold," he told Mel, and she laughed – she'd not done that in a while, she seemed to be softening.

"It's at least fifteen degrees, Roger, come on, please don't get your duffel coat, not in the middle of summer," she pleaded, trying to toughen him up.

The car journey was pleasant enough; Dave drove and Roger sat beside him with an A-Z even though there was satnav. He gave a running commentary on where we were which was irritating Dave.

"And just around this corner, we should see a fork in the road… And there it is, so we'll take a left soon." Our destination was literally signposted every 100 metres, we had no need for anything but the signs but still he continued to navigate.

"Roger, put that book down, mate, please, it's not the eighties, we've moved on from that," Dave said abruptly, unable to take it anymore. Roger tucked the A-Z into his satchel and put his headphones in: "I'll just listen to a podcast, I think." And he shut his eyes.

THE BIG HOUSE

My sister and I sat in the back together observing our husbands – they could not have been more different. If Dave got a cold, he would have a chicken madras and a hot bath to sweat that bastard out. Roger, on the other hand, would have his bloods done privately to test for everything but the common cold. 'They found no traces of Lyme disease but they're questioning kidney stones,' was the type of shite we heard after just one sneeze.

Dave would also 'get on with it' in times of crisis. Like when Michaela ate a spider as a toddler whilst in Roger's care. "If it's a false widow David, she'll be unconscious and foaming at the mouth by noon." He was writing an email to the spider department of Chester Zoo titled URGENT.

"Or, Roger, she will be able to spin a web from her thumbs and scale the Eiffel Tower within seconds," Dave had replied jokingly. They were just cut from different cloth and their interactions were highly watchable.

"Right, well I fancy a wander down to the water," Dave announced, stretching as he took in the view when we parked up.

Roger shook his head. "David, that water will give you chilblains and it looks quite mucky too. No, thank you, I am going to see if I can find a bookshop to browse in. Melanie, will you join me?"

"Okay, let's go on a busman's holiday shall we, riveting." Mel sighed as she put her bag on her shoulder.

I pointed up to the high street where the cafés and shops were. "We'll be on the beach for a little while and then perhaps we'll meet up there for lunch." We all agreed.

Dave was quiet as we plodded along the sand next to the waves. He was still walking next to me and at my pace but there was a sort of distance between us, his mood seemed to have plummeted and he was pensive and quiet. I toyed with the idea of telling him how I was feeling

THE BIG HOUSE

but I didn't feel it appropriate to open up about us, particularly with the murkiness that had been unfolding in my other world. Something told me that unless I was prepared to tell him everything then nothing was the best option. I was comforted by the fact I had not cheated, I had not even looked at another man since Matt, so everything I had done, should it ever come out, was completely in Dave's best interests; I was, and would continue to be, a good girl.

I had once been called a 'wanton hussy' by a mate's mum when she caught me in their downstairs toilet with said friend's brother. I remember giggling at my new title that was straight from one of the Testaments. We were only snogging, and it wasn't even pleasant as he had a crusty zit just under his nostril, which was very off-putting. His mother was very protective, a "don't mess with the mama bear" type – (Holly Willoughby, 2019).

She was so upset with me that she used that term before slinging me out of their house and told me I would no longer be welcome. I walked home unbothered; it was just a way to fill a boring afternoon. That zit, by the way, turned out to be a rather nasty and infectious case of impetigo; I ended up with face like a buttered crumpet for weeks afterwards, that was the real punishment.

Anyway, it was the name 'wanton hussy' that really stuck with me and I endeavoured to use it one day just because it sounded good. I never imagined that it would be used to describe me.

"You're quiet, Dave, is everything okay?"

"I guess so, just had a bit on my mind," he replied cryptically.

"Like what?"

"Oh, work, really, and it's sad to see my mum and dad decline so much physically, it makes you think."

I grabbed his hand, and he let me, but it didn't feel like he was really holding it back.

THE BIG HOUSE

"People get old and I'm sure they will be fine as long as they keep moving, you know," I told him.

He nodded. "I don't feel good about myself, Raquel, morally. I feel as though I let them down doing what I did last year."

Well, this was new; he had done what he did for the family and as far as he was concerned that was what was most important. Why was he letting him affect him now? I shrugged it off.

"What they don't know can't hurt them, right, isn't that what they say?"

"They do know, my mum does anyway," he admitted.

I stopped dead in my tracks and let go of his hand. "Your Mum knows what exactly?"

He rubbed his head. "She knows that you messed up and there was another guy involved. That's all."

"That's all?" I shrieked. I couldn't believe that CeeCee was privy to this information, that my mother-in-law knew what I had done. "But how does she know, Dave, and how much does she know?"

He sat down on the sand so I joined him. "I told her that things had been strained between us for the past year, Raquel. We talked about it because she knew something wasn't quite right when she came here. I needed to offload and she's my mum."

"But she'll hate me Dave, I can't bear it." He gave me nothing, no reassurance at all.

"Raquel, what happened was massive and what I ended up doing for us still keeps me awake at night. Don't get me wrong, I would do it again in a heartbeat, it's just hard, you know. I broke the law Raquel and I am supposed to uphold it." He dug a hole in the sand with his hand, he seemed a little helpless.

I guess Dave hadn't been coping as well as I had thought and he did harbour some resentment towards me. I had felt that shift, so in a way

THE BIG HOUSE

felt lighter for knowing I hadn't imagined it. I was now only focussed on CeeCee's opinion of me, as most of us would be. It truly matters what our husband's mothers think of us.

"What did she say, Dave, about me, about what I did?"

He looked at me coldly and said, "What, her actual words? Do you really want to know?"

"Yes!"

"Wanton hussy," he told me, and I gasped.

You know that feeling when you've just been slapped but nobody has laid a finger on you? I felt it then. Being called a slut, a slapper even a whore is like water off a duck's back when you're young and beautiful-ish. One of my mates was known as 'Slutty Maria' for years and she loved it; she runs the PTA now, so we tend not to use it so much. But as a woman of a certain age, having a label like that was just downright grimy.

"I'm sorry, I had to talk to somebody. I thought I had got over it, but things have just come flooding back recently."

I was frightened to ask why. I didn't want him to mention Miles and I really did not want to let any more untruths leave my 'wanton' mouth. So I just played it down.

"It was never going to be a smooth road this marriage thing, eh."

Dave smiled and nodded. "No, for better or worse and all that."

"Come on, let's go and have some lunch and wind Roger up until he combusts."

"Well, it can't hurt to give it a go." Dave perked up a bit at this prospect.

We headed into the town to find the other two and I tried to be as upbeat as possible just hoping now I knew he was struggling; I could try and make more effort or do something to get things back on track. We sat in a quiet little café on the front waiting for the others whilst

THE BIG HOUSE

watching the world go by, it was actually quite peaceful. I never really got those couples who sat in silence but now I did. After more than twenty-five years of chatting much shit, sometimes silence is just a beautiful thing. My phone rang on the table disturbing our moment.

"The butchers, what do they want?" Dave asked, noticing the call.

"Oh, it will just be about one of my orders. Can't be arsed with that now. I'll call them later."

Dave nodded, "You need a break from food, you're supposed to be on holiday."

"People always have to eat, Dave, it's not just work," I said trying to be casual but my heart was pounding. I told Miles to never call me, only message me and even if he must do that, he would need to make it cryptic. Why was I surprised this little tit couldn't take instruction? He couldn't even steal stuff without getting caught.

Another beep indicted I had a voicemail, just great! His creepy little whispers no doubt incriminating me on my voicemail for anyone to access. I needed to delete it, and fast. I excused myself to the toilet and quickly locked the door behind me, pressing my phone as hard as I could against my cheek because that felt somehow safer to listen to it.

"Raquel, it's me. I know you said not to call but this is somewhat of an emergency. I have made contact with this Gemma Wild and she's coming up to Scotland. She wants to meet you face-to-face, she has some info that's too sensitive to talk about on the phone. She'll be at The Hotel tonight. You need to get over there later, she says she'll come up to the house if not. Okey-dokey, darlin', see you soon."

I deleted it. I pressed delete multiple times just to make sure. I did not want to meet this woman under any circumstances, I didn't want dragging back into this mess. I was turning into one of those people where everything they touched turn to shit – not gold, actual shit. I would just have to wing it, reminding myself that I only needed to ask somebody to

THE BIG HOUSE

visit somebody else in prison. No transporting immigrants, no looking after drugs and most of all, no heavy petting with the neighbours. I could not have her rocking up at The Eagle Lodge, hell no. I made my way back to the table to see that Mel and Roger had arrived and they were questioning a waitress who looked incredibly stressed.

"Are you're saying the eggs are organic or are they free range?"

"I don't know the difference, sorry." The young waitress was pale.

"What about the chicken in the salad? Is that organic or is it corn-fed?" She shrugged and looked back to the counter in search of her boss. Mel was picking this menu apart and this girl who wasn't much older than Sam was beginning to tremble.

"Come on, guys this is a caff, not Soho House. Just pick something will you, for God's sake," Dave said, putting a stop to it.

Mel handed her menu back and sighed. "Okay, I'll have a goats cheese salad and a bottle of mineral water, then, that seems safest."

She was really taking this clean eating far too seriously; it was annoying and actually quite depressing, as we were on holiday.

After a very measly lunch which left me unsatisfied because I felt too guilty to order chips with my sandwich, Mel and I took a walk along the front. Dave and Roger went for a game of crazy golf although there would be nothing crazy about it.

Mel's phone rang as we walked and as she looked at the screen she was nervous and her hands shook slightly. "I have to take this call, I'll be a minute." She rushed off into a shop doorway and talked animatedly to whoever it was. She wasn't long and when she re-joined me she seemed more relaxed, happy even.

"Who was that?" I asked nosily.

"Somebody who will make my dreams come true." She smiled. This was my chance to try and find out just what the heck was going on because I doubted Dave would be calling her with Roger by his side.

THE BIG HOUSE

"There's someone else isn't there, Mel?"

"There will be if my plan comes to fruition," she beamed.

"What about Roger? The love of your life… apparently," I said scornfully.

"Roger is not enough, not anymore, Raquel."

"Who is then, Mel, who is going to complete you?"

She paused so I filled in the blank.

"It's Dave, isn't it?"

She re-opened her eyes and frowned. "Your Dave?"

I nodded. She needed to stop playing dumb because I'd had enough of this act.

"Yes, my husband. David!"

She smiled, she even laughed a bit. I suddenly felt embarrassed.

"No, idiot. Not your Dave, you don't think that, surely? Have you been actually thinking that?"

Immediately I felt a little bit stupid with my sensible sister now observing me as if I needed a lobotomy.

"You're actually serious, aren't you?" she stopped and faced me.

I tried to explain.

"Well, it's just the lack of contact over the last year, the weight loss, the yoga, the weirdness. And then there's Dave's keto, and you don't seem to like your husband anymore." Her eyes suddenly displayed sympathy.

"Sit down, I'll tell you everything," she said as we reached a bench looking out over the water.

"Firstly Raquel, you're an absolute clown."

I agreed. "Yep, noted."

"Secondly, I have no interest in Dave, for God's sake, how absurd. But, I do have a problem and things have not been good for Roger and I."

THE BIG HOUSE

I got as comfortable as I could on the iron bench, immediately feeling better this wasn't about Dave.

"Raquel, you know I have always wanted kids but Roger wasn't keen. I tried to fill the hole with Walter, but although I love him I still never felt fulfilled."

"I had no idea you still felt this way, I thought the dog was enough," But she just shook her head.

"I made the decision last year that I wanted to have a baby and I got him to agree after much persuasion."

This was a massive deal, especially at her age and I was gutted not to have been included in this.

"Anyway, I decided I would get healthy so I could stay alive long enough to look after my child – I'm nearly fifty, it wouldn't be fair to do this unless I was at my best. I am still having regular periods so my body has not shut up shop just yet. So, I took a sabbatical to focus on getting my mind and body ready for a mid-life pregnancy."

Okay, now the new-and-improved Mel was beginning to make sense.

"Roger and I started trying, I bought the ovulation kit, took all the right vitamins and we went at it like rabbits, I mean, we were doing it every day, Raquel."

I felt considerably queasy, the thought of Roger at it like a rabbit was absolutely horrible. I wondered if he wore his socks during sex. I bet he did.

"Nothing happened for the first three months and every time I got my period I felt like a failure. Roger was supportive and we just went at it again. Month after month in every position under the sun we tried to make a baby, but it never happened."

More visions of Roger using sticky notes in his copy of the *Kama Sutra* entered my brain, I wondered if he cried after sex. I bet he did.

THE BIG HOUSE

"Eventually last month, after nine months of trying, I booked us in for tests. I was fit, I'd lost weight, I wasn't stressed with work. There had to be something wrong."

That sounded fair, and I nodded.

"On the day of the test, just before we were due to leave, Roger asked me to sit down at the kitchen table as he had something to tell me. And do you know what that wanker said?"

I shook my head.

"He told me that he couldn't have children, that he was firing blanks, that his swimmers didn't swim."

I stood up and gasped.

"You what? No way! Poor Roger."

"Poor Roger? Are you having a laugh? He's always known, he knew this before we even got married, the absolute bastard. He has been leading me up the garden path this whole time."

Tears ran down her face and both her fists were clenched in anger.

"I see what you're saying, Mel, but maybe because you said you didn't want children when you first got married, he didn't think there was a need to tell you," I said, attempting to be the voice of reason.

"Are you actually sticking up for him, Raquel? Well, this is a first! You said you wanted to throw a toaster in his bath last year and now this." She was right, I had made some comments about electrocuting him but I was in a really bad mood at the time.

"Do you know how much sex I have had to have this year? I'm absolutely knackered, I don't even like sex."

I smiled inside. Roger the absolute dog had used this situation to get more sex than any married person had ever had in their lives. I didn't think he had this sort of deceit in him, maybe he did have a personality after all. And really, how many people are asked to prove their fertility at his age? The guy must have been in turmoil having this

THE BIG HOUSE

landed on him. But I had to be on Mel's side, no matter what, she was my sister and I only had the one.

"This is very bad, Mel. We should electrocute him, actually, but what are you going to do without his swimmers?"

"Oh, I am not letting this stop me. I've decided to get a sperm donor."

My mind yet again sent me down Weirdo Road.

"Whose sperm? You're not having any of Dave's, before you get any ideas."

She rolled her eyes, "No, Raquel, I do not want any of your husband's jizz, you absolute freak."

"Phew. Well, that's good. Whose jizz, I mean semen, are we using and how do we get it into you?"

This would be an interesting exercise going around the country milking high-flying professionals so that Mel could produce a top-quality product with a place at Oxford before it's even born.

"We don't, Raquel, a fertility clinic will do it so you put your Calpol syringe away, let's leave it to the professionals. I've been to see them twice, had all the necessary tests and now my dates are aligning and I need to get to London later this week and be inseminated, that was them calling me in."

"What does Roger think about bringing up another man's child?" She rolled her eyes.

"He actually stuffed my fertility chart into his mouth and tried to swallow it. He's not coping very well." I didn't tell her I'd witnessed it.

"Oh, Roger, he must be feeling pretty traumatised right now."

She shrieked. "I don't care, Raquel, he's a liar."

"Why haven't you told me about any of this, Mel?" I couldn't help but feel hurt she hadn't confided in me.

"You had enough on your plate, we're all still reeling after last year.

THE BIG HOUSE

I thought you needed your space."

She was right, I had been caught up in my own shit, and working on my marriage. Mel knew that and she respected that. I was actually a shit sister.

I wondered if this was the right time to tell her that it has been me who had insisted Roger came over to Scotland. I had made a big mistake with that one and she would kill me if she found out. I needed to make sure Roger never leaked the fact I had asked him to come, and if he did I would need to make sure the toaster reached the bath.

"And you're going to London soon?"

"Yes, in a couple of days." She was excited. "This is it Raquel!"

I jumped up and shouted "Yeah!" like Tom Jones – it just felt right.

But then I remembered something that had made me wonder if there was a piece missing from the puzzle.

"Miles, what about your secret meeting with Miles?" She sighed.

"You really are a nosey bitch, aren't you?"

"Yes, I am a self-professed nosey fucker, but you knew that. Why did you meet up with him then lie about it, Mel? He's not a possible donor, is he?" She visibly recoiled.

"Are you actually nuts?"

"Well, I saw you in his house and then you denied ever talking to him?"

"Oh, Raquel, your imagination is wild. I just wanted to talk to him about some local yoga classes and whether he knew of any raw local dairies. Nothing more than that. I didn't tell you because you always had something negative to say about my new lifestyle."

I heaved a huge sigh of relief that my sister wouldn't be giving birth to a tiny little chain-smoker.

"So what's the protocol? How will you pick whose sperm you use?"

"Well, it's like a menu, really. You can even get some pictures of how they looked as a child."

THE BIG HOUSE

"No way!" She nodded.

"Plus, you get a pretty detailed report on medical history, educational achievements, even personality traits."

"Wow! I'd get someone with straight hair, Mel, this bog brush has been the bane of my life." I tugged on my knotty bun. "And if possible, you should get a tall one. Tall people never seem to lose in life. Apart from Kylie and Ronnie Corbett there are no other really small successful people."

She looked at me with real concern and said, "Would you consider Ronnie Corbett a success though, Raquel?"

"I would, actually. But I'm guessing a tiny comedian is not what you're looking for." She agreed, that would be her worst nightmare.

"Oh, and check whether or not there's any addiction in the family. You don't want it reaching for the sherry the minute your backs are turned." She gave me a look.

"What, like you did as a kid and still do now, come to think of it." I agreed, I did have a liking for the booze.

"So what do they do? Take it out of the freezer and just fire it up?" I was genuinely intrigued.

"Well, I would like to think that they may use a gentler term than 'fire it up' but yes, I suppose that's about the size of it."

She patted her stomach, it was very flat these days but not for long. Once you've carried a human for nine months, it's only a matter of time before the vagina and stomach become one. A very cruel joke on us ladies from Mother Nature.

We continued to walk, the wind picked up and the breeze from the water was quite biting at times. She linked my arm, possibly for warmth but it felt good we were close again.

It had been strange day out, we all had things on our minds so there were plenty of silences and staring out of windows. Sometimes, quiet

THE BIG HOUSE

reflection was necessary and although we went together, we each had some time on our own: mine was spent in the toilet on the phone to a criminal, Dave went off and had a long chat with a young PC he saw walking down the street in uniform. Roger had enjoyed some time in a bookshop, if you could call WHSmith a bookshop. And Mel, she took a call from the clinic and prepared herself for a life-changing journey. Perhaps this was middle age, wandering around with your hands behind your back wearing a waterproof. Perhaps sitting across from your spouse and saying nothing in a cafe was how things were from here on in.

Back at the house, Mum greeted me at the door with an apron on. "You've missed a great day! We've had an absolute ball."

"Who has?" What ball could be had without me, I wondered.

"All of us, wait until you see what we have in store."

Mum smoothed her hair back and played with her pearl studs nervously, which was never a good sign.

"Well we were a bit bored so we all got together and we played 'bake-off'." She giggled. "I'm afraid we've made a bit of a mess, but I think you'll like what we have achieved."

At the words 'a bit of a mess' I pushed past her to see what they'd done to my kitchen. I was faced with a sea of people covered in flour, and my food mixer, which was a 'do not touch item', was in bits in the sink, including the electrical plug. Sam was putting the finishing touches to a deconstructed Black Forest gâteau; I only knew this because it was labelled and not because it resembled one.

On the kitchen table were a number of other cakes, one a brownie with what looked to be marshmallows going through the centre, there was an apple turnover that was slightly burned on the top and had a bowl of split whipped cream sitting beside it. Meanwhile, CeeCee was glazing some sort of giant pink iced bun, glancing at me briefly but nothing more.

THE BIG HOUSE

"What do you think, Mum?" Suzy came bounding over, "We all made something for our holiday bake-off and guess who is going to be the judge?"

I did a quick scan just to make sure Noel Fielding hadn't turned up on his broomstick.

"Who?" I asked, praying to God I wasn't going to have to taste some of these.

"You, of course, our resident chef. We've all worked really hard and we want you to judge it like the telly." Suzy was brimming with excitement; she was really turning over a new leaf. A couple of weeks ago this sort of thing would have been 'totally lame'.

I smiled. A warm feeling came over me, proud of their efforts, so I tried to ignore the mess which was annoying me. Every single pan, oven dish and utensil had been used and there was frangipane splattered onto the kitchen window, but I put that out of my mind and began to try the contestants' entries.

The only thing I felt was inedible, and I feel guilty for saying it, really, was Babs' offering. She'd probably never seen the show as she was busy in a war zone or travelling under a lorry. On a silver platter lay a very long and slim pastry parcel. I could have used my finger to slice it as it was basically sitting in a puddle. When I asked what was inside it, she ominously said, "Surprise."

Hoping the surprise wasn't a dead dog, I reluctantly took a slice but smelled it first. "What is this? It smells very meaty."

Mum shrugged, "I was concentrating on my turnover, no idea what that is, although she did go to the butchers, come to think of it – your dad drove her down there."

Blood seeped out of the sides of the 'dessert' and I tried not to look alarmed. "Mmmm, delicious. Is this from Syria?"

Babs shook her head, her apron was smeared in raw meat and

THE BIG HOUSE

she was expecting me to put this into my mouth when it smelt like a sanitary towel and it looked like one too. Luckily, Tom came over and shed some light. "It was supposed to be a sweet Christmas pastry stuffed with mincemeat, you know, the spicy one with orange zest, but she got mistaken and ended up using pork mince. It should still be nice, though, like a sausage roll."

"Tom, she hasn't even cooked the mince, she's put it in raw."

"And?"

"And we'll all be dead if we eat this."

"Well, what about steak tartare? I bet you eat that, you picky bugger." He snatched the tray from my hand and shuffled off towards the oven, Babs tutted at me and followed him.

I looked at the others, they all seemed disappointed that I hadn't played along. But come on, I would have a better chance of survival by taking forty paracetamol than trying that. Luckily, Suzy and Arif presented a damn good effort in the form of a Swiss roll, and the fact they'd rolled it without breaking it was very impressive. "We just follow recipe in book and bing bong," Arif told me using another of his new phrases.

"Well it really is very professional and the sponge is perfect." He and Suzy gazed at each other with pride and I noted what a good influence Arif was becoming on her.

I tried all of the entries and spent time wandering up and down the table pondering on which was my favourite, milking my moment.

"Well, who is the winner of The Eagle Lodge bake-off?" Mum asked impatiently, gesturing not so subtly towards her turnover. Which, by the way, was very good and could have been the main event in some apple pie shop in Ambleside. Suzy was convinced that she would be crowned queen and on looks, the Swiss roll was the best. Sam's flavours in his gâteau were good but the presentation was

THE BIG HOUSE

certainly deconstructed, and that's being generous about it. I looked at my notes, I had made them to look important. I looked back at the desserts and then at the contestants.

"And the winner is..." Dave made a drum-roll noise as I delivered a controversial decision that would piss everybody off.

"The pink iced bun by CeeCee," I shouted. There was a silence and CeeCee went pink herself. Discontented murmurs began, somebody coughed and said 'bullshit' at the same time, even my mother-in-law was confused. And then Mum just couldn't hold it in any longer.

"Excuse me!" she shouted as she took her apron off and slammed it onto the counter. "That's basically just a baguette and icing sugar. Paul Hollywood wouldn't give that to his damn dog."

Dave locked eyes with me and smiled. I was building bridges with CeeCee, one crap cake at a time.

BRANDY & COKE

No dinner was needed after the bake-off; there had been all-day nibbling and afterwards the kids made big bowls of popcorn and decided to put one of the DVDs on that were kept in a cabinet under the telly. A heated discussion eventually resulted in *Uncle Buck* making the cut that evening.

"I need to nip into town and send some work in." I excused myself, edging my way towards the front door with my laptop visibly under my arm and a pen behind my ear for my alibi.

"Can't you just send it from the basement?" My knob of a sister offered a reasonable solution.

"No!" I snapped. "It takes too long to upload the photographs and they send low-res because of the bandwidth," I bullshitted, stepping further out of the door.

"I think I'll come with you, I'll have a G&T whilst you work," Mum announced, alarmingly, starting to put on her cardigan. I tried not to scream it but my voice was noticeably very high-pitched.

"No, sit back down. I need to concentrate, you'll only end up distracting me."

Mum buttoned up the cardigan and started applying her lippy. "No, I won't, I'll sit quietly and people-watch."

"Mum, stop smothering me. I need some space to do my important work," I said exasperated.

The movie-watchers turned around, Dave screwing up his face and Dad raising his eyebrows. They waited for Mum to let rip. She was silent for a second or two and then she started to laugh. "She writes about mashed potato, and she acts like she's running the country. Come on, we can have a good chat on the way." And she left the house

THE BIG HOUSE

getting into my car and there was no telling her otherwise.

I couldn't protest any further, it would have been too obvious, so I would have to sort her out once we were out of the house. As soon as I switched on the engine, she started.

"Well, are you going to tell me just what all that was about?" She clunk-clicked and folded her arms.

"What?"

"You giving CeeCee the top spot for a hot-dog bun."

"Oh that." I realised, relieved her ulterior motive was to get the dirt on my judging.

"Yes, that, I thought you knew your food, you were supposed to be a professional judge, I thought you were going to do it like Mary does."

"Oh, it's just Mary to you is it? Look, I'm sorry about that but I was doing some damage limitation. Well, creeping, really."

"What do you mean?"

"She knows Mum – about me and Matt Dennis," I explained.

Mum gasped. CeeCee was not from a long line of cheaters like I was, she'd only ever slept with Gary, and this sort of thing would rock her world. "Oh, Jesus Christ above, Raquel. That is hideous."

"Thanks, Mum. That makes me feel much better."

"Well, CeeCee's not like me, Raquel. I'm easy-going, chilled, a laugh, a people person," Mum said with a straight face.

I laughed my head off at her description of not herself but Emma Willis.

"I thought I'd let her win to try and smooth things over. I'm warning you now though, Portugal might have to be on the cards at Christmas again."

Mum slapped her hand on the dashboard. "Are you trying to kill your father and I? We don't know how many Christmases we have left and year after year you take our grandchildren away to a foreign land

THE BIG HOUSE

and leave us to rot," she said with her eyes shut for effect.

"Mother, it would be the third year in the last twenty-five, stop exaggerating. You're welcome to join us, you know that," I reasoned.

"Do British Airways fly to the Algarve?" she asked after a few moments, and I smiled.

"Well, they fly to the capital. You could go to Lisbon for a couple of days beforehand, that would be lovely, wouldn't it?"

"Hmmm Lisbon, yes there are some galleries there I would like to visit and apparently the restaurants are top notch."

I continued, "Just think, a lovely weekend break followed by Christmas with the family. What's not to love?" Now I was really getting her on-side.

"Okay perhaps, but I can't do easyJet again, not after the last time. I am boycotting that airline until the day that I die."

I agreed, easyJet and Mum just hadn't been a good fit.

"I know, I know. We'll get you and Dad out to Lisbon with BA and then you can join the rest of us, the great unwashed, for Christmas."

She made a murmur of agreement – I had her where I wanted her.

Six years previously, Mum and Mel had taken a trip to Salzburg in Austria to visit the place where apparently the von Trapps lived high on a hill and all that. They loved the movie and decided to combine a Christmas market trip with a *Sound of Music* tour. I was invited but I told them straight, I would rather be buggered by a Nazi than do any of those things. Anyhow, the only way to get to Salzburg out of Manchester was with easyJet, which sounds fine unless, of course, you're a massive snob like my mother and Mel.

The journey got off to a bad start with the flight being delayed for four hours because Manchester Airport was on its knees due to baggage-handling strikes, and according to Mum, the skeleton staff that they had working the desks were nothing but 'plebs and blobs'.

THE BIG HOUSE

Eventually when called to go to the gate, speedy boarding was not applicable due to an admin error. For this reason, there was a charge for the gate with much shoving and pushing between passengers and cabin crew. Mum was so aggrieved, she ended up prodding some guy on the forehead with her brolly. 'Some guy' was the actual pilot and although he said he would let it go this time, she should keep her hands to herself in future. My sister unleashed her lawyer's spiel and that seemed to work, as Mum was still allowed to fly even though she had physically assaulted the driver!

Once on the plane, it turned out that Mel's PA had failed to seat them together and Mum was wedged in between a child with a permanent runny nose and an addict with the shakes. It was a very messy flight in terms of Mum's cream overcoat.

What had topped it off was at baggage reclaim where Mel and Mum waited for their carefully packed suitcases full of silk, cashmere and Merino wool ready to do the Austrian hills the justice they were owed. But, easyJet had sent both bags to Cairo by 'accident' and they were currently somewhere over the Red Sea. Mum had put her head on the desk and sobbed. However, as a token of their sincere apologies, easyJet were kind enough to award a voucher of £25 per passenger that could be spent in duty free.

"Oh, well!" Mum had screamed at Salzburg's lost luggage desk. "We'll get fifty quids' worth of fucking Toblerone and wear them, shall we?"

They had both been escorted out of the airport by security and for the following three days they wore Lederhosen and looked absolutely frickin' ridiculous. It was then that Mum's relationship with easyJet came to an end and she stated on TripAdvisor: "If you like travelling in a flying wheelie bin, then easyJet is your airline."

THE BIG HOUSE

* * * * *

We arrived at The Hotel at about eight and I still had no real plan as to what I would do with Mum. But, knowing her, she would immerse herself in someone else's business within minutes and I could slip away to this Gemma Wild's room, introduce myself, insist she visited her brother-in-law, preferably with a naked picture of Gina, and that would be my part done.

"After what I just heard, I'm having a double." Mum stormed through reception and straight into the back bar. It was fairly busy and there was music playing, which was good. Plenty of distractions for Mum and not so much focus on me.

Right on cue, a group of walkers sitting on the table politely said good evening and Mum immediately asked them what route they had taken that day. I ordered the drinks, mine a mineral water and Mum her usual fuel.

"We're staying at the big house on the hill. Maybe you've passed it, it's our wedding anniversary, you see, so we thought, why not, let's push the boat out." People's chairs were moved and Mum had a new group of friends which was my cue to exit.

"Just nipping to reception, the connection is strongest there," I pretended, but Mum barely noticed me leave the bar.

Climbing the stairs, I must admit I did have a knot in my stomach. It was the first time I would meet one of Gina's relatives and I had no idea what to expect. If she was as cold and calculating as her sister, this could be a tricky ten minutes. Ten minutes was all I had before my mother would ask questions. Miles had sent me a message with nothing but the number nine so I presumed this was her room number.

I knocked on the door gently, being covert. The door opened slightly and I edged my way in. A figure wearing a cap shut the door

THE BIG HOUSE

and locked it, the curtains were drawn, it was hard to see anything but then I heard the voice.

"Raquel, how are you babe? Long time no see."

My heart dropped; my arse actually dropped. This was not Gemma, this was somebody I never thought I would have to see ever again.

"Gina! What the actual fuck?"

She put her hands up to calm me.

"Now, Raquel, don't do anything silly, I only want to talk. Nobody knows I'm here, we're safe."

I stepped back and stuttered "I can't be in here with you, I can't even talk to you, this can't be happening."

She took her cap off and turned on a small lamp, an attempt to put me at ease. She looked tired, a little plumper and certainly not the tanned Colombian drugs baron I had imagined.

"Just give me five minutes, Raquel. That's all I need," she pleaded.

Although my instinct was to run – she had stuff on me, she had stuff on Dave – I needed to at least hear her out.

"Sit down, have a drink, I'll explain everything," she said, seeming gentler and quite calm, actually.

I sat on the bed, not daring to go to the window seat in case I was spotted or snipered.

She mixed two drinks in silence from the mini-bar.

"For the shock, brandy and Coke. Sorry, I've got no ice."

I took at the drink and then I smelt it – what in the Hammersmith Palais possessed her to mix such a sweet and rancid cocktail? Even though it took me back to queuing for hours just to have a wee and walking home without any shoes, I sipped it anyway for Dutch courage.

"It's nice isn't it, maybe you can feature that in one of your articles."

I looked at her bemused. Firstly, she remembered what I did for work and secondly, she was suggesting a brandy and Coke would make a good news-worthy recipe. I almost forgot that she was a cold-hearted lunatic who nearly ruined my entire life.

"Gina, I have to be quick. My mother is downstairs."

She immediately smiled. "Ahh, I love your mum, she's right laugh, Suzannah is."

Why did people think this? If repeatedly being poked with a cocktail stick was funny then yes, she was an absolute comedian.

"How are you here, in this country? Why on earth have you come back, Gina?" I was in disbelief that she would risk everything to have a chat with me.

"Me mam's not been well, and I had to see her before the end."

I gulped. "Oh, gosh, so sorry to hear that." She nodded and looked at the floor.

"It is what it is, but I have to say goodbye to me mam, she's worth the risk. It wasn't easy mind, getting in and out of this country on a false passport, but here I am and so far so good."

I felt terrible. You don't think about this sort of thing when people abscond, the fact they may have elderly relatives that won't last forever. If this were me, I think I would have done the same.

"And have you seen her?" I wondered.

"Yeah, it wasn't nice but I got to hold her hand one last time."

"God, that's so sad. I'm not sure what to say."

"Our Gemma tells me you've heard from my Matt," she said, swiftly changing the subject.

I nodded. "Yes, a family friend shared a cell with him in prison. They made the connection and now Matt is sending me letters via Miles. He wants your sister Gemma to visit him. He's sent her visiting orders but she hasn't responded."

"Yeah, well, that's too dangerous, they'll be watching and waiting for any clue as to where the rest of us are."

THE BIG HOUSE

"Will they?" I had no idea the police were this thorough. I was still waiting for them to do something about a white-van driver who'd moonied me at the traffic lights.

"I really need to contact Matt myself but I can't risk leaving any clue as to where I am located. Raquel, there are things he needs to know, stuff he has to see." She sat a little closer to me, I didn't like it. I drained my drink and put the glass on the bedside table.

"I am sorry about your mum, I really am. But I was dragged into this mess and basically blackmailed, I'm just not sure what you need from me now."

She sighed. "None of us got into this business intentionally. We're not born criminals, it just sort of happens. We all have a backstory."

I wanted to mention Charles Manson who was born to raise hell but I didn't have time for splitting hairs. "What do you want Gina? Give it to me straight!"

She faced me. Her eyebrows were faded, the Botox had dissolved and her hair was now a dull brown, not the liquorice black it had once been. She was make-up free but looked a damn sight better than me even with my full face on.

"I need you send him something via your guy Miles, The Mule."

"He's not my guy and what do you mean 'The Mule'?"

She obviously thought I knew, and she said flippantly, "Well that's what he's known as, that's his nickname, The Mule. He can get anything, anywhere, at any time. How do you think these letters have been getting in and out jail cos it ain't the Royal Mail, that's for sure?"

She was right, Miles did seem to be easily communicating between Matt and I very quickly. So that was his thing, eh, moving things from A to B.

"He even got a photocopier into one the jails you know, he knows his stuff."

THE BIG HOUSE

I rolled my eyes; yet another hardened criminal who I was now all pally with.

"What is it then, what do you want to send to him?"

I got ready to be handed a grenade that Miles would have to stuff up his jacksie and smuggle into the wing, imagine that, being blown up via your anus. She reached into her purse and handed me a small photo. It was of a baby in a car seat and on the back it said, 'R Liam'.

She stood and walked over to the bar for a refill and with her back to me she said, "That's our baby, he's only three months old."

"What, yours? Yours and Matt's?"

"Yes, Raquel. I had a baby. I had no idea I was pregnant. I'd been feeling shit but I put it down to stress. Anyway, when I got to South America, I saw a doctor who confirmed it."

I looked at the photograph of the innocent newborn, he was actually lovely. "Er, congratulations, he's gorgeous."

"Kids need two parents, Raquel, you know that. I need Matt to know what he is missing, I heard his sentence has been extended but he has a family waiting for him on the outside, it's important he knows about the baby."

"Okay, I understand. So you just need me to get Miles to send this photograph of your son, R Liam, to Matt. Are you sure he'll understand he is the father, because he's not the brightest?"

"I'll leave it up to you to make sure he does and tell him that Gemma will visit soon but only when we think it's safe. But if the prison or the police find out he's got a kid or that he's heard from me, it will shine a spotlight on us all over again."

"And then that's it, that's all you need from me?" I checked, eager to wash my hands of this situation.

"For now, but if anything else crops up, I'll let you know via your ex."

THE BIG HOUSE

"He's not my ex and I don't really like the term, 'if anything crops up'. We're not friends Gina, you did a very bad thing to me, in case you have forgotten."

"Yeah, I know that, and Matt took the hit for you and your man so we may not be friends but we're both mothers and we'll do anything to protect our family. Nobody must know I am in the country, Raquel, not Miles, not Matt, I mean no one. If I get caught, R Liam will end up in the care system and I will have no choice but to tell them everything that happened. That means most of your family will be in serious shit. Let's do this for our families, you know what I'm saying, girl?" She definitely meant business and had a sternness to her voice.

"Okay, I'll get this photograph to him. I hope this is the last meeting we have," I sighed, fed up of this already.

"Let's see how things play out, babe." I went to leave but added, because I was a writer and mistakes bothered me, "Just a thought, Gina, perhaps you should write 'our' Liam instead of just the letter 'R.'" She frowned, possibly insulted that I was correcting her homework – R Liam sounded like R Kelly's nephew, which wasn't a good thing. "Do it my way, he'll understand what that means, babe."

I left the room clutching the photograph of the mini-criminal – I was in no doubt he would end up in the bottom set for maths.

I got back to the bar where Mum was trying on another hiker's walking boots and testing out their Nordic walking sticks.

"Here she is, this the daughter I was telling you about, not the lawyer, the other one," she said, as cutting as ever.

The walkers all raised their glasses and waved. A bearded man wearing a large crucifix who seemed to be the guide kindly asked me if I would like a drink.

"Yes!" I said very firmly. "A double brandy and Coke."

Mum and I walked home that night for obvious reasons. She was

THE BIG HOUSE

excited because she had arranged to join the walking group for a fairly flat walk just outside of Edinburgh a couple of days after.

"I've always fancied myself as a rambler, you know. I've got good calf muscles, you get your good big legs from my side of the family, my mother's were like elephants, you're so like her, Raquel. Your dad's legs have always been on the spindly side so I never liked him in shorts. And since his veins have started bulging, even less so. He wears a chino very well, though, I'll give him that, always has done. Are you listening to me, Raquel?"

I wasn't listening, I was miles away, I was in the hotel room with my enemy who was now some sort of protective lioness doing what she could to feed her cub. That was annoying, she'd only been a mother for three months, I had eighteen years under my belt. Her words rang through my head, just what was she capable of? Was she genuinely just very sad that her 'baby daddy' (Facecock) wasn't able to be with his son? She seemed genuine, and in a way I did feel a little bit sorry for her, remembering being a first-time mother, and I felt small and pathetic. Almost in disbelief that the universe trusted me to keep somebody else alive.

"Anyway, tomorrow we shop. We'll head over to an outdoors centre and get kitted out. I need to have walking boots properly fitted. I can't use my M&S UGGs, can I? No, they don't have the correct ankle support. This has turned out to be a really interesting jaunt, hasn't it, Raquel, full of surprises."

I caught the last bit. "Yes, Mother, very surprising indeed."

The only people awake when we got back to the house were Dad and Gary, who were playing cards at the table. It looked to be quite a serious game as there were twenty-pence pieces scattered in piles all over the table.

"Gambling, eh?" I patted my dad on the shoulder.

THE BIG HOUSE

"Oh, hello, you've been ages. Where's your mother?"

I pointed to the porch way where Mum was trying get her UGGs off without bending over. It's harder than you think when they have zips. We watched for a while as she said 'fiddlesticks' repeatedly until eventually they came off.

"She's had a few," I warned him.

Dad nodded, "Evidently."

"I'm going to bed if anybody is interested," Mum said a bit too loud, as she stumbled on the first stair.

Gary groaned. "Looks like the old boiler needs a service, Phillip." Dad went red not knowing which way to go with that comment.

"I'll be coming soon, up you go, Suzannah." They went back to their card game and I headed down to the cellar to pen yet another note to dumbo, print it out and deliver it at my second uncomfortable meeting of the evening.

Dear Matt, I'm sorry to hear you were assaulted by the governor, I would let that one go if I were you. Not sure you should be rocking the boat any further right now.

Hey, I heard something interesting today through a friend of a friend. Someone we both know had a baby three months ago, somebody who lived on the same street as us and it's not me or my daughters. He's a beautiful little thing by all accounts, I wonder if he looks like his dad. Green eyes, dark hair, tall, etc. Anyway, I found a picture of him which I enclose. I wonder if you can recognise any of his features? His mum is doing well and she is really looking forward to the day the baby can be with both of his parents as one of them is away right now on some sort of self-inflicted trip. She hopes it can be as soon as legally possible. Also, that girl you wanted to see will come and visit soon, she has been super-busy but has promised to make time for you in the coming weeks. Just try and be patient.

THE BIG HOUSE

I hope you're enjoying your lessons with Big Mike, he is very creative with such limited ingredients, perhaps one day I will see his recipes online, wouldn't that be something. In the meantime, I thought I would share one of mine. It's cheap as chips and could become a firm favourite on your pudding menu. Please pass it on to Big Mike, I think he will thank me.

I do hope your cellmate has stopped the dirty protest, the smell will be forever inside the walls. Unfortunately I learned that first hand when one of my kids took a full nappy to the tiles of the downstairs loo. The grout never ever recovered.

Your life on the outside once you are released will be waiting for you and hopefully you are able to understand how important it is to behave properly for the next eight years or is it now nine, I forget.

Take care, keep well.

R

I made sure all the upper lights were off before I made my way down the kitchen garden and through the gate to the rat's cottage.

He was once again in his night attire, but it was late evening, and this was his house, so I had to be tolerant on this occasion.

"Come in, would you like a wee dram?"

"No, I would not!"

He shut the door and the curtains; the fire was lit but it was just the embers burning away. He was watching a film which he put on pause, and he waited for me to tell him what our next move would be.

"So, this Gemma, what did she want?"

"Well, she said she would visit at some point soon. In the meantime, she wants you to get a letter to Matt directly from her."

THE BIG HOUSE

"Okay-dokey, then, that won't be a problem. We'll get it in through the food delivery, which goes in most mornings, I've got a good contact with the wholesalers. Is that it, just a letter?"

I nodded. "Yes, just a letter but it has to go straight to him. it's important nobody else gets their hands on this."

"Okay, not a problem."

I handed him the envelope. I had sealed it with red candle wax from the Christmas candle (something I saw on *Outlander*). I didn't have my own stamp, but if I did it would an imprint of a large dick, because that is what I was.

"If the seal is broken, then she'll know it's been tampered with, and you'll be in big trouble."

"Wow, this is like working with MI5," he said sarcastically. "Don't worry, darlin', the seal will stay intact."

Not appreciating his rudeness, I ignored this snide comment.

"Okay, so you know what to do, and this is the end of it?"

"Well, not quite," he reminded me. "Have you managed to find out what my folks are planning yet?"

"I haven't seen them, really, and as far as I'm aware they're having a wonderful time in Edinburgh," I bluffed.

He shook his head. "Aye, but they're not in the city, they're in a shitty wee caravan about three miles from here."

I widened my eyes. "No way, why would they be doing that? And why lie about it?"

He folded his arms, they were heavy with tattoos that he'd probably acquired in prison to make him look hard on the outside. "Look, ma dad works in the butchers and ma mum is selling all of our furniture. Looks to me like they're in debt and they're running out of cash. This is my money they're playing about with; I need to put a stop to it, Raquel."

THE BIG HOUSE

"Hmm, I see where you're coming from, it doesn't look good. I'll do some more digging," I said, trying to buy some time.

Great, I'd almost forgotten that was another thing I had to do, deciding whether to tell Morag that Miles was on to them or to just keep it to myself and make sure the little creep stayed away. We only had two weeks left, which wasn't long to juggle things. Once we'd left, the distance would help massively, plus with Miles not being allowed to go out after dark, he couldn't go very far, which always tickled me.

As I went back into the house, I just hoped the letter was clear enough for Matt to grasp the point. Hopefully Big Mike would help, he sounded intelligent, and with my jam roly-poly recipe handwritten on parchment he would be forever grateful to me and perhaps return the favour. If this guy had the know-how to use aquafaba (juice of chickpeas) to bake a cake then he was alright by me. Once he was released, he should write his own cookbook and do signings at Waterstones. People loved a book with a dodgy background – crime definitely sells. *Cooking in the Clink*, *Smokie in the Chokey* or simply *Big Mike's Kitchen Tales*. Gosh, this was superb idea; I could be his ghostwriter. I would need to be anonymous, though. A policeman's wife writing a convict's cookbook and bringing his recipes to life, well, that was scandalous but genius all at the same time. If it wasn't my idea I was describing, I would have pre-ordered it on Amazon.

I focused on the matter at hand, hoping he'd get the message. I couldn't have made it more obvious without actually telling him, could I? That letter and photo was surely enough to keep Matt going. The news that he was a father plus a visit from Gemma would have to quieten him down for at least the next couple of years giving me enough time to plan my permanent removal from their situation. By the time he got out, I would be out of that cul-de-sac, possibly out of the country. I couldn't live like this on a permanent basis or I'd end

THE BIG HOUSE

up with a pacemaker. If Dave retired at sixty, I could have learned Portuguese by then and be cooking Christmas dinners on the beach in the sun. Saying hello to complete strangers and talking to yucca plants suddenly seemed like a retirement plan.

WHITE STUFF

On Wednesday morning, Mum and Dad headed off to meet their new Nordic walking friends for a full day's hike and then they were planning to have dinner at The Witchery at the foot of Edinburgh Castle where they would stay for two nights. Even though it was a mid-week getaway, Mum kept referring to it as 'a dirty weekend'. I was incredibly jealous, not of their bedroom antics, good God no, it was The Witchery's cheese trolley that grabbed my envy. It was so spectacular that I would rather sit next to that for the afternoon than have any sort of sex.

Dave, CeeCee and Gary had taken Sam off to Ibrox, Glasgow Rangers' football stadium and then to some burger joint where they were having a triple burger that threatened to 'put you on your back' – that was actually written on the website. The other kids were just doing their own thing and Tom and Babs had set up a little camp by the lake which I delivered tea and biscuits to on a regular basis.

Mel and Roger were still not talking about the 'baby in the room', so when the time came for Mel to book her flights and start packing her bag, Roger flipped. Well, I say flipped, his version of flipping was very mild. He ran down to the lake and looked out over the water for twenty-five minutes and she didn't follow. He then locked himself in one of the bathrooms for over two hours, but she just left him to it. And then, he kicked over Walter's water bowl, stubbing his bad toe, but Mel didn't care, just refilling it before handing him a mop. It was no good, his cries for help were not heard. During all of this, I quietly pottered around the kitchen sautéing chicken livers and shallots for my pâté.

"Tell her, Raquel, tell her that pregnancy at her age can be very dangerous," Roger said, trying to garner my support. He was standing

THE BIG HOUSE

in front of me, mouth open, waiting for me to back him up – I owed him one, remember. But instead, I popped a small amount of pink liver into his gob and asked him, "Do you think this needs more thyme?"

He immediately spat it into to the sink, exclaiming that offal was hideous and he would need to be tested for BSE.

"It's chicken, you wally, ask them to test for salmonella instead," I teased.

He stormed off at this point, up the stairs and into bed. I couldn't very well get involved with such a sensitive situation, it was not my place.

"Thanks, sis," Mel said affectionately afterwards, glad for me standing with her on this one. However, if I really had to dig deep and give my honest opinion, I wasn't at all in agreement with Mel. She had married this sap of a man, she had accepted him not 'wanting' children many years ago. Changing the goalposts now was bound to have a catastrophic effect on their marriage. She could have done this with a little more kindness, I actually felt quite bad for my brother-in-law. So as Mel prepared to leave for London to be fiddled with, I decided to be kind to Roger for once.

On Thursday morning, I watched Mel load her small suitcase into the boot of her car from the library window. It was slightly ajar so if I stood back with the curtain slightly over my body, I could hear everything that was being said.

"They won't put it in you on this visit will they, Mel? At least promise me that." Roger's soft Dublin accent made this all the more pitiful.

Mel shut the boot and turned to Roger who was wearing a tweed waistcoat and carpet slippers.

"Go back inside, you'll end up with flu, Roger. I'll be back as soon as I can."

THE BIG HOUSE

"You'll not come back with it inside you, though, will you, Mel?"

She folded her arms and sighed impatiently. "Roger, it makes no difference when it goes up, I mean, is inserted, the point is that it will be going up there no matter what."

"But I just need more time to talk about this, you're being very rash, Melanie. It's not like you." he whimpered.

"Now look, there is no more time at my age. Every day is precious, so I am getting on with this as soon as biologically possible." She got into the car and shut the door but she leaned out of the window so they could continue their conversation.

"It's not the end of the world, nothing has to change between us, it's just a baby, you used to deliver the damn things for a job."

Roger put his hands on the roof of the car and cried out, "But it's not our baby, Melanie."

"It will be my baby, Roger, and if we're strong enough, you'll grow to love it, if we're not then, well, we'll have to have a chat won't we."

He tried another approach.

"What if it's Chinese? I read in a medical journal that they can't be one hundred per cent sure of the origin of all of this 'stuff'. Sometimes it gets up mixed up in transit."

"Then we'll have a Chinese baby to look after, won't we?" Mel said, not rising to it.

"But people will know it's not mine, they'll think you had an affair on a business trip to the Far East. In fact, really this is an affair, Melanie, you letting some man insert you with his stuff."

"No, Roger, the doctor will not put his personal 'stuff' up there, it will be somebody else's 'stuff'. Now I have to go, please move away from the car. Your magnesium sleep spray is next to the bed. And can we stop calling it 'stuff.'" She started pulling away with Roger still clinging to the door.

THE BIG HOUSE

"But you said you didn't want children, Melanie, why are you doing this to me?" he called after her, having to let go and watch her drive away.

Sir Walter sat on the steps of The Eagle Lodge looking forlorn that Mummy had gone to dirty London to get a new baby and that Daddy was as sad as a Dogs Trust puppy that couldn't find his forever home.

"Are you okay, Roger?" I asked as he wearily wandered past me in the hallway accepting that this was not his day.

"Well not really, Raquel, she's going to get herself pregnant." He clasped his hands over his face. "I cannot believe I am saying that sentence about my own damn wife."

"Come and have a cup of tea, Roger, or something stronger maybe?" It was about midday and it had been a fraught morning for Roger.

"I think I'll take a whisky, Raquel. That is a condemned man's drink."

I poured him one from Tom's personal decanter, the old guy wouldn't notice. "You're not condemned, she just wants a baby. She's not saying she doesn't want you."

He sat at the kitchen table as I started to cook.

"It won't be ours, though, Raquel, and she'll end up thinking I'm in the way. I've only just got used to having him." He pointed to Sir Walter who rolled on his back and wagged his tail.

"Well he likes you now, look. He used to growl at you in the beginning. It will be the same with the baby, you'll see." I tried to reassure him.

He sighed. "I'm too old to wait for a baby to stop growling at me, that could take years. They just want their mothers when they're small." He had a point, my three looked straight past Dave and at my nipples for the first year of all of their lives.

"How come, if you don't mind me asking, couldn't you have any of your own?"

THE BIG HOUSE

Roger refilled his glass again this time without stopping halfway. "Have you heard of the mumps?"

"Yes, I've heard of the mumps." I smiled, he made the mumps sounded like a travelling folk band when he said it like that.

"I got them when I was just a boy and it travelled south and ruined things for me in the baby department. My testicles were the size of oranges." He winced at the memory and no bleeding wonder.

"I was in hospital for months, it was one of the worst cases they'd ever seen. Anyway, at the end of it, they told me that sadly my chances of having children were nil. I didn't care at the time. I was just glad to be alive, plus I was only sixteen and nobody cares about fertility at that age."

He was right, if I had been told I couldn't have kids at sixteen, I probably would have high-fived the doctor, having had it drilled into us at my Catholic high school that a baby would ruin my life. At sixteen, I only really cared about myself, my FILA trainers and Michael Jackson. But then, once you hit mid-twenties and everybody else started reproducing, turning down all-nighters in favour of gutting the house, you then start to think about what you want out of your life. This must have been a difficult time for Roger, he may have felt left behind.

"That sounds bloody awful, I'm so sorry to hear that." I patted his shoulder. He shrugged, clearly having accepted it and moved on. He was well past middle-age, it must have been a huge shock to have to dredge all this up again.

"And that's why I knew Melanie and I were kindred spirits, we wanted the same things out of life, we had the same dream and one that did not involve our own children, Raquel."

"What was the actual dream, Roger?" I asked out of interest. He relaxed a little and smiled, fondly remembering why he and Mel were right for each other, originally.

THE BIG HOUSE

"A career, of course, a comfortable house, the ability to travel wherever and whenever, private healthcare, nice things, good food, nothing holding us back."

"And now?" I wondered, wanting to probe a little further.

"Well now she's lost it, quite frankly, and she's having a baby with somebody else and I'm expected to be absolutely on board with this. It's like she's inviting a stranger into our life." His expression soured.

"I see your point, I really do. But, Roger, plans change, and we have to become adaptable to new situations, if this is true love, you'll find a way."

Roger put his whisky down and swivelled on the chair towards me.

"Aren't you the philosophical one these days, it was only last year when you were at it with that tearaway from across the street."

And then he stopped and blew his nose on a hanky that he kept up his sleeve. I said nothing.

"I'm sorry, Raquel, I'm just at my wit's end, I shouldn't take it out on you." His apology ended with him putting his head down the table and wailing.

I started on my roly-poly, massaging cold butter into the flour, but I continued the chat, I wasn't offended by what he'd said, we all make mistakes and the term 'tearaway' to describe a grown man was hilarious.

"Is that why you are obsessed with medical conditions, then?"

He looked up. "What do you mean 'obsessed'?"

With my back to him I said, "Because you were so unwell as a child, spent time in hospital. Is that why you always think there is something wrong with you?"

There was a short silence, the whisky must have relaxed him up because he thought for a while before speaking again.

"Do you know what? Perhaps it is. I never thought of it until now.

THE BIG HOUSE

I just presumed I was cautious, maybe a little on the anxious side. You may have a point, Raquel."

This was a breakthrough moment, Roger and I having a deep and meaningful and me not thinking he was just a big soft Irish man-baby.

"There's help out there, you know. Not just for this but for you and Mel, you could see somebody together. That's what Dave and I did."

I felt disloyal telling Roger that Dave and I had seen a therapist, but disloyalty and all that came with it was part of my every day. Plus, I felt it was something he needed to hear.

"You and David, seeing a shrink?" He nodded slowly as if it all made sense somehow.

"Well not a shrink, more of a relationship therapist. Julian took the approach that we should answer our own questions, he doesn't tell you what to think he makes you work it out for yourself."

Roger nursed his whisky and looked pensive, mulling over the idea. "Are you suggesting that this Julian has kept you and David together? Because to be honest, I thought after what you did you were done for."

I dropped my raspberries into the sugar for the jam that would coat the inner roll of my sponge. "Well, Roger, it turns out that Dave and I were much stronger than we thought, and it took just a few sessions to work that out." I said this with smugness, why, I don't know.

"This Julian, I like the sound of him. Can you send me his number?"

I was about to grab my phone but then I had a better idea. "Actually, I have a session with him tomorrow on Zoom. You know what, you can join for the last five minutes and I'll introduce you. He will be grateful for the business."

Roger was chuffed, delighted to hear that there would be somebody out there who would listen to his opinions and see his point of view. Even if it would cost him £120 for the pleasure.

"Raquel, would you like to join me a little later in the garden for a

THE BIG HOUSE

cocktail or two and a game of gin rummy?"

I felt a bit fuzzy, I'd made a new friend which was most unlike me, and although he was a bellend most of the time, today I quite liked him. "Yes, I would be honoured to take your money, Roger. You're on."

Roger went up for a long soak, one of his knees had swollen after the dog-bowl kicking incident and so I went down to the basement to email my agent.

Jane Aldgate @Eatmedia

Hi Jane, just thought I would give you an idea of my menu for the 'going back to basics' feature for Good Housekeeping. Let me know what you think. Since this is out in November, I have gone filling and warming. I also interviewed my uncle who was a small boy during WW2, could be some good stuff here to pad out the feature and give it some authenticity. He has agreed to put his name and face to the article if they want but he does have a look of Claude Greengrass, so he'll probably need a makeover. I think I have created a three-course dinner that would have been not only low cost but also using ingredients that were actually available during the war. I have used a key so you can see how the ingredients could be sourced. In today's money, this entire menu could be created for less than £5 per head, they just need to get to Aldi or Tesco for most of it. It makes you think, doesn't it? How did we go from this to Super Noodles and Findus Crispy Pancakes? It's mental! Things are okay here up in Scotland, not seen up a man's kilt yet, though there's still time. LOL

Anyway, here it is, instructions to follow if they agree:

THE BIG HOUSE

Chicken liver pâté

> Livers – *cheap cut*
> Shallots – *garden or supermarket*
> Garlic – *garden or supermarket*
> Thyme – *garden or long-life dried*
> Brandy – *store cupboard but not essential*
> Butter – *rationed*
> Bay leaves – *garden or long-life dried*
> Stale bread for toasting – *baked at home during the war*

Oxtail stew

> Oxtail – *cheap cut*
> Flour – *more available than a miserable face*
> Lardons – *cheap*
> Carrots – *garden or supermarket*
> Celery – *garden or supermarket*
> Onions – *garden or supermarket*
> Bay – *garden or long-life dried*
> Garlic – *garden or supermarket*
> Tomato purée – *long-life*
> Cooking wine – *store cupboard*
> Worcester sauce – *more available than a miserable face*
> Potatoes – *garden or supermarket*

THE BIG HOUSE

Jam roly-poly & custard

Butter – rationed
Flour – more available than a miserable face
Caster sugar – rationed
Milk or water, can use powdered milk with water – store cupboard or allocation per family (Everybody had a regular supply of milk particularly if they had children.)
Shredded suet – store cupboard
Jam – store cupboard or garden made using picked fruit, Sugar and gelatine – (store cupboard)
Birds Eye custard powder – store cupboard can be mixed with water/milk. Or freshly made using milk, eggs, vanilla essence, sugar and cream if available.

I cooked everything and photographed it that afternoon and I left it out for a family dinner once the day trippers had returned. Dave wasn't hungry as the burger was weighing heavy on him apparently. The kids all ordered pizza, stating that an ox's tail was one of the foulest descriptions of a meal they had ever heard. So I just had Tom, Babs, CeeCee and Gary who were all of a generation where they would appreciate what I had done so I watched them tuck in. Babs was delighted by the creaminess of the pâté on toast, which I actually rescued from the bin – somebody had left the loaf out to go stale so I thought like a woman with a ration book and wasted nothing.

The oxtail had been slow-cooking all day, which is how it would have been when Tom was a child. The stew would be bubbling for hours so by the time he got home from school the meat would have been so rich and tender it would dissolve on the tongue. I added whole potatoes to this dish because I imagined that dealing with the

THE BIG HOUSE

fear of your house being blown to bits and waiting for news that your husband had been killed really left little time to do sides. Also, the three courses that I had created were more than enough to fill the bellies of a family of four. And to be fair, this was based on a Sunday lunch during the war, which would have been pushing the boat out at that time – a lovely weekly treat where the food would temporarily take their minds off the Jerries.

At the end of the meal, I sliced the jam roly-poly and served it at the table. The diners watched silently as I drenched each slice in my crème anglaise. Halfway through his pudding Tom caught me watching him and he put his spoon down and hobbled over to me.

"Now that, Raquel, was absolutely perfect. I shouldn't say this, really, but it would give my mother a run for her money! That was proper food, my dear. Well done." He slapped my back and went back to finish the rest. My work here was done.

CeeCee finished her dessert quietly, still not meeting my eye since Dave had told her about my infidelity. "Did you enjoy the meal, CeeCee?"

She looked up and nodded. "Very nice thank you, Raquel. I'm very tired, though, so I think I'll have a brew in bed."

Gary showed his concern. "Are you alright, Cee? You've been to bed early the last few nights."

She stroked his cheek, "I'm just enjoying my rest, Gary, it must be the air up here."

He nodded, "Yes, I feel quite tired too. I'll join you. Thanks for dinner, Raquel, it was tremendous."

I watched my in-laws leave the table before 8 pm and I knew it was because CeeCee couldn't stand the sight of me, I needed to talk to her soon, we couldn't go on like this.

"I'm playing cards in the garden with Roger if anyone fancies it," I

THE BIG HOUSE

announced, as the diners left the table. There were some murmurs but nobody was particularly interested. Even Dave, who normally loved a good game of rummy, said he had some work emails to respond to and headed down to the cellar with his laptop.

"I guess it's just me and you, then," I told Roger, who appeared wearing a smoking jacket and for some utterly bizarre reason had a Panatella cigar behind his ear. His card-playing costume had me thinking I was acting in a play.

"Where did you get that cigar?" I pointed to it frowning.

"I found it in the kitchen drawer and I feel like this is a night to sail close to the wind." I smiled.

"Feeling reckless Roger?"

"I think perhaps I am." Reckless Roger raised an eyebrow.

"Have you heard from Mel?" I asked hoping this wouldn't upset him too much.

"I did a 'find my iPhone' on her handset and she's staying in some sort of Ibis near St John's Wood. And tomorrow she'll visit a sperm shop, no doubt where she'll be impregnated with an alien."

I nodded sympathetically but said nothing. I had to be careful I didn't go against my sister, so I supported Roger but very subtly.

I had my Zoom with Julian the following morning and luckily Dave had a meeting in Manchester in the afternoon so he was setting off early and would be gone for the day. He would be none the wiser that I had put Julian back on the payroll – he didn't need to know about that for now.

I just had to hope and pray that this was not another mystery trip that involved lying to me; I had put the thing with Stu to the back of my mind for now because I had enough going on. I was trying to trust that Dave was still in it for the long haul and that love conquered all in the end. I could have chinned myself letting dross like this tamper

THE BIG HOUSE

with my mind, I was more realistic than that. I wasn't a romantic or a fantasist, even, I knew deep down that actions have consequences because Julian had told me this and I had agreed. Julian wasn't by any means the Dalai Lama, I wasn't as gullible as to let some flaky therapist with a qualification you could buy online shape my future. He was just a sounding board who allowed me look at my situation from the outside, that was all it was.

Roger and I ended the evening rather bizarrely playing a game of 'Ideal Family' after many Moscow mules. It was a bit like the dinner-party game where everybody chooses their ideal guest list. It was usually the likes of Frank Sinatra, JFK, Madonna, Amy Winehouse, etc, that would end up at the table. This game was a little different, more serious, more current in light of what Roger's wife was about to do.

So the rules went like this: you choose the ideal co-parent, it can't be the one you already share kids with. That could be anyone, any sex but normally famous. Then you pick how many kids you have together and you can choose what your kids do for a living and you basically create your perfect family on paper. It was very interesting and caused a lively debate which we both thoroughly enjoyed, mainly because of the mules.

I decided that the father of my kid would be Michael Whitehall, Jack Whitehall's dad. My argument for him was that he was not only dry, witty and intelligent but he was also a family man with good solid values. I had seen him show warmth at times but not too much. I liked the fact he said it how it was, plus he had managed to produce some okay-looking kids, so that was my decision and I was sticking with it. Mine and Whitehall's child would be a heart surgeon, that way he would not only be paid very well but he would also be able to save my life when my ticker packed in.

"Why would your heart give up, Raquel?" Roger asked with real concern.

THE BIG HOUSE

"Well, once our son was a fully-fledged surgeon and is called Mr and not even Dr, I will probably smoke quite regularly, but don't worry, I'll stub them all out with my Jimmy Choos."

"Why would you smoke, Raquel? This is very confusing," Roger said as he scribbled down my answers, not letting his imagination run wild like you were supposed to.

"Ah, but I do in this imaginary world, Roger, plus I'll have a dirty martini every day at five which Michael, bless him, will mix for me. Oh, and our son will be called Xander Whitehall and he'll be the only surgeon ever to have a topknot and be taken seriously," I said, trying to keep a straight face.

"Will you and this Whitehall chap have any other children or will he be too busy restarting your heart?" Roger asked whilst chewing the pencil.

"Yes, we'll have twin girls and they will own a restaurant called 'Raquel's' with two Michelin stars."

"Good grief, this is very detailed!" exclaimed Roger, struggling to get into character as easily as me.

"Your turn." And I took the pad and waited for him to play right into my hands.

"Well, my child's mother would be Melanie. I was going to say Helen Mirren but she made a bit of a show of herself as Jane Tennison and Melanie has better legs." (This was definitely not the case.)

"Boring, you could have had anyone, Roger."

He lit the Panatela, I'm not sure he'd ever had one before, he held it whilst it smoked and I hoped that was far as it would go.

"I don't want anyone else and I can have her because we don't already have children."

That was true, he was technically playing by the rules.

"We would have one daughter who would be named Bernadette, a good solid Irish name, and one of my favourite saints, come to think of it." I laughed because who on this earth has a favourite saint? He continued to fantasise. "She would of course be a writer, a historical fiction writer focussing on periods of turmoil but capturing some of the finest moments of our time."

I yawned. If our little Bernadette had crossed my path at school, I know for sure we would not have been friends. She sounded like a cross between Annie Wilkes and Frank McCourt which was extremely depressing. Nevertheless, if Mel did have a donor's baby and Roger spent enough time drip feeding his Irish literature into the Blue Cross pram, I'm sure that they could become a happy little family.

Roger and I parted company with, in my opinion, a newfound respect for one another. I know we were chatting pure shit, I know that most of it made no sense, but this was the first time I had experienced a nonsensical evening with Roger that I actually enjoyed. I went up to put my pyjamas on which were under my pillow. Dave's laptop was open on the bed and he must have been off somewhere brushing his teeth. I shouldn't have, I had no right to, but I clicked the screen to see what he had been doing.

So spreadsheets weren't my thing, I wasn't a woman who put things in boxes in an organised fashion, I was more of sticky-note girl. But I was switched on enough to realise what this was about and as I read through it, the fear that had been creeping into my heart became bigger with every line.

This looked to be the family finances, with columns showing our outgoings and incomings. It was standard that somebody had to have control of the finances for a family of four living their best life in Cheshire – it wasn't cheap by any means. But this was very detailed and precise, and even had a figure for fuel. Maybe it's just me but I fill up my car when it's empty and I go where I need to go. I would never

THE BIG HOUSE

set a budget for this; it was very anal. It was not anything I had seen before and I had never been made aware this balance sheet existed, which raised my suspicions.

"How was your evening with Roger?" Dave asked as he climbed into bed next to me, shutting the lid of his computer and putting it on the floor.

"It was a laugh, we had fun."

"Really, with him?" Dave frowned and I nodded.

"He's not so bad, he's going through some shit."

Dave grinned. "Never thought I'd see the day."

"You're off to your meeting first thing, then?"

"Yep. Stu needs a bit of guidance on a case, I'll be back on Saturday, I'll let you know what time when I can."

I turned over. I bet Michael Whitehall didn't tell lies.

ROASTED

On Friday morning, I had another session with Julian. With Dave gone to his meeting and Mum and Dad still away in Edinburgh, at least I could do my session uninterrupted.

"This is definitely confidential, yes?" I asked Julian when he appeared on screen.

Julian smiled, putting his hands behind his head. Sweat patches underneath his arms immediately annoyed me.

"Of course, Raquel, that's a given."

"So you're still on holiday, then?" He was on the same balcony with the palm trees blowing in a light breeze behind him.

"Yes, we fly home tomorrow, so if you want a face-to-face I will be back in the office next week."

"No, this is fine thanks," I said. Somehow I didn't want to go back to the office where Dave and I had done our sessions. I liked the distance as it felt like it was me I needed to work on.

"Who's 'we' by the way? Your partner, kids, friends?"

"I don't tend to discuss my private life with my clients, it can create problems."

"Okay, so you get to know all my secrets but you can't tell me anything about yourself?" That didn't seem fair.

"That's about the size of it, yes. In my line of work, people can become a little too attached, it's best to keep that sort of thing separate."

"Attached? What, like in a stalky way? Have you had a stalker, Julian?" I asked, my interest piqued.

Julian shook his head, not to say no, just to tell me to back off. I was apparently encroaching on his personal space. What a joke! He knew more about the workings of my brain than I did and it felt only

THE BIG HOUSE

fair I should at least get to know who he shared a bed with. If I had to hazard a guess, he would be married to an estate agent. She would have a bob and I bet she got their dinners on the meal deal at M&S. She would drink Prosecco in a business suit whilst he would ride the Peloton in the bedroom. I knew his type; I was good at this.

"How has your week been? Any developments?" He asked, trying to refocus. I sensed that our sessions were like a juicy episode of Corrie that he was looking forward to watching.

"I think that Dave is having an affair and it's not just a hunch anymore," I admitted. His eyes widened, this was juice alright.

"On what evidence?" He rubbed his hands together.

"He has lied to me twice about who is with, and now, last night I found that he is combing through our finances. I think this means he is planning on a split, he is working out how we will afford to live apart."

Julian nodded. "Okay, so what does he say about all of the above?"

"I haven't discussed any of it with him."

"And why not?"

"It doesn't feel right."

"In case you've got it wrong?"

"Well, yes."

"So you're not absolutely certain?"

"No."

"So why not ask him and find out if you're right?"

"I don't want to, what if it's true?" And there was the crux of it, I was scared.

"So what's your plan here, Raquel, to ignore it and hope everything just goes away?"

"It's not the worst idea." I shrugged.

"So why are we talking if you're going to ignore it? What is the point of this session?"

THE BIG HOUSE

"To see what you think," I explained.

"What I think is irrelevant, you have to make that decision yourself. Do you want to address it or ignore it?"

"I just want the old Dave back where I never had to question our relationship."

"I'm sure he would want that too but unfortunately, Raquel, you took a brick out of your wall and now it isn't as strong as it once was."

That prickled me, I didn't like being the one who weakened us and I didn't like this stupid analogy. "I thought you were supposed to help me to rebuild this so-called fucking wall."

He raised his eyebrows at my bad language and rubbed his beard. I noticed that it had turned slightly ginger, the sun had bleached it. I felt an overwhelming urge to point and laugh at it but I didn't.

"It's up to you to strengthen the wall, we did discuss being open, vulnerable and transparent last week, but as I remember you said it reminded you of…" He looked down at his pad. "Channel 4's *Married at First Sight*."

I nodded. "Yes, that's right, that's the lingo the experts use, perhaps you went on the same course as them."

He shook his head. "I would take the term 'experts' with a pinch of salt, Raquel."

"Have you watched any of it?"

"You can't get Channel 4 in Barbados."

"So you've tried then?" I smirked.

"Only to see if I could watch *Countdown*."

"Okay, Julian, if you say so."

"So I take it that you have decided not to share your thoughts and feelings with Dave at all?"

I shook my head. He pulled a face I had seen before from people when I had a fringe cut in. Yes, I knew at the time I was making bad choices, no I wasn't listening, and okay you might be right but take that look off your face.

He leaned closer to the screen and lowered his voice. "If he's leaving then it would be best to know so you can either accept it or try and change it. If he's cheating, then it would be best to know the details and what you're up against."

"Up against? What do you mean?" I asked, freaking out.

"Well, if there is somebody else. Is it a fling? Is it love? How long has it been going on? Is it woman, a man? Who, if anyone, is your rival, Raquel? Know your enemy, as they say."

I felt rashy and hot all of a sudden, thoughts of the Tesco woman that looked like Suranne Jones drifting into my head. I imagined Dave and her going on a date. I bet she would actually go to watch Arsenal with him, she probably had a season ticket and a scarf. They would sink pints together after the match and then, afterwards, they would go and watch an action film at the cinema. I hated the cinema and I could not stomach action movies. Later, they would go back to her flat in Didsbury and do it with her on top. I hated going on top, everything jiggling about at a very unattractive angle.

"Having some tough thoughts there, Raquel?" Julian had got to me.

I jumped. "Yes, actually, I feel a bit sick. So thank you for that."

"You don't want to live like this, do you? Wondering all the time? It's not healthy." He shut his pad and tilted his head sympathetically. "Try and open up, you'll thank yourself one day. Let's leave it there for today, I hope you can make some progress before we next talk."

I put my thumbs up to the screen, it was a half-hearted attempt to tell him that I had listened but also a way for me not to actually verbally agree to anything. I couldn't plan on which way to go; I would need to think on it.

THE BIG HOUSE

"I was wondering if I could quickly introduce my brother-in-law to you, Julian? He's in desperate need of some advice. He is available on Zoom anytime but I was hoping he could just say hello now to see if you would work with him, he's waiting upstairs."

Julian looked at his watch, he didn't show any gratitude for the potential business but said, "Okay, I have five minutes." I shouted up the cellar stairs for Roger who was waiting patiently for his turn with the oracle. He came down and pulled up a chair next to me before waving through the screen to Julian. I decided to do the introductions.

"This is Roger, married to my sister Mel. He can't have any children because of the mumps but, well, that's a long story. Anyway, my sister has gone to London to be inserted with some donor's sperm. It will be of high quality knowing her, but, anyway, Roger isn't happy. He's quite old as you can see and he also has hypochondria, don't you, Roger? So you'll need to address that at some point too. We only really started liking each other yesterday because before that I thought he was a bit of a cock, you know, passive-aggressive and underhand but I think he's alright really."

Nobody had said anything at all, bar me. I turned to Roger who had his mouth open. Julian was wiping his head with a napkin.

"Well that was quite the introduction, Raquel but I think I will take it from here." Roger pointed to the door urging me to basically go the fuck away.

"I'll message you, Julian, about our next session. Safe flight." I hurriedly said my goodbyes because crikey, he had a lot to unpack with this family.

Back in the main hall, I saw that my parents had arrived home after their little trip with the walkers. "How was it, guys, did you enjoy?"

Mum slammed her coat onto the table and kicked off her shoes aggressively. Dad shook his head at me trying to warn me there was a tale to be told and it wasn't a happy one.

THE BIG HOUSE

"The Witchery was stunning as always; the walk, not so much," she moaned, folding her arms.

"Oh, why, was it a tough walk?"

"Tough doesn't come close. And it wasn't the walk, it was the company that was really trying."

I looked over to Dad who smirked and said, "Your mother made a bit of a booboo, didn't you, darling?"

"Yes, I bloody well did! Do you know, Raquel, that your dad and I were almost radicalised yesterday?"

"By who?" I asked, wondering who'd want them in their cult.

"By an evangelical Christian walking group who failed to give me the name of their actual organisation until we were halfway up a mountain; well, to be fair it was a hill, but it was very steep." She rubbed her back, feeling sorry for herself. "If I wasn't as sharp as I am, I would have ended up selling the cottage and giving the funds to these lunatics for their 'charity work'. They really set about us with their begging bowls; wanting a van to transport the Christians about the place, wanting flights to Utah so they could meet their master and then apparently they need a new church roof which they expected your father and me to foot the bill for."

I saw Dad snigger as he threw his walking boots down the cellar steps knowing he would not be needing them again.

Mum continued. "That church was actually a semi-detached house in Acton. Church, my eye, it was just a premises where they forged cheques and stole the identities of retired professionals like your father and I."

She threw her new cagoule to Dad who sent it in the same direction as the boots.

"And, when I told them that my daughter was a television chef, they had the brass nerve to ask me what kind of money you earned."

THE BIG HOUSE

I shook my head. "But I'm not a television chef, Mum, I'm a food writer."

She flicked her hand. "Yes, well that doesn't sound as good so that's what I tell strangers you are."

I tried to ignore that jibe and find out how it had all gone down. "So what happened? How did it end?"

She looked at me with some shame. "We had to do something. I'm not proud of it but needs must."

"Do what?" I asked, wondering if there were a group of Christians tied up at the top of Arthur's Seat.

"I had endured three hours of them talking non-stop of virgins and wholesomeness, some tat about meeting Our Maker the same way we came in. I presumed that meant naked and skint. So, I had to shake them off."

"Go on, how did you shake them off, Mum?"

"Well, I had to tell them you'd been in an accident and we needed to rush to your aid."

"What sort of accident?"

"A sort of kitchen nightmare."

"Go on…" I was dying to hear this.

"I said you were cooking fondue in the Alps, and with it being the Alps there was an avalanche."

I coughed. "Excuse me? I was cooking on a mountain and was taken out by an avalanche?"

"Yes, it was all I could think of at the time."

"So did I survive?"

She shrugged. "You're still missing, presumed dead," she added as if that would make me feel better.

"Thank you, Mother, that's got to be some seriously bad karma right there."

THE BIG HOUSE

"Raquel, you were breaking boundaries in the Alps, though, darling, I said you were roasting a squirrel on a spit at four thousand feet."

"Oh well, fuck it, then, at least I was dipping vermin in melted cheese whilst I was buried alive."

"I was being creative. Anyway, we managed to get away from the group and within the hour I was in an Emperor sleigh bed with a dressing gown on. It took us all of yesterday to get over it, didn't it, Phillip?"

"Too right it did," Dad muttered.

"At least you're okay then, Mum. Hope these Mormons say a prayer that I will be found safe and well."

She laughed. "Move on, Raquel, what's done is done. Anyway, now we can spend some time with family, that's why we're really here, after all."

The pickings were a little slim that day with the guest list. Suzy and Arif had gone into the woods foraging, apparently. Michaela was still up in her room with her nose in a book for the next module of her summer course, only coming out for herbal teas and to throw a few insults at anybody she met en route to the kettle. Sam was nowhere to be seen and he'd started lying in until midday and spending huge amounts of time in the bathrooms – if he wasn't fishing, he was in a bathroom somewhere which I worried meant the teenager had fully arrived in the building.

I'd mentioned it to Dave before he left. "What can he be doing for seventy-five minutes in a bathroom?" I probed.

"Watch out for stiff socks in the laundry, that's all I'm saying," Dave had told me whilst laughing his head off.

"What is this sock nonsense? It's utterly gross. Surely a sandwich bag would be more hygienic – you'll need to have a chat with him,"

THE BIG HOUSE

I'd said, but I'd started picking through the washing basket with Marigolds on just in case.

I filled my mother in on where everyone was. "Dave has gone to Manchester and Mel is in London. So we're not a full house at the moment. CeeCee is still spending a lot of her time in bed, she feels lethargic, apparently."

Mum frowned and looked knowingly at me. She knew this was a result of her discovering that I was a hussy. "So have I missed anything?" She wanted to know.

"Actually, you missed my wartime feature meal last night, although it was oxtail stew so I'm not sure you'd have liked it."

Mum grimaced. "I think I would prefer the squirrel. Yuck, I'm glad we weren't here, I couldn't stomach the tail of anything."

Roger emerged from the cellar door, his eyes swollen and red. He was wearing that tweed waistcoat I disliked but this time he had teamed it up with a shirt with a grandad collar, which surely had an impact on his outlook on life. It was a miserable outfit that said, 'I travelled on the lower deck of the Titanic.' We had to sharpen him up somehow if he was to stay married to Mel.

"How did it go? Did he help?" I asked hopefully.

"I guess so, he helped me see things from all sides. I've booked a session with him next week, he thinks I'll be needing quite a lot over the next few months, especially if the worst happens." I sighed, there wasn't much more I could do but try and keep his spirits up. He went off to take Walter for a walk, it was his turn and I insisted he needed the fresh air. Reluctantly he put his overcoat on, the final piece to the 'sinking ship' outfit, and off he trudged.

I was quite pissed off to say the least to find Morag and Miles in the greenhouse when I went out to have some time reading on my chair. I know she was sneaking back at night to pack but I didn't expect to see

THE BIG HOUSE

her hanging around in the daytime too.

Miles was smoking inside the glass box which made it difficult for me to see in and hard for them to see out. The smoke, however, did not affect the sound and I heard the tail-end of a conversation.

"All I asked for was a couple of thousand to put into a small investment, Mum, and that was last week, yet I still haven't seen this money in my account."

"That's because it hasn't been done, Miles, and it will not be done, son, so you'll need to find it elsewhere."

"This is very disappointing, Mum. I've promised the guy I will send the money, I can't let him down."

"Miles, I will tell you again, your dad and I just haven't got it spare." I heard Miles's little foot stamp onto the floor in a paddy.

"We'll see about that. I'll speak to the organ-grinder, shall I? We both know he'll sort this for me," Miles threatened.

"Not this time, son, no he won't. I've taken over the finances and there will be no more cash for your hare-brained schemes."

"Listen, woman, it won't be long until I'll be the one who decides which home you go into. I'd be careful if I were you."

"Now come on, Miles, let's not get nasty. You've had enough out of us. Time to get a job, son, away you go."

The greenhouse door slid open and Morag backed away. I was so shocked by how he had spoken to his mother that I forgot to even hide or pretend that I'd overhead everything.

* * * * *

"Oh, kids, eh. Who'd have 'em, Raquel. I just came to feed the tomatoes, they need an awful lot of attention, particularly the sugar drop variety." Morag sniffed, dabbing her eyes.

THE BIG HOUSE

"Are you okay, Morag? He was really quite vicious."

She shook her head. "He doesn't mean it, he's just a silly wee boy. He needs to grow up a bit, that's all." She dismissed it.

I said nothing else but was beginning to understand their need to get away. If this is what they had to deal with on a regular basis then moving to France was the best plan.

"I've got to go and pick up Robbie from the butchers but your mum invited us to dinner one night, so I'll see you soon." I did my best not to scowl, Mum really should be consulting me before offering my services, yet again.

"Oh, and, Raquel, there's a letter with your name on it next to the chillies in the greenhouse. Not sure where it came from, perhaps it's a wee love letter from David." Morag shouted back to me.

Dear Rackel,

I had to write after receiving the photograph of R Liam. I have been wandering about on cloud nineteen. Big Mike has told me that what you said meant that R Liam is my baby. I can't get over that me and Gina are parents, I mean I am in shock but in a good way. I wonder what language he speaks and what team he supports. I know that I have to behave, I'm a dad now and if I want to be part of his life, I will need to really concentrate on getting out of this place as soon as possible. I grew up without a dad and look where I am now, in the Big House as Miles used to say. Maybe if me dad had stuck around, I would have had my own business and had something to pass down to my kid.

Anyway, Gemma has agreed to visit me in a few days, I am hoping she can tell me a bit more about my family. This news means everything to me and it's all thanks to you for helping.

Also, cheers for the roly-poly recipe. Nan used to make that for me

THE BIG HOUSE

and it made me think of when I was little, one day I will make it for R Liam and then he'll make it for his kid. Big Mike made it for dessert at the weekend and the guvnor came down and tried a bit cos it's his favourite too, he said it's the best he's ever had. Me and Big Mike found two vapes and a Crunchie under our pillows that night, as a thank you.

The screws are doing a surprise for the guvnor's birthday next week and they've asked us to make a big one and shape it like a 60, cause it's his 60th and they are having a buffet in the staffroom. That should get me in the good books and maybe they'll shave a few years off my sentence if it goes well.

Thanks for everything, babe.

Matt

After I finished reading, I realised that there were a few things I could take from this letter; I was right, giving this guy some hope will keep him off my back. He now had a reason to pull himself together. No more talk of discussing the truth with a solicitor and no more veiled threats, so that was a relief. He had his visitor, a photo of his kid and the knowledge that Gina was waiting for him no matter how long it would take, so he'd be in a better frame of mind. Also, I realised a good deed goes a long way. My recipe had cheered up his wing and would now be the main event at a sixtieth birthday buffet. The last bit just really cemented what an absolute buffoon Matt really was, to think he would have his sentence reduced due to a pudding and custard. I did giggle a little, he was quite funny.

This letter was the best news I had received since I landed in phase two of my nightmare with the neighbours. I could see the light and I relaxed a little. Now he'd heard from Gina and got Gemma visiting he

THE BIG HOUSE

wouldn't be needing to go through me again.

I spent the afternoon in the garden weeding the veg patch and cleaning out the chickens, grateful to have no interruptions.

Just before my evening shower, I took a pile of Suzy's washing up with me and placed it on the floor outside her door to free up a hand to turn the handle. But, just before I entered, I could hear a rhythmic squeak and some light moaning coming from the other side indicating that Suzy was 'busy'. And then, when I heard a deeper voice, a man's voice, my blood ran temporarily cold.

If Miles had been anywhere near my daughter I would have caved his head in with my rolling pin, but thankfully, once I heard the term 'tickety-boo' being used followed by hysterical laugher, my murderous thoughts dissolved. I double-checked Arif's room, which was empty, and when I sniffed the collar on a jumper he had been wearing, it smelt of Suzy's perfume. I didn't know how to feel if I'm honest, he was nineteen, she was eighteen. He was lovely, she was not. I left the washing outside the door and went for a shower, wondering how to broach the subject. It was a strange one, it felt as though a shark had befriended a cockapoo and I was the shark's mother.

We decided to go for a bar meal at The Hotel that evening, nobody could be arsed with any more washing up and CeeCee and Gary only had three more days until they flew back to Portugal. I really needed to get out of the house instead of just lounging in bed, and needed talk to her to smooth things over.

The menu that night consisted of tasty bar snacks. Small panko-covered haggis with a mustard dipping sauce particularly took my fancy and I ordered two portions knowing they would be moreish. Different boards with bits and bobs were on were constantly being passed around the table and it was actually a nice way to all be together. Apart from when Tom sneezed in the direction of the Scotch

THE BIG HOUSE

eggs which, for that reason, I passed on and let the others risk catching syphilis.

CeeCee had simple tastes and all she wanted was a ham and cheese toastie to nibbled at whilst looking out of the window nervously. Because she was sitting in the window seat, I saw this as my opportunity to make some effort to communicate.

"Budge up," I said. I actually didn't like people who said that, it was a complete disregard for a person's personal space and the word 'budge' was just bad mannered. However, she did budge, leaving me a little space to sit beside her. "Penny for them?" I asked as she continued her gaze out onto the road just below the hotel.

"I'm wondering what time Dave will be back."

I frowned. Dave had given me no indication of what time he would be back, in fact he hadn't even read the three messages I had sent him today. I presumed he was consumed with work, I hoped that was the case. And with my head buried firmly in the sand, I would believe it no matter what.

"Oh, I'm sure he'll message when he's setting off."

She put down the toast and turned to me. She couldn't have looked evil even if she tried, she was plump with curly blonde hair and she had a jazzy jumper on, we were in bingo-calling territory with CeeCee.

"Maybe I can come bring him back here and buy him steak and chips for lunch," CeeCee suggested.

'Well he won't eat the chips, he's keto," I laughed.

"Oh, yes, I forgot, he's trying to lose weight and be younger and fitter and all that." She said this with distain, clearly not happy about this.

"Don't you want him to be healthier, CeeCee?"

She sighed. "I just want my son to be happy."

"And don't you think he is… happy?" I said nervously.

THE BIG HOUSE

"No, unfortunately I don't, Raquel," she said, her eyes narrowing as she bore into me. "He is trying to be somebody that he isn't for some reason."

I gulped. I wanted to defend myself, I wanted to say that nobody was perfect and that I was sorry. I wanted her to tell me I was a silly sausage or something like that but she just sat looking at me blankly.

And then she suddenly stood and started waving at the window, her heavy gold bracelets jangled. I looked down and was surprised to see Dave all suited and booted and climbing up the steps, when he'd told me he'd be back tomorrow.

"I have to talk to my son." She pushed past me and towards the reception where she would be finally reunited with Dave who'd only been to Manchester for a few hours.

"Oh, hell, no, it's the Christians, Phillip, they're coming in here," Mum shouted, lifting my mood as I watched her grab her bag and scarper. She threw her credit card at me and said, "See you back at the house."

With that they both fled through the bar and out of a side door to escape any further radicalisation. I nipped to the loo, leaving the group arguing over a profiterole tower and who had had three and who'd had two. I knew for a fact the Sam had one wrapped in his napkin but I said nothing. As I washed my hands at the sink and had a good look up my left nostril because it looked smaller than the right, I heard a noise coming from the cubicle.

"Oi, Raquel," a voice hissed.

I turned and frowned. Was I starting with a fever?

"Raquel, come into cubicle next to me."

I recognised the voice – the high-pitched scouser, my neighbour from hell. Why was she still here in Scotland? Why hadn't she gone back to her kid and her cartel? I locked the door and put the toilet seat down to perch on it.

THE BIG HOUSE

"What are you still doing here?" I whispered.

"Got some stuff to sort out," she explained.

"What do you want? He has the photo," I hissed angrily, thinking I was done with all of this.

"I know, ta, babe, just wanted an update, really."

"He's very happy that he's a dad and he is going to behave."

I felt her smile through the wall.

"So, when can he get out?" Who was I, Judge bloody Rinder?

"Err dunno. Eight years or something, maybe less if he's good." There was a deep sigh.

"I told him you'd wait for him, Gina."

"What, for eight years?" she snorted.

"Yes, unless he gets a reduction for good behaviour."

"Hmm." I sensed she knew that may not be in the bag.

"Me sister is going to see him next week. But in the meantime, can you send him something through Miles?" she asked.

"Well, not really, it's my parents' wedding anniversary soon and we have a lot on."

"Oh, come on, babe, it's no skin of your nose."

"What is it?" I checked.

"It's just a Babygro and a teething ring, you know, so he can smell R Liam. Babies smell amazing don't they!"

It was true that for some reason the smell of a freshly bathed baby was one of the most wonderful scents known to man. Their little feet in cotton socks, the curl on the top of their heads. It was a wonderful memory. Now all I had from my baby boy was stiff socks and Clearasil gel.

A small brown package gently slid under the cubicle before I'd even had chance to agree. "This isn't your knickers, is it, Gina?"

She laughed. "No, love, it's a Babygro and a toy, you can check."

I opened the bag tentatively; I knew this woman was a slippery one. However, inside the bag was a little white towelling suit from Mothercare. It had tiny little pearl buttons down the front and teddy bear ears for collars. It was actually lovely. I inhaled the scent deeply and sure enough notes of Johnson's Baby Lotion took me right back to a time when everyone loved me. Behind it, there was a velvet pouch with a blue rubber ring with a giraffe in the centre that squeaked.

"He's not used that yet, his teeth aren't through, but it's a nice reminder for Matt, don't you think?"

I murmured, "Guess so."

"I have to go. Take care, babe." I heard the latch on the door release, footsteps and then a creak. She was gone and I just hoped that was the last time I saw her.

MUM'S THE WORD...

On Sunday morning, before I embarked on bog duty with Dad, I left a package in the greenhouse to be collected and delivered to prison. Saying that out loud was so ludicrous but the alternative was Armageddon. I normalised what I was doing by pretending I was starring in a gritty drama, so that I didn't feel as afraid. I'd also written a letter to go with it.

Dear Matt,

I wanted to express how pleased I was to hear that one of my recipes has put a smile on some of the inmates' faces and some of the staff at your place. Quite honestly sometimes I wonder what the point of my work is, whether it's worth it and am I making any sort of difference out there in the world of home cookery? I don't really know why I am telling you this, you will probably wipe your arse on these letters if you run out of loo roll. Anyway, because you've massaged my ego a little, I was wondering if you could pass on my recipe for oxtail stew to Big Mike. I am really enjoying working on dishes where the availability and budget are limited. It's amazing what a nutritious and hearty meal you can create by being resourceful and thrifty. Not sure if you remember my Uncle Tom – he was the one who broke Malik's cheekbone with a catapulted rock. Anyway, he was actually alive during WW2 and he has given me some real food for thought. So, in light of that I would like you to ask Big Mike to give this stew a go; I achieved it for £1.40 per head.

Anyway, I'll get to the point, I enclose a gift for you from an old friend of yours. You'll understand what it is and who it belongs to when you see it. I hope it brings you comfort and the determination to get through the rest of your sentence.

R

THE BIG HOUSE

Yet again, I'd packed up the note and the baby items and sealed it with some red wax, it had become a ritual. Now that I had Miles's number, I'd sent him a message and told him I'd left a small package in the greenhouse that needed to be sent to Matt immediately; that meant I could avoid going into his grubby little lair and potentially being spotted by Dave. It wasn't so bad all of this, I was becoming to prison food what Jamie Oliver did to school dinners. Perhaps one day, I would be recognised for my efforts and awarded in some way.

That morning, Dad and I had volunteered to do the bathrooms together, we hadn't had anytime alone so strangely I looked forward to doing something I would normally rush through. Holding two bottles of bleach and some of those gel discs that created bubbles every time you flushed, we began our chores with the toilets. I was actually a shit-hot cleaner in my own house but once other people's fluids were involved, ones that I did not give birth to or marry, it was a quick wipe whilst retching and looking in the opposite direction.

"I've got your mother something very special for our fiftieth wedding anniversary, Raquel, can you keep a secret?" Dad said with a hushed voice. I nodded, shutting the door and taking my surgical gloves off. Dad reached into his pocket and pulled out a set of keys with a yellow satin ribbon holding them together in a neat little bow.

"What's this?" I asked, praying she wasn't handcuffed to a four poster somewhere wearing a leather basque.

"I bought your mum a cottage," he announced proudly.

"But she already has a cottage," I said, confused. Perhaps he wanted a break from time to time.

"Yes, but this isn't just any old cottage, Raquel, this has a certain *je ne sais quoi*." He said this with an affected accent, I hated it. Memories of my parents pretending to be from the continent whenever they left the country resurfaced. Mum in her jaunty berets and Dad constantly

THE BIG HOUSE

asking for *un croque monsieur* even if he wasn't hungry because he thought it sounded good.

I sat on the floor and leaned against the back of the bath; Dad clearly wanted to make this revelation a big thing so I let him.

"I was going to wait until Mel got here but she's not even answering my calls. I think we need to leave her be for now," Dad said, and I agreed. Mel was completely offline to the world doing God knows what with Christ knows who.

"Go on then, Dad, explain the keys," I encouraged him.

"I've purchased a small house in the South of France. A lovely little getaway that your mother and I can just pop off to whenever we fancy."

"Oh, wow, that's unbelievable. She'll be blown away, she really will."

Dad beamed. He knew he'd done good as this would give Mum a completely new village to go at. "It's only half an hour from Le Moulin. You know about Robbie and Morag's new place?"

I nodded.

"Best decision they ever made, there's no use them staying here and running this old place. It's a money pit in more ways than one." He winked. We both knew he was referring to Miles.

"I think it's an absolutely stunning gift. Mum has always wanted to have a second home and to think she'll be able to meet her friend whenever she likes for coffee or more likely a gin," I said enthusiastically, wanting Dad to feel proud of his efforts. I hoped that one day in the future my husband would buy me a home in the French countryside. I would have to behave, obviously, and stop telling lies, perhaps giving up my new hobby of sending letters to inmates. But if I managed all that, maybe it would be me being handed the keys to a two-bed cottage with original beams that was in strolling distance of a *boulangerie*. What a way to go out, I thought to myself. Dad was a diamond – in his own way.

THE BIG HOUSE

"Now, only Morag and Robbie know all about it because we've been sharing the same solicitor to do the paperwork, but that's it! It's a total secret so keep shtum. I'm going to give your mother the keys in bed on the morning of our anniversary."

I nodded. "Okay, I'll be sure to bring up a glass of champagne."

"Add some orange juice, Raquel, we're not animals."

We chatted about freshly baked croissants, crème brûlée and warm French sunsets whilst we scrubbed debris from three of The Eagle Lodge's toilets. It sounds strange to say it, but this was probably up there with the best hour of the holiday so far.

Just as we were finishing up in final bathroom, I heard a scream from the top floor, then some shouting and then a door slammed. Dad and I both rushed up. We were met by CeeCee hobbling down and clinging on to the banister, she looked as though she'd seen a ghost.

"Are you okay?" I worried seeing her struggle to get her breath. Dad sat on the stairs next to her and put his arm around her shoulder.

"What's the matter, old girl?" he asked her gently. He sounded like he was talking to a sick horse. She caught her breath.

"I went up to see Suzy, I wanted to see if she fancied doing something with me before we leave and… oh my God." She covered her mouth.

I realised what she was going to say next.

"She was doing it… with the Syrian boy." Dad raised his eyebrows and removed his comforting hand from her shoulder.

"I think that's my cue to leave," he said rather awkwardly, and immediately left the corridor.

"Did you know about them, that they were at it upstairs?" she asked, and I nodded.

"Try and put it out of your mind, they're just kids, well, adults, but you know what I mean," I said.

"How can I unsee that? You should have a word with your daughter,

THE BIG HOUSE

she shouldn't give herself away like that, and to do it with her parents and grandparents in the house is very disrespectful," she ranted.

I sort of agreed so I shouted up the stairs, "Why can't you do it in the park like we had to at your age?"

CeeCee glared at me. "Or they could try NOT doing it at all, how about that!"

She didn't have to say anything because it was clear that she thought my loose morals had been passed straight down the gene pool to my children. I just hoped her next stop wasn't to Master Stiff Socks' room where she would probably have a mini stroke. "Sex sex sex, it's insanity," I heard her saying to Gary as she poured herself a rosé in the kitchen before noon. "It's my David I feel sorry, it's no wonder he's doing what he's doing, the whole family are out of control, Gary."

"Now, Cee, just take another one of your pills and have a lie down, will you. We'll be gone tomorrow and you'll be back on the balcony in the sunshine. Go on, off you go, my love." He calmed her down.

I waited in the hall for her to pass me, but she didn't look at me. I got that she was clearly upset but what did she mean 'It's no wonder Dave is doing what he's doing?' Just what was he doing and who was he doing it with?

Whatever happened, CeeCee would have to forgive me at some point, I was the mother of her grandchildren, and apart from a small lapse in judgement I had been a very good wife to Dave. How much longer was I to live under a black cloud of guilt, worry and judgement? I was actually becoming quite irritated by the whole damn thing. I was still trying to balance the scales; I was still feeling the pressure and this time I was handling it all alone just to ensure that everyone else had a good holiday.

Neither Suzy nor Arif appeared after they were rumbled by CeeCee, which I could understand. Not only was it mortifying to be discovered

THE BIG HOUSE

by an elderly relative mid-bonk, but Suzy also knew the rest of the house would know by now too. Arif was possibly terrified that Dave would give him a good hiding, that's normally what British men did when their daughter's had been defiled. I did feel slightly sorry for them, so I went up to talk them both and clear the air. They were in their own bedrooms when I went up, so I started with Suzy first.

"Have you got something to tell me?"

She shrugged whilst lying on the bed, pruning her nails with her teeth.

"You and a certain boy." I tried again and she covered her face, groaning.

"Yeah, go on, what about it?"

I wasn't sure what I was asking here as they were only doing what teenagers did. "Is it serious?"

She burst out laughing. "No, no way."

"So what is it, then?"

"It's just a bit of fun."

"Does he know that?" I checked protectively of sweet Arif.

"Know what? That it's fun, errr, yeah."

"Suzy, you know what I mean. Does he know it's not serious? I don't want you hurting him, he's been through a lot."

"Mum, if you're asking if I will be calling him my boyfriend, I will not ever be doing that. What happens in Scotland stays in Scotland," she said confidently.

"Yeah, but, he won't be staying in Scotland will he! He'll be going back to Granny and Grandad's, and you will see him all the time."

"Well, we'll deal with that when it happens, Mum." She shrugged.

"Family friends are really tricky to shake off, Suzy, believe me, I know," I tried to explain.

"Well, you do know everything don't you, Mum," she said sarcastically.

THE BIG HOUSE

"Yes, I think I probably do. You don't get to my age without learning a thing or two."

She stood and walked towards the door. "You bring us up here with no Wi-Fi, not sure what else we were supposed to do to be honest, Mum."

"There's garden Jenga, croquet and fishing." I gave her three other options to choose from other than getting it on with the nearest person to her. But knowing that there was no getting through to her, I left and went next door to Arif. He was nervous, wringing his hands and pacing.

"Listen, Arif, we were all young once."

He looked at me with his huge eyes. "I sorry, we like each other, we laugh together. I sorry."

"It's okay, calm down. You need to be discreet and you need to be careful." He went into his bedside drawer and pulled out a box of condoms and showed them to me.

"Well done, that's very responsible," I said trying to overlook the fact they were 'cheeky cherry' flavoured and a size large.

"What about David... Mr Fitzpatrick...will he, er, take me away?"

I laughed, imagining how full the cells would be if all sexually active teenagers were locked up. "No, he won't take you anywhere. I'll talk to him. You're fine."

He heaved a big sigh of relief.

"Just keep the noise down and wear them!" I pointed to the drawer. He nodded, and after that I needed to get out of the house for a bit.

I drove over to Stirling on my own that afternoon, needing a break. I was having one of those days where things kept going wrong, the sort of day that in hindsight should have resulted in me going back to bed when the second or even third thing went wrong. I should have realised that it would be a trying day when I caught sight of my

THE BIG HOUSE

bare backside in the bathroom mirror and it reminded me of a rhino's hide. Going back to bed would have been the better option when I discovered there was a hole in the surgical glove that I had worn to clean the toilet with and I had been hacking at some dried poo with my bare fingernail. The day was dealing me low blows on a constant basis so I needed a change of scene.

Although the journey there wasn't as calming as I'd hoped when a lorry-driving woman wearing a leather spiked collar threatened to peel my eyelids back after I stared at her for a little too long at the traffic lights. After I sped off to lose this sado masochist, my boot flew open and my brand-new cool box was ejected onto the street. I watched as 'Trucker Bev' flattened it under her big fat wheels.

I needed some retail therapy after that – my version of this was wandering up and down the aisles of the supermarket and reading all the labels and buying interesting ingredients I could play around with. When I got to the till with all my new bits and pieces, my debit card was declined. Not just once but three times, people behind me were huffing and puffing and one guy who was very impatient, not to mention rude, shouted, "Either pay the fucking bill, sweetheart, or put it all back."

Eventually, I found my Amex at the bottom of my bag and whacked it all on there. I put the bags in my boot and headed off to the first place that would serve me some hard liquor. A day from sheer hell so far!

I sat in a pub called The Roebuck and logged in to their Wi-Fi to check my online banking and why the hell my Halifax debit card had left me looking like a complete tosser in Waitrose. I called them and they treated me like the 'Tinder Swindler', passing me from pillar to post only to be eventually told I was required to attend any Halifax branch of my choice with my passport, my birth certificate and a fucking unicorn by the sounds of things. Please, put your hand up if you carry this sort of ID around in your handbag on a staycation.

THE BIG HOUSE

Four grand from our joint and current account had been used to pay off two credit card bills and a large lump sum was paid off my car loan. The remaining £800 had been transferred over to Dave's personal account leaving a grand total of £130. He was paying off debts and tidying things up, it felt like he was separating himself from me financially and this was the start of a bigger separation. I considered how I would manage without Dave's wage, how I would keep up with Suzy's obsession with Vicky Beckham's mascara or Michaela's £200 'built up' trainers. Would I be the one on a prison budget, using tinned tuna inside my wellington, Spam as a filling for my pies and, God forbid, Findus crispy pancakes as the main event at my Sunday lunch? Financially I would really feel it, but emotionally it would crush me. I stomped off up the high street starting to believe that Julian's suggestion to actually talk to Dave may be the way to go. How many more clues did I actually need before I had to accept that bad shit was going down?

As I was almost back at my car when the final blow of my crap day was bestowed upon me. Angus Ferguson, the young butcher who had assisted me with my August Christmas, was getting back into his van after delivering a number of butchered lambs to a Turkish restaurant. He waved at me and wandered over with his cheerful smile. "Hello, Mrs Fitzpatrick, how are things going?"

I took a deep breath; a friendly face was just what I needed right now. "Hello, it's Angus, isn't it? Yes, things are going great, thank you for asking."

He nodded. "You remembered my name, well done, you – people get us Fergusons all mixed up."

"The pheasants were absolutely fabulous, I'll be sure to send you a copy of the feature when it appears later this year, perhaps you can put it on the wall of the shop?" I offered.

THE BIG HOUSE

"Yes, that would be lovely, let me give you my card, it has all my details on it." He reached into the top in the pocket of his butcher's coat.

"Oh, I don't need another card, Angus, you already gave me one at the house, remember? When you said I should call you anytime."

He looked a little embarrassed. "Sorry, yes, I did, I was just hoping that, well, you'd possibly, well it's a bit inappropriate actually Mrs Fitzpatrick but I wanted to ask you if…"

I stopped him, poor thing suffering like this. "Look, I'm very flattered, Angus, I really am, but I am happily married woman. I'm sure there's someone out there for you but it's not me, I'm afraid, bless you." I ruffled his hair to comfort him.

He looked up at me with nothing but horror. "Oh dear, I think you might have got a little bit mixed up, Mrs Fitzpatrick, I didn't mean for you to call me."

I stopped him again, he needed help. "Don't be embarrassed, Angus, I get this a lot," I assured him.

"Do you?" He looked confused. "I was sort of hoping your daughter might call me. The blonde one – she came in for sausages once and we had a sort of moment."

I looked at the sky for help. A cartoon mallet basically donged me on the forehead and an animated donkey kicked me up the arse. It was Suzy who was the wanton hussy not me, spraying her wicked scent all about Scotland. I walked away slowly, my head hung low in embarrassment. There it was, the cherry on the shit-day cake.

He shouted after me. "I'm just not into that sort of thing, Mrs Fitzpatrick, but I could ask my dad, though, if you want."

The old penniless maid drove home knowing that the only attention she got that day was from a big butch lorry driver called Bev who wanted to physically assault her.

THE BIG HOUSE

Back at the house, the last supper for Gary and CeeCee was upon their request: fish and chips! Dave had been to collect it and mine was in the oven. CeeCee was a little bit out of it, the shock of seeing Suzy getting some had forced her to seek solace in the last of her rosé and her hip pills. The old girl was even dipping her chips in gravy which I have been told on many occasion was against the law if you're from anywhere south of Birmingham.

"She's cheered up, then." I gestured to her as I sat down at the end of the table next to Dave.

He nodded, "Yeah, she'll be okay. Will just take time."

"Got some news for you," I whispered.

He looked at me worried. "What now, Raquel, what have you done?"

"It's Suzy, well Suzy and Arif, actually."

"What's she done to him?" he asked, which had also been my first thought.

"Well, I went up there with some washing this morning and he was in her room. I heard some noises, you know... noises?"

He shook his head. "Don't tell me anymore, I don't want to hear any more about the noises. But mark my words, this will end in tears and they won't be hers."

"Your mum caught them at it. She was very distressed, had to take even more pills." Dave rolled his eyes. "I've spoken to both of them, had the talk, so not much more we can do."

Dave looked over at Suzy and shook his head. "To be honest, she could do a lot worse."

Now that seemed to have eased the tension, I decided to ask him about the bank account. "My card was declined today in the supermarket as," I said, seeming confused.

He nodded slowly. "Ah yes sorry about that, I was rejigging the finances and I forgot to top the account up." He then ate a chip! A carbohydrate! Mr Keto was falling off the wagon before my very eyes.

"Why are we rejigging Dave?"

He ate another chip, and then some battered cod. "I just think we need to tighten our belts for a while."

I frowned. "I don't want a tight belt, I like mine loose, actually."

He grabbed a buttered bread roll and stuffed it with more fried potatoes. "Well, I think we're going to have to, I'm afraid," he said quite forcefully.

"Don't I get a say in any of this? And why haven't you discussed this with me? I looked homeless in Waitrose," I told him.

"Maybe Waitrose is somewhere you'll have to rethink," he said abruptly.

My mouth dropped open; this was bad. I was not a spendthrift by any means, I never bought designer clothes or handbags, we didn't fly business class. I even bought my copper pans on eBay. Not being 'allowed' to shop for food where I wanted to, considering the job I did, was a right kick in the dick. "What the hell is going on Dave? I need to know. I wanted to ignore your odd behaviour but how can I when you're moving *our* money without consulting me?" I hissed.

He continued to bring on his carb coma, carefully stuffing a bread roll with all he could get his hands on. With a serious look on his face, he said, "Yes, love, we do need to talk but not here. Later, when we're alone."

I felt like I'd been winded. He had something to tell me and I just knew for certain it was going to be unpleasant. This was the very reason I had avoided talking to Dave until now, I somehow knew it would be unpleasant. Julian was wrong, Julian was an idiot. No I did not want to be transparent and vulnerable because that would hurt me and, duh, nobody actually wants to be hurt.

THE BIG HOUSE

I sat quietly as the family ate their supper; I didn't want them to finish because it got me closer to the 'chat'. CeeCee and Gary's flight was booked for tomorrow evening, thank goodness, and Dave was driving them over to the airport. At least I wouldn't have to endure an awkward car journey with their judgy faces in the rear-view mirror, sitting in the back like I was some lady cab driver, messing with the heating and putting the windows up and down like a pair of toddlers with ADHD.

"We'll be hitting the hay soon, people, thanks for a wonderful trip. Sorry we can't stay for the actual anniversary but we'll see you all soon." Gary raised his glass. Everybody cheered back and that was the end of their stay at The Eagle Lodge.

"Before you all leave the table, I have an announcement to make," I said, clearing my throat before I made a manipulative attempt to regain some sort of respect from my mother-in-law. "We have decided that we will be coming to Portugal for Christmas this year. Mum and Dad will be joining us, so you'll have your family altogether again." I looked over at CeeCee and got ready for her to faint with excitement. But she just glanced at Dave and then back at her plate barely lifting her head.

"Oh well, we're not sure what we're doing this year. We'll let you know," she said meekly.

I wouldn't normally use the word 'unprecedented', even in my own head, because I fucking hated it, but there was no other description for this reaction. Sure she was pissed off with me, maybe she even thought Suzy was a little tart, but come on, I was prepared to transport her whole family over to 'her manor' for Christmas and she said, "We'll see!" I was stunned into silence.

Mum gave me a look across the table to show she didn't understand it either. CeeCee must have been in a very bad place not to jump at the chance. My shoulders dropped, I felt defeated. I had a horrible feeling of being an outsider in my own family. The diners dispersed and there was nothing left to say on the matter. My grand gesture had failed and if that didn't work then I had no place left to go.

Dave said he had some work calls to make but then he would meet me in the kitchen garden for the big chat. I felt absolutely hideous – was CeeCee fuelling this plan for us to split, doing a Peggy Mitchell and telling him to 'take out the trash'? He had been okay until she arrived. We'd done therapy, had regular sex, travelled, laughed, talked. All the things a married couple are supposed to do on paper over the last year. I couldn't have tried any harder, I mean sure, I did say no to him going through my back doors but I said yes to literally everything else. People had done worse than I had for fuck's sake, so why was I being hung out to dry by his mum? I started to wind myself up more and more, I wasn't a bleeding serial killer. I made the decision that no matter what Dave had to tell me, I wasn't going down without a fight and CeeCee would not break up my relationship. With 'one on me' I went storming up the stairs to what actually should have been my master suite but had been very kindly handed it over to Mr and Mrs Shit Hips. I banged on the door; Gary opened it with his toothbrush hanging out of his mouth. "Raquel, if this is about Christmas, don't worry, she'll come around."

I folded my arms. "I want to talk to CeeCee alone please, Gary." He looked back at the bed and then nodded to me before wandering off down the corridor dribbling toothpaste on the carpet.

"What is it, Raquel?" she asked, sitting up in her frilly nighty and putting her Catherine Cookson book down for a minute.

"I just came to say that I am very disappointed in how you are treating me, actually, and even after what I did over a year ago, I don't think that is a reason to break up my marriage," I said firmly.

THE BIG HOUSE

She put her book down and took her glasses off. "I don't actually know what you did, Raquel, I mean, I know you had some sort of fling but by all accounts it wasn't serious."

I unfolded my arms and softened a little. "No, it wasn't serious, it wasn't even anything. It was just a stupid mistake. We all make them."

She nodded. "Your generation does tend to muck things up, I agree."

"So why are you being so cold, why are you encouraging Dave to leave me? And why is he sneaking around and lying to me?"

She didn't seem shocked at my accusations and shrugged before saying, "I am not encouraging him to leave you. And perhaps he is trying to save your feelings by keeping things from you." That caught me off-guard – Dave's Mum would normally have reared up like a python at anybody calling her son a liar, so what did she know?

"And just what is that supposed to mean, CeeCee?"

Quite smugly, she said, "You'd better ask him that, hadn't you."

I was starting to get quite het up with all of this, something was happening, and for me, it didn't look good. I had tried to ignore it, but since we'd got to Scotland Dave had been different, distant, and my gut told me that my time may have come to pay the price.

"Look CeeCee, I'm all over the place here. If there's something going on and I need to know."

"Oh, you're all over the place, are you!" She raised her pencil thin eyebrows. "Well he's the one dealing with something life-changing right now, not you, Raquel."

I gave up trying, she was not on my side and never would be. I left the room without saying another word, I needed to see Dave.

* * * * *

THE BIG HOUSE

Down in the garden, Dave sat on a chair holding a beer whilst rubbing his head. I parked myself next to him, hoping that if I didn't face him it might not hurt as much.

"Talk to me, Dave. What's this life-changing decision I hear you've made?" My heart was pounding wondering what my fate would be.

He sighed. "My mum?" I nodded.

"I thought we'd made progress, really great progress. Why are you leaving me?"

He turned to me and smiled. Jesus, I loved this man when he looked at me like that, his smile was like a massive hug. He put his arm around me and said, "I'm not leaving you, Raquel. I am leaving the police."

We locked eyes, there was such a sadness in his. This was something I never thought I would hear from Dave.

Dave leaving the police was like Gary Barlow leaving Take That, it just didn't work. I wasn't sure who Dave was without it.

"Why the hell would you leave your job and why haven't you told me any of this?"

"I needed to be sure and to make the decision without your influence. You would have tried to stop me, wouldn't you?"

I nodded. "Of course I would."

He took a swig of his lager and held my hand. "I've had a lot on my plate, Raquel, stuff has happened."

Suddenly I wanted answers, none of this made any sense. "But where have you been going when you said you were going back up for work?" I questioned him, as if I were the police.

"The first time, I went to meet my bosses to discuss my exit. The second time, I went for a meeting about a new opportunity, which could be good, but the money is nowhere near as much," he explained.

"Ahh, hence the rejigging and tightening of belts," I realised, as

THE BIG HOUSE

everything started to fall into place.

"Yes. Although bloody hell love, you do spend a shitload of money on food, that needs addressing either way."

I couldn't believe all of this was going on under my nose. I had immediately thought the worst of him and all along he was leaving behind the thing that meant almost as much to him as I did.

"You know I thought you were having an affair?" I said, shaking my head at myself.

He nodded and smiled, almost laughed actually. "Of course I knew, dipstick."

"And you were fine with that, were you?" I asked, my temper slightly rising.

"Yes, it was quite nice you being jealous." He grinned.

"I thought you were running off with that Tesco delivery woman, do you know who I mean?"

He laughed. "Yes, Christ she was fit."

"And my sister – I thought you and her were at it at one point." He shook his head.

"When you said you were with Stu, I nearly lost my shit."

"Because you know he's in Australia, visiting his daughter?"

I nodded, hating to admit to Dave that I'd been through his phone but I suspected he already had an idea.

"Maybe it's you that should be a detective, Raquel, and not me." Dave smiled, although I could see that he was hurting because being in the police was all he'd ever known. "I didn't want you to feel bad about this so I wanted it to be all sorted before I told you. I compromised myself last year – it was my decision and so is this. I'm a big boy, it will all be fine, Raquel," he tried to assure me.

"But why now? Things seemed fine until a few weeks ago, this has come as such a shock to me, and to almost find out from your mum."

THE BIG HOUSE

He picked up his beer and leaned back into the seat and then he said.

"Well, it all started when I got a letter from Matt."

LIGHT RELIEF

It turned out that Matt had been hedging his bets and had initially sent Dave a letter from jail hoping that he could persuade him to get news on Gina. He did after all have our address – we used to be neighbours so it was very easy for him to get somebody to push it through the door.

The first letter had arrived a couple of weeks before we left for Scotland. Dave had been a bit startled by it, but he had decided to ignore it. It was basically just a plea for news on Gina, and Matt hinted that he would reveal the whole truth if he didn't at least get some intel. He presumed with Dave being in the police, he would have more of a chance of locating Gina than anyone. Although Dave had felt uncomfortable, as you would, he put it down to Matt having a bad day and had chucked the letter away.

However, another letter arrived the day before we left for Scotland, this time directly to the station. This one was more forceful and Matt invited Dave to check the visitor's list just in case he was unsure of how serious he was. After a little digging, Dave then found out that Matt had indeed been visited by a solicitor and it was one of those nasty Rottweiler types who would keep digging for dirt before calling the *Daily Mail*.

Even then, Dave tried everything to stay positive, hoping that Matt would just settle down. A solicitor could have been visiting for many reasons, he had after all just had his sentence extended for locking the prison chaplain in the stationery cupboard.

"Did you consider trying to locate Gina, you know, on the quiet?" I asked Dave, hoping that something inside him had at least tempted him to play along."

"Did I bollocks, Raquel! You don't bow down to people like that –

THE BIG HOUSE

once they've got you on the inside, you're basically one of them," he said sternly.

I gulped, this truly was the moment I should given myself an uppercut. Julian's words 'open and honest, transparent and vulnerable' rattled around head. This was my chance right then to give him my account so far, but I couldn't do it. I couldn't allow him to be disappointed in me all over again. Not when he was leaving his job, not when he was worried about his parents being so frail and not when he had only just forgiven me for my last dickhead move.

"When I got a call from the station, the day we were having our massages, to tell me a visiting order had come in requesting to see Matt Dennis, that was it, Raquel. I just knew that I couldn't carry on being a police officer. I can't go into work with my head up anymore, love. It's not who I am as a person. And if this does come out, I can't cope with being fired, it would kill my mum," he said looking crushed.

Of course I felt absolutely disgusting, lower than a snake's belly, actually. This was all down to me and I should have known better than to think for one second this could go away so easily. "I'm so sorry, Dave." I was getting sick of constantly apologising to him. "I wish I could make this better."

"What's done is done. We need to move on, we want to be together, and mistakes have been made," he said to me kindly. "But, I had to tell my mum about this, Raquel. She needed to know that I was leaving the police before she goes back to Portugal, I don't want her getting any nasty shocks, especially at her age."

I agreed, Dave did have a close relationship with CeeCee and this sort of news was huge to her. Although, it did leave me looking like a career-ending harlot.

Telling Dave at this point about my letters, my connection with Miles, my previous French connection with Miles, the discovery of

THE BIG HOUSE

Gina in the hotel, the birth of R Liam plus my newfound hobby of writing the weekly menu for B wing was not a good idea at all. When you listed it out all like that, it was simply too much.

So, after the big chat, Dave and I went to bed and we put on a funny movie I had downloaded on the iPad and we ate a family-size bag of Minstrels. Dave put a big red cross in his keto diary before he went to sleep, his first cheat day in months.

I lay awake that night combing through the situation in my mind – I'd come this far, there was a chance that I could somehow salvage this, and so far nobody had squealed. (Prison lingo I was quickly becoming accustomed to.) I really believed that Matt had no intention of ever doing anything sinister, and Gina had too much to lose as well. As worrying as all this was, the odds were still in my favour, and now I'd sent that final letter I should be free of it.

Therefore, my plan was to keep quiet until we got back to Cheshire, once we were home and in a safe environment away from Miles, then maybe I would tell Dave all about what had happened. Doing it now would just over-complicate things, plus I would have to reveal my filthy secret with Miles in the vicinity and things were just too sensitive for that. It would look like I had a thing for criminals undoing my bra and I didn't, not really. I also had to work out what to do about Morag's secret and Miles's demands for information – that little cretin was lingering in the background with his own problems. So much to do and only me to do it, as usual.

I have to admit, I did feel lighter that Dave's secrecy was about his job and not Tesco bitch. It was a huge weight off my mind and so I slept better than I had in days.

CeeCee and Gary were on an evening flight out of Glasgow and spent most of the next day looking for their stuff – most of which was in front of them or already packed. I could not understand why

THE BIG HOUSE

yesterday's newspaper was important or whether it really mattered if they had an umbrella. They were going in the car to an airport and from there basically to a beach. Eventually they accepted they were packed and ready to leave but made Dave promise to do a sweep after they'd left. "If you find a packet of Polos, they're mine. Can't seem to remember where I put them," Gary said lifting up the cushions on the sofa.

"We'll send them over if we find them, Dad," he promised.

"You do that, David."

I shook my head. What the actual hell. I hadn't really enjoyed their company on this trip and both of them had been royal pains for most of their stay. Add the fact that CeeCee hated my guts, let's just say, I was itching for them to go.

We waved them off from the steps, and as Dave's car left the gravel drive there was shared relief. Particularly from Suzy and Arif who must have felt better knowing they weren't going to have to make small talk with CeeCee after what she'd witnessed.

A couple of days went by and not much happened; people just got on doing their own thing as we tried to enjoy the last week of the holiday. I certainly felt some light relief, a little bit of honesty from Dave made all the difference. Because I wasn't as tightly wound and because I could see the light, during those two days I tried to spend some time with everybody and I tried to be nice. I ran out of niceness about 4 pm on the second day after Old Tom said that my legs had seen better days. Vowing never to wear shorts again, I went out into the garden and collected my book from the greenhouse where I'd left it. I wanted an hour of calm before I started dinner but as I opened the page where I thought my bookmark was, it had been replaced with an envelope.

THE BIG HOUSE

Dear Rackel, you have no idea what it meant to me be able to smell my son. It had made me even more determined to get out of here and be with him. This is the sort of thing that is keeping me going. I understand that you won't be in Scotland for much longer and unfortunately after that, we won't have Miles to help us communicate. For that reason, I have to ask you one final favour. I really need access to some more cash in here, it works on a card basis. If I had a card with a balance, I would be able to call my nan more and buy more fruit from the tuck shop, at the moment I am struggling to make ends meet. I know if you get yourself up to The Hotel, my associates would be able to help out with that and you could simply give it to Miles and he can get it to me. It's hard in here, Rackel, you have to hustle almost every day. A bit of extra cash would make it so much easier whilst I continue to carry the can for others. Have a think, I would be very grateful.

You'll also be pleased to know that Big Mike added your oxtail to the menu on Sunday. Rackel, people were queuing for seconds. Somebody who tried to lick the serving tray was thrown into solitary, even though we are in prison, we still have to have manners. The guvnor has looked over the new additions and is super-chuffed that we're saving money and cooking real food. He has even given permission for us to make a veg patch outside the kitchen, so we're saving money which the government will be pleased with too.

The dirty protest has now stopped, my cellmate has literally run out of shit. He was straining for two hours the other day and nothing happened so he is thinking of another way to get attention. I suggested he try and escape but this place is watertight with the screws looking over all of our shoulders so he'll have to think of something else.

Gemma came to see me yesterday, she told me that my Gina is doing well and can't wait to see me in 2030. It's a long way off but at least I'll have a family waiting for me like you've got.

THE BIG HOUSE

Anyway, this could be the last letter you get from me so I want to say thanks, just knowing someone has my back even if it is a copper's wife is good to know.

Enjoy the rest of your holiday and perhaps one day we'll meet again.

Matt.

So, the oxtail was a success, plus it came in on budget, so yet again I had smashed it in the food department. However, having to get yet another object and send it to Matt was really very inconvenient, but I knew it would be the last time we ever communicated and I felt this was the closure we both needed.

* * * * *

Mum and Dad were happily chatting in the kitchen when I walked in.

"Only five days until our anniversary, Phillip," Mum said, whilst washing a cup with her finger. Why did that generation always swill teacups out using their digit fingers? Why didn't they use the brush?

"Yes, we'll have a wonderful morning and then later on, Mel has organised a very special surprise for us," Dad teased.

"Ooh, has she?" Mum was not previously told about this but Mel had told Dad not to plan anything on the day of their 50th wedding anniversary but to dress nicely and be ready for 11 am. In fact, we were all going somewhere and it was to be a full day of celebrations courtesy of Mel. I'm sure she'd planned all of this just to upstage me.

"Let's just hope she turns up," said Mum. Nobody had heard a thing from Mel since she went sperm shopping just under a week before. Also, Mel had not informed me of any surprise, nor had she asked

THE BIG HOUSE

me to go halves with her, which was typical Mel. Trying to look better than me at every opportunity, but she would be sorely disappointed as I had already sorted my gift and unless she'd got Arif a book deal, she would not come close.

We ate dinner at the table that day as the weather had turned again, so soup and sandwiches with the fire lit was what that day was all about. Cauliflower cheese soup was an invention of mine using the leftovers of a Sunday lunch. It's basically cauliflower cheese made the traditional way, roast potatoes, vegetable stock, some double cream, a ton of grated parmesan and a quick whizz in a blender and voilà. I sprinkled some smoky bacon bits on top and served it with a crusty slice of buttered granary. I wondered as I spooned it into the bowls if perhaps this would make a good meal for the inmates. On a cold winter's day, those prisoners would welcome a bowl of this creamy delight. I made the decision to add that to my very last letter to Matt, a sort of goodbye gift to them all.

Morag knocked on the back door just as we were finishing up and she looked quite stressed. She beckoned Mum into the utility room where they whispered for a while before emerging both with angry faces.

"What's up?" I asked Mum, as Morag slipped off upstairs to fill some more of her secret boxes.

Mum fumed. "It's that bleeding little shit, Miles. He really is a piece of work, Raquel. He's managed to get Robbie to transfer some money over to him yet again! It really has to stop."

"Why has Robbie done that, hasn't he learned his lesson?" He really was a dumbo, why was he feeding the little monster?

"Well he's an old softy, really, and apparently Miles is his 'wee boy'. He feels sorry for the lad – he doesn't have many friends and apparently he's dogged with bad luck. But he just wastes all the money

THE BIG HOUSE

and comes back for more. Morag says he's waiting for the house to be sold as that's where the real money is."

I nodded, she was right, that was exactly what he was hoping for. A big cheque from the proceeds of the house that he could squander away on fags and heavy metal T-shirts.

"It wouldn't surprise me if Robbie and Morag weren't both found at the bottom of the lake, you know, he's been wanting the cash from this house since he got out of… erm… left Hong Kong," Mum carried on dramatically.

Hong Kong, my arse, and they had no idea that Miles was still heavily involved in criminal activity, so he wasn't exactly turning over a new leaf. No wonder he needed money, he was probably in debt to some awful people. His job as 'The Mule' mustn't have paid much, as he only really sent messages, baby items and now recipes thanks to me, so I wasn't sure how he was getting by.

"They really need a good break from him, there's something about that little weasel that puts me on edge. At least you're not permanently on the scrounge. Anyway, your dad and I are going for a nap, we'll see you later." She winked twice.

"Is there something wrong with your eyes?"

"A nap!" she said and nudged me in the ribs. I frowned.

"All I'm saying, Raquel, is don't come in our room without knocking."

"Too much detail" I shouted after her.

She whistled to my dad who dropped his tea towel and almost ran up to their room.

"On that note, I'm taking Sam into town and I'll be glad to be out of the house," Dave said, having overheard the horrendous conversation with Mum.

"Don't blame you, I need to find my noise-cancelling headphones."

THE BIG HOUSE

I patted Dave on the back as he exited the sex den as quickly as he could. After they'd gone, I sent a quick message to Miles, determined to put an end to this and save Morag and Robbie from his scrounging.

Are you free to talk?

Always x

I'll come over to the cottage.

He sent a thumbs up.

I figured with Dave out with Sam, and Mum and Dad doing revolting things, this was a good time for me to make one final visit to Miles and sort a few things out.

* * * * *

"How are you, my darlin'?"

"Fine, thank you," I said curtly. He looked particularly grubby that day and smelt of washing that hadn't dried properly.

"So, I have some info for you about your mum and dad. You were right to think something was up," I said, knowing he'd fall for this.

"Go on." He rubbed his hands together in anticipation of his pay-out.

"It turns out the house is mortgaged up to the hilt. My parents have had to pay their utility bills and help them out. Mum told me because she's worried about them. They're completely skint, mate." I shrugged and pulled a sad face with my bottom lip out.

"Mortgage? As if, they paid that off years ago." He furrowed his brow.

THE BIG HOUSE

"They had to remortgage, Miles, a long time back. They've never told anyone because they were embarrassed, why do you think we're here? They need the money." The little twit clenched his fists.

"Is there any equity left in the house, is there a penny for me to inherit?" he shouted, his voice sounding squawky and pathetic.

I shook my head. "There's nothing. Not a penny. It's likely it will be repossessed and they will have to go stay with my parents."

"Fucking idiots." He lit a cig and took a drag while the cogs slowly turned in his little brain.

"Well, I'm absolutely scuppered now, I owe money everywhere, I need to come up with a plan."

"Sorry the news isn't more positive. I'm sure something will come up." I patted his arm making a mental note to bleach my hand soon after.

"Aye, if you hear anymore, let me know okay."

I nodded. "Oh, I have one more letter for you to send over to Matt, can you help?"

"Just leave it in the greenhouse and I'll get it there in a couple of days. Thanks again for the info, Raquel, I knew I could rely on you."

I really hoped to God this didn't make him feel like finishing off his parents on the back of what I said. There would surely be no point if they had nothing to leave him. Anyway, I had to focus my attention on getting this money card for Matt. I certainly couldn't let Miles know Gina was in the country, he would probably use it to blackmail me, or even Dave, especially now he was desperate. I would have to communicate with her myself. I was almost home and dry and slipped out with everyone else distracted.

Up at The Hotel, the bar was busy. I ordered a pot of tea and took my laptop out, making sure I was seen. I poured the tea into my cup and then asked the bartender to keep an eye on my stuff as I was nipping to the loo. I made my way up to the floor where Gina had been staying,

THE BIG HOUSE

hoping and praying this would be the last time I would ever see this woman. I knocked quietly a few times. An eye appeared at the spy hole and then the door was opened quickly with the occupant hidden behind the door.

The room was dark with the blinds down at both sash windows and only a small lamp provided light. There were a couple of holdalls on the bed and Gina was dressed like she was going on a trip.

"Hiya, babe."

"Going somewhere, Gina?" I asked while she put on her lipstick in the mirror.

She nodded. "Yeah, it's time for me to head back to South America now, R Liam is waiting for me."

She reached into her purse and pulled out a plain black plastic card. "Pass this to The Mule will ya, babe. It's one of those cards that never runs out of funds." She laughed. "Not that there's much you can buy inside, like, but at least he can make calls and buy vapes whenever he wants, it's the least we can do, eh, girl."

I put the prison credit card in my purse, wondering if I should try it in Waitrose on the way home just to stock up on some expensive items before my food budget was dramatically cut. I had no idea how Gina could have created a card that never ran out so quickly and from inside a hotel room, it was very clever and also very illegal. But actually, with years ahead of him locked up like an animal, perhaps Matt did deserve a perpetual credit limit just to take the sting out of it all.

"Gina. You will wait for him, won't you?" I asked before I left.

She smiled, her teeth were still pearly white and unnaturally straight. "Course I will, babes, we're soulmates, and now we've got R Liam, we need to be a family again."

Although she was dodgy as fuck, I believed her. She would sell her own arse for a wrap of whizz but this honour amongst thieves thing was definitely a thing. I reached for the doorknob but heard a shuffling in the bathroom.

"Who's that?"

"Just the wind, babes," she claimed.

"That wasn't the wind, it's not even windy, Gina."

"Who've have you got in there?"

"Just a mate, they don't want you to see them, Raquel. Go on, off you fuck."

And there she was, sinister Gina was back in the house with her foul mouth. I didn't want any more nasty surprises and needed this situation wrapping up once and for all.

"Tell them to come out or I won't be responsible for my actions. I need to know who is listening to our conversations."

Gina sighed, "Fine! Malik come out, love, come say hi to our old friend Raquel."

"Malik! What the heck is he doing here?" I gasped as the little bald tyrant strolled into the bedroom.

"He came back into the country to help me out Raquel, I wasn't going to travel alone, was I? Who'd carry all me bags?" She giggled.

This was insane. These people had been given a free pass to a new life and now they were holed up in a hotel room around the corner from my holiday home. Malik had been nothing but a nuisance last year and you would have thought he had learned his lesson when my Uncle Tom shattered his cheekbone with a catapulted rock.

"Good evening, Raquel," he said to me in his baddy voice.

"I am sorry to say this is not a pleasure whatsoever."

He grinned. "We'll be out of hair as soon as possible. Please pass my regards to Arif, he was good boy."

Gina scoffed. "He was a liccle twat, Malik, he's the reason we're in the mess."

THE BIG HOUSE

Malik nodded slowly. "Yes, probably right, Gina, probably right."

"I hate to break up the party but I best be off. And so had you two. If you're found here, you'll both be inside for a very long time."

Gina nodded. "I know that. Thanks for everything, please make sure that Matt gets the card."

I nodded and left. Downstairs, I wrote the letter on my laptop in the hotel bar.

Dear Matt, as requested and for the final time, I have a gift for you from a friend. I hope this will supply you with an endless supply of vapes, fresh fruit and the means to call your nan daily.

I would also like to enclose a final recipe that is not only cheap and delicious but is made from leftovers. I think that Big Mike is going to love this one. This comes in at under £1 per head, enjoy this ultimate comfort food.

I am travelling home quite soon so this is where our communication must end. I have to say that I am very impressed with the way you are handling things, I think you'll make a good dad someday. Try not to think too much about the time you will spend apart from R Liam and just focus on the time you'll have once you are free.

From here on in, I really do need to look after my own family, I hope that I have done enough to keep your spirits up.

Take care, Matt,

R x

THE BIG HOUSE

I rushed backed to The Eagle Lodge to print and package up the letter with the cash card in the envelope. With Dave and Sam still out playing football in the garden, I slipped it under Miles's front door and walked away feeling relieved.

So there we have it, the crims were heading back to their cartels, Matt was tucked up nicely in jail with a picture of R Liam and a few bits that smelt of Johnson's, he had a card full of cash so his next few years would be as comfortable as possible. Miles was under the impression that his parents were brassic so he would have to find another income source, and all I had to do was celebrate my parents' anniversary, pack up my shit and get the hell out of dodge.

"I'll have a lot more time to play football now I'm unemployed," Dave said when he came into the kitchen for a glass of water.

"Don't shut that door fully just yet, Dave. Let's wait until we get home and have another conversation about it, I might have some good ideas."

"There's nothing you can say, love, I can't have this hanging over my head and do my job properly. Matt's got nothing to lose, nobody waiting for him, he's just brooding and plotting. I've made up my mind," he told me.

I didn't say anything and just hoped I'd be able to persuade him otherwise when we got home and I explained everything to him.

"Come sit with me whilst I do the chickens, they have a calming effect." Dave shrugged and followed me out.

Roger was sitting out on one of the garden chairs staring at the floor, he barely looked up when we approached him. "Mel will be back soon, you know," he said glumly.

"Well that's good, though, right?" Dave said cheerily.

"Not if she's with child."

Dave glanced at me with concern. "You're having a right mare aren't you, mate?"

THE BIG HOUSE

Roger nodded. The brothers-in-law shared a moment. There isn't a man alive who would be happy for his wife to be impregnated by a stranger.

"She won't know if she's pregnant for at least a couple of weeks, though, mate." Dave patted his shoulder.

"What if it's an alcoholic?" Roger suddenly piped up.

"Give the kid a chance, mate, I doubt it will be staggering about Dublin anytime soon."

Roger groaned. "David, you know what I mean."

"Well that could happen with anyone's child, Roger, even your own flesh and blood, look at her." He pointed to me and winked.

"What if it's a headcase? I don't want to have to pad the feckin' walls in my own house, thank you very much."

Dave looked away. It was hard not to laugh listening to Roger when he was being wet. "You don't even know if she's actually pregnant yet, Roger, let's do this one step at a time."

Roger checked his wristwatch; he had another session with Julian booked and I was really hoping that perhaps the therapy would start to have a positive impact on his state of mind. He suddenly froze in his seat, only moving his eyeballs and mouth very slightly.

"Can you move that dangerous animal away from me, it looks very cross?" Roger said through the corner of his mouth, as a nice brown hen sat on his slippered foot looking the absolute opposite of cross.

"Oh Christ, I think it's about to go for me." He shut his eyes presumably to save them from being viciously pecked out. Slowly, I lifted the hen under my arm allowing Roger to make a run for it. He didn't look back as he headed for the house, in his mind that had been quite a close call.

* * * * *

THE BIG HOUSE

"Suits you this *Good Life* look," Dave said, admiring my ability as a hen whisperer.

"Maybe we should think about a complete change in lifestyle, not just hens and veg, maybe we should move?" I suggested. To be honest, I had enjoyed many elements of a rural life, even catching feelings for these smelly birds. There was a lot that I could embrace outside of suburbia, but without doubt, wherever I was and whatever I did, we would not be without Wi-Fi.

Dave sat deep in thought, perhaps a move was what we needed, a fresh start. Living across the road from 23 was actually a permanent reminder.

I heard the crunch of the gravel soon after and I was pleased to see a very healthy-looking Mel marching up the driveway with a smile on her face.

Roger met her as she reached the bottom of the steps and I watched out of the library bay window as they awkwardly hugged and neither knew what was appropriate to say. Roger carried in Mel's bag even though she was physically stronger than him and they both went straight upstairs for a talk, that was a good sign. Mum had been watching them over my shoulder and had the same idea as me to stay out of it but still wanted to witness it.

"What a bloody mess, Raquel, I can't imagine how this will end," Mum sighed.

"It will work itself out, Mum, we've all been through worse," I said.

Mum nodded. "Yes, you're talking sense for once. Hopefully she can't get pregnant and they'll just get another dog."

"Mum!" I said, shocked. She knew that Mel wanted a child, so this was a surprising opinion.

"She's nearly bloody fifty, what on earth does she want a baby for now? I mean, he's over the hill already, it's not exactly fair on the child.

THE BIG HOUSE

They have such a nice life, why ruin it?"

I understood what she was saying but once Mel got something into her head there wasn't much that would stop her. Roger was a tragedy of a person, only this sort of thing could happen to him, and he'd be facing fatherhood so late in life. The mumps ruining his reproduction was a dot on the landscape for the relentless unlucky situations Roger had endured. He'd broken his shoulder on a visit to the cobblers whilst he was staying with us once. I didn't know we still cobbled shoes, I just thought we threw them away once the heel was worn down and if we did still repair shoes then surely we had updated the name. But anyway, he'd called Mel from the Manchester Royal Infirmary, screaming in agony just as they were taking him down for surgery. The highly amused paramedics had explained to Mel that Roger had unexpectedly been caught up the Manchester Pride parade. He had turned a corner and ended up right in the middle of a gang of over-excited drag queens on roller boots, they collectively lifted him above their heads and carried him for a quarter of a mile until they threw him onto the pavement as he was struggling quite a bit. They apparently had said that he was 'no fun at all' and a 'boring bastard'.

He had a long pink eyelash stuck to his cheek when he came around from the anaesthetic, a memento from Manchester Pride. The boots, by the way, never got cobbled.

THE BARN DOOR

As the holiday drew to a close, I noticed everybody being that little bit more helpful, enjoying their surroundings and soaking up the benefits of being in a different place. The last few days of a holiday are when you actually appreciate being away.

My mum and dad were retired so every day was like a holiday for them; however, they still made the most of the final few days by acting like newlyweds. Calling each other 'honey' and 'sweetie' and at one point I caught them actually snogging, clearly feeling smitten with the upcoming anniversary. There is no noise worse than the sound of your parents' tongues meeting up for a dance, unless of course they took it further. Tom and Babs, who again did fuck all worth talking about at home, suddenly mustered up the energy to take some trips out trying to squeeze the life out of the remainder of our wee break. Watching them trying to work out a bus timetable was amusing because neither of them could read it with it being so small, and then finally, once they had their magnifying glass, it turned out there were about eighty-three stops between our town and Fort William and the train was really the only sensible way to go. But they had their hearts stuck on a bus ride so as far as I was aware they rode round and round in circles on a bus eating cabbage sandwiches.

Dave and Sam fished for as many hours as the light allowed; they were catching and throwing back like pros whatever the weather. It would also seem that Suzy and Arif had broken the curse of the family cringe and had not only been to Edinburgh for a day out but they also continued to get along and were happy in each other's company.

What had become apparent is that I had spent most of the holiday, apart from the odd trip out, doing exactly what I did in Cheshire, if

THE BIG HOUSE

not more. I'd either been fretting over the various dramas I had in my life or cooking for large groups. I'd been working, I'd been parenting a bit and I had been actually doing more than I did at home.

So, when I did return home, I would look into booking a break for Dave and I. Probably Tenerife in a tacky hotel, flying easyJet so it didn't break the bank, and I would leave my food snobbery at home and eat shite whilst lying on my back with a burnt face. I would do aqua aerobics with a burger in my hand and, if that wasn't enough, I would wear a high-waisted tankini to cover up my bulging front bum. That, in my opinion, was a proper holiday!

Mel came to chat to me whilst I folded some sheets in the utility room. She shut the door behind her. It was Thursday morning, four days until the anniversary and there was a buzz building about the house. Mainly created by Mum who kept saying, 'only four more sleeps'. Mel and I hadn't had a chance to talk since she'd got back the previous evening because her and Roger had been out together for a drink and a chat.

"How did it go?" I asked my possibly pregnant sister.

"We'll see in a couple of weeks. Got to wait and do a test." I could tell she was excited, I knew she was trying not to show it.

"Are you feeling okay?"

"I feel good, I'm so glad to have started the journey, it just feels right."

"And Roger, how is he?" I remembered my downtrodden brother-in-law who trudged instead of walked thanks to Mel and her wanton womb. I hoped Roger was handling this okay.

"He'll be fine. He's mellowed slightly. He said you've been a great comfort," she said, sounding surprised.

"He said that?"

"Apparently, you're not so bad after all."

THE BIG HOUSE

I was a little bit chuffed to hear that, proof that I was a nice person sometimes. "Dad tells me you've organised some huge surprise for all of us for the anniversary. So do I get to know what the plan is?" I asked, hoping it was an open-top bus ride, which I knew Mum would not like.

"No, you can't keep your mouth shut, Raquel. I don't want you leaking it out when you've had a few."

I laughed, "I am the soul of discretion, I have more secrets than Prince Andrew."

"Okay. Promise, you'll make sure you keep it quiet?"

"Yes, for fuck's sake, go on."

"I've booked a special lunch up at Cameron House for everyone, do you know it?"

Oh, I knew it – who didn't? Cameron House was a beautiful stately house on the shores of Loch Lomond, the setting looked breath-taking and I imagined the food would be too.

"Oh, is that all?" I said with some childish envy, annoyed I hadn't thought of that.

"No, that's not all," she said, and I tried my best to not look rattled. "They do private flights by seaplane to the Isle of Jura from the shores next to Cameron House. So, after lunch Mum and Dad will go off on a flight together and return in the evening."

God damn my sister and her bottomless bank account. Even if I'd been that thoughtful I never could have afforded it.

"Just brilliant, Mel, well done." I smiled, barely hiding my fury. "When did you have time to arrange all this?" I asked, wondering why she couldn't have included me so I could have claimed credit.

"The week we arrived, why?"

"Oh nothing, just surprised you managed to bag a table in peak season for so many of us."

THE BIG HOUSE

"I have my connections," she said smugly.

"And it's a Monday so they managed to pull it all together in time. Anyway, what have you got them?" she asked with a smile that I could have slapped away.

"A voucher… for a spa… in Birmingham," I said glumly.

"Right, well, how thoughtful, well done." She walked away chuckling to herself, knowing she'd truly one-upped me. Good gracious we were immature at times.

Later, I googled the Isle of Jura as I really had no idea where or what that was. I pretended to when Mel asked me because I couldn't be bothered listening to her explain it all to me like I was five years old. It was an island in the Hebrides that was gorgeous, with breathtaking views, one hotel and a couple of distilleries. This was a perfect gift for Mum and Dad and a fabulous way to end the trip. I just wished I had been the one to think of it. To be honest, though, I couldn't have afforded it, not with my new budgeting sheet and tight belt.

That evening, we had a dinner planned, with Morag and Robbie joining us, so I was cooking with Arif helping out.

"Do something special, Raquel, as a thank you for letting us use their home," my mother said, yet again losing touch with reality when we had paid to be here.

"A thank you? From me to them? You actually mean that don't you, Mum?"

"Yes, what of it?" she snorted.

"I really don't know where to start. There's no Wi-Fi, they keep turning up uninvited, their son stinks and the kitchen is shit. And let's also not forget that we paid them to be here. Is that enough or shall I go on?" I said cockily.

"Raquel, why do you insist on complaining about everything? She's my bestest friend and I won't see her for a long while. And remember,

THE BIG HOUSE

lady, this holiday was about you mending fences, so go mend some." The brass nerve of the woman!

"This holiday, Mother, has been about a little more than that! But, we will discuss it another time," I warned her. Then, I nodded very slowly whilst maintaining eye contact with her. According to TikTok, that's how you deal with a narcissist.

Frustratingly, Mum nodded back in exactly the same manner – it would seem she had learned this trick too. Nevertheless, she had orchestrated this entire trip around Morag and Robbie's need for cash and as a ruse to distract Miles. Mum pretty much used her family to help their cause on the quiet. And now, I was to say thank you, to them. She really was deluded.

Due to the fact I was starving and really fancied a big meal, I decided to stay in the holiday spirit and to cook some stuff. Hearing of Big Mike's jalfrezi got me thinking about Indian food, and Arif and I set to work on making two curries, one spicy and hot with strong punchy flavours and the other a creamy mild chicken korma with fluffy naan breads to soak up the sauce. We had quite a nice afternoon tasting and testing, burning endless poppadums until we go the oil to the right temperature. I started to wonder whether the right path for Arif was a cooking school, not a university where he would have to write constant essays in perfect English. A practical education doing something he was actually already good at was a much better idea. I planned to take this further with him when we got home and really felt that I was on to something that would help him build a good life for himself.

The girls set the table, Babs ran a hoover around and the family got ready for a night of Indian food in a Scottish castle. There were some grumbles from Mum and Tom over the choice of cuisine. Tom had never been a fan of anything super-hot and Mum would just

THE BIG HOUSE

prefer meat and two veg. But you can't please a dozen people every day for four weeks so the pair of them would have to suck it up or go to the chippy. Morag and Robbie arrived around seven, they were both thrilled to hear the menu wasn't traditional and I think they were just glad to sit in a room where the bed didn't double up as the dining table.

Just as we were all tucking into the bhajis and samosas, the tikka and the dips, Dave's phone rang in his pocket. He looked at the screen and immediately got up from the table. "I'll need to take this, it's my boss."

I liked that, that he still called whoever that was 'his boss', that meant that he still thought of himself as a police officer and so did they if they were calling him at night. I nodded as he walked past me and towards the front door, he took the call outside on the driveway.

The rest of the family and our guests seemed to be enjoying the meal. Even Mum, who had positioned herself next to Morag, was dipping everything in, well, everything. The conversation flowed and it was turning out to be a really lovely dinner. My phone pinged, I glanced down to see it was Dave.

Come outside. I need to tell you something.

I frowned, this must have been serious for him to interrupt me mid-meal and be so covert. I immediately made my excuses and went straight out to see what it was.

"You're not going to believe what I've just been told."

"What, oh God, it's not your parents is it?"

He looked shocked. "No, that was my boss, Raquel. He felt I needed to know something."

I looked at him blankly waiting for him to tell me what was going on.

THE BIG HOUSE

"It's Matt Dennis."

"What about him?" I said trying to stay calm.

"He's escaped, Raquel, he's escaped from jail and he is on the run."

"I'm sorry what, what did you just say?" I gulped.

"He's out of prison, he broke out."

Dave put his hands behind his head and looked up to the sky. "This is insane, Raquel, you won't believe what they fucking did."

My legs started to shake as I processed what was happening. I'd only written to him a few days ago, he was going to behave.

"Who's 'they', Dave, there was more than one?"

"Yesterday, him and this other guy, Michael something, well they had jobs in the kitchen. They were responsible for doing a buffet for the governor's sixtieth birthday. All the staff attended, it was in the staffroom, you see."

I nodded; I was already aware of this.

"Okay, that's nice for the governor." I don't know why I said that, I was just terrified of what was coming next.

"No, it's not nice, Raquel! They drugged the fucking lot of them. Put some stuff in the food, and by 5 pm they were all out of it, I mean completely asleep on their desks, on the floor, everywhere."

I gasped. "Oh my God… but why would you eat food that an inmate had cooked? That's just an accident waiting to happen, right?"

Dave narrowed his eyes and said sharply, "Well they did eat it, Raquel! Apparently this Mike guy was a top chef and they trusted him. Somehow, they've managed to lace the entire buffet with some sort of sedatives and whilst they were all dribbling and snoring, Matt and this other guy managed to get out in a catering van using the fobs they took from the unconscious guards."

I thought for a while, pacing up and down the gravel trying to make sense of the situation. There had been no mention of this, nothing had

THE BIG HOUSE

led me to believe they were planning this. It must have been a last-minute decision from the stupid pair. At least I hadn't done anything which could implicate me in this, just sent a few letters when he was feeling lonely.

"They won't get far, surely, Dave. They'll be caught soon." He looked pensive, trying to work out what his next move should be.

"It took over six hours for the alarm to be raised because everyone was out cold, so they could be anywhere by now. That's why they called me, they wanted to give me advanced warning to keep my wits about me, warning me I could be a target." Dave scanned the bushes with his phone light.

"He's not coming for you or for me, he's not like that. He just wants Gina, you know that – we know him remember, he's not dangerous, he's a bit dim that's all."

"Maybe so but, Raquel, if he gets caught, he'll be in so much shit. He could end up telling them everything, about us and last year. You know what I'm saying?" Dave panicked.

So were we actually hoping for Matt to have got away? I think we were. Knowing that Gina was heading back to South America only a couple of days before led me to believe that he would go find her. I wasn't scared of Matt, he was pretty stupid but he wasn't evil, he just wanted out of jail, I started to wonder whether this was perhaps a positive thing.

"This isn't as bad as you think, Dave. Perhaps him being gone is actually the best thing for everyone."

"Ah, so you think a prisoner escaping is good for me, a police officer? You see this is why I'm leaving my job. This is all just very wrong." Dave heard a rustle in one of the bushes and jumped backwards clenching his fists.

"It's just a bird Dave, calm down."

THE BIG HOUSE

Dave took a few deep breaths to pull himself together and I continued to reason with him.

"All I'm saying is that he wasn't happy in jail, he was actually a liability in there, sending letters and meeting solicitors from what you told me."

Dave slowly nodded, he perhaps started to actually hear my point. "Fuck's sake, Raquel. I hope you're right; I can't take much more of this."

Dave bit his nails and the skin around his thumbs during the rest of the meal, slowly processing the situation. That was natural, I thought, completely normal to be a bit on edge that the guy you put away was now roaming the streets. But it wasn't any old criminal, it was a criminal who spelt my name 'Rackel', it was man who I was sure sucked a teething ring at night. He was no threat to us; his wife, on the other hand, was a little trickier, but she should be long gone. We finished the curry, played a few games and then watched telly. I know I should have been more worried than I was but quite honestly with him gone and R Liam having both his mam and his dad meant they had no business with me.

Friday morning was three days before Mum and Dad's anniversary. Although I hadn't organised a flight over the Highlands with a distillery visit or purchased a house in France, I had got them a lovely card and a voucher for a spa in the Midlands. A couple of facials and a day wearing dressing gowns was in my opinion what a couple of their seventies should be doing. It's all well and good sticking them on a plane over the glens, but with Mum's indigestion and Dad's vertigo it would all end in the tears of a pharmacist in a Scottish Boots. After that little trip, they would have that many new ailments to report that people would realise a spa just north of Birmingham was actually the sensible option.

THE BIG HOUSE

Dave hadn't slept much the previous night, and he was up and down at the window with every creak. "Did you hear that? Did you hear this?" I just ignored him mainly and snoozed through it. Eventually at five in the morning when the light came up, he settled down and fell into a deep sleep. I wasn't able to relax, so at six I got up and made my way out to the kitchen garden with a cup of tea and my book. There wouldn't be many more mornings with Sister Sledge, nor would I be able to inhale this delicious lake/heather combo.

I padded around the garden barefooted, pulling out weeds and hydrating the thirsty vegetables. I wasn't a keen gardener by any means, but I knew watering should be done out of the daytime sun, something about scorching. I checked for eggs and one of the chickens was in the middle of laying when I opened the cover to their box, I felt like an intruder, a pervert even, so I put the lid back down. Imagine if some nosy women had walked into my birthing suite as I was pushing, I would have gone blumin' mental. So I left her in peace and it would seem she accepted my deepest apologies.

Once everything in the garden was watered, I headed to greenhouse to give the sugar drops some attention – I had actually listened to Morag when she gave me a lecture on the needy tomatoes. Just as I connected the hose and got ready to drench the tommies, releasing that odour than encapsulates a British summer in one sniff, I noticed an envelope leaning up against the chillies.

If I had one of Roger's cigars, it would be now that I would light it; if I had one of Miles's orange-ends, again I would be puffing like a dragon. Perhaps this was the last letter before the escape, perhaps it was a thank you from Big Mike or maybe it was just creepy wee Miles returning my thirty-year-old knickers, realising that they had no value now that I was past it and had the big front bum. I took the letter and sank into a garden chair, pulling my glasses over my eyes and I began to read.

THE BIG HOUSE

Dear Raquel, I must thank you for all you did to get me out of the hell hole. It must have been difficult being married to you know who. Anyway, you did me proud you really did. The twenty buttons on R Liam's baby grow were a whole Temazepam each and the liquid in the teething ring was the strongest form of GHB known to man. A combination of that lot in your roly-poly absolutely finished them all off, it was brilliant to watch. One of the guards fell asleep whilst he was bollocking me. It's comedy gold, it really is. Anyway the guvnor had the biggest portion and he was nicely tucked up under his desk within the hour. Nighty night, ha ha ha. We couldn't help it but we did draw a couple of things on some of the guards' faces, it would have been rude not to.

So anyway, me and Mike are free to go wherever we want to, see whoever we want to and finally I get to go to the toilet without somebody watching. I mean it wasn't all planned but the minute the guv tasted your pudding we knew we wouldn't be able to hold him back. He's a right fatty, you know.

Only a few more things to sort out now before I can be on my way and I know you'll help us. Have a chat with The Mule, he will give you your next instructions and then I will be on the beach like you said I would be, just like Andy Dufresne. Great movie recommendation, babe, I really enjoyed it. Big Mike downloaded it to his phone and we watched it together, it gave us hope.

Speak soon, friend.

M XX

Holy fuck! This escape had me all over it: the drugs, the recipes, the frigging film I recommended all played a part in these two busting out of prison and putting the entire staff to sleep. The Mule, who was

THE BIG HOUSE

being described by many as my cousin and my ex (there are some dark incestuous undertones to that description) played a big part too. And now, I was to await further instruction? Like what? Which cocktail they should order and what strength sun cream they should use. Surely this was over, surely they had the brains to have left this country by now. I felt sick, stunned by what had happened, this was not something I had expected, not at all. And how the hell had Big Mike got a phone? This prison was more of a Center Parcs; I wondered if there was an ASK Italian on the top floor and a waterslide down to solitary.

And there was one other thing that niggled me, all of a sudden, he did actually know how to spell my name correctly. I had a look through the keyhole of the gate to see if there was any movement at Miles's cottage. It was just after six in the morning, but if he was up this would be the perfect time for me to speak to him without anybody, namely Dave, noticing.

Miles's front door was actually slightly open and I could smell fags, so he was already smoking, filth bag that he was. I screwed up the letter and put it in my dressing gown pocket and decided that I would have a face-to-face with him, as uncomfortable as it would be.

"I wondered how long it would take you," he said whilst stirring a pot of tea.

"You know you're all totally stupid, don't you?" I said angrily.

"You'll need to include yourself in that statement, darlin'. You've been just as involved as the rest of us."

"I had no idea they were planning on escaping, I just did it for my own reasons." Miles put the lid on the teapot and then put a cosy over it.

"Raquel, that guy went to jail and his wife went on holiday. You didn't think that he would be able to stomach that for long, did you?"

I felt a bit stupid at that point. "Well, actually, if I'm honest, yes I did."

THE BIG HOUSE

Miles shook his head, he pitied me and my naivety. "Come on, darlin', I spent enough time with Matt to know he's not built for jail. And Gina needs him now with the kid and everything."

I gasped. "You knew about the baby – how?"

"I make it my business to know stuff, I can't do what I do without knowledge."

I was livid, yet again I had stepped in the shit without looking where I was going. What's that old saying? 'Fool me once, shame on you, fool me twice blah blah blah'. We'd need a few more verses for me. The last one being, 'Fool me umpteen times and then have me sectioned.'

"It was you who sent those drugs into the prison and you let me go and pick them up and then pack them up with my own fucking seal."

He laughed. "Ah, yes, the special seal. Anyway, it's what I do, I move things from A to B. But let's face it, I'm on a curfew, I wear this." He pointed to his Salford anklet. "It's likely I'm being watched from time to time. I couldn't very well go and visit a woman on the run with her sidekick, could I, I needed you for that and you didn't disappoint." He laughed.

I fumed, what was wrong with me and how could I have let this happen? "So you knew Gina was there at the hotel all along with that tyrant Malik, you sent me there knowing it was them."

"Like I say, it's what I do."

"So now what? They've gone, right, away for good?"

Miles poured two mugs of tea and added an alarming amount of milk to both cups. "Not quite, there are just a few things to sort before that can happen."

"Like what?" I said in disbelief.

"Well, like they'll be needing a brew and probably some breakfast I would think."

THE BIG HOUSE

"Who would?"

"Our guests."

I shut my eyes and clenched my fists. "You haven't…"

He giggled a little. A man giggling, I mean really. "I have." He gestured towards the old barn, the one that had bits missing on the roof, the one whose door sat at an angle because its hinges had basically decayed. The barn, that in my opinion, was not a good hiding place for anybody and was the least secure building I had ever seen.

"Are you telling me…" I took a deep breath, "that you have some escaped convicts in that barn?"

"Aye, that's where they are for now, but they'll be on their way soon enough."

"Why the hell would they come here where my husband is… my police officer, drug squaddy husband?"

"Well because you're here, Raquel, and we know you'll help them. You have no choice if you want to keep yourself out of trouble, stop your husband from losing his job and you possibly taking their place in jail." He nodded slowly, I joined in, he was right on all fronts. "So, if you can just pop over with these teas, I'm sure they will both be glad to see you, they've not seen a woman wearing a nightie in a while. Well, not in the flesh, anyway."

Stunned, I picked up the two cups of milky tea and left the cottage to walk the few metres over to the old barn. It was very strange time to have noticed this but it was a glorious day, a day you would start cleaning down the barbecue and make potato salad. I wondered how many more days I would enjoy where I even saw the sky or got to think of such normal things; the way things were going, they seemed numbered.

The barn was freezing, and I didn't even need to open the door as the gap was big enough for me to walk through. It was two storeys but the top floor was open, the stairs leading to the top floor looked as if

THE BIG HOUSE

they would collapse if I blew on them. Old farm-type machinery took up one corner, a few empty wine boxes another corner and against the back wall there was a huge antique armoire that really should have been restored and placed in the main house. The place was silent, there was nobody in there, Miles the little bastard had been winding me up. I felt relieved – okay, I was the butt of a joke again but this time I was happy to be so. I turned to leave but as I did, I heard somebody cough. And then I heard somebody else say, "Ssshh." My heart sank.

"Miles, is that you?" somebody whispered. Somebody else again said, "Ssshhh."

"No, it's Raquel." I whispered.

The door to the armoire slowly opened and Matt Dennis sat awkwardly in the bottom of it, smirking.

If this had been a dream, I would have written it down and sold it as a movie. But it wasn't, it was my actual real life on a Friday morning before 7 am. Somebody on the top level crawled out of the shadows and a big head appeared over the edge. This head belonged to Big Mike, my cooking buddy and now stowaway. I put the cups down onto the floor and stood in the middle of the room, my heart doing backflips wondering what came next.

"It's so good to see you, babe." Matt crawled out of the wardrobe on all fours and dusted himself down. Prison had been kind to him, he was still great looking, a bit skinnier, but that really helped his jawline. He was wearing a prison guard's uniform but the trousers were too long.

Big Mike gently made his way down the wooden staircase, being careful to miss all the gaps. He too had a uniform on, but the trousers were far too short. I wanted to ask them why they didn't swap, that surely would have been the wise thing to do. But were these two wise men? I highly doubted it.

THE BIG HOUSE

"Pleased to meet you." Big Mike held out his massive hand, a bear's paw was more apt. It was hairy and it was huge, so was the rest of him. He was somewhere around six foot five with a full dark beard and a skinhead. "Pleased to meet you, Raquel, I heard lots about you." He had a West Country accent, perhaps Bristol.

I shook his hand, not wanting to be rude. "What are you… I mean why are you… what the hell are you doing here?"

They looked at each other. "We're here because we escaped, Raquel," Matt said in that stupid accent that I sort of loved and hated at the same time.

"I know that, but why here at this house, my holiday home, you know Dave is in there." I pointed to the house.

"We had no choice, really, the place we stayed at yesterday didn't feel safe."

"And where was that?" I asked crossly, like a teacher who'd found some louts in the toilet.

"The Hotel, in the town, do you know it?'

"Of course I know it. What, you just booked a room and checked in?" I found this incredibly brazen.

"No, we had a room already booked, we took Gina's room, but she left and we replaced her and Malik. Remember she gave you the key."

I stopped to think – the card, the damn cash card. "That was a key to the room?"

"Not just the room," Matt explained. "It got us into all the external doors, it's a master key they give to residents who've been out late at night."

"It saves them paying a night porter you see, Raquel," Big Mike added, seemingly having all the industry secrets.

"Well, why did you leave there to come to this?"

Big Mike chuckled a bit. "It was my fault, really, the menu got the better of me and I ended up ordering room service. I knew I shouldn't have but there was a triple club sandwich that I just couldn't stop thinking about."

"And, what happened?" I asked, wondering how a club could have been the reason I was in this mess.

"Well because the room had been paid for with cash, they wanted a credit card number for the extras and clearly we don't have access to that. We panicked, to be honest."

"And then what?"

"We did a runner down the fire escape and we came here."

"Too risky, just for the sake of a sandwich, don't you think, babe?"

Matt shook his head at Mike. "Always thinking about this, aren't ya, Mike?" And he tapped his belly as if he were his wife.

"I'm sorry guys, I just cannot believe you're here, of all the stupid…"

Matt interrupted me. "We're really sorry, we didn't mean to ruin your holiday. Dave doesn't have to know we're here. We've got Miles sorting things out for us this time, he's very good."

I looked over at Mike, he was slurping the tea down and then he wiped his mouth with his sleeve.

"And why are you here? Why have you escaped?" Mike had a kind face and he had no qualms telling me.

"I was sick of it, being stuck in there day in day out."

"Well that's prison, that's the point, right?"

"Eh, she's sharp this one," he said to Matt and laughed, a big booming laugh that would wake up Aberdeen if he wasn't careful.

"What did you do anyway?" I asked him, praying and hoping it didn't involve kids or animals.

"Bank job, back in '15. The Halifax, Maida Vale," he said proudly.

I heaved a sigh of relief. But then I suddenly wondered. "Did you kill anyone? Was anybody hurt?"

THE BIG HOUSE

He shook his head. "Never got the chance, I got tasered after the shutters went down – there was a copper in the queue behind me. I didn't even have time to get my gun out."

"Right, so a rubbish bank robber and a drug-dealing trafficker, what lovely friends I have."

"Told you she was funny," Matt said and elbowed Big Mike in the arm.

"So what are you planning on doing, what is the big plan now you've escaped?" I said, realising I'd have no choice but to help them get away to save myself.

"We'll sit tight until Miles finds us a way to get us out of the country," Matt said, as if it were that simple.

I rolled my eyes. "Miles has to be in bed by nine, so you'll have to do it in broad daylight. This plan seems shit."

"We could take your car," Big Mike piped up, suggesting he just take my 4x4 and drive it across the sea.

"Don't be ridiculous, that will connect you to me and you do know there is water between here and other places? We're an island, you know. And where's Gina? Didn't she wait for you?"

Matt shook his head. "No, we can't get caught together – R Liam needs at least one parent."

"And she's gone, back to her hiding place?"

He nodded and then shifted nervously before asking me for yet another favour.

"Look, Raquel, if it's not too much to ask, could you bring us some food, please? We're starving. We'll work out a way to get away from here soon but in the meantime if you could just do us a picnic or something." Matt asked this with a completely straight face.

"Ooh yeah, let's have a picnic." Big Mike's face lit up as mine got darker.

THE BIG HOUSE

"You're not starving, you've only been gone twenty-four hours and you had access to a hot buffet yesterday." Matt looked disappointed.

"What do you mean by picnic anyway?" I asked wanting to know what an ideal menu was for 'men on the run'.

Big Mike then reeled off all the things he had been fantasising about for the last seven years. "A gazpacho, a red pepper one with some basil and fresh garlic served with a crouton, perhaps a little burrata. And then something fishy, a tiger prawn salad, maybe with some gravlax and a lemon mayonnaise. Ooh and a Scotch egg but the yolk has got to be runny so you'll need to get your timings right. Matt, what do you fancy?"

"Erm, I'll take a beef Wellington if it's all the same to you, Raquel."

After getting over the downright cheek of their request, I hissed into their faces. "I will get some sandwiches and a packet of crisps, that's it! I have to go. Do not make a fucking sound."

I took the cups and left the barn with my head wedged firmly up my arse.

OPERATION CAMBODIA

When I headed back into the house, everyone was gathered around a television set that was so old it would have fetched a good price on *Antiques Roadshow*. It was turned up to its absolute max volume and Mum shouted out, "Be quiet everyone! It's on!"

And so it began, a special Friday lunchtime news report about two escaped convicts who were on the run after drugging the prison staff and making off in a catering van. Dave looked out of the library window and listened as opposed to watching it – he had been very quiet since the phone call last night.

"Ooh, look, Tom, we've met him, remember?" Mum was so excited to actually know the man in the mugshot.

Tom glanced at me. "How could I ever forget, eh."

Barbara and Arif held hands whilst watching the programme, terrified that they could be shoved into the back of a lorry and tortured for info.

The news reporter, a woman in a pencil skirt, stood outside the high security facility in Liverpool looking very sombre, and then she said: "It is thought that a jam roly-poly was the culprit in this very strange and serious escape. Two men who were trusted in the kitchen to make a special dessert for the governor's birthday party took it upon themselves to lace it with sedative and render anybody who ate it unconscious for a number of hours." *(Dramatic pause.)* "And then, whilst the guards were incapacitated, the men made their escape." *(A pause even more dramatic than the last one.)*

The camera then panned to a guard who had just been released from hospital after being checked over and was prepared to be interviewed. He was wearing what was classed as civilian clothes because his uniform was worryingly removed whilst he slept.

"I don't know what they did to me whilst I was out, it could have been anything." He was visibly uneasy.

The pencil-skirt wearer appeared to smile slightly. "Well, what we do know is that they're very handy with a Sharpie." The man nodded and then he turned his head to one side.

"Look at this, it's sick is what it is." He pointed to an image of a large penis with some sort of liquid spraying out of its bulbous end. He then turned his face the other way to reveal a large pair of breasts drawn on the other cheek. He then got animated: "They even drew a swastika on the governor's forehead," which drew a gasp from the reporter before he added, "and his next-door neighbour's Jewish, can you imagine?"

The reporter shook her head but I still didn't get the feeling she was taking this seriously. "I suppose this was their idea of a joke, was it?" she asked whilst desperately trying not to laugh.

The guard started to get pissed off: "Eh, it's no joke, I'm getting married next Saturday and this won't come off, not even with nail polish remover." He folded his arms in a huffy way.

She regained her professionalism. "And what can you remember about the attack?"

The guard rubbed his forehead. "Only that we all had a good big slice of the dessert and then as we started singing *Happy Birthday* the governor slithered off his chair and under his desk. We all thought he was drunk but then the rest of us started dropping like flies and we realised something was up but we couldn't do anything."

The reporter nodded sympathetically. "Gosh, that is really scary stuff. What can you tell us about the men involved?"

The guard shrugged. "To be fair they weren't bad lads, they seemed to get on with it mostly. Nobody could have imagined they were planning this – we just weren't expecting it."

THE BIG HOUSE

She raised her eyebrows. "Evidently," she said, quite sarcastically. "So what does this tell us about the security in this establishment? That two hardened criminals were able to provide the food for a party held during working hours, they put you all to sleep and then they waltz straight back into the community?" she said, her tone more serious and pointing the finger of blame at this poor guy. He looked behind him at somebody off camera, pulled his microphone off and stormed off towards the car park.

Mum jumped in the air. "How exciting being on the run, I wonder where they'll go."

Tom said, "My money's on Cambodia, it's cheap and they even let the likes of Gary Glitter in, so a couple of likely lads shouldn't be a problem."

Dad looked over at me. "Are you okay, love, you're not worried, are you?"

Out of earshot of the kids, as they knew very little about last year's mishap apart from the fact that their dad had locked up one of the neighbours, I told him I was okay and that everything was fine.

I went over to Arif and Barbara. "Look, it's all good, nothing for us to worry about. Enjoy the rest of the holiday and stay calm."

Matt's face was on every channel, they called him a 'gang leader', a 'drug lord' and a 'crazed lunatic'. They called Big Mike, 'Mike The bullet O'Hara'. I wanted to tell my family that Mike never actually fired a bullet and Matt was not a lord, or a leader of fucking anything, but I couldn't. The public were being whipped up into a frenzy, being told to lock all their doors and windows and not to approach the two maniacs if they spotted them. There was also talk of recalling all jam roly-polys from the supermarket shelves in case this was a mass attack. With all this going on, I just sat sipping a cup of tea waiting for the right moment to make 'The Bullet' and 'The Lord' a picnic lunch.

THE BIG HOUSE

Once the excitement had calmed down and people had stopped obsessing over the news, I made a decision, on account of the weather and because we had visitors in the barn, that we would have lunch down by the lake away from the house. I stood in the kitchen making egg mayonnaise whilst jumping every time anyone went near the back door. I started to stress about the practicalities of living in a barn. Where would they go to the toilet? How would they brush their teeth? They couldn't cross the courtyard to Miles's place, that would be far too dangerous.

"I'm going to feed the chickens," Sam said.

I snapped, "No, it's already done, stop overfeeding them. In fact, stay away from them."

He shrugged and walked away.

"Shall I go and get some radishes from the garden for the salad?" Roger offered, attempting to get out of the back door, which I had locked and safely pocketed the key.

"Stop interfering, this is my picnic, Roger. Go read a book."

He raised his eyebrows. "Blimey, where is nice Raquel? Please tell her to come back."

"I'm sorry – sorry, Roger. Time of the month," I pretended.

He patted my arm sympathetically, no doubt he'd experienced crippling PMT at some point. "Shall I make you a nice G&T? That should calm you down."

I looked at the clock, it was midday, which counted as G&T time on holiday. "Thank you, Roger, that would be much appreciated."

"I'll get some cucumber from the garden, shall I?" And again, he headed for that god damn door.

"No, no cucumber, just the drink with nothing in it." I was snappy again, verging on aggressive, this was a very serious case of PMT so Roger decided he would double up on the gin and completely negate the garnish.

THE BIG HOUSE

I couldn't very well go on like this and there was no real reason for anyone to go through that gate. Beyond the gate there was Miles's cottage, the orchard and the old barn, nothing else. I needed to calm down, if they wanted to go into the kitchen garden I had to let them. However, to be on the safe side, I plugged in a CD player that I found in a cupboard and stuck Andrea Bocelli on full blast just to drown out any suspicious noises that could draw attention. One cough or one booming laugh could have Dave charging down there with his taser.

When I'd calmed myself with two gins and prepared a very large picnic, I sent every member of the household down to the lake carrying all the plates. I gave everybody a job, be it putting up umbrellas or setting up blankets and once they were all out of the way and completing their tasks, I took a bag for life busting at the seams with food and legged it to the barn.

"You're a fucking star, girl," Matt said as I handed him the bag. "What we got?"

"Egg mayo on brown, ham and mustard on white, pork pies, sausage rolls, two apples, two bananas, a family bag of Wotsits, two cans of Carlsberg, a bottle of water each, oh, and some chewing gum. I figured you wouldn't have toothbrushes or paste."

Both he and Mike were delighted. "And there's some sandwich bags in case either of you need a number two, you can knot the top to stop the smell." I almost gagged saying that.

"She's thought of everything." Mike put his arm around me and I let him, it was an incredible effort from me, really. And then he said to Matt, "We've got beer, fucking cold beer, mate." So they sat on the floor of the cold, dark barn and started to unpack their lunch. As I walked away, Matt called after me, "What's on the menu tonight, Raquel?"

I ignored him, which is the only correct response to an escaped criminal asking for a dinner menu. That food should have kept them

THE BIG HOUSE

going for at least a couple of days so they would be full and would stay in the barn and be silent.

This was a secret that I was hoping would never have to be told. The men would somehow get out of the barn, across the ocean and never be seen again. The police would see this as a waste of money and forget about following them. Gary Glitter managed to go undetected for years and compared to these two he was the Devil himself.

Once I had fed the crims and my family, I made a big decision, one I could live to regret, but the risk was necessary. When your mum and dad are in the winter of their life, your sister is possibly in the very early and fragile stages of a pregnancy and your husband is already exasperated having you as a wife, who do you turn to in your hour of need? Not the guy who grassed you up the last time, not the man who you had only started to get along with very recently, that would be madness, right? But that's what I did, I turned to Roger for help.

We took a walk into town together and it felt good to be away from the house for a bit. Roger had been allocated the task of dog-walking as Mel wanted to rest, so I joined him, telling people I needed the exercise. Initially we walked in silence, enjoying the day, the greenery and the fresh air.

"Can I just say something to you, Raquel?" Roger said softly as we walked along.

"Yes, of course."

"Well, I've not had the chance to thank you actually for being there for me through a wretched time." I wanted to laugh out loud at the word wretched, I hadn't heard that since my granny was alive.

"You're welcome, I really hope things work out for you and Mel."

"You know what, I really believe you when you say that, Raquel, I don't detect any nastiness at all."

"That's because there isn't any, I am being genuine."

THE BIG HOUSE

"I wouldn't have come to Scotland you know, had you not sent me that message, and I truly believe Mel and I would have grown apart." He was possibly right; Mel had arrived on this trip with a strong mindset to go it alone.

"You think there's hope for you both, then, even if she has a baby?" I asked.

"I think what's meant to will be but we'll never know if this can work if we're apart, will we?"

"That's a good way to look at it, Roger, and just for the record, I think you'd make a very good father, actually, I think you'd be a great role model for Bernadette."

He smiled, recalling our silly game. "Stop, you're making me blush so you are."

But I continued with my charm offensive; "It doesn't matter how old you are or whether you share the same blood as this child, Roger. Any man can be a father, but it takes a real man to be a dad. Jeremy Kyle said that."

"Who the heck is Jeremy Kyle?" he wondered.

"Don't worry about it, someone I used to spend my mornings with." He frowned, how on earth did somebody miss the entire television career of Jeremy Kyle?

"She's not perfect, you know, Raquel, she's high maintenance, your sister."

I laughed. "You don't have to tell me, she'll end up exactly like my mum."

Roger's eyes widened. "Mother Mary of God, do you really think so?"

"A milder version, but they're similar in many ways," I said trying to play it down.

"Anyhow Raquel, I wanted to say that you've been a real friend to

THE BIG HOUSE

me, a rock actually. I just hope that we continue along this path after the holiday."

"I can't see why not, we've had a breakthrough, an awakening, don't you agree?" He nodded although I got the feeling he expected me to crack a joke at any time, but this was not a time for jokes, this was a time to get serious. We continued to walk, both quite happy that the hatchet had been buried, years of feuding had come to an end, Roger and I had eventually become allies; the common goal was to save our marriages.

I picked my moment as we hit a quiet patch on the gravel path. "Can I trust you, Roger, I mean really trust you?"

He stopped. "Now what's this about, Raquel, you've got me all nervous now."

"Answer the question, I need to know I can trust you before I tell you."

He thought for a while. It was unusual that somebody would take this long to respond. He really had to think about it.

"Yes, I suppose you can trust me but I'll warn you there are certain things I cannot stomach."

"Like what?"

"Well I suppose if you'd killed someone on purpose and you wanted me to keep quiet."

"Okay, anything else?"

"Erm, if you were planning a terrorist attack on, say, a government building."

"It's none of the above Roger."

"Oh, if you were to abduct a child and I knew about it, I would have to say something in that case."

"I've not done that either."

He shrugged. "Okay, well, in that case, you can probably trust me."

THE BIG HOUSE

That was a close as I was getting to a yes, so I began. "Now try and stay calm, this a lot to take in but I think you know I am a good person. I hope you know that I have got your back, I've been kind with all this baby business, haven't I?" He nodded. So, I told him everything as we continued towards the town, dumping my latest dirty secrets onto his tweed covered shoulder pads.

The first thing he said was this: "I think I'm going to be sick; this is pure madness." He'd leaned against a tree and went a little green.

"I know I know, this is completely fucking bonkers. But, think about it, once they are gone, it's over, I mean really over."

Roger dropped his chin to his chest and shut his eyes. "Raquel Fitzpatrick, what on earth have you done this time woman?" I pleaded my corner.

"Roger, how could I have predicted that some family friend would end up in a cell with Matt? That's how this whole thing got started up again, it was a huge shock to me."

He shook his head. "Perhaps it was fate, perhaps karma came to bite you on your arse," he added unhelpfully.

"Yeah, maybe, but I have to deal with the here and now. I have to get them away from here and I have to make sure it's permanent this time."

He gasped, slithering a few inches down the trunk. "You don't mean… kill them? You'll go to hell so you will, you devilish woman."

I laughed my head off. "No, no, of course not. Just permanently out of the country, away from me, from us basically."

He massaged his temples in relief before saying, "And David, what on God's green earth will he have to say about all this because I can't imagine he'll be very happy. Convicts in the barn, sending recipes to a prison, you sleeping with your cousin."

I ignored the last bit, I would have to accept that is what people

THE BIG HOUSE

thought he was. I helped him up from his brace position and linked his arm offering him support as we continued to walk.

"Ah, well, that's where you come in. You have to take Dave away from the house overnight, let me see what I can do without him here."

"What, me and David?" Roger frowned. "Where on earth would we go, me and David, alone?"

"It doesn't have to be just you and Dave; you see I have a plan."

Roger and I sat in a café, and I told him what his movements must be for the weekend. I told him that if he fucked this up, we'd all likely go to prison and he'd be bummed every night, haemorrhoids or not. He flinched at the thought and that's when I knew that Roger was going to be my unlikely ally and play a crucial part in 'Operation Cambodia'.

WOULD YOU RATHER...

"A stag night? We've been married fifty years, I think it's a bit late for that," Dad said when Roger told him about the 'surprise' he'd been planning for weeks.

"Yes, Phillip, all the boys are going up to Gleneagles tomorrow morning, staying overnight for a real knees-up."

Dave's ears pricked up. "Gleneagles, seriously?"

Roger nodded. "Yes, David, let's give Phillip a proper send-off."

"Who is actually going on this impromptu trip? First I've heard of this." Mel was surprised that Roger had kept this from her. He couldn't hold water normally.

"Not impromptu, it's a surprise, there's a difference. It's not just you that can arrange surprises, Melanie, I wanted to do something special for my father-in-law." He was milking it for all it was worth, overlooking the fact that I had paid for the three rooms on my very tired Amex card to avoid falling foul of Dave's budgeting.

"Just the boys, Phillip and Robbie, Dave, Sam, Tom and Arif if he'd like to." Arif nodded excitedly.

"Thanks Roger, that's a really lovely gesture." Dad was chuffed to bits – he could get a break from Mum and was made to feel a bit special.

"No strippers, hookers or eyebrow shaving," Mum called out as she went upstairs to help Dad pack a case.

"Erm, Gleneagles, Roger, when was this decided?" Mel asked again, not letting it drop.

"Last week when you were in London. I thought, why not, it's about time I had some fun."

"Have you ever held a golf club in your life, do you even know what way round it goes?" she asked quite rudely.

THE BIG HOUSE

I stepped in to help him out. "Oh, come on, Mel, it's a nice thing he's doing. Dad will love it."

She went back to her book on hormones but wasn't at all convinced. This was so out-of-character for Roger, doing things on a whim, heading to a facility where he could be struck by lightning on the ninth hole.

Dave was a bit apprehensive. "I'm not sure I should be going anywhere with Matt on the loose, perhaps I should come back tonight so you're not on your own."

"Don't be ridiculous, you need this to take your mind off things. It's half an hour up the road, if anything happens, I promise to call you. Please go relax and make sure my dad has a great time. I think you both need this," I persuaded him.

"I think I'll call work and see if there's any word on their whereabouts, they may have been caught already." He went off upstairs to make the call and probably to scan the gardens from an elevated position.

"And, am I having a girls' night?" Mum asked, feeling envious of Dad. Mel and I looked at one another, we hadn't planned a bleeding thing.

But, so she didn't feel left out, Mel came to the rescue and said, "Yes, of course, we're going into Edinburgh in the morning to get our nails done and then we'll have lunch, all the girls."

Mum beamed. "Phew. I thought we would be doing chores whilst they lived it up."

"I'm not going to make it, Mum, I have a huge piece to write up but the girls are up for it, aren't you girls?" Suzy and Michaela were both less than enthusiastic, but I gave them the look. And when that didn't work, I gave them my debit card. They didn't need to know it didn't work anymore.

"Any luck?" I asked Dave when he returned.

THE BIG HOUSE

"No, nothing. The boss said they'll be gone by now and it looks like they'd been plotting it for a while. They will have had plans in place and help on the outside."

Unwitting help, I thought to myself. "Well, let's just enjoy the rest of the week. Knock a few balls around, let your hair down." He would normally have laughed at that, being bald, but not this time. We all went to bed early that night but I barely slept. There was a lot that could still go wrong with Operation Cambodia.

The following morning, the boys left first. Morag and Robbie turned up in the butcher's van as their car had apparently taken its last breath. Morag was in high spirits and had brought a bottle of champagne for the hens to drink before they left. This was dragging on and I urged them to down their drinks quickly and get gone.

"Make sure he has plenty to drink, I don't want him driving back here tonight," I whispered to Roger, gesturing at Dave before they finally set off.

Roger agreed. "You promise you'll be rid of them by the time we get back, Raquel. I can't believe I'm doing this to be honest."

I gave him a push out of the door and whispered to him, "I am doing this for the family and so are you. Now go!"

The ladies were going to get a taxi and then a train, that way nobody had to drive and they would be out for longer.

"What about her?" Mum asked, looking over to Babs who was already a little lost without Tom and was keeping herself busy polishing the dining table. "Is she staying here with you?"

My heart suddenly skipped a beat. "No, no way, you have to take her with you. You can't leave her out, Mum, that's cruel to exclude her," I said, knowing this would make her feel bad.

"Look at her nails, though, there's not much to work with." Babs's nails were indeed very stubby but that would not hinder my plans.

THE BIG HOUSE

I passed Barbara her coat and beckoned her down from the table. "She can have acrylics, it's fine, please take her, I'll pay."

Mum smiled. "You just want the house to yourself, don't you? A bit of peace and quiet at last."

"You got me, ha ha," I shrugged but it worked.

At long last, the house was empty. I took a moment to gather my thoughts, to process just what I had ahead of me, the stupid risks I found myself taking again. But unless I put my neck on the line the alternative was more frightening. This situation reminded me of the questions Sam used to ask me on the way to school.

"Would you rather be eaten by a lion or a tiger? Would you rather sink in a boat or crash in a plane?" The best one was, "Who would you rather snog, Grandad or Uncle Tom?" Each question in the game of 'Would you Rather' had to be answered or you would have to face both. It was very silly but it passed the time on the school runs.

Right now, my 'Would you Rather' question was this: Help some criminals leave the country or go to jail and ruin everybody's life?

I knew what had to be done.

I got dressed all in black, which felt appropriate, and then I went to visit the inmates. I could hear hushed voices as I got closer to the barn and was disappointed to see that Miles was there having coffee with them like it was some sort of rustic Starbucks.

"Morning, or is it afternoon?" Miles muttered looking at his watch. I hated people who said that. Who gives a shit? What a waste of words said by certain people around the midday mark. These were the same people who if they didn't have their watch on, they would use the phrase, 'Freckle o'clock'.

"Have you brought us any grub?" cheeky Big Mike asked me.

"No! I'm here to find out what the plan is. I've managed to get everybody out of the way for the day so you two need to leave soon.

THE BIG HOUSE

You can't hang around here," I said firmly.

Miles lit a cigarette; he bit his nails pacing around the barn. This did not look like a man with a plan – typical, shit at absolutely everything.

"I thought you were 'The Mule', I thought you could move things. Move these two, will you," I told him.

Miles took a big drag. "Yeah, I have plan it's just that there's been a development."

"What development?" I wanted to know, although maybe it was better if I didn't.

The three looked nervously at one another. Matt tried to explain.

"Thing is, Raquel, we dumped the catering van in Carlisle before we came here."

"And…" I asked confused as to why that was relevant.

"And we just got word that they've found it. So they will know we've headed north and Carlisle is on the way to Scotland."

"Where did you dump it?"

Matt sighed. "Asda car park, Carlisle."

"Oh that well-known hiding place that is a supermarket car park. Well done, lads," I snapped furious at their stupidity. They nodded like schoolboys knowing that was a very silly thing to do.

Miles continued: "So there will be CCTV of the lads getting into the second vehicle and that went as far as Edinburgh."

"And after that?" I asked.

"Well, we should have gone under the radar after that because we kept off the main roads and hid in a trailer."

"But they know you've got as far as Edinburgh?" I said in disbelief.

"Yes, and knowing the filth, they'll start to put two and two together and start thinking about my ex-cellmate and whether he has helped in any way, maybe offering a safe house," Matt realised.

"Aye, that's about the size of it," Miles nodded.

THE BIG HOUSE

"So, what are you actually saying, they may suspect you're here with him?"

Mike explained whilst looking out of the barn door to the sky, presumable checking for helicopters. "It means they are closing in and it means we are pushed for time – they will be thinking about any Scottish connections that we have."

"You two are the shittest criminals I have ever met. Who goes to Asda when they're on the run?" They both looked blankly at me.

Miles, who I think was the most intelligent of the three, said, "We've got a plan to get them out of the UK but they can't actually leave the country until Monday. Staying here is not an option, it's too dangerous. I know a place not far from here but we have to get them there."

I rolled my eyes. "Oh, it's we, is it? And then what, what will they do once they have reached this place?" I was losing faith in this so-called plan.

Miles tried to convince me he knew what he was doing. "It's safe for a good for forty-eight hours but they'll need a disguise. This is all over the news, we need them to blend in."

Matt looked at me with his ridiculously good eyes and then asked very nicely, "Can you please help us one more time, Raquel?"

I tore around upstairs in the house looking for things that could help. Big Mike was absolutely massive and I was struggling to find anything to fit him. Miles was on it too, so I got what I could, heated up some leftover curry and we met back at the barn within half an hour.

I had never watched a transformation more intriguing. Without a beard, Big Mike looked like Tom Kerridge, and once he'd shaved it all off, he said he felt chilly. I told him to belt up, armed robbers didn't feel the cold and if he were to survive the long trip he had ahead of him he

THE BIG HOUSE

would have to be a big boy. There wasn't much we could do with Matt's hair but we figured if we gave him a skinhead they would look like recruiters for the National Front, so we just swept his hair back with plenty of Uncle Tom's hair cream and then I set it with Mum's Elnett. I had also found the plastic moustache from my Christmas cracker so I secured that to Matt's top lip using Suzy's nail glue – there was no way that could fall off anywhere between here and his final destination.

Matt put on a pair of jeans that I had stolen from my dad's wardrobe – they were from M&S and they had stitched-up turn-ups and a built-in belt which made him look older. Unfortunately, the only person even close to Mike's stature was Morag so he ended up wearing a pair of her floral gardening trousers which had an elasticated waist and were slightly flared.

"They look absolutely fucking ridiculous," I said, standing back and looking them up and down.

"Ah but you've not seen the finishing touches," Miles replied, reaching into a plastic bag and pulling out two butcher's jackets and two hats.

"Ta-dah. Nicked them from ma dad's work van."

"Course you did," I said, raising my eyebrows.

They put on the outfits and laughed at one another. It was the best we were going to get.

"What now?" I asked, confused as to how this was going help get them out of an airport or ferry port.

Miles threw a set of keys at Big Mike. "Van's round the front, you know what to do and where to go, and if anyone asks, you're from Ferguson and Sons, right?"

They both nodded and after licking the bowls I had given them my curry in, they were set to leave. From a distance they looked completely plausible.

THE BIG HOUSE

"Goodbye, Raquel. Wish us luck," Matt said as he put his arm around me.

"For God's sake, go and don't come back, okay? Please let this be the end of it."

Big Mike went to hug me too; he really was a cuddly one for an armed robber. "Thanks for the recipes, I'll always think of you when I make them, and when I have my own restaurant, I'll name a dish after you."

"Please don't."

"Okay," he said.

And that was it, they pulled away at a respectable speed in the meat van and there was nothing suspicious about it. I really didn't think anybody would suspect them, they definitely blended. My heart rate slowed down a little bit after that, knowing I was going to have to put my faith in the fact they would be able to lay low until the opportunity arrived for them to get out before they were caught. Perhaps The Mule was quite the professional when it came to his job after all.

I left Miles to take control of the disposal of three sandwich bags with something inside that I'd rather not say to remove all traces of the visitors. "Don't worry about the van, once they get to where they need to be, I've got somebody bringing it back up here. My ma and pa will never know it went missing," he told me.

I preferred not to know the logistics, but they couldn't have been going far if the van would be back by the evening. I just had to trust he had this under control.

"We're done, you and I! And you're sure you have done enough to ensure they will get away?"

Miles smiled. "Fingers crossed, darlin'," which was not the guarantee I was looking for.

"Told you we make a great team didn't I. See you soon, I'm going for long soak."

THE BIG HOUSE

I headed back the main house where I would crack open a bottle of heavy red and drink it whilst staring moodily out of the window like they did in the movies.

MAGICAL MAGNESIUM

I spent the rest of the evening on my own, but I won't say it was relaxing exactly. Dave kept messaging and calling, each increasingly more frantic than the last. The first one was just a check-in to see if I was okay. There were a couple more containing pictures of Sam and Arif holding various golfing apparatus, I had to walk up to the lane to get them to download. Then, I had a call to say that my dad was still a total rascal and he'd winked at a buxom barmaid and ended up with a drink in his face. She wasn't buxom, she was heavily pregnant, apparently, and she didn't take kindly to old perverts, I laughed at that. And then at about nine-thirty I got a message that had eight exclamation marks at the end just to drive the point home.

THEY FOUND THE CATERING VAN IN FUCKING CARLISLE!!!!!!!!

I responded very calmly. *WHO CARES!*

Immediately a call came in from a drunken Dave. "I'm coming home, they're coming for us," he slurred.

I heard Roger in the background trying to manage him. "David, come away from the phone, it's your dad's stag do, so it is." I then heard noises of a struggle and Roger said, "Ouch, you beast."

"Shurrrrup, Roger. Matt's on his way, he's coming for us."

"Roger, put him on the phone, will you." Roger somehow pinned the phone to Dave's ear, whilst holding him up against a wall by the sounds of things, so I could try and talk some sense into him.

"No he isn't, Dave, I promise, everything will be okay... we're all completely safe."

He then became agitated. "Lock the fucking doors, the girls, shit, the girls."

THE BIG HOUSE

Eventually Roger wrestled the phone from Dave and said, "Jesus, Raquel, he's outta control. But one thing's for sure, he certainly cannot drive." He was whispering at this point so Dave must have been very close.

"Roger, it's good. Let's just say that Operation Cambodia is complete, I repeat, complete."

He whispered back, "Okay, I hear you, good work. Quite honestly this is like looking after a pack of monkeys. Your Uncle Tom is a disgrace, he used a paperclip as a toothpick at the table, and don't get me started on your dad. I never knew he could be quite so inappropriate." He then started to shout at somebody again. "Hey, put that down! Give me strength, put that down right now! I'll have to go, Raquel, Tom has just picked up a meringue from a lady's plate, help me Lord."

The phone went dead and I patiently waited for further updates. Eventually, I was finally able to relax when I received a photo of Dave asleep in a bed. Roger had very kindly tucked him in and sprayed him from head to foot with his magnesium. I received another message with a picture of the spray next to him.

That should be him now, Raquel. I used enough to put a bison to sleep.

I went to bed before the girls got back, but judging by the messages I'd had from the hen party a great time was had by all. Babs had ended up with longer nails than Missy Elliott, and although she couldn't pull her own knickers down, she could eat a sirloin steak without a knife or a fork. Mum had been made to feel special, my girls had both had a few glasses of champagne, so ended up being nice to each other, which was good news as it easily could have gone either way. Mel got all the credit and Morag made the most of not being treated like shit for once.

THE BIG HOUSE

I woke up the next morning with a feeling of being on the home straight. I hoped Matt and Big Mike had a good night, that they were warm and that the curry had kept them going during what must have been a stressful time but hopefully they were laying low and keeping quiet. I thought about Gina and the baby, wondering if she was waiting for news, whether she and Matt had been able to have a conversation at all, perhaps even a FaceTime with R Liam. I wanted everyone to come out of this well, with me at the top of the list, obviously. In a few more days I would be back in my own house, the washer would be whizzing around and the familiarity of my home would be like my very own teething ring. Instant relief from an uncomfortable and unpredictable month that had felt like giant molars ripping through my gums at times.

I had felt some levels of guilt towards Matt Dennis, not Gina, but him. When he went to jail to save his wife, although he had been a massive shit I admired the gesture. I have to admit, I had a soft spot for him and although the initial sexual attraction was just me and my pathetic ego needing a cuddle, a grope and a cheeky kiss, once I had realised this was temporary blip, I realised that he was a nice guy.

As for Big Mike, ah, Mike 'The Bullet O'Hara, well, in another life we would have been friends, colleagues even, sharing a passion for food, ideas on recipes and a mutual hatred for the Halifax.

* * * * *

Mum wore her sunglasses all morning as she'd clearly overdone it on the ale. When I pulled open the library curtains to let the light in, she sat bolt upright from the sofa and said, "Oi, what's your problem?" like some lad outside a nightclub who'd caught me eying up his bird.

THE BIG HOUSE

In response, I made a big pot of coffee and I left it on the dining table with a few rounds of white toasted bread smothered in Lurpak. This was my hangover Elastoplast.

Mel, who was completely fine on account of her possible pregnancy and having only drunk water, took me to one side. "Matt Dennis on the loose, what do you make of it?" she asked, looking to gauge how I was feeling.

I acted like I was completely indifferent, sighing, "Silly Matt, he always did make daft decisions."

"Yeah but escaping from prison with an armed robber – pretty serious, Raquel. They'll catch him, you know, he won't be able to get out of the country, no chance," she warned, and I immediately felt defensive.

"Well, they let enough people in so why can't he get out? Maybe they should concentrate on securing the incoming borders for once."

Mel gasped. "Raquel, considering the two house guests we have and what they have been through that is incredibly insensitive. Have you forgotten what they did, Matt and that wife of his?"

"Of course not, I just think that there are more pressing issues for the police than catching Matt and some half-wit bank robber."

She nodded. "Perhaps there are, but we have a system for a reason, you can't just drug people and walk out of a prison."

I controversially jumped to defence of the wrong side. "Well apparently you can," I said sarcastically. "I mean come on, Mel, inmates making lunch, governors having shindigs metres away from rapists and muggers, robbers and fraudsters. They almost deserved it – let this be a lesson to them."

Mel was disturbed by my attitude but I had to hold my nerve. Just in the nick of time before we got into an argument, the crunch of the gravel indicated the return of the stags.

THE BIG HOUSE

"Oh good, the boys are back!" Mum and Morag lifted their heads momentarily but it didn't last long.

The people carrier pulled up on the drive, and as the door opened Dave almost fell out, having been leaned up against the window for moral support. Roger was in good spirits; he never went too far with the booze so he bounced up the driveway whilst the others almost crawled. Being made to feel useful suited Roger, having a purpose and a friend, namely me, was something that perhaps he'd not had for a long while. He nodded as he passed me to greet Mel. He'd done good, I had to admit.

Roger and I had a brief chat in the library when we were sure we couldn't be heard. "Have you any idea where they've gone?" he asked nervously.

I shook my head. "Nope, and I don't want to know, I'm just glad that they are gone."

"Mel says they'll be caught before long, she reckons that it's extremely unlikely they'll get far," he warned me.

"Yes, well, Mel needs to stay in her own lane," I sneered and Roger smiled.

"Anyway, how are you feeling about the whole baby thing now? I'm sorry I haven't asked, I've just been caught up in the mess," I admitted, feeling like I should have checked in more on his emotions.

"I have to say that Julian has been a great comfort. He has given me a new attitude towards this situation, whatever the outcome."

"Wow, I had noticed you being a little less, well, stressed about the whole debacle."

Roger exhaled dramatically. "I'm not going to lie, if she has another man's child, it's going to hurt. It's not what I want and it won't be a conventional arrangement. But, if I stop her or persuade her to change her mind, she will resent me, possibly forever."

THE BIG HOUSE

I nodded; he had that one right. Imagine sitting and looking at your husband with scorn and sadness for the rest of your days, wondering what could have been? This is why people smother their spouses whilst they sleep, years and years of fury eventually triggering a pillow-over-the-face jobbie and a light sentence due to stress.

"I'd rather she loved me with child than hated me without one. And, as Julian said, if I don't like it then I have options. It's not just her that can make changes."

Well, well, well, a backbone was starting to develop within Roger, it was something that Mel would find attractive and would keep her on her toes too. I knew her well enough to know that she would like this new Roger, one that let things be and didn't incessantly complain. Julian the sly fox had actually got into someone's head at last. Not mine, obviously, as I had a skull as hard as platinum and not even Freud could infiltrate my good side.

"I'm planning to take up golfing when we get back to Dublin, I rather enjoyed the camaraderie at Gleneagles. There's a beautiful course and club at Portmarnock, it's quite exclusive so they'll be no riff-raff. Plus, I need to start enjoying myself at my age." Roger left the library with his new life all planned out and that didn't involve crying into his handkerchief every ten minutes. I hoped Mel wouldn't blame me that she was to become a golf widow/single mother, but knowing Mel she would probably employ a Kensington nanny and she'd just do the good bits.

I had hired a babysitter once who spent almost the entire summer holidays with us. She was patient, kind, loving, young, full of energy, blah-de-fucking-blah. Meanwhile, I was juggling, I mean really trying to hold it together with two young kids, one on the way, a job and a husband who was constantly on stake-outs. It was as though the universe had sent me an angel and she came each morning all

THE BIG HOUSE

refreshed from her good night's sleep in her parents' house and played with the kids, took them to the park and made jelly with them. All those nice things we do with our kids were done by her that summer. Whilst she did this, I did the shopping, housework, chores, gardening and my actual job. It seemed to be a good arrangement but one day on a Friday she'd said goodbye to my daughters telling them she'd be back on Monday.

There were tears, by God there were tears. The kids were howling, Suzy hid her car keys and Michaela even said, "Please don't leave us here with her." 'Her' was standing in a dressing gown at 5 pm with elephantiasis of the ankles. The poor girl had tickets to see Katy Perry that night and she was being held hostage in my house.

Eventually after finding the keys and releasing her, the girls sobbed at the window, almost choking on their tears as she drove away. I didn't have her back after that, I would rather be absolutely fucked than the girls prefer somebody else. My children were fickle, they would drop you like a hot potato if something better came along.

That evening, Dave and I and our three decided to go out together as a family. There was a lovely little pub in the town that did some good classic grub, there was a pool table, darts board that sort of thing. We thought it would be good to have some family time. Dave had recovered from his big night at Gleneagles and with there being no news on Matt and Mike, it looked to him as though Scotland wasn't their destination after all.

"They'd have been here by now if they were coming," he said. "And I've looked at reasons they went up towards Carlisle."

"So what you thinking?" I was interested in this, because perhaps whatever his theory was it could help me understand where they were now.

"Carlisle is close to the coast and there are so many ways to leave

THE BIG HOUSE

the mainland. You've got the Isle of Man, and it's easy to get a ferry over, and from there you've got Northern Ireland."

I liked this – it did seem like a good way to escape. Island hop and lay low until it's safe to go further, so hopefully they were well on their way.

"All the scousers have Irish relations, I bet he knows someone to help them out over there." Dave sipped his pint, clearly not keto any longer after the stress of the past few days.

"And another thing, that Big Mike's not so dangerous, he's a bank robber but the job went tits up. They are both just petty criminals who saw a chance and took it." He was right but I needed to see what the police would do about them once they were at their final resting place.

"But what about this mass hunt and them not stopping until they are brought to justice, that's what it said on the news?" I wanted to know.

Dave shook his head. "The crucial period has gone, Raquel, everybody knows they will be a long way away by now. We have to say that we're doing everything we can but once they're out of the country, realistically, it becomes somebody else's problem."

"Oh, right, so I guess it's sorted then, don't you think?" I urged him to agree.

Dave didn't say either way, he was not a man who would admit the bad guys winning was a good thing. "Look, Raquel, if they were deemed a serious danger to the public, they would throw everything at this but we're stretched as it is. The prison staff are all in big trouble and blame is almost certainly being laid at their door."

As Dave was talking, I could hear Julian's voice in my head, urging me that this was the moment to tell him the truth, but I couldn't, I needed to wait until they were definitely gone.

"Do you think you could reconsider you leaving the police?" I

THE BIG HOUSE

asked nervously, hoping this would be enough for Dave to stay in his beloved job.

"I'll have a think but I'm not sure." So, it wasn't a no, that meant there was still a chance.

He opened a packet of nuts and shook the entire contents into his mouth.

Suddenly Dave noticed somebody talking to Suzy. "Hey, isn't that one of Ferguson's sons from the butchers in town?" Over at the bar giggling and arm touching was my daughter Suzy and Angus Ferguson.

"Yes, that's Angus, he delivered the meat for my Christmas feature."

Dave grinned. "Ah yes, didn't you say he fancied you?"

I sighed. "Yes, it came across that way. Looks like it wasn't me he was after, he actually left his card hoping Suzy would call him."

"So it wasn't you he wanted?"

"No, it would seem not."

Dave burst into laughter. "Not the MILF you thought you were, then, eh." And he laughed some more.

Suzy continued to be openly flirtatious with Angus so Dave turned his chair around to face the other way, not wanting to see.

"She's turning into trouble that one," he said and I had to agree. She was brazen and she really didn't care. When she came back with our drinks, I told her to tone it down.

"Tone what down?" she asked, confused.

"Flirting with him, the butcher."

"What's up with flirting?"

"What about Arif, Suzy, he probably really likes you."

She shook her head and rolled her eyes. "Arif and I are just hooking up." Which was enough for Dave to drain his pint.

"Why are you flirting with him, if you hook up with someone else?" I probed, trying to get her to see the problem.

THE BIG HOUSE

"Because I want to, and if Arif wants to do the same then that's cool. It's not that deep, Mum, we're not a thing."

She then reached into my bag and put some of my lipstick on, rubbed her lips together and went back over to the bar to wind up the horny butcher a little bit more.

"This generation have no shame. At least we have the decency to hide our bad behaviour at that age. She wears the badge with pride," I seethed.

"At least she's honest about who she is – no surprises with our Suzy," Dave noted.

I had to hope that wasn't a dig at me, but even it hadn't been intentional it still had an impact. Perhaps the new open-and-honest policy all the kids seem to follow these days wasn't so bad. It does, however, explain why parents of my age all seemed to be saying stuff like, 'I would have had a good hiding'. Or, 'My mother would have killed me.' It's because these days, our kids tell us everything, and if they don't tell us, we break into their phones and find out for ourselves. 'Back in my day', another old-person saying I was now using, my mother knew the bare minimum of what I got up to because I hid most of it, for her own good, might I add.

SANTÉ

"Happy anniversary!" I shouted through my parents' bedroom door on Monday morning before I entered with the requested Buck's Fizz on a tray with my cards and gift. It was nine o'clock in the morning of their fiftieth wedding anniversary.

Mum had tears in her eyes when I went in, shaking her head and saying, "I just can't believe it," after Dad had told her about the new house. I handed them their glasses and they sat up in bed with the keys and the French property details in front of them.

"You're happy, then?" I asked her. She turned to Dad and said in her most hideous and over sexualised voice, "Oh, Monsieur, you have spoiled me in more ways than one this morning." Dad became embarrassed and took his glasses off to wipe them.

"I think we'll talk about it downstairs when you get up." I left the room immediately. "I think they've just had sex," I mouthed to Dave, who was waiting behind me to wish them well. He shuddered and retreated back to our room as well. Monsieur could spoil Madame all he wanted but not with us in earshot.

There was a buzz to the house that morning, as we were all having a trip out and the holiday was coming to a close. We all sat at the breakfast table and cheered when the happy couple arrived downstairs. Mum chatted excitedly to us all about the 'pied-à-terre', yes, that's what she called it.

"I for one cannot wait to just pack a bag and bugger off for months on end, it will be glorious. And we'll get a little car, a Citroën, something French, with a soft top. That way we can gallivant around with the sun on our faces," she said, showing Arif the wonderful fireplace that was completely open and the vine that grew across the back of the house.

THE BIG HOUSE

"We'll be able to make our own wine, you know, people do that."

Arif was impressed but he said to me, "You'd like that wouldn't you, Mrs." I gave him the look.

"Oh, and there's a boulangerie, a bistro and a market on Friday mornings. So we'll not need to go the big supermarkets, you know, we'll buy local." Mum nodded to me for my approval. She went on and on, how she'd be picnicking riverside, doing watercolours in the meadows and cooking rustic French casseroles in the autumn that would bubble away in the Lacanche.

"It's got a Lacanche, Melanie, you know what I mean, don't you?" Mel wasn't impressed, Mel didn't cook, so ovens were by the by. But I wanted a bloody Lacanche more than I wanted a breast lift. It sounded idyllic, picturesque and charming, and with Morag a fifteen-minute drive away, would Mum ever be at home?

"How often will you go there?" Suzy asked her grandmother.

"As much as possible, even the winters are lovely down there."

Dad agreed. "Yes, crisp and fresh in the mornings, warm in the afternoon."

I suddenly felt a feeling that I never expected to, something that I would never really have to face until the actual end of my mother's life. I would miss my mum, and knowing that she was just twenty minutes away with the potential to ruin any one of my days at the drop of a hat suddenly felt comforting. This French dream that was now a reality sounded much better than the north of England, with its dog-walking racists, neighbourhood Karens and the shitty little Tesco on every corner.

With Mum and Dad away for entire seasons, Mel living in Dublin and Dave's parents abroad, my family was suddenly diminishing. The only one left close by would be Tom. I looked over to him to seek comfort but he was reading the paper whilst picking his nose with a biro.

THE BIG HOUSE

* * * * *

As we cleared away the breakfast things, Mel said nervously, "I really hope they enjoy my surprise."

"Why wouldn't they?" I asked.

"Oh, you know what I'm like, I just like everything to be just so." She twiddled her diamond studs and smoothed her trousers.

"You could have asked me to help out, Mel, you've had a busy few weeks." I pointed at her stomach.

"And you've spent the summer cooking for everybody and had the kids to look after. This is supposed to be my thing, and anyway, I knew you'd only try to take the credit for it if I asked you to help."

I smiled; she was absolutely right.

Three cars set off in convoy making our way over to beautiful Loch Lomond. We all had made the effort that day with our outfits, and we looked like a very nice and respectable family celebrating a wonderful milestone. Dave had a new crisp white shirt for the occasion and a pair of jeans that actually fit him. I wasn't sure if this was weight loss or the new jeans, either way, he looked pretty good in them. Obviously, Mel looked annoyingly amazing and Roger, bless him, had a T-shirt and a jacket teamed with a pair of slim-legged trousers. I had never seen this modern look on him before.

"You scrub up well, Roger, very nice," I said to him as we got out of our cars at the hotel.

"Thank you, I went to Reiss in Edinburgh the other day. The lady was absolutely lovely and she put together a couple of outfits for me."

Mel raised her eyebrows. "Lovely, was she. Interesting." Roger winked at me – he was learning to walk on his own now.

Mum and Dad had been planning their outfits for months, the usual beige silk and satin combo for Mum, and Dad was in his silver

THE BIG HOUSE

suit, the one he always wore for special occasions. The house itself was impressive, it definitely pissed on the chips of The Eagle Lodge. The location was stunning, and when the sunlight hit the windows, it put a warm glow over the whole building. It was a 'wow' location.

I caught Mel checking her phone. "Everything okay, Mel? We're here now, it will be fine I'm sure."

As we approached the door, a very slick-looking maître d' met us on the steps of the hotel and greeted my parents by their names. He showed us into a plush lounge and a waitress promptly arrived with a tray of champagne flutes. Mel looked over to me and put her thumbs up, this was a great start.

We were shown into a bar with circular sofas all upholstered in tasteful tartan, a wonderful selection of rare whiskies were displayed in a cabinet across one wall, each bottle was lit tastefully to be admired. Dave and Sam met a man from Norway in the lounge who had been fishing that morning and they were discussing what could be caught in such a deep loch. The atmosphere was relaxed, there was much positivity and this was a seriously beautiful place to celebrate my parents' half-century as a relatively happy couple.

After a nice, civilised chat overlooking the water, we were then taken through to a beautiful dining room, where the table was decorated with Mum's favourite flowers as the centrepiece. Because it was a long table, they had placed cream roses in tiny white teapots in a line down the centre, which was a nice touch from Mel. There were personalised menus that had Mum and Dad's wedding date at the top and then the words 'Anniversary Luncheon' written across the centre in gold letters. Mum clearly liked the word 'luncheon' because she gasped and pointed to it when she first saw it.

"This is simply exquisite!" she said to Mel as she sat at the head of the table, revelling in being the centre of attention. Seeing that

THE BIG HOUSE

everything was going so smoothly, Mel the perfectionist relaxed. If we had asked Mum how she had wanted the day to go so far, this would have been the blueprint, this would have been Mum's dream day, so Mel had literally nailed it, even without the help of a PA. Although, I did have to remind the children and Old Tom to remember their manners even before the starters arrived. Unfortunately Sam felt the need to use a bread roll as a missile to fire at Suzy as she was reapplying her gloss and she retaliated by calling Sam a 'knob jockey' which made the waitress giggle but made Dave furious. "Have some fucking respect, you two, and grow up," he barked at them.

Old Tom also let the side down when he rudely revealed he'd always preferred Valerie, Dad's first girlfriend who apparently was a "right little goer and good laugh too". It turned out that Valerie was the local bike and Mum had no idea that she and Dad had dated. Mel stabbed Tom in the leg with her fork when he started that story and it took a good few goes before he realised that this was not the day for this sort of revelation.

The food, when it arrived, was to die for, I couldn't fault it, and the service was on point, Mel had picked an absolute winner here. It was a proper family event and although Arif wasn't really Barbara's nephew, it felt as though he was one of us, so this mish-mashed family enjoyed a very snazzy meal at the expense of my super-rich sister who would come out of this with many brownie points. I actually took pictures of all of my dishes, hoping to re-create them at some point. Cullen skink to start, a braised lamb shoulder for main and to finish, a banana soufflé served with a dark chocolate ice cream. Food tasted so much better when somebody else had cooked it and almost even better when the washing up was taken care of. I was tired – tired of cooking, tired of serving and although this was my parents' treat, I greatly appreciated eating beautiful food and having nothing

THE BIG HOUSE

to do with the preparation for once.

After the dessert plates were taken, we raised a glass to my parents, congratulating them. There were many years that I resigned myself to the fact that they would not be together once Mel and I were adults. I had planned two Christmases many a year, presuming that the lawyers would be instructed at any moment. My dad was a good guy, a great father and I am sure he was a wonderful friend, cousin and boss, but as a husband, he'd been a shit. In this day and age, he would have ended up handing over everything he had to Mum and then some. He would have been labelled as a sex addict and a disgrace so to see them happy and relaxed, planning a future together in their French gîte having worked through both of their flaws was actually so much more meaningful than if had been plain sailing.

Dad insisted on making a speech. It was a fairly standard thank-you speech, mentioning his daughters for putting up with him, his sons-in-law for taking his daughters off his hands, his grandchildren for making him smile every day, his cousin who was also a crabby bastard but had a good heart and finally his wife was also a crabby bastard with a good heart. We all laughed at that.

"Joking apart, this woman," he said looking at Mum, "this woman is many things, some good, some terrifying, but she has stuck by me and never once wavered. So I thank you, Suzannah, for the last fifty years and hopefully looking ahead to a few more." He picked up his glass and raised it. "Santé et merci beaucoup," he said. We all repeated it back to him. I later found out that apparently meant 'cheers'. There would be a lot more of this wanky French stuff coming my way.

During coffee, I went and sat next to Mum and Dad. "Are you enjoying yourselves?" I asked, knowing the answer.

Mum beamed. "Well this has been fantastic, in fact the whole trip has been spectacular."

THE BIG HOUSE

Dad agreed. "It's been great, Raquel, and this food, although it's super, it's not a patch on yours." He winked at me.

I appreciated Dad bullshitting to show his appreciation for the hours I had put in at The Eagle Lodge. This felt like a nice moment to privately celebrate the end of the holiday and closure from this summer's escapades.

"Do you want your present from me?" I suggested and Mum nodded excitedly. "I wanted to get you something to remember, an experience as opposed to an ornament." She looked deflated – Mum loved a bit of Wedgwood. I pulled the envelope out of my bag and handed it to her. Mum put her reading glasses on and read through the voucher.

"According to this, we're to go to the Midlands for a spa weekend, Phillip."

"Are we?" Dad frowned.

"When do we have to go?" Mum asked almost panicky.

"You can go anytime, well, within twelve months."

"Do they have Zumba?" she said, scanning the voucher.

"I don't know."

"Is there a golf course?" Dad asked, putting his glasses on and grabbing the voucher.

"I don't think so."

"When do we have to go?" he said, almost worried it was within the hour.

"You don't *have* to go, Dad, but you need to use it within twelve months," I said, getting exasperated with the conversation.

"Do they have any other branches that aren't in Birmingham?" Mum grabbed the voucher back and turned it over to see what it said on the back.

"Not sure, why?" I smiled through gritted teeth.

THE BIG HOUSE

"I wonder if they have a French branch."

"It's not a bank, Mum, it's a spa."

"Phillip. Give them a call and ask if they have a continental branch." Dad reached into his pocket for his mobile phone.

"Give it to me!" I snatched the voucher back and stuffed it into my handbag. Ungrateful beasts I thought to myself. "We'll sort it out tomorrow."

"Turn that frown upside down, Raquel, your face will stick like that if the wind changes," my mother warned.

"But it won't, Mother, will it? It's not actually scientifically possible for that to happen," I hissed at her before walking back to my seat.

"Thank you, by the way," Dad shouted after me. "Very thoughtful." And then they whispered to one another, shaking their heads. Dad mouthed 'Birmingham' to Mum and she threw her hands up incredulously.

"Time for phase two." Mel nudged me as we were leaving the dining room, "This will be super special. Let's get everyone to see them off at the shore."

Mel delivered the news that my parents would be taking a short flight to the Isle of Jura as we put on our coats in reception. "Fancy taking a little trip to make the day even more special?"

Mum and Dad turned around with genuine shock, they thought the lunch was enough, so having something further to celebrate put huge smiles on their faces, especially after the disappointment of the facial in Brum.

"A sea plane, oh, how exciting. I haven't brought a headscarf, though, my hair will be a state, will they give you the goggles on the plane?"

"A seaplane does not have an open top, madam, your hair will be just fine and no goggles are required," the maître d' assured her, amused that Mum somehow likened herself to Amelia Earhart.

THE BIG HOUSE

Dad rubbed his hands together. "This should be something to remember, thanks, Melanie, thanks so much."

"Not a problem, Dad," she said, smiling widely. "Come on, we'll come down to the jetty and wave you off."

Mel led the way as the family prepared to watch my parents take off on their own private flight over Scotland. Mel and I went to the reception desk near the jetty to check them in. Mel muscled her way to the front, obviously.

"Good afternoon, we have a booking for my parents to fly over to Jura, their names are Suzannah and Phillip."

The guy behind the desk looked at a clipboard. "Their fiftieth wedding anniversary?"

Mel nodded. "Yes, we booked a return flight and some excursions on Jura. Oh, and a bottle of champagne and some petits fours on the flight." The guy immediately logged into his system but looked very confused.

"Erm, is there a problem?" I asked reading from his expression something was up.

"There's a big problem, I'm afraid," he said shaking his head.

Mum and Dad overheard and walked over to the desk. "What's going on here? Is there bad weather coming in?" Dad asked, he always had something to say about the weather.

The guy shook his head. "The weather is glorious, sir, a perfect day for a flight."

"So what is it, then?" Mel was becoming agitated.

"It's the timings of the flight, really. What time did you say you were booked for?"

"Two-thirty… pm… obviously."

I laughed nervously and nudged Mel. "Have you booked it for in the morning?

THE BIG HOUSE

The guy looked at me seriously. "We don't fly in the middle of the night, that would be pointless, you wouldn't see anything. But unfortunately it was for one-thirty."

Mel thumped her hand onto the desk. "Well that was somebody else's mistake and we were having lunch at that time so they couldn't have flown then, could they?" she said sharply raising her voice.

"Okay, not to worry, when is the next available booking?" I tried to smooth things over. The man beckoned somebody in from the office behind him, a lady who also looked very concerned. She was wearing pearl earrings and a green tartan skirt with a pin holding it altogether.

"Can I help you?" she said in a very soft and delicate voice.

The desk guy looked at her. "These are here for the anniversary flight we had booked at one-thirty, apparently they thought it had been booked for two-thirty."

"Suzannah and Phillip, going to Jura?" she said, frowning.

Everybody in the room said, "Yes!" at the same time.

"So you two are Suzannah and Phillip?" Mum and Dad both nodded. She whispered to her colleague but loudly enough for us to hear. "If they're Suzannah and Phillip then who the hell was that that got on their flight?"

THE THROUPLE

Dave and Roger took everyone back up to the reception of the hotel whilst Mel and I waited with Mum and Dad for someone of authority to arrive to try and sort this mess out.

"What a pickle. They need to get their administration sorted out." Mum sank back into a big leather armchair whilst the rest of us leaned against the desk. There seemed to be a heated discussion going on between all of the staff and paperwork was being pulled out of filing cabinets and scrutinised. Eventually Mel had seen enough, she pressed the bell relentlessly until they all came out to the desk to face her.

"What the hell is going on? I arranged this for my parents and frankly this is just not on. Are you going to take my parents on this special bloody trip or what?" She was quite fierce, annoyed at what a mess it had turned into.

The receptionist tried to explain: "The problem is, according to our records and eyewitnesses, 'Suzannah and Phillip' already boarded their plane so the aircraft is not here."

Mel screwed her face up. "Eyewitnesses? What do you mean? And this is Suzannah and Phillip right here." Mum and Dad both waved cheerily.

A smaller man who was red and sweaty stepped forwards. "Good afternoon, my name is Jimbo. It was actually me who helped them to board. I watched them take off after I served them champagne and petits fours."

"Yes, I arranged that, it was me who requested that," Mel said as she took a notepad out of her bag. "Right, well this is fraud, somebody has stolen my parents' gift and you let them. I want your full name immediately – 'Jimbo' cannot be a real name."

THE BIG HOUSE

The softly spoken woman stepped in and offered a little more information: "There was something a little different about them, wasn't there, Jimbo?"

Jimbo nodded, he was clearly scared of Mel and could barely look her in the eye.

"Like what?" Mel demanded to know.

"Well one of them…" he stuttered and then paused.

"One of them what?" Mel said.

"The biggest one, I think was a cross-dresser of some sort, I can't be sure, but she was pretty manly and a little large for a lady, the make-up was bit off, too, quite over the top."

Mel threw her hands up. "How is that even relevant Jimbo? The point here is that we are out of pocket and I want to know what you'll do about it." But then he continued his description of the odd couple:

"And Phillip, the husband, was also kind of strange, his moustache was so shiny, I think it was fake. His voice, well, it was almost as if he was masking an accent. When they initially arrived, I have to say, I thought they were in fancy dress." Jimbo looked ashamed as he said that, he knew judging was not acceptable in his line of work.

"We get all sorts and who are we to pass judgement on anybody, my own brother moved in with a man last year." The lady with the pearl earrings was trying to be as open-minded as she could.

Mel was getting very agitated now, and no amount of staring at the sun with no shoes on would calm her down now. "This is bloody ridiculous and it's too much of a coincidence that they had my booking reference and my parents' names. This is deliberate!"

"And they had the paperwork and they called themselves Suzannah and Phillip, you say?" Dad rubbed his temples. "This is really very odd, don't you think, Raquel?"

I stayed completely silent; I was doing all I could not to faint.

THE BIG HOUSE

Realisation that the fraudulent Suzannah and Phillip sounded incredibly like a couple of cons I used to know was not only terrifying but also confusing. How could they have known about my parents' flight? Was it a coincidence? And how was it possible for them to have changed Mel's booking?

Then, Mel said, as if a lightbulb had been switched on: "But how do they expect to get away with it? They have to fly back here, don't they?"

All the staff nodded, Jimbo even put his finger on his lip like Dr. Evil. The cogs in that room were turning swiftly as everybody attempted to make sense of this very strange event and I just hoped they wouldn't ask too many questions. I willed them all to instantly fall asleep, where is a bottle of super-strength GHB when you need it? And just when you need your mother to have an afternoon nap, she piped up, "Looks like we may have a hijacking on our hands, how exciting." And that was all it took to create absolute carnage.

We sat in the bar of Cameron House and waited for news on when it was appropriate for us to drive home. Of course, the police were called and they were buzzing around the hotel talking to each other and on their radios. I overheard many of the conversations, as far as they were concerned we were the victims so they made no attempt to shield their calls.

"Looks like a couple of chancers managed to get into the flight booking system and took themselves a free flight, only trouble is, nobody can get hold of the pilot," said one officer on the phone to someone whilst swigging a can of Tizer.

A female officer who was only in her early twenties shouted into her radio to somebody:

"A man in a dress and his partner have commandeered a sea plane, we think they may be activists, why didn't they just go to Pride?"

And then a plain-clothes person, probably a detective sat next to

THE BIG HOUSE

me on his phone to either his partner or a family member having a good old laugh telling them: "We think the pilot may have been in a throuple, it's possible the three of them may have headed for Amsterdam. Pilot's wife is on her way down here and she's baying for blood after going through his search history."

I sat quietly with a pot of tea staring blankly at the wall. Mel stormed over and elbowed me. "I've just put the phone down to Miles, Christ he is rude."

"Why are you calling him?"

She went a little red. "Well between you and me, I got him to organise the whole thing."

"Miles, why on earth would you…" I started but she cut me off.

"Because he said he was here to help with anything and I was very preoccupied with stuff and because I have no PA, Raquel."

I gulped.

"You should have asked me to help."

She folded her arms and rolled her eyes. "Yes well, I didn't want to give you the satisfaction of knowing I was completely unorganised."

"But Miles, he's just so untrustworthy." How could she not have got that feeling from the smokey weasel?

"Is he? Since when? I thought he was very helpful, and to be honest, he knows everybody up here, he used to supply the wine to this hotel, he has connections, or so he said."

I shook my head, I knew from that moment this was about to become very complicated.

"He literally said he would take care of everything, and he's got everything right, the flowers, the menu, it's all been perfect so far, I didn't have to lift a finger."

"Who paid for it all?"

"Me, I gave him my credit card details."

THE BIG HOUSE

I groaned. "You'd better check your statement Mel, there's probably a Ford Escort and ten thousand Embassy Number 1s on there."

"Don't be ridiculous, he's not a thief. He's a sommelier, a wine and food supplier."

I didn't challenge that. Now was not the time for challenging.

"Anyway, he said that he booked it for two-thirty as requested but he did it online, I mean I could have done that myself. I thought he would be arranging it personally."

The plot continued to thicken. "What else did he say?" I asked, hoping that I had not been mentioned.

"He said I should stop shouting and that he had to go as he was watching Martin Lewis."

Eventually the detective came over to tell us we could go, and Mel should contact the bank in relation to any fraudulent activity on her credit card. Dave shook the officer's hand, thanking them for their help and introduced himself. "What do you know about the perpetrators, officer?"

"To be honest not much to go on, however we do have news, the plane and the pilot have been located and he's heading back in now, so we'll know more then."

"And the perpetrators, are they with him?"

The officer shook his head. "No, strangely they decided to stay over on Jura. They apologised for the mistake and gave him the cash for their flight. It looks to have been a practical joke perhaps, we're really not sure. It's a weird one."

Dave looked at me, he breathed in deeply. Without saying anything I suddenly realised that he knew I was somehow involved. He wouldn't have managed a career in the police without working this one out: two men on the loose last seen heading our way and now two men in disguise flying in a plane that was supposed to be for my parents.

THE BIG HOUSE

I mouthed to him. "We need to go now."

But Mel could not leave it at that and was starting up again until Dave cut her off. "Okay, Mel, that's enough, let these officers get home to their families. No real harm done, eh?"

Mel went red, she was not used to being quietened down and she certainly didn't enjoy the fact her gift had gone wrong. She went to say something else but Dave said very loudly and with some desperation, "Mel, enough!" He moved his eyes to the side in my direction and showed her that there was more to this story. And suddenly Mel dropped her head to her chest and sighed. She knew, Dave knew, and if the police took this anymore seriously then they would too.

"Yeah, you're right. No harm done. Just a little bit of fraud, it happens every day. Not to worry, let's get home to bed, it's been a long day." She walked past me without looking at me and gathered her things. I had an awful lot of explaining to do.

We drove home in silence and the kids napped in the back. Roger drove my parents and Arif, Tom and Babs went in Mel's car. The atmosphere between me and Dave on that journey was so tense that I'd have preferred to walk home on my hands.

The four of us, my sister, Roger, Dave and I waited very patiently until everybody had gone to bed. There would be so many questions and I would have to answer every single one of them. My parents didn't do the maths and wonder if the two convicts whose escape vehicle was found on the edge of Scotland could have been the very same criminals who had stolen their trip and neither did anybody else. Perhaps their big day had worn them out and with Mum obsessed with her French getaway she really gave no shits about the plane ride anyway. In fact, according to Roger, they had both expressed some relief that the plane thing didn't happen.

"It wasn't meant to be, I've never been one for cheap flights anyway,"

THE BIG HOUSE

she'd said to Roger on their journey home. "And anyway, we've got a spa weekend in Birmingham to look forward to from Raquel. That's more up my street."

Dad had also agreed. He wasn't one for heights or pissing around in the sky, apparently. He had been concerned in case they did a loop-the-loop. "I think that's the Red Arrows, Phillip, not sure they do that with pensioners over Loch Lomond, my friend," Roger told him. So it transpired that Mel's present wasn't as amazing as she'd thought, anyway.

My sister, husband and brother-in-law sat at the table in the grand hall in silence. After my parents and the kids had gone upstairs, Mel and Dave sat me down at the kitchen table, rounding up Roger too. They were all waiting to hash out my mistakes once again; it felt like a scene from *Game of Thrones* where at the end I could possibly have my tongue cut out. I had resigned myself to telling them everything, I really had to at this point, but before I told them about my 'summer horribilis', there was somebody I needed to see.

"You'll need to give me five minutes, there's something I have to do."

I made my way out of the back door and I stormed down the path to Miles's cottage. I would give him a piece of my mind and I needed to know that this time they were definitely gone. I needed assurances, guarantees, that this nonsense was over. But the cottage was in complete darkness. I banged on the door and it opened on its own. I expected Miles to appear in his disgusting blue dressing gown but there was silence. He had to be there, he wasn't allowed to be out after nine and it was nearly eleven. I searched the house, there was no sign. Perhaps he was lurking in the main house, I hoped not. I didn't want Dave anywhere near him, that would not end well since Dave would soon know that he booked the flight.

I rushed back up to the house in a frenzy but just before I reached

THE BIG HOUSE

the back door, I noticed the greenhouse door was open. We never left that open, it attracted the slug and snail community to come in for a midnight feast on the veg and Morag had explicitly warned me not to do that. I wondered if Miles was hiding in there, stupidly thinking that the police couldn't see through glass. As I stepped in, I immediately saw it and I knew what it meant. I don't know how anybody could get an ankle tag off without cutting into the bone, they put them on tightly as far as I knew so it would be difficult to abscond. The grey Salford Anklet was severed in just one place, and it sat on top of an envelope that just said 'R' on the front.

Hi darlin, I couldn't go without saying goodbye. I'm hoping by the time you read this, you'll understand that I have decided to join the others and start a new life.

I feel bad that I didn't get to say goodbye to my ma and pa but what life would I have had without the house I have waited so long to inherit?

Don't worry about the pilot talking by the way, he's one of mine. We've been pals for years so he made sure the boys got on a boat and you'll not see them again.

Sorry I had to use your parents as a decoy, at least they got to enjoy the lunch, it really is special up there. I made sure at least that went well.

It's been a pleasure, I know you've had to do some stuff that wasn't ideal but sometimes you just have to go with it.

The police will arrive soon, they'll be looking for me because I've absconded. Do me a favour and throw my tag in the lake, that will buy me some time.

I won't forget you. Good luck with everything.

Miles

THE BIG HOUSE

So this was the part where I threw this story, the whole damn thing into the bottom of the lake where it belonged. I picked up the tag and I screwed up the note and made my way around the house and ran straight down to the lake. Dave was at the front door as I passed it and he shouted, "What the fuck? Where is she going?"

"I'll be back," I yelled and I headed to the shores of water and hurled the tag as far as I possibly could into the middle. I soaked the letter into the water until it was nothing but mush, making sure that it could never ever be reconstructed. I could just see it, some nosy little forensic person sitting for hours with a hairdryer and some No More Nails. So I turned it to mush and walked away. It was over, it had to be over. Satisfied it had suitably disintegrated, I walked back to the house to explain just how Matt Dennis and Big Mike had managed to take my sister's gift and use it as an escape route.

"I think you'd better sit down and start at the beginning." Mel folded her arms.

"Firstly, before I start to tell you what I have been through, please know that what I did was because I had no choice, I didn't tell you what had been going on because I wanted to save you from any more stress. This is a continuation of last year's situation, nothing new, just me trying damage limitation."

"Have you broken the law, Raquel?" Dave asked, meeting my eye.

I thought for a while. "Not intentionally, no."

"Have you had any relations with Miles?" Dave continued not to make eye contact.

I hesitated and he looked up. "Have you? Have you been with him?"

"Well, yes, but…" Dave's eyes grew wide, he looked at Mel who shook her head in disgust. "How could you? Of all the people, what is wrong with you?" he yelled and then he smashed his fist onto the table. I waited for everybody to quieten down and then I told them.

THE BIG HOUSE

"Calm down, I did do it once… in the nineties before I even knew you."

Mel started to laugh. "Good grief, you must have been pretty desperate, what on earth possessed you?"

"Actually I was very drunk." They all nodded, that made sense to them. Dave seemed to retreat a little once he knew that the 'incident' had happened BD (Before Dave).

"Please, you need to listen to the entire situation and then afterwards tell me what else I could have done, what you would have done." Dave clutched a glass of red wine whilst staring down at the surface of the table. "Okay, so don't interrupt me, we don't have long until the police turn up looking for Miles."

And so for the following ten minutes nobody said a word. I told them how I'd wanted to spare Dave from any more exposure to this nasty business. I wanted to make sure Mel didn't become involved as she was going through so much with her fertility and her marriage. Mum and Dad were simply too old to help so I handled the whole thing on my own, trying to make sure everybody came out of this okay.

The only real knowledge I had that I was breaking the law was when I sort of harboured two criminals for less than forty-eight hours and fed them. But I figured by doing this and making sure Matt got away it would save us all from having to face some extremely serious charges.

"I am so sorry, I hope that this is finally over and I hope you can all forgive me. This was all done for the right reasons and, well, it sort of grew legs and I couldn't stop it." I was apologising and really meaning it.

All eyes were on Dave at this point, his reaction was the crucial one, what he said and did next would shape what followed. But he hardly reacted.

THE BIG HOUSE

With absolutely no emotion, he stood up and all he said was, "I didn't hear any of that, I think I'll need my ears checking when we get back to Cheshire. I'm off to bed. Goodnight." He rinsed his glass in the sink, put it the wrong way up on the draining board, which was very annoying, and then he went upstairs. We watched him leave and then Mel turned to Roger and myself.

"I cannot believe you've kept all this from me. Both of you sneaking around behind my back."

Roger wasn't fazed by Mel being cross, he almost seemed smug to have been the one in the know for once. "Now, Melanie, come on, be fair. You've been very distracted and you admitted yourself you didn't want any stress whilst you were doing this whole baby business."

"That doesn't mean you and my sister can become Scotland's version of Bonnie and Clyde. That's three criminals on the run, not one but three. Not to mention the rest of the bleeding gang that Dave let go last year."

"Hardly his fault, though, Mel, all he did was take the lads over to Gleneagles, nothing more."

"I knew that wasn't your idea! I bet that was you, wasn't it, coercing him?" she shrieked, pointing at me. I felt like bending her finger back until she screamed for mercy.

"Well, I asked for his help, if that's what you call coercing. And please stop being a bitch, I've been very stressed myself." She sighed.

"I just don't know what to feel to be honest, Raquel, I can see why you've done some of this but yet again you are heading for a big fall."

"I had no choice, Mel. I have a better chance with Matt gone than I did when he was languishing in a cell missing out on being a father, wallowing about his wife who, by the way, is still capable of anything, even from the other side of the world." She cupped her chin into her hands, I could see that Mel understood that I had a real 'Sophie's

THE BIG HOUSE

Choice' with this one and I just did what I thought was for the best.

"Perhaps, Raquel, but..." She didn't get to finish her sentence because we heard a car approaching.

"Okay, that's the police. You both know what to do, right?" I stood up getting ready for the grilling.

Roger suddenly looked uneasy. "Actually, I'm going to bed, I don't trust myself, I could say the wrong thing."

Mel agreed. "Yes, you get to bed and stay there. We'll take control of this."

Roger scurried away; I think he'd really pushed himself far enough for one year. Mel looked at me with some warmth. "You okay?"

I shrugged. "I don't know, really."

"We've got this, okay? Let me do all the talking, I think you've done quite enough." So my big sister Mel stepped in and did what she could with the police.

The officers came in fairly casually, I had expected a SWAT team and a bit of muscle, something with more oomph, especially from the Scottish. Two extremely young male PCs showed their identification and they asked to go and look in Miles's cottage. I pointed them in the right direction and told them if they needed anything we would wait up.

"He'll be in bed, I expect, so you'll need to knock loudly," I shouted after them as they made their way around the house to the rat's lair.

The two officers came back to the house nearly an hour later, with Mel and me pacing around whilst preparing ourselves for a long list of questions. We didn't offer them tea but we allowed them to sit at the table and make themselves at home. And so they began:

"When did you last see Miles? Did he have any visitors? Were you aware that his old cellmate had escaped jail and was last seen in Edinburgh?"

THE BIG HOUSE

"Cellmate! He's been in prison?" I asked with a good amount of shock and fear.

"Yes, he has, not sure if you heard of the two guys that broke out of a jail down in England?"

"Not really, we've been very busy, I'm afraid. Why, what's that got to do with this, are we in danger? Gosh, how worrying."

The policeman tried to assure us and keep us from becoming hysterical. "Now don't get silly, ladies, it's probably nothing, I doubt there is a connection at all. Just a coincidence."

Get silly? Who did he think we were, The Cheeky Girls? We were the least silly of all the people they would interview this year. "Little twerp," I mouthed to Mel when his back was turned.

Twerp continued with his list of questions. "Are you aware of any medication he may have been taking?"

Mel started to lose patience. "Oh, come on, purrrrleeease. How could we know that? We hardy know the bloke," she said scathingly. The police boy wrote a few words on his pad and showed it to his colleague who nodded. Probably 'rude bitch', something like that.

"Okay, where exactly are his parents?"

"In an apartment in the swanky part of Edinburgh." Mel flicked her hand towards the north.

"That should be easy to find then." He grinned at his partner. "No address or phone number for them?"

"No, I'm afraid not. My parents may have the address but they're very very old and in bed asleep."

"Did he have a girlfriend, boyfriend any romantic connections?"

Mel and I looked at one another shaking our heads. They tried to ask further questions but Mel shut them down again.

"Look, officer, we are renting this house, we know nothing about this man or his acquaintances. Had we known what an unsavoury

THE BIG HOUSE

character he was, we would have probably asked him to leave. Now, please, if there's nothing else…" Mel shuddered as if she felt all dirty with him living so close by.

The officers then made a few calls and then went out to stare at the lake for a while. After that, they said they'd be in touch and went off quickly because a call had come in that somebody had kicked the window of Greggs in and they were the closest. They sped off with their blue light flashing because somebody needed a pasty.

"So what do you think will happen now?" I asked, dreading her answer.

"Not sure, they clearly don't think he's in the lake or we'd have had more of them here with torches and that sort of stuff."

"Okay, so we wait and hope it goes away?" I asked hoping she would agree.

"They'll be a warrant out for Miles, it's likely that they probably think he's gone out drinking and cut the tag thing off in a moment of madness. I doubt it's too high on the priority list. Unless they really believe there is a connection with him and your friends on the run."

"Maybe they think that was him at Greggs."

She nodded. "Perhaps they do. Are you sure he can get out of the country without being apprehended, is he really that intelligent?"

"You know what, Mel, I think he can. He managed to organise a prison break, that's not easy."

"Yeah, with your help," she reminded me harshly.

"Not intentionally, though," I said defensively. "He knows pilots, he seems to have a contact with boats, he told me that he could get anything, anywhere, and so far it's been true." She couldn't disagree.

"Let's go to bed and hope tomorrow is less dramatic," she suggested, and we locked up, wearily going up to bed at two o'clock in the morning.

On the landing I caught her arm. "So sorry about all this, Mel," I said genuinely. "This fling thing with Matt Dennis was the gift that kept on giving. But this time, now he's left the country, I really feel it has gone away for good." She didn't say anything, she just gave me a hug, a hug that I actually needed.

The next morning, our penultimate day at The Eagle Lodge. I woke late due to not sleeping until well past three. I heard quite the commotion downstairs and went down in my pyjamas hoping that I wouldn't find the police waiting for me. Morag and Robbie had returned, having been awoken in the dead of night by the police on the telephone looking for their wayward son. The police had said the signal from Miles's tag was pinging from the bottom of the lake which almost gave poor Morag heart failure. After they had almost killed the woman by telling the story the wrong way round, they then said that he couldn't have been down there with it as they had found a small piece of it in his kitchen. This proved it had it had been removed in his house.

"Out on a tag, eh… well well well. I had a feeling he was a wrong 'un," Tom said as he sipped his coffee.

Morag snapped at him. "He might be a 'wrong 'un', Tom, but that's certainly not for you to say."

Tom grumbled, "Had we known we were so close to a lunatic, we'd have come on this holiday tooled up."

"He's not a lunatic, either, he just had some financial problems," Robbie said forcefully, clearly explaining why he'd been such a soft touch giving him all that money.

Mum put her arm around Morag. "Now try not to worry, he's probably face down in a pile of vomit in some flat with a prostitute and just simply lost track of time."

Morag groaned at my mother's version of comforting. "He'll end up back in the big house, Suzannah, he has to be inside by nine at

THE BIG HOUSE

night, that's the terms he agreed to with this probation officer."

Robbie called Miles's phone from his mobile for the umpteenth time but shook his head and hung up after a few seconds. "The number's dead. It was only a pay-as-you-go thing, perhaps he's got a new SIM card."

"Shall we go and have a look for him, Robbie?" Dad offered, trying to show support to his old friends after seeing Morag start to cry.

Tom stood up from the table. "Okay okay, fair enough, let's go around the local brothels and see if we can capture this young scallywag, now where's my wallet?"

"You will not!" Mum snapped. "Leave it to the police. Besides, we all need to start packing, we leave tomorrow morning, first thing."

Mum went off for a chat with Morag, although I found my usual spot to overhear them in the library. "He's a grown man who makes his own decisions, you mustn't let this stop you with your plan to move, Morag."

Morag dabbed her eyes and nodded. She was a broken woman, a mother without her son, even if he was a shit.

I needed to somehow let her know that her son wasn't dead or in a brothel. I definitely couldn't leave it like this, it wasn't fair, so I would think of something to alleviate her stress before I left.

Unbelievably, I hadn't any conversations at all with Dave since the night before when he went to bed. He was asleep when I got up there and asleep when I got up this morning. The strange thing was that he had held me during the night. Normally when he was pissed off with me, he would physically blank me, sometimes even building a pillow wall between us. I would end up staring at his back the whole night wondering what he was thinking, knowing that he was aware I needed affection but was holding back. But last night he slept with his arm around me, his legs over mine, and he didn't let go.

THE BIG HOUSE

We spent the rest of the day packing, there was plenty of arguing due to tiredness, but also a sense of excitement to get home. It doesn't matter where you go or how long for, getting home always felt good. We had decided to pack most of our things and give the place a good clean and then we would have a takeaway, eating out of the trays to avoid any more washing up. I fed Sister Sledge for the last time, feeling a sadness that they had been the only ones who hadn't caused me an ounce of stress. I heard Morag and Robbie in Miles's cottage, emptying bins, washing up and making the place look presentable. Miles had treated the cottage like a doss house, but according to Robbie it was the police who had left it in a complete state during their search. Robbie again was not being realistic about his son and who he was.

Dave joined me in the garden. "You should grow your own when you get back, you've enjoyed this, haven't you?"

"Yes, this garden has been the best part of the trip for many reasons." He smiled with his eyes; he did that sometimes. Unable to muster up the energy for an actual full facial expression, but unable to control the eyes, they had a life of their own.

"You're tired, aren't you?" I touched his arm as I said this, an intentional move as I needed and craved him to tell me it would be okay. He reciprocated and put his arm around my shoulder.

"I never knew it possible to be this mentally exhausted, Raquel." His words hung in the air as I knew it was me who had sucked the energy out of this man. I had removed his integrity, his faith, his trust, it was me that had left him unable to look at me with his whole face. He was battling so many opposing emotions: love, hate, anger, passion (possibly). It was an awful lot for one simple man to process. A guy who was previously happy to go to work, come home, eat his dinner, watch telly and do the deed once a week in the missionary

THE BIG HOUSE

position. All of a sudden, he had been plunged into a situation so dramatic that it was equal to watching back-to-back episodes of *MAFS*. My shit had taken its toll on my husband, and it didn't feel good. Had he been shouting at me, ignoring me, eating three Twixes one after the other, that would have been good. But this exhaustion, was horrible.

"I take it you don't want to talk about it, then?" I offered him the opportunity to berate me, to tell me what I did was insane or even to congratulate me on my quick thinking and spot-on judgement.

He squeezed me tighter. "I'm not sure whether I would have done things differently to you Raquel, I think you did what you thought was best. But whilst I am still in the police force, I cannot discuss any criminal activity with you. I think that we should leave it there, don't you?"

There was nothing to say, I couldn't make him talk about this, I needed him to be in control of what happened next. I would have to accept that sometimes the silence was a good thing and that time was a great healer.

For the final time, and presumably forever, I wrote my last letter that morning in the basement and put it in an envelope with a thistle on the front. I had found it in one of the kitchen drawers and felt it appropriate to use for this particular message, which I read many times to check it sounded legit.

Hi Mum and Dad. I am safe and well. I decided that I wanted a better life, one where I can fend for myself without relying on you. Don't worry, when I am settled, I will find a way to contact you, logistics is what I do best. I am sorry for the way I treated you both and I appreciated all you did for me.

Please focus on what's best for you now, you deserve to have some

THE BIG HOUSE

enjoyment in your life. I know it hasn't been easy.

Love to you both,

Miles

X

I left it in the greenhouse propped up against the chillies and I hoped that would be enough to put Morag and Robbie's minds at rest. The way I saw it, this could have gone a few ways; Miles would end up back in prison as he wasn't towing the line anyway with this mule business so it would be bound to catch up with him eventually. If he stayed, he would bleed his parents dry until one of them or both keeled over with the stress. So perhaps this was the kindest way for everyone. Him doing a runner with some other like-minded people and starting his life again somewhere far far away and hopefully, somehow, he uses his 'skills' in other ways to live happily ever after.

I slept very little on that final night, it's possible that I may have started with these hot sweats that Mum had warned me about. It was hard to know; who wouldn't sweat like a hog having just been through the summer that I had? I was the right age for the change but perhaps it was just pure relief leaving my body via the pores. All I know is, my pyjamas were soaked through at 2 am and I ended up sleeping on top of the sheets wearing just my flimsy satin dressing gown. I woke again at 5 am, re-saturated as the heat just kept on a-coming. By 8 am, I had piggy eyes and I was all over the shop – time for my own bed and a break from this mental anguish.

I had no idea if I'd packed everything, I prioritised my kitchen equipment, selfishly. Anything else could have been sent on or binned,

THE BIG HOUSE

I just wanted to get home. I craved the local Karens, the shitty little Tesco and Wi-Fi so disgustingly fast it could blow up the house.

As the last boot was slammed shut and everybody had hugged everybody, we all finally left The Eagle Lodge. This house had been the venue for round two of my role as an involuntary gang member, but this would be the very last time I ever rubbed shoulders with criminals.

LASAGNE

I'd had quite an enjoyable time since I'd returned to Cheshire, the 'out of sight, out of mind' concept was a real thing. What happened in Scotland felt like a dream or a movie I'd watched on Netflix, and I was glad to put some distance between it and me. Especially because it didn't feel as though it had actually happened to me. Mum and Dad were busy organising what they would take to France with Mum having signed up to online French lessons and insisting on talking with an accent, it was painful. She had been to "le supermarché" when I called her late morning.

"I got some lovely pommes de terre from le supermarché, Raquel."

"Okay, you got some potatoes from Tesco, did you?"

"Oui, Madame, and tonight your dad and I are going to a wine-tasting in Manchester, we need to brush up."

"Right, very good, Mother, don't forget to wear a beret otherwise you won't get in," I teased her.

"Ooh, you're right, where is that beret? I'll need to dig that out for next month."

"Mum, you do know you are a cliché?"

"What do you mean? I'm immersing myself in my new way of life."

"British people who wear a beret in France look embarrassingly even more British."

"I don't agree, I think it's called making an effort, actually."

"Mum, this is exactly like Jolene wearing those cowboy boots for months just because she had visited Graceland," I reminded her.

Mum snapped. "It is not, Raquel. Jolene is a sad bastard with a terrible choice in footwear."

"Mum!" I was shocked. "A sad bastard? That's your niece."

THE BIG HOUSE

She sighed, "I know I know, God forgive me. Anyway, think of me as Coco Chanel, or even Édith Piaf, what I am not is a Dolly Parton Fan Club member with a loyalty card at River Island."

"So when are you leaving?"

"Mid-September, we're driving down to Calais and we will slowly make our way over to the Dordogne, making two overnight stops on the way."

"And how long are you staying?"

"There is no plan, we'll just play it by ear," she said, giving no shits about me. "I need to furnish the house, Raquel, and introduce myself to the village. Could be a month, could be two, perhaps three." She laughed, and even that was in a haughty French accent.

I sighed. "Well, you'll still come to Portugal for Christmas, won't you?"

There was a pause. "We'll see. Anyway, need to go now and prepare le déjeuner, au revoir." All of a sudden the need to be with us at Christmas had reduced significantly now she had her own life. A French one, which I was a little bit jealous of because it didn't involve me, but also I was happy about because it didn't involve me.

Suzy and Arif hadn't seen each other since we returned from Scotland – Arif had been very busy applying for catering colleges, and between us we had created a CV for him declaring that he was currently a private personal chef for my parents. We also added that he was a highly trained cook who had worked at various exclusive establishments in Syria, all of which had now closed down for obvious reasons so no references could be sought. On the back of this masterpiece, Arif had an interview for a part-time job in a very nice French restaurant in Manchester and I was confident they would take him on. Suzy was a little put out by all of this and voiced her concerns to me when he had blanked her messages.

THE BIG HOUSE

"It's been ten days. What do you mean he's busy? Busy doing what? He works at Granny's, he can answer his phone," she moaned at me, almost blaming me.

"He's forging his future, he is broadening his horizons, and when Granny and Grandad are in France there won't be much to do at Duck Cottage so he needs to start thinking about himself," I told her.

"And, what's that got to do with answering his phone?"

Dave looked up grinning. "Looks like his world doesn't revolve around you, Suzy."

"Erm. I thought you said manners were important. This is just bad manners, he could at least reply," Suzy answered back.

"Maybe he's just not that into you," Dave said, trying to hold back laughing.

"Oh, is that one of your olden day sayings is it?" she said moodily.

Dave and I looked at each other in shock. Was a saying from *Sex and the City* that resonated with everybody who dated in the days that Sarah Jessica Parker told us all how to actually date, now considered to be from the olden days? She was acting as though it had been said by the Corinthians.

"Suzy, Arif has interviews, he has his braces coming off next week and he hasn't had the same opportunities as you. He has to work twice as hard to get anywhere."

Sam, who was lying on the sofa quietly listening to her complain, suddenly spoke up: "And he's got two dates, so he'll be really busy with that too."

Suzy spun around. "You what, you little shit, what do you mean?"

Sam casually explained. "Yeah, he's been talking to some girls, one from his maths class and one that he met at The Hotel in Callander. Remember that hot waitress? She served us a few times."

Dave nodded. "Oh, yeah, pretty little thing, beautiful actually."

THE BIG HOUSE

Suzy's mouth dropped open. She huffed, folded her arms and stomped off. She could say nothing, Arif had played her at her own game and it looked like she'd lost.

On the last Friday of the school holidays I had eventually completed the mountain of ironing that had kept me busy for most of the week after we'd got back. The kids were out seeing friends and Dave had been into the office even though he was still officially on leave while he was considering his next move. He'd done a lot of thinking since we returned but he kept most of his thoughts to himself.

My phone rang and I swiped to answer.

"I'm pregnant! I've fucking done it, sis!" Her voice was breaking with emotion.

"Oh my God, seriously?"

"Yes, I did an early detector test and there are two blue lines."

"Okay, you're sure that's not a Covid test because it's normally a cross, isn't it?" I wanted to make absolutely sure she was correct.

"Raquel, I'm not stupid, the thickest and bluest line."

"Well in that case, congratulations! I am so pleased for you." Wow, she had been successful at her first attempt, this was some seriously strong 'stuff'. "How's Roger coping?"

My sister snorted. "Raquel, I don't know what you've done to him or this therapist slash witch doctor Julian, but he's been amazing. No crying, no snivelling, no nothing."

I smiled at the phone, relieved that he wasn't in an absolute state over this. "Well that should make things much easier with him on board, you need minimal stress, particularly through the first trimester. So tell me again about the father?" There was a pause.

"Roger is the father!"

"I know but biologically, what we getting? What flavour?"

"It's not a packet of crisps, it's a baby."

THE BIG HOUSE

I laughed. "Yeah, but I want to know a little bit about my niece or nephew's bloodline."

"Let's just say, I went for brains, height and a sort of honey colouring with waves through the hair."

"Honey? What does that mean?"

"Well like a strawberry blonde, I suppose."

"What?! You did that on purpose?"

"Yes, I did, Raquel."

"Why?"

"I figured with me being a blonde and Roger having dark brown hair and eyes, that would make it look like it was part of both of us."

"You know I'm imaging Ed Sheeran, all I can see is him."

"It might be a girl."

"Exactly, a girl version of Ed Sheeran, good grief."

"Raquel, you have to think of the child, it's nice for them to resemble you physically to feel part of you both," she reasoned.

"Right, well, I'm sure you know what you're doing." Although I still thought she didn't have a clue what she was letting herself in for.

"Why what would you have gone for?" she asked tersely.

"I probably would have gone down the Chinese route just to see Roger's face."

"Stop it, you're terrible," she laughed.

"So we'll call this baby Ed until it arrives shall we?"

"No, we shall not, we'll just call it a baby."

"Look, I have to go in a minute, Dave's just pulled up outside with a colleague. He's been in meetings all day and I am praying he has retracted his resignation and we can all get back to normal."

"How is everything in that department?" she asked with genuine concern.

"Well Dave's been okay… just deep in thought, I guess. He was a

THE BIG HOUSE

little worried when he heard the police had been back to search The Eagle Lodge for clues as to where Miles has gone. Morag told Mum they'd turned the place upside down."

Mel didn't seem fazed. "Well, it's been a while now, Raquel, they'll be lucky to locate him at this point."

I added more positive news to the list. "And no news on the other two, either, Mel, they'll have new names and an ocean view by now, I think we're all home and dry."

"So you did it!"

"Erm, they did it, Mel. Please don't include me in that sentence."

"Any more developments from Scotland?"

I watched Dave through the window but, he was deep in convo with dickhead Stu. I had enough time to fill Mel in without him hearing. "Well, only that the pilot, the one who flew them out from Cameron House, was interviewed and he said that he had no idea what was going on. The passengers asked him to divert the plane slightly north because they thought they had seen a school of dolphins in the water. He obliged because he thought they had some learning difficulties on account of how they were dressed and how strangely they interacted. Anyway, one of them had a funny turn, a panic attack of some sort and started hyperventilating. He had to land the plane on a very remote small body of water because of all the flailing about."

She gasped. "Go on, what next? Christ, this was very well executed."

"Well once they landed, the two passengers gave the pilot some cash for the flight, said that they had enjoyed the ride but this was where they would disembark."

"They actually used the word disembark?"

"Yeah, apparently so."

"And off they went onto some shore laughing and joking."

THE BIG HOUSE

"What the heck did the police make of this story, Raquel?" She tutted disapprovingly at just how easy this all was for a couple of crims.

"They are still looking into it but as far as they're concerned they think it was some sort of prank, part of a stag do or something. They also wondered if the pilot had been given something, some psychedelics maybe."

"Why would they think that?" she asked. I could tell she was getting annoyed at how good this plan actually was.

"The pilot went off grid for an hour and didn't answer his radio and then he seemed to be dazed and confused when he returned with the plane."

"Blimey, I mean they have some connections these friends of yours, don't they?"

"They're not my friends, Mel, you cow. I suppose you meet many useful people in jail, though."

"Yes, like middle-aged food writers with a thirst for a bad boy," she said, taking the piss.

"Ssshhh, not on the phone," I scolded her.

"Take it easy, Mel, and I'll call you tomorrow. Say hi to Ed from his Aunty Raquel," I said. The line went dead.

I peeked out of the window and saw the Joneses, the new family who'd moved into number 23, were charging their electric car. When a new family moved into 23, it really cemented the end of our troubles. The family looked extremely boring and they were the perfect neighbours for me to see when I looked out of my office window: the Joneses, sensible and quiet, just like their car.

"Stay away from that window and stop being so nosy," Mel had said when I sent her a photo of them which I had taken from through the slits of my blinds. "Look where that's got you in the past."

THE BIG HOUSE

Anyway, once I was satisfied that the neighbours weren't worth spying on, I went into the kitchen to check on the chicken lasagne I was making for dinner. Sometimes I did that when I fancied something a little lighter. Basically, you swap out the beef for shredded chicken thighs and chopped smoked bacon, add summer vegetables to a rich and smokey tomato sauce and then to ensure the ooze of white sauce when you cut through it, add dollops and dollops of mascarpone. With a parmesan crust, this was a slice of pure heaven.

"Did you have a good day?" I asked when Dave walked in the door, he shook his head miserably but I knew what would cheer him up.

"Guess what I made?" I asked him.

"Smells Italian." He mumbled.

I nodded. "Keep going."

"Penne arrabbiata? I don't know, Raquel," he exhaled.

"No, keep going." He seemed agitated, I got the feeling he'd already eaten even though I'd told him not to.

"Spag bol, lasagne… I really don't know."

"Ah, but what type of lasagne?" I said, probing him for more.

"Vegetable, maybe?" He shrugged, he didn't seem arsed.

So I bent down to open the oven to show him how crispy and golden the top was.

"It's chicken, Dave, and get a load of that top layer, imagine the crunch."

He didn't say anything at all, he must have been so impressed that he couldn't actually express it and he was rendered speechless. Dave wrapped his arms around me very tightly and kissed me on the forehead.

"I love you," he said firmly.

"You too!" I said back. I'd have to make this dish more often if this was the response.

THE BIG HOUSE

Eventually he let go of me and stood back whilst facing me, he momentarily shut his eyes and gulped: "Raquel Fitzpatrick, I am arresting you for perverting the course of justice, you do not have to say anything…"

The rest of it was a blur, I didn't even listen to my rights. It was at that moment the gates of Hell were opened and I slowly went through them. I was taken and put into the back of Stu's car. Dave did not come with me, he just stood on the street with his arms folded and his head down.

I have no idea if anyone ever ate that lasagne, it could still be cooking for all I know. I'd put a lot of love into that dinner, it was a terrible shame.

It was a dressing gown that ruined things for me in the end, the satin one that I'd soaked with my night sweats on the final night. I'd put it into the laundry basket and never retrieved it. That dressing gown had a very incriminating letter in the pocket that I'd forgotten about. I was so overwhelmed and ridiculously tired on the last day I just forgot to empty that one basket. When the police searched the house, they found this letter and, well, that was the reason I was sitting in an interview room having been arrested by my own husband.

According to a pleasant enough female officer, Dave had insisted that he be the one to bring me in – as hard as it was, it was the right thing to do. He didn't want me being man-handled by anyone else or humiliated any further than I needed to be. Big Dave, always the gentleman.

Had it not been for that letter, I would have served that lasagne to my family and we would have eaten it sitting in the garden with a crisp green salad and some homemade garlic bread. I was offered a Pot Noodle that night, chicken and mushroom or sweet and sour. When I refused both I was given a cheese sandwich with a fingernail in it and a bottle of warm water. It really was a dark day.

THE BIG HOUSE

My interviews were long and laborious, but I endured them as best I could. Mel had sent in the best person she knew to help me so at least I had some guidance and support. Most of the detectives were friendly, some were unreservedly disgusted in me, showing their disdain for the wife of a police officer who had flouted the law. The two that conducted my final interview were the worst of the lot. A woman with a pointed nose and bloke with really thick eyebrows. Neither knew Dave and they were particularly mean. I mentally named them Brows and Beaky, that made me feel better.

So, on a diet of black coffee and body-part paninis, I sat and I recounted my story over and over again and I did not waver. Yes, I had a soft spot for Matthew Dennis, I thought of him as a friend. I inadvertently helped him and Mike 'The Bullet' O'Hara escape from jail because I felt sorry for them both.

"We'll ask you one more time, Mrs Fitzpatrick, did you have a sexual relationship with Matthew Dennis?" Beaky said with one eyebrow raised.

"No," I said firmly.

"But you wanted one, didn't you? And that's why you helped get him out, so you could get your dirty mitts on him," Brows barked at me horribly.

"No, that's not true," I yelled. "I love my husband, Dave."

"Ah, but it is true. It's all here in this letter. 'Thanks for helping to get us out of here.' That's what he wrote to you." Beaky pointed to the document on the table with her finger and her nose. I defended myself as best I could but the detectives had a photocopy of the letter and they had a highlighter pen.

"Look, I didn't deliberately help get them out, I had no idea there were drugs in those items, I thought they were keepsakes from his baby boy," I said.

THE BIG HOUSE

"Don't take us for fools, you must have at least suspected that these criminals were capable of doing something well… criminal." Beaky smirked at Brows, chuffed to bits with her 'play on words'.

"Ahh, I see what you did there, you're good," I sarcastically said to Beaky, who went red with fury.

Brows sank back into the chair and folded his arms, attempting to be good cop. "Mrs Fitzpatrick, look we know it's hard for you. An unappreciated housewife with a husband who is just not at all interested. We get it, you were bored, you got in with the wrong people. So, tell us where they are and let us do our job."

I shrugged. "I don't know or care! All I want is a coffee made from actual beans and don't mention my husband, he is nothing to do with this."

"This 'R Liam'. Did you ever see him?" Beaky said, changing the course of the interview.

"Well, I saw a photo of him, he was beautiful actually."

The detectives looked at each other and pulled faces. "So you are telling us that you genuinely believed that this Gina woman had given birth after she absconded just from a photo she showed to you?"

I nodded feeling stupid, I suppose that picture could have been of anybody.

Brows then leaned forwards and got close to my face. He had dandruff in his eyebrows, and I was glad.

"So this mystery baby with the silly name, this is the reason that you have pretty much ruined your own life? There has to be more to it."

I sighed. "Well, there isn't. I felt sorry for Matt, being in prison and not seeing his kid. I taught him to cook when he lived on my street, we had a friendship. It was Gina who was the real villain."

"Why not shop her, then, Mrs Fitzpatrick? Why allow her to go free? You could have alerted the police when you knew she was in that

THE BIG HOUSE

hotel." Beaky made a good point but she clearly wasn't a mother.

"That would mean them both going to prison and R Liam would have been an orphan, like Annie."

"The heart bleeds," she muttered, but then she went in hard, probably something she'd learned from *Cracker*.

"Mrs Fitzpatrick, did you have a sexual relationship with your cousin Miles?" she shouted into my face, almost skewering me with her nose.

I paused; this was getting tiresome. "Not recently, no," I said with exhaustion. There was a sharp intake of breath from everybody in the interview room including my solicitor who grimaced before writing something on her pad. "Hang on a minute. It was back in 1996 when we had a 'one afternoon stand', but that was it and can you please get it on record that *he is not my fucking cousin*," I shouted that into the tape recorder and smacked my hand on the desk.

"Now you better calm down or we'll have to cuff you, Mrs," I was told by Brows, which was extremely degrading.

And it went on and on and on until eventually they accepted my story. They surmised that Detective David Fitzpatrick was a very unlucky husband to have me for a wife and was completely oblivious, shocked, hurt, etc, etc, while I was just some silly tart who had fallen in with the wrong crowd.

There was nothing that my sister or Dave or even Judge Rinder could do for me now, I would have to face a judge and be judged like everybody else.

This is going to sound strange but I had made peace with my situation after my arrest. I wasn't hysterical, I didn't even cry. Of course I had fucked up very badly and I would be paying the price for these mistakes for a very long time. But, when you're at rock bottom, there's only one way to go and that's up.

THE BIG HOUSE

Dear Matt, I hope you are well and have the sun on your face. I wonder how you are getting on as a father to R Liam, I imagine he's crawling by now perhaps even walking.

You're right about jail being a pain in the arse, it's no wonder you left. The food in here is so appalling that I have managed to lose a good bit of weight, you wouldn't recognise me without my bingo wings.

Talking of wings, a woman known as Muggy Marie has taken me under hers, she's in here for a while because after a bad bout of PMT where she unfortunately ran over her husband in her car. He's physically recovered but he has developed an acute fear of Mercedes-Benz, they're everywhere you look so he is having some exposure therapy. He still visits Muggy Marie so she can't be that bad.

Sadly, Dave left the police force after what happened, it was impossible for him to enjoy his job with his wife doing time. He's set up a company with an old friend doing security for footballers and celebs. Apparently, the Neville brothers get right up people's noses so they take up most of their time.

My children are thoroughly disgusted in me, it's embarrassment more than anything, really, I'll make it up to them when I get the chance. Dave is doing his best with them and my sister is helping out when she can. When I get out of here, we have been talking about moving abroad to make a fresh start, just like you have, really. So at least Dave is sticking by me, despite everything.

My parents are living their best life, and although it's not ideal to have a daughter in prison, they haven't let it get them down. Mum has become quite pally with the governor and they plan to meet up in France later in the year.

My sentence was quite lenient considering the charges, my defence threw in the menopause card in at the beginning of the trial and the judge was a lady so she sort of got it. She gave me 18 months and said

THE BIG HOUSE

that I was 'quite a stupid woman'.

It shouldn't be more than twelve months so long as I stay out of trouble and I'm trying to. Marie asked me to look after some pills the other day in my bra, she said they were HRT but I'm not sure they were. I took one and I saw a neon lizard on the ceiling of my cell.

One of the screws, Linda, has taken quite a shine to me. We talk quite a lot and when I complained about the quality of the food, she promised she would bring me her big fish pie one night next week. She's really kind.

Anyway, Matt, I'm not sure you'll ever get this letter. 'I will give it to my mum who will pass it to Morag and she will somehow get it to Miles who will hopefully pass it to you.

I genuinely hope you are dangling your feet in the ocean right now and that you are happy, I have no ill feeling anymore, we were all victims in one way or another. It's my time to pay the price.

It's true what they say,

'Fear can hold you prisoner. Hope can set you free.'

Take care and good luck my friend.

Rackel x

CAULIFLOWER CHEESE SOUP

After a Sunday roast, I always have leftovers. Soup is a great way to use these up and it can be frozen so no need to eat immediately. This soup has become a favourite in my family, so much so, I have started to make extra roast potatoes and a giant cauliflower cheese just so I can whizz this little beauty up and have it when I need a food hug! This soup is not keto, paleo or Zumba friendly so you might as well thickly butter a slice of granary and dunk the damn thing right in.

Just in case you want my own recipe for the king of the Sunday roast sides, here it is; I like to prep this the day before, it helps with the flavour and putting it into the oven from cold avoids it going watery.

Cauliflower Cheese
Serves approx. 6

Ingredients
1 large cauliflower
100 grams of butter
1 litre of full fat milk
70 grams of plain flour
150 grams of grated mature white Cheddar
25 grams of Red Leicester
25 grams of parmesan cheese
1 level teaspoon of mustard powder
Sea salt and black pepper
Fresh nutmeg
Olive oil

Method
Preheat the oven at 180 degrees.
Break the cauliflower into large florets and drizzle a little olive oil over the

THE BIG HOUSE

top and sprinkle with sea salt. Then place into an oven proof dish and roast for about 8-10 minutes.

Make a roux

Melt the butter in the bottom of a heavy based saucepan being careful not to burn.

Add the plain flour gradually and make a smooth paste.

Add the whole milk slowly whilst whisking into a smooth sauce. Keep going until you have a good amount of white sauce and the consistency of custard.

Slowly add the mature white cheddar cheese and stir in until melted.

Add the mustard powder.

Grate some nutmeg into the sauce

Add salt and pepper and then take off the heat.

Now remove the cauliflower from the oven, some bits should be a crispy and golden.

Pour the sauce over the cauliflower and grate the Red Leicester and parmesan over the top, then allow to cool.

When ready to eat, cook for 25-30 mins again at 180 degrees.

The Soup

Ingredients
1 chopped white onion.
3 cloves of garlic chopped finely.
1 tablespoon of butter
1 tablespoon of olive oil
Approx. 2 pints of chicken or vegetable stock
1 sprig of rosemary
Chopped smoked bacon or lardons.
Leftover cooked Cauliflower cheese, approx 450 grams or more
Chopped left over roast potatoes, approx 4 or 5

Method
Sauté a white onion and three cloves of chopped garlic in salted butter and a splash of good quality olive oil being careful not to burn.

THE BIG HOUSE

Once soft and lovely, add in your left-over chopped roast potatoes and gently continue to heat until soft.
Heat two pints of chicken or veg stock in a pan and transfer to a jug.
Now, add the potatoes and onions to a blender or soup maker, the left-over cauliflower cheese and half of the stock, whizz up until smoothish.
Keep adding more stock until a soup like consistency is created.
Add the soup back to a pan and heat gently.
You can adjust the consistency to your liking with more hot stock.

Whilst the soupy is warming, fry some lardons or smoked bacon with some chopped rosemary until crispy and golden.
Pour the soup into bowls and sprinkle the bacon over the top.

ACKNOWLEDGEMENTS

Huge thanks to all who have supported me during the creation of my second book. My family have been right there throughout the entire process, relentlessly interrupting me and winding me up.
Without them, I would have completed it yonks ago. Also, if anyone would like advice on how to write a book with a dog on your knee, drop me a line.

I have to mention the lovely readers of 23, the reviews and comments I received after releasing my first book were so encouraging, I decided to give it another shot.

AUTHOR BIO

NJ Miller is an observer of people; their quirks and flaws are what makes her tick.
Having spent over forty years storing amusing memories in her head, she has finally decided to share them through the writing of books.
Apart from that, she is a self-appointed gravy connoisseur, is outwitted by her children on most days and relies on red wine to solve all of her problems.
Even after the wonderful response to her first book 23, she would still prefer to remain anonymous and has no desire to ever meet any of you in person.
She's very grateful though, from a distance.

Printed in Great Britain
by Amazon